The Fortune Teller of Berlin

What readers are saying about J. C. Maetis

'One of the best books I have read'
*****

'A compelling story of bravery, love and survival'
*****

'The twists and turns will keep you engrossed all the way through'
*****

'Powerful and truly moving'
*****

'Amazing work. A masterpiece'
*****

'This is one of the finest novels I have read'
*****

'A wonderfully written historical novel'
*****

'A gripping story with a very interesting cast of characters'
*****

'A remarkable piece of writing'
*****

'Haunting and complex . . . Really well-paced and affecting'
*****

'A gripping WW2 novel with a personal touch'
*****

'Powerful and heartbreaking . . . a moving story'
*****

'A brilliant and enthralling read'
*****

'We need more books like this'
*****

'This will appeal to fans of Philip Kerr, which is high praise!'
*****

The Fortune Teller of Berlin

J. C. MAETIS

PENGUIN BOOKS

PENGUIN BOOKS

UK | USA | Canada | Ireland | Australia
India | New Zealand | South Africa

Penguin Books is part of the Penguin Random House group of companies
whose addresses can be found at global.penguinrandomhouse.com.

First published 2024
002

Set in 12.5/14.75pt Garamond MT Std
Typeset by Jouve (UK), Milton Keynes
Printed and bound in Great Britain by Clays Ltd, Elcograf S.p.A.

The authorized representative in the EEA is Penguin Random House Ireland,
Morrison Chambers, 32 Nassau Street, Dublin D02 YH68

A CIP catalogue record for this book is available from the British Library

ISBN: 978–0–241–99890–8

www.greenpenguin.co.uk

In memory of my mother and father, who met in a special operations unit of the RAF during the Second World War and played their own part in Hitler's downfall.

Author's Note

While there was much speculation both during and after the Second World War regarding Hitler's sudden about-turn in going to war with Russia, this novel deals with it purely under a 'fiction' heading. Indeed, part of that speculation was that 'outside forces' had a hand in guiding Hitler, but the suggestion of SIS (British Intelligence) involvement in *The Fortune Teller of Berlin* is, in turn, equally 'speculative' fiction rather than fact. Similarly, I have taken a few historical liberties for the sake of the plot.

Hitler had two Fortune Tellers . . .

One foretold his rise to power . . .
The other aimed for his demise.

Prologue

Deià, Mallorca, October 1973

She always stopped at the same point on her walk up through the village.

It might have been due to the steepness of the walk, which now she was over sixty left her slightly out of breath, but she liked to think it was mainly because of the view: a small ridge with a drystone wall and a field beyond of fig and olive trees, flanked by the terracotta roofs of village houses, then a haphazard patchwork of other rooftops interspersed with green, pink, burgundy and yellow from bougainvillaea, palms, grapevines and hibiscus before dipping into the deep blue Mediterranean beyond.

Teresa Delmar stopped to catch her breath as she admired the view. Early October, it was still warm, mid-seventies, the oppressive high-summer temperatures tailing off, the first hint of cooler breezes rising from the ocean. One of her favourite months of the year. The villa she was heading for, owned by Deià's most notable long-term resident, the writer Robert Graves, had more of a mountain and valley view.

She lingered a moment more on the sea view, in part to compose herself, because this time she'd be sharing her story with an audience of two. 'I have a good old friend visiting who I know would love to hear your tale,' Graves had told her when she'd met him in his favourite village shop, Estanco, two days ago. 'I think it would be of particular interest to him.'

Always a lover of intrigue, Graves didn't tell her who this 'visiting friend' might be.

She took a last couple of calming breaths before continuing on, the road dipping down after that point, then the last three hundred metres of narrower village lanes and a farm track leading to Graves's villa, Ca n'Alluny.

Graves rose from his chair on the terrace and greeted her effusively as she approached. 'So glad, Teresa, that you could come and see us today.' He held a palm towards a more diminutive man with a shock of tight-curled greying hair who rose from his chair a second after. 'Allow me to introduce my good old friend, Jacob Bronowski – although he's usually termed affectionately as "Bruno" by friends.'

She nodded, smiled and shook his hand. 'Pleased to meet you too.' Graves pulled a chair out for her and they sat down at an oval terrace table. A bottle of white wine and a jug of water were on the table alongside three glasses, two of them half-filled with wine.

'Will you join us?' Graves gestured.

'Just some water, thank you.' She smiled as Graves poured from the jug. 'A bit early in the day for wine for me.'

'I used to follow the "sun over the yardarm" rule too – until I lost track of what time of day it was.' Graves eased a sly smile.

She'd heard stories in the village about Graves's increasing senility but if he could acknowledge it yet jibe about it at the same time, at least it hadn't reached too advanced a stage. There was little about Graves's life that wasn't the subject of village gossip – part of it in fact also involving Jacob Bronowski. Of course, she'd instantly recognized the eminent scientist from his recent *Ascent of Man* programmes on the BBC, but she hadn't realized he was now back in Deià. Graves and Bronowski had been firm friends years ago, and stories had abounded in the village of the wild bohemian parties held at Graves's villa. Quite commonplace in the Swinging Sixties, but these parties had run through the 1940s and 50s, as if Graves and his circle of friends were laying a blueprint for a new generation to follow a decade or two later. Deià had ever since been known as a haven for artists and hippies.

But there had been a falling-out between Graves and Bronowski years ago, and the smidgin of recent village gossip that there'd been a reconciliation between them she hadn't paid too much attention to – until now, with the proof before her.

'I thought that Bruno would be particularly interested in your story,' Graves said, 'because he lost half his family in the Holocaust.'

Bronowski nodded, but flushed slightly. 'That isn't a tale I like to spread too widely or frequently, for obvious reasons.'

Teresa met his gaze sombrely. 'I understand.'

Graves held one hand up, as if in apology that he might have been indelicate. 'The point I'm trying to make is that Bruno here has far more interest in a story about that bastard Hitler's downfall than the rest of us.'

Bronowski smiled at the attempted patch-up, took a sip of wine. Allowances were obviously already being made for Graves's dementia and uneven behaviour, Teresa thought.

She'd in fact only previously shared the bones of the story with Graves before he'd deferred hearing the full version. Perhaps already thinking of Jacob Bronowski to share it with, or it could have been the couple who'd disturbed them at their café table just as she was getting started.

'From what little I have been told by Robert, it sounds a fascinating story regardless.' Bronowski shrugged, held a hand out. 'But, yes, perhaps I have more interest than most because of my family's tragic plight.'

Teresa nodded sympathetically, took a sip of water. 'Where best to start, though?' She looked into the distance for a moment, and suddenly she was back on her favourite village ridge looking towards the sea. But the sea had turned a deep cobalt blue, almost black, as if she were back looking at the dark concave glass speculum and its murky, shifting images beneath. 'Yes . . . Paris, 1940. I think that's the best place to start for the tale of Edith Creutzen,' she said almost breathlessly, feeling those shifting images come to life, drawing her in. 'The young woman who single-handedly changed the course of the Second World War.'

I

Paris, June 1940

It wasn't much of a choice.

If he missed, the return fire would kill him. And if he hit his target, the same; or, worse still, he'd be captured and tortured to inform on his co-conspirators before being executed.

Either way, he was going to die. *Un choix qui n'en est pas un*, a Hobson's choice.

Henri Benoît contemplated his fate as the seconds ticked by, his hands starting to tremble and sweat increasingly on the Lee Enfield rifle in his grip. At just twenty-six years old, he felt he was too young to die. But then no doubt many had said the same in this war so far; what made him so special?

It would be three or four minutes before the motorcade carrying his target arrived, the last radio message had informed him. He adjusted the wavelength on his radio for the next message, *if* there was one. The rumbling vehicle carrying Adolf Hitler and Albert Speer might just appear two hundred metres to his right, the first visible point, and he'd have to concentrate on timing and steadying his aim.

Hitler's visit to Paris had come suddenly, without warning, only eight days after the French capital had fallen to the German invaders. Over half of the city's inhabitants had fled, and those who remained mostly stayed indoors, fearful of being stopped and questioned by the SS or the Gestapo. The streets of Paris were like those of a ghost town. The city of light had suddenly become a city of silence and darkness, especially with a 9 p.m. curfew now enforced.

The sun had risen almost two hours ago, but still the streets were eerily silent; with little other traffic, the rumble of a motorcade would be clearly heard.

Nevertheless, the radio alert came: *'They're approaching. You'll see them soon. And important to note: our target is in the front passenger seat of the third car.'*

The suddenness of Hitler's visit had caught the Resistance unawares, scrambling to make preparations – which had obviously been the intention. Hitler's assassination in the city would be a gigantic coup that would wipe out the glory gained by the Nazis' takeover, so Reich Security wished to avoid that at any cost. The Resistance had only heard of Hitler's impending visit the day before, but had no idea which route he'd take. The only places they felt sure Hitler would visit on a lightning tour were the Eiffel Tower and Napoleon's Tomb – so it was agreed Benoît would be positioned on the route between the two landmarks with his rifle at the ready. An empty ground-floor apartment with a clear view over Avenue de la Bourdonnais was quickly found.

The radio signalling had been particularly tricky. If messages were intercepted, Hitler's convoy would simply change direction or halt. But radio signals usually took eight to ten minutes to pick up on, and what was actually said couldn't be heard until you'd tuned in. So the Resistance radio signallers changed location every five minutes and as an added precaution also changed wavelengths. Only those receiving the messages, like Benoît, had been given the sequence of wavelengths for each signal.

Benoît heard the growl of vehicles approaching, gauging the convoy's distance and speed before returning his focus to his rifle sights. His barrel poked through a small gap in the open window, net curtains shielding his presence. He glanced again at the approaching motorcade – no more than twenty or twenty-five seconds before they were upon him.

He gripped the rifle tighter to try and quell the trembling in his hands. Yes, he'd probably die from the return fire, but think of the glory. *The man who killed Hitler!* His name would go down in history.

But the SS and Reich Security had been equally cagey with their preparations. His Resistance colleagues had soberly informed him that there might also be two decoy convoys with Hitler lookalikes. So the man he was planning to shoot now might well be one of those. His own life lost for nothing.

His stomach sinking at the thought, he tensed harder as the motorcade came closer, starting to track it through his rifle sights fifty metres to his right, willing himself on. No, it *would* be Hitler. Glory, glory . . . *glory*!

Thirty metres, twenty. He got his first clear view of Hitler in his light-grey trench coat through the glass of his Mercedes, as notified sitting in the front next to his chauffeur, an SS Officer and two Führerbegleitkommando security men in the back. Hitler's profile was suddenly clear: trademark toothbrush moustache, a forelock of black lank hair trailing down before being smoothed back into place.

He fired as the Mercedes came directly in line but – whether from the pressure and enormity of his action, sudden second thoughts, or the kick of the rifle – his shot was fractionally too high, zinging off the roof of the Mercedes. He quickly fired off a second round as the car passed, but this also missed.

Two motorcycle outriders were suddenly in motion, one with a rifle, the other with a machine gun, swinging round and halting – using their sidecars as part protection as they fired a volley of shots his way. Benoît ducked down below the windowsill as shattered glass and window-frame splinters fell around him like a blizzard. Hitler's Mercedes had stopped briefly, the SS officer emerging, gun raised, before the car continued steadily on.

'*Stop!* I am on your side,' Benoît shouted. 'I have information that can help you.'

A last couple of shots rang out from behind the sidecars before the SS officer raised one hand. 'Throw out your rifle and raise your hands,' the officer commanded. 'Then come out so we can see you.'

Benoît nodded and did as instructed, clambering over the windowsill and raising his arms. The SS officer kept his gun trained keenly on Benoît, his expression scowling and sceptical.

'If you are on our side, why the shots?'

'I was put up to it, didn't want to do it . . . that's why I fired high,' Benoît said. The SS officer nodded thoughtfully, but still didn't look wholly convinced. 'But I have valuable information on the people who –'

Two gunshots – one to Benoît's shoulder, the other through his neck – cut off any further speech as he slumped to the ground.

Xavier Achard felt both sadness and regret firing the shots, especially as he'd introduced Henri, only three years younger than himself, into the Resistance, and they'd become firm friends over the past eight months. Only the day before, he'd argued strongly on Henri's behalf, saving him from other Resistance colleagues who'd wanted to kill him there and then.

'Stop! I'm on your side. I have information that can help you . . .'

But those words had proved Xavier wrong, so there had been no choice.

It had been a week of dramatic change and shifting allegiances. Those who feared the worst or felt in danger, which was over half of Paris's population, had promptly fled when the German army rolled in. Most of the remainder were either apathetic or slightly for or against the occupiers – none of them presented any danger to the last hardcore ten per cent, the Resistance, who had vowed to stay and make life as difficult as possible for the Nazis.

But a few previously strong Resistance members now felt they should switch sides – even going so far as to build favour with the Nazis by providing valuable information on their comrades – and they *did* present a danger. Henri Benoît had fallen into that category.

The damning information on Benoît had been delivered by the assistant Préfet de Police for the 11th Arrondissement, Philippe Joubert, who presented himself as a Nazi sympathizer, so was one of the first people those wishing to defect would contact. But Joubert was playing a double game, providing vital intelligence to the Resistance on possible defectors who might present a danger.

Benoît was picked up the very next day and questioned by a group of six key Resistance members, including Xavier Achard. Benoît had protested that he was still a devout Resistance member, that he had just been 'testing the water' with Joubert. His account hadn't washed with the group. The vote was in favour of him getting a swift bullet to the head, but Xavier had argued that he should be given a chance to prove himself.

The leader of the group, Pierre Meunier, mid-forties with already a touch of grey, became thoughtful. 'It stands to reason, Xavier, that you would stand up on Benoît's behalf – because you've become closest to him. But you risk putting the rest of us in danger, including yourself.' Meunier held out a palm. 'And what sort of test did you have in mind for him to prove himself?'

Xavier took Meunier into a side room and laid out his case. Hitler arriving the next day had caught them on the hop. They had a raised-level sniper, himself, to fire from a third- or fourth-floor window, but still lacked a street-level sniper. Meunier nodded pensively. Two snipers offered better odds. Firing from a raised level was more difficult, with the higher angle and greater likelihood of the bullets deflecting off the glass – but the chances of getting away were good. With the street-level shot, the odds were higher on penetrating the glass and hitting the target – but the chances of getting away were virtually nil. In essence, it was a suicide mission.

'If he accepts the task, at least he will have proved himself,' Xavier concluded.

'That he will. Along with becoming a household name for ever.' Meunier looked up at Xavier. 'And you'll still take the higher-level position, in case he lets us down?'

'Yes. About eighty metres along. But probably best he doesn't know about that – he might simply use that as an excuse to chicken out.'

'Or let him know that it's ostensibly a suicide mission?'

'I think he's bright enough to work that out for himself. But on the off-chance he's not immediately killed by return fire, if he does a practice escape beforehand up to the second floor and out through a window at the back – he might have a twenty per cent chance of escape.' Xavier shrugged. 'Far better than his odds now.'

After Benoît had accepted the mission, they'd kept him close under their wing for the remaining eighteen hours, never letting him out of their sight. Not only to go through final preparations but also in case he got cold feet and ran off to tell the Nazis all about their grand plan.

But after Benoît had made his plea to the SS officer and come into the open, Xavier was faced with a dilemma. He was the back-up sniper to take out Hitler, and Hitler's car was almost level with him. Yet if he left Benoît, he'd no doubt be hustled away after that first shot, and within days their Resistance unit would be ripped apart.

No time to decide! He angled towards Benoît and took two shots, then swung back to Hitler's Mercedes, already thirty metres past by that point. Two starbursts appeared in the rear window as he took the shots, but Xavier wasn't sure if they'd penetrated.

With the shots that felled Benoît, the SS officer had looked back at his men at first, wondering if one of them had been too trigger-hasty. But the following shots to Hitler's car immediately pinpointed where they'd come from.

The return barrage was instant. Machine guns and rapid rifle fire, the SS officer now also firing his pistol as he ran at full pelt towards the apartment's entrance below, three other guards from Hitler's security entourage joining the chase. Xavier leapt away from the window as it shattered in a hail of bullets behind him and started his run. He left his radio where it was – too cumbersome – and threw his rifle down after only three paces – a man carrying a rifle was an open target. His only remaining weapon, a Browning HP, was tucked deep in his jacket pocket.

He bolted along the corridor outside the apartment and up the stairway at its end. Halfway up, already he could hear the rapid clattering of boots heading up the same stairway three floors down.

At the top, he risked a glance back, caught the glimmer of an SS helmet. Probably the young guard who had leapt off his bike after his shots at Hitler, so with a twenty-metre lead on his colleagues.

A bullet came his way, but he was already out of sight and heading along the corridor on the fourth floor. He knew his escape route off by heart by now: into the second turn-off dog-leg in the corridor, out the window at its end, then down the four flights of fire escape to his bicycle in the passage below.

But the young guard leading the pack of soldiers was quick, and had already appeared at the top of the stairs before he'd reached that dog-leg turn-off. A shot was fired his way, just missing him, and he instantly drew his gun, turned and fired back – only realizing his mistake a moment after. In that split-second, the guard had seen his face before leaping for cover behind the wall facing the stairs.

Xavier fired twice more. It was vital he kept the guard pinned down, so that he didn't see exactly which way Xavier had gone – too risky a gauntlet to run down the four flights of stairs under fire – then he leapt into the dog-leg, along and out of the window, making his way frantically down.

He was three flights down before the first shots zinged past, one bullet kicking up brick dust close by. He fired back a couple of times as he ran down the fourth flight, but with a spidery network of iron steps in between, the shots were mostly pot-luck; the main aim was to get the guard to pull back in and stop firing for a moment – give him a breathing space to leap on his bike and escape.

Thankfully, the soldiers with rifles and machine guns were a bit behind – though the flurry of bullets did kick up cobblestone chips and dust uncomfortably close as he pedalled frantically away and into the first passage turn-off twenty metres along, out of sight and gun reach.

2

Xavier knew he still had one hell of a gauntlet to run. Half of the SS and Reich Security would be tracking him down in a city they now controlled. *The man who'd tried to kill their beloved Führer*. Or perhaps those shots *had* reached their target, that hunt even more acute, and in addition his face had probably now been seen!

A wave of hopelessness washed over him, his breath already falling short from his frantic pedalling. He should slow down soon, so that he didn't stand out from any other Parisian heading to work or home.

Almost five-foot ten, broad shouldered with an unruly mop of chestnut hair and hazel eyes, Xavier was good looking, but not startlingly so; he could blend in and get lost easily in a crowd. Even more so with his garb now: black cloth trousers, worn and soiled brown wool jacket, dark-grey cloth cap pulled sharply down – the dress of many Parisian factory workers. And pedal bikes, with fuel shortages already biting, were by far the most common form of transport. Motorbikes and cars were increasingly sparse, most of those driven by SS or Wehrmacht soldiers.

As Xavier turned into the first main thoroughfare, Rue de Monttessuy, he tempered his pace, hopefully appearing like any other Parisian casually making his way along. As he approached the two guards at the sentry post on the corner of Avenue Rapp, his nerves bristled, but thankfully they were busy examining the papers of two young men – one in a suit, the other with a sports jacket – and paid hardly any attention to him as he rode past. He doubted any radio alert would have reached them yet, let alone a description.

As he turned into Avenue Bosquet and then, shortly after, Rue Saint-Dominique with its pavement cafés, he was more on edge. Half the patrons there were German officers, sipping at coffee and biting into morning pastries. Portable radios were still extremely rare – but some of these officers might be high-level enough to carry them to receive urgent security messages.

They were also quite large, half a metre long, and he couldn't see any on the tables. He noticed two cyclists ahead wearing clothes not too different from his own and they didn't seem to attract any attention, so hopefully he'd be the same. Unless any security alerts were yet to come through.

Then Xavier's nerves leapt as he noticed a middle-aged Reich Security officer take out a radio from a holdall at his side and start talking. But the officer appeared to be gazing unfocused into the mid-distance, nodding at intervals as he responded – didn't appear to pay any attention to Xavier on his bike as he drifted past.

Xavier let out his breath as he passed all the main cafés, took the next turn into Rue Malar. A quieter street, the safe-house rendezvous point was only two-thirds of a kilometre away now. But still he remained alert, in particular for anyone that might be following him.

That was practically Pierre Meunier's first question after Xavier had tucked his bike into a downstairs hallway alcove and made his way up to the second-floor apartment.

'No, I made sure nobody was tailing me,' Xavier answered, recovering his breath after the tense ride. 'In fact, there was hardly any other traffic at all in the last half a kilometre.'

Still, one of the other three Resistance men there glanced out of the window anxiously for any vehicles pulling up in front while Xavier filled them in on what had happened.

Meunier nodded soberly. 'You shouldn't feel any guilt over Benoît. It gives me no pleasure to be proven right. At least at the final moment you did the right thing.' Meunier held a hand towards his colleague, Bernard Calvier, mid-thirties and resembling a Latin matinee idol with warm brown eyes and slicked-back black hair, hunched over a 50cm square radio set. 'And of course we've been able to piece together much of what happened from the messages coming in.'

'Was Hitler hit?' Xavier pressed. 'Did I get him?'

'No, it appears not.' Calvier sighed, looked up. 'We're not even sure he was wounded – unless the SS and Führerbegleitkommando are keeping that under wraps. Or you hit a decoy Hitler.'

Xavier looked dejected and Meunier patted his shoulder. 'Don't feel discouraged. You did your best, and we knew the odds from the start, with the more acute firing angle.'

Calvier was in fact the only one of their unit who was Jewish. When the Nazis rolled into his hometown of Amiens, he moved to Paris. He was a master radio technician, but Meunier had to balance that benefit to their unit against the risk of having a Jewish member. Not an easy decision, but as an extra precaution they'd had Calvier's identity papers changed to those of a devout Catholic from Corsica – which more or less matched his looks.

It was Calvier who had devised their system of five-minute-maximum broadcasts, then immediately to shift location and wavelength for the next. They never used the safe house to broadcast from, only to receive messages.

'Where is Hitler and his entourage now?' Xavier inquired.

Meunier answered. 'We expected him to go next to Napoleon's Tomb. But it appears he's taken an unexpected diversion.' He grimaced. 'Perhaps a clandestine meeting with Marshal Pétain he didn't want anyone to know about.'

Calvier consulted a notepad by his radio. 'An address in Rue Oudinot, to be precise.'

Xavier felt his breath catch. 'Which number?'

'Uh . . . number forty-seven,' Calvier responded, a shade off-balance with Xavier's sharp tone. 'A small theatre, it seems.'

All eyes appeared to be on Xavier as his expression darkened. 'I know that theatre. It's where Edith Creutzen holds her sessions.'

'*Sessions?*' Meunier quizzed.

'Yes. She's a clairvoyant – a fortune teller.'

Meunier still appeared puzzled. No doubt a difficult mental leap from a meeting with Pétain to a fortune teller. 'And how do you know this Edith Creutzen?'

'Because she's best friends with my girlfriend, Teresa Delmar.'

3

An added darkness seemed to appear in the speculum as the six men entered the small auditorium. It could have been a trick of the light – the lighting in the room was finely balanced, and some figures briefly obscuring the faint glow from the entrance could have cast that extra shadow.

Half of the theatre's auditorium had been curtained off, the remaining space ideal for a small group of thirty arranged in a semicircle around the main illumination in the room: a large spotlight suspended low over a central speculum. The light reflected off the concave dark glass, giving a ghostly glow to the front rows.

As the six men moved into the room and took seats at the back of the semicircle, I tried to shift from my mind that it was a portent, an omen. Even in that fleeting glimpse from the entrance light, the figures were unmistakable: Reich Führer Adolf Hitler, Albert Speer, Arno Breker and three Führerbegleitkommando security guards. No doubt another four or five Führerbegleitkommando were outside guarding the theatre entrance. Where the six men sat now, they were in near darkness.

A few in the audience had turned to look at the approaching group but had quickly averted their gaze back to me and the centrally lit speculum, as if openly staring at the Führer might invoke some hitherto unforeseen punishment.

The mood, the spell, had been broken briefly. I needed to bring it back.

'I'm sorry . . .' A moment more staring into the dark speculum before lifting my eyes to the middle-aged woman in front of me – hazel eyes, auburn hair touching the shoulders of her burgundy velvet jacket – I lightly touched the back of her hand to make the connection again. Yvette Massin, the second subject of this morning's session. 'I don't see your brother here.'

Yvette nodded slowly, cast her eyes down. 'I know. I feared as much. He died seven months ago.'

It could have been a trick or a purposeful test – it wouldn't be the first time that had happened – but I let it ride simply as confusion. 'If you're keen to know how he's faring or wish to make contact with him, then perhaps you should have sought a medium. I deal only with lives here – in this case *your* life and what it betokens.'

'I know. I'm sorry.' She looked to one side awkwardly. 'It's just that I talk to him now and then still while alone in my room. I miss him so.'

Her contrition appeared to be genuine. I smiled understandingly, cast my eyes back to the speculum. 'But I do see another man here – though he's only recently arrived in your life, so certainly not your brother. But he is quite close to you and appears to have strong influence over you.'

Yvette sat forward keenly. 'Yes . . . *yes*. That would be Claude. My brother Pascal did so much for my mother and me that, when we lost him, an enormous gap was left in our lives. And then Claude came along, almost as if heaven sent, just when we needed help. Do you think that Claude will help fill that gap?'

It would be so easy just to tell people what they wanted to hear, let them leave satisfied. But as I looked back into the speculum, that wasn't what I saw. 'Of course, nobody can replace your brother. And this new man appears different, has his own aura.'

'In what way?' She seemed concerned at first, but then clung quickly back to the hope she desperately sought. 'Will he not in the end be good for me and my mother, even if in a different way to my brother?'

I couldn't dance around it delicately any more. I might be putting her and her mother at risk by misleading her. I looked across levelly. 'I'm afraid not. I see this other man as quite charming, but also manipulative.' I looked back at the dark shifting shadows in the speculum. 'He could well take advantage of you and your mother. I don't see his end intentions as good.'

But I wondered whether some of those darker shadows were due to the other presences now in the room, and I was being unfair to her, my reading maligned.

Yvette looked down for a moment, gently shook her head. 'But he seems so nice.'

I felt sorry for her, clinging to this last vestige of hope. 'Yes, he would need to be, in order to take you and your mother into his confidence.'

And now some other images in the speculum: *flames licking around the edges of a large building*. But I knew that it had little to do with the woman before me now, my memory leaping back to the Reichstag fire.

The main event that had led to the death of my mentor, Erik Jan Hanussen, Germany's leading mystic and fortune teller. His execution ordered by the man now sitting at the back of this audience, Adolf Hitler.

'What do you suggest I do?' A look that carried the weight of limited options rather than hope. 'Should I simply ask him to leave and not see him again?'

'That I can't advise either way. You could, though, wait to see the signs of these traits I've foreseen – then make your decision. But meanwhile don't put yourself and your mother in a position where he could take advantage.' I grimaced tautly. 'So certainly don't give him any money or sign anything over to him.'

Other speculum images now too: *Hugging two of my fellow Hanussen protégés after his funeral, myself the youngest of the group by two years, a slim, willowy blonde nineteen-year-old. All of us tearfully lamenting his death, but me holding back on why I might feel that loss more than they.*

Was that what Hitler was doing here now, having obviously sought me out? Not content with ordering Hanussen's death, he was now hunting down his remaining acolytes. I hadn't been in touch with the others in over five years. Were they even still alive?

'Thank you. It's been very enlightening.' Yvette nodded, seeming to finally accept. 'I will take your advice.'

'I hope things work out well for you.' I smiled graciously and held one hand out to indicate the session was finished, and as Yvette Massin made her way back to her auditorium seat, some murmurs of approval and light applause broke out from the small crowd.

As it died off, a voice I recognized as Albert Speer's broke through boldly from the back. 'The Führer has asked whether you see a success of the Reich's recent takeover of France?'

I realized why Speer had voiced the question. His French was fluent, and while Hitler would know that, as a Berlin-born and raised girl, my German would be fluent, he wished this exchange to be aired also for the benefit of the audience.

I felt my stomach tighten. This could be a test. If indeed the Führer had sought me out as one of Hanussen's protégés, perhaps my *final* test. I looked into the speculum briefly again and answered cautiously.

'There has been some opposition, of course – which you will no doubt have seen first-hand yourselves. I see an unsettled period continuing for a while – but part of that is fear of the unknown. As things settle down, I see that improving.'

Some words were exchanged between Speer and Hitler, then Speer looked my way again.

'Will that opposition perhaps be too heavy? Or do you see us finally prevailing?'

Another momentary glance at the speculum before looking back at Speer and Hitler. 'I see continuing strong opposition. But you have much support too, a number in Paris who see bright days ahead under the Reich. So, yes, given the might and strength of the German army, I see you prevailing.'

Speer related my comments in German to Hitler. He remained stony-faced, thoughtful for a moment, then with a brief nod to me he stood up, his entourage following as they made their way out.

Hitler's expression had given nothing away. Hanussen

had no idea that he was about to be executed after the Reichstag fire – in fact, having predicted the fire, he felt that he was still very much in favour with the Führer. And no doubt the same lack of prescience would apply to me if I'd unwittingly sealed my own death warrant with my last words.

Xavier didn't tell Meunier about possibly being seen until towards the end of their brief rendezvous.

'Was it just the one guard?' Meunier asked, his expression concerned. 'Or did other guards get a look at you?'

'Just the one. He was ahead of the rest of them, and it was only fleeting.' Xavier gestured. 'I had to look his way to fire back, keep him pinned down for a moment while I escaped.'

Meunier took out a pack of Gitanes and lit one as he sank into thought. A heavy smoker, his habit increased even more when he was anxious. He offered Xavier one almost as an afterthought. Xavier smoked no more than a few a day, so usually he'd decline. But Xavier felt anxious in that moment too, so took one with a tight smile, lit up and eased out some of his wire-taut nerves – which had been like that for almost two hours now – on his first exhalation.

'I doubt there will be any artist's sketch until tomorrow.' Meunier took a heavy draw. 'But best you don't stay at your own place for a while, in case neighbours recognize the drawing.'

'There's been a radio alert already, what little we've been able to pick up on the airwaves,' Calvier commented. 'But it's a fairly vague description – twenty-five to thirty-five, black trousers, brown jacket, grey cap – it could fit half the working men of Paris.'

Meunier nodded. 'Still, might be safer to wear a different coloured jacket and style of cap.'

'Or perhaps even dye your hair,' Calvier interjected. He smiled tightly. 'Light blond is increasingly popular now.'

Xavier shrugged. 'With rationing, hair dye is becoming as rare as gasoline.'

'Yes. Perhaps we can use bleach for the time being,' Meunier said. 'And do you know somewhere else you can stay meanwhile where you won't be recognized?'

'I don't know.' Xavier looked uncertain. 'My parents don't have any spare room, nor my girlfriend. Besides, I'm at her place so often, I'd risk having the same identification problem there with her neighbours.'

Meunier sank into contemplation again, appearing to search for options when Xavier hit on a thought.

'Though Teresa's friend Edith might be a possibility – the fortune teller I mentioned earlier. She has a large apartment with a music room for her young daughter and a spare bed there. She might be able to put us up for a while.'

Meunier paused a moment more, his lit cigarette held suspended a few centimetres from his mouth. 'And would you be safe there if anyone untoward were to call by?'

'It's a large place with a lot of back rooms where we could tuck away,' Xavier commented after a moment's thought.

Meunier nodded. 'It would only be for four or five days, a week at most, until we can find you a more permanent new place. Do you think she can handle that?'

'I think so. I can get Teresa to ask her, at least.'

'OK. But approach Teresa about it tonight, so that you're at this Edith's place by tomorrow morning, before any artist's sketch might appear in the newspapers.' Meunier finally took a draw, a wry smile touching his lips. 'And while there, perhaps you can ask Edith why the almighty Führer might have deigned to pay her a visit? Kill two birds with one stone, so to speak.'

4

My life, I felt, had been forged by five main events: my acceptance into a select Swiss music academy when I was only eleven, contracting meningitis and almost dying when I was fourteen – my fight against it toughened me for the battles ahead – being appointed as one of only five Erik Jan Hanussen protégés when I was just eighteen; the death of Erik, shortly after my boyfriend, Christof Lange, had been killed in a motorbike accident, and finally the birth of my daughter, Louise. I always lumped Christof's and Erik's deaths together, because they were so close together – only two weeks between them and not connected, but the effect on me had been the same: I felt as if I'd been thrown into a grey bottomless pit, which it took me over a year to crawl out from.

My first action to get out of that pit was to move from Berlin – too close to what had happened with Christof and Erik, and I no longer felt safe there. Hitler was on a rampant rise, and I didn't like what I saw coming – even though my mentor had predicted it. I had a good friend in Paris, Teresa Delmar, who had been at the same Swiss music academy as me. I asked Teresa if I could stay with her for a while until I found my own place. 'I'll only stay in Paris a year of so . . . two years at the most. Hopefully, Hitler's star will have faded by then.' But of course it didn't fade, only grew stronger, and by the time of his visit to my session earlier that day, I'd been in Paris seven years.

My daughter, Louise, had in fact been born in Paris, and it was she who had finally lifted me out of my grey slump – or rather my jaded reaction to her. If it hadn't been for Teresa's help at feeding times and with changing nappies, I'd have been sunk. My own breast milk was unreliable – possibly still a reaction to Christof's and Erik's deaths – and Louise had to be heavily supplemented with bottle feed. Then one evening when I was switched off and had forgotten Louise's feed, Teresa had finally snapped: 'You can't stay in this grey mood for ever, Edith. Your baby needs your love and attention. Don't let the shroud of Christof's and Erik's deaths hang over your baby as well.'

That had woken me up like a jolt from an electric cattle prod. My eyes filling with tears, I picked up little Louise and hugged her tight, vowing never to neglect her again. And I didn't; from that moment on, she became the primary focus of my life. Having Louise also carried the benefit that I gained weight; a curse I know to many women, but in my case it was much needed. Until then I'd been painfully thin, and it put a pleasant roundness to my hips and bust, turned me from a waif-like girl into a woman.

Folding some of Louise's dainty clothes and putting them in a drawer, I smiled contentedly as strains of the Moonlight Sonata came from the next room. If I hadn't been able to pursue my own music dreams, I'd make sure my daughter would be able to.

Swiss born from Basel, my father had been a leading

bookbinder, but the demand was far stronger in Germany so he'd moved his business to Berlin – which was where he'd met my mother. When I was only seven, my father had given me a potted history of how the Gutenberg press had transformed the book business: 'Even now, I stitch many books the original way rather than just using glue.' I recall vividly going into my father's workshop, the smell of printed paper and glue heavy in the air. A noxious smell to many, but I revelled in it – still to this day open and lift a newly printed book and inhale its aroma.

When the depression hit in 1929, my father's business was affected. He could no longer afford the music academy fees, and I moved to a Berlin state school. Any German or French family worth their salt had a piano in a spare room, so when I'd finally got back on my feet in Paris with my clairvoyance sessions and started to attract regular audiences, I'd chosen an apartment with extra-large rooms and opted for a grand piano. Nothing was too good for my little Louise!

A strong regret upon leaving Berlin had been that I'd also be leaving behind my younger brother, Tobias, an 'acute case' mongoloid. My parents had raised and taken care of him, and as I'd grown he'd remained trapped in that same childlike wonderland we'd played in as children. I recall one day not long after Hitler had come to power, an SA official calling at our door, commenting, 'I see you have a mongoloid person with you. Shouldn't he be in a special home or asylum?'

My mother had found and handed over the papers

from our family doctor that assigned Tobias to my parents' care – pointing out that she preferred us all to refer to Tobias's condition by its medical name, Down syndrome rather than 'mongoloid'. Already rumours were circulating about Aktion T4 euthanasia programmes to rid the nation of the mentally ill and infirm, and my parents were desperately afraid that Tobias would be taken and sent to an asylum for 'special care'. People like Tobias were seen as much if not more of a problem than Jews because, to the Nazis, they stood as uncomfortable proof that the Aryan race might not be perfect after all. It was the one area where, despite their praise for what Hitler had done to improve Germany, my parents were critical of the Nazis. 'We are quite capable of taking care of him, thank you,' my mother had responded firmly.

The choice between my own and little Louise's welfare and staying to help my parents with Tobias had been a close one.

And through it all, my clairvoyance skills, which took me a while to recognize. *A gift or a curse?*

The first signs of my ability came when I was only six. My mother was holding my hand crossing a main road, but it was me holding her back at the last minute. Then a second later a van careened around the nearby corner and swept past. She hugged me tight.

'Thank goodness, *Liebling*. You heard it when I didn't.'

Except that I hadn't heard it. I'd had a clear vision of the van swinging round the corner before it actually appeared.

Then I also had clear visions of Tobias staying in a childlike state as he got older, even before his diagnosis – which didn't happen fully until he was five years old, although there were tests along the way. I'd been nine at the time and had been getting those images for almost two years, but hadn't said anything to my parents, fearing that they might find it strange, or perhaps clinging to the hope that the images meant nothing, that I was wrong.

But the main transition was my near-death experience when I contracted meningitis, as if almost dying opened up an extra portal. After that, I'd get far darker, more troubling visions that often related to people nearby to me, albeit briefly, rather than myself or my family. I had trouble making sense of these at first, and there was little I could do to prove them real. I could hardly reach across to the woman on the tram whom my gaze had been drawn inexplicably towards and ask her if she had an infirm sister she was concerned about. Even if I had, the last thing she'd want to hear was that her sister would soon die.

So I'd simply shut my eyes against the images, try and shake them away.

My first opportunity of proving they had any substance was when I'd joined Erik Hanussen as a trainee – seeing his advert in the *Berliner Tageblatt* as almost preordained, meant to be. Question-and-answer sessions with applicants quickly put them to the test; eighty per cent of trainees were rejected within two months.

Hanussen had commented after observing me in that first period, 'You're a natural.'

I countered that it was nothing compared to his own

feats, and he admitted to part of those being carefully crafted showmanship, which left me slightly puzzled.

'If you have a real skill, why bother with showmanship?'

'Because when I draw on those skills, it leaves me drained, and I wouldn't be able to sustain a two- or three-hour show. You don't seem to tire in the same way.'

But the main thing I learned from Hanussen was how to read the speculum – my presumption that it was mainly for showmanship or to lend atmosphere quickly fading as I became skilled at interpreting its rapidly shifting shadows and shades like a sea captain reads waves.

After settling into my tutorship under Hanussen's wing, one day he asked what was my first recollection of having clairvoyant skills, and I'd told him about seeing the careening van in advance and pulling my mother back sharply.

But as I told him, it was suddenly me in my mother's place and a little girl pulling at my hand. I wasn't to realize until later that it was my own daughter, Louise, or the significance of it striking me in that moment.

As two knocks came on my apartment door, I broke off from putting Louise's clothes away and went over to the spyhole: Teresa and Xavier. I was delighted to see them, but their expressions looked heavy, concerned.

'Yes, of course you can stay for a week. A month or two, if necessary.' Given our friendship and how Teresa had helped me after Louise's birth, it was the least I could do. 'The only thing I ask is that when you both wake up, you spend most of the day in the main lounge here, so Louise has her music room free again for her practice.'

'I'll probably just spend some nights over,' Teresa commented, 'because you only have the single bed there.'

'You can stay over as much as you like.' I glanced towards the music room. 'I have a spare mattress tucked under the bed you can pull out. I got it two years ago when my parents and my brother Tobias came to stay.' Their first opportunity to see little Louise, I'd been delighted to have them, but part of their visit had also been stressful, my mother asking when I was returning to Berlin. '*Hitler's not as bad as made out in the foreign press. At least he's lifted us out of depression and got the economy moving again.*'

I hadn't wanted to go into the detail of how and why I could never trust Hitler and his henchmen after they had ordered Erik Hanussen's death, so simply explained that I'd built up a good business and income in Paris and Louise was settled in a good local school, '*So probably not for a few years.*'

The reason for Xavier having to lie low for a while had alarmed me at first, but now I looked at him admiringly, raised a brow. 'So, the man who tried to kill Hitler. Fame at last.'

Xavier shrugged and gave an awkward smile. 'It would have been a more deserved fame if I'd actually succeeded.'

I noticed Xavier's eyes linger on me for a moment. Something else was clearly on his mind. But he averted his gaze as Teresa asked, 'Shall I get some of our things, then?'

'Yes, of course,' I said. 'Bring over whatever you need.'

It was agreed that Teresa would make the collection. Xavier had already packed a case and left it at Teresa's – the less he was seen in public on the streets or close to her place, the better – and meanwhile I'd make a fresh pot of coffee for everyone and refresh hers on her return.

I broke off to put Louise to bed. 'Tante Teresa will be staying for a while. Isn't that exciting?' Louise beamed back. Teresa was like a second mother to her, and Teresa blew Louise a kiss and gave a little wave as she went out the door.

But having settled Louise down to sleep, after a while sitting alone with Xavier over coffee, the small talk and niceties – '*So kind of you to let us stay like this, how's Louise getting on at school? Good. It took almost a year for her to really settle in*' – ran out of steam, and I could tell that whatever had been on his mind was back.

'I'm sorry to bring this up,' Xavier said on the back of a sigh. 'And tell me to mind my own business if you don't want to talk about it. But some of my comrades earlier told me that you had a surprise visit from Hitler.'

'Yes, I did.' My sigh in turn was more laboured. I should have guessed that Xavier's Resistance colleagues would have tracked Hitler's every move. 'But it came as more of a surprise to me, I can tell you. Over seven years since I've seen that ogre of a man, only weeks before he'd ordered my mentor Hanussen's murder. And suddenly there he is before me.'

'Any idea why he decided to pay you a visit?'

'He didn't declare any reason while he was there, simply watched my session for a while, had Albert Speer ask a couple of questions in French towards the end – then left.' I held a palm out. 'So I'm as much in the dark as you.'

'Do you think it might be connected with Hanussen?'

'Yes, I'm sure. I can't think of any other possible reason.' I went on to explain about Hanussen being Hitler's coveted fortune teller before he had him put to death.

In fact he had foretold Hitler's dramatic rise to power, 'And now only four of Hanussen's protégés remain, plus me.' I shook my head. 'I feared at first that, not content with Hanussen's death, Hitler was now hunting the rest of us down. But then realized I was probably just being paranoid based on his reputation.'

Xavier looked at me solemnly. 'There are as many who regret underestimating Hitler's ruthlessness, including your past mentor.'

I waved one hand over my coffee, a dismissive motion. That was a fear I didn't want back on my shoulders. 'Or it could just be curiosity. My posters have been over the city for a number of years now, with the bold proclamation at the bottom: Protégée of the Great Erik Jan Hanussen.'

'I suppose.'

Xavier didn't look wholly convinced, but then neither was I, if I was honest about it. The reason for Hitler's visit to me remained a mystery.

Teresa arrived back shortly after, and I spent the next half hour with them sorting out wardrobe and drawer space. Then, with a mixture of tea and bleach, Teresa and I set about trying to lighten Xavier's hair. Pure bleach would have left his hair too white – we were aiming for dark corn-blond, which after an hour we more or less attained.

The next morning Teresa went out and bought a dark-green jacket, maroon beret and brown trilby. She'd also bought a couple of newspapers, one of which carried an artist's sketch of '*Hitler's would-be assassin*'. She slapped it down on the kitchen counter at our side, waggling one hand. I let Xavier look at it first before I moved in to study it closer.

'Some semblance, but not close enough to be worried about,' I voiced. 'Particularly now with your hair lighter and different clothes.'

From the next room came the syncopated cadences of Louise fifteen minutes into her piano practice.

We were halfway through judging Xavier's new look, getting him to stand in front of a long mirror as he tried on his fresh clothes – still basking in the reprieve of that less-than-accurate artist's sketch – when three heavy knocks came on my apartment door, making my heart leap suddenly into my mouth.

I went to the spyhole: an SS officer in his fifties, some grey at his temples, stood there, a younger junior officer just behind. My stomach sank: obviously a neighbour of Teresa's or mine had seen a likeness in the sketch which we hadn't seen, and sent them here!

Having shooed Teresa and Xavier away and whispered a couple of possible hiding places – my voice hopefully masked by Louise's piano playing – my stomach still in knots, I turned back to the door with trepidation and opened it.

5

The older officer, having introduced himself as 'SS-Sturmbannführer Gustav Strehl, third in command for Paris and its environs', spent a while silently perusing my main drawing room before commencing with polite small talk. 'Quite a nice place you have. Just you alone here?'

'No. My young daughter is here with me. That's her playing the piano you can hear now.' I nodded towards the music-room door to the side. I hadn't asked Louise to stop playing, in part because I hadn't alerted her that we had new visitors, but also hopefully her continued playing might mask any faint sounds from Teresa and Xavier hidden away.

'And how old is your daughter?'

'Only seven.'

Strehl raised a faint brow, listening to the piano playing more keenly for a moment. 'Very competent for such a young age, if I may say.'

'Thank you. She practises regularly and also has a tutor.'

Strehl was quite stocky and ruddy faced, which made his watery light-blue eyes look odd in contrast. He nodded slowly, continued walking around the room as if he owned it – perusing paintings, the many leather-bound books on shelves on the far wall, photos, one of Louise's framed music competition awards on top of a walnut side cabinet – before looking back at me keenly. 'Still, quite a grand place for just you and your young daughter.'

The first moment I felt he suspected that someone else was here.

I forced a smile, prayed that my nerves didn't show. 'She's only a little girl, but her grand piano is quite large. Only large rooms would accommodate that.'

Strehl's gaze stayed on me for a moment, his eyes seeming to bore through me, before he nodded a slow acceptance and looked away.

At that moment, Louise's piano playing stopped, the only sound to reach us muted street-noises from Rue du Bac two floors below. I prayed that no faint shuffling noises might be heard from elsewhere in the apartment – I had no idea whether Xavier and Teresa had finally chosen the shower with its frosted glass screen or the far end of the kitchen larder. But neither would stand up to even a moderate search. My own pounding heart and blood-rush to my temples seemed to swamp all other sounds for a moment before Louise's piano playing resumed.

'If I may?' Strehl held one hand towards the music room. But it was more of a confirmation than a request, as he'd already started moving towards it. I nodded numbly. *The first room no doubt on his checklist.*

As he opened the door, Louise looked up at him, startled, her playing abruptly stopping.

'No need to stop on my account, little one.' Strehl smiled. 'I was just commenting to your mother how fine you play for someone so young.'

In the background, I nodded towards Louise, and after responding with a brief tight smile she resumed her playing, Beethoven's Sonata in D Minor, but more hesitantly now.

Strehl waved one hand for a moment in time with the rhythm, then with a curt nod towards Louise, 'Very good,' gently shut her door, went over to the nearest armchair and sat down for the first time since his arrival. The young SS officer had stood silent throughout and hardly moved from his position by the door to the hallway.

'Anyway, to business,' Strehl said summarily. 'You are no doubt wondering why the Führer paid a visit to your modest establishment the other day.'

'I . . . I had begun to wonder, yes.' Sudden relief that it wasn't a targeted search for Xavier. But it was quickly replaced by my earlier concern that I, as one of Hanussen's protégés, was the target.

'You probably surmised that it was to do with your past mentor, Erik Jan Hanussen?'

'Yes, well . . . it was the only possible connection I could think of.' My throat felt dry as I met Strehl's steady stare as evenly as I could.

Strehl looked aslant for a moment, appearing to gather his thoughts. 'The Führer has taken a particular interest in Hanussen's remaining protégés, had their progress followed over the years. Two of them pursued other professions a while after, didn't continue with the path of fortune telling. And of the remaining two that did – yourself and Ehren Graf – you by far appear the strongest in following Hanussen's guiding light. A worthy protégée.'

I forced a strained, gracious smile.

'And that is why the Führer has asked me to see you now to make this generous offer.' Strehl held out one arm, a circus ringmaster presenting. 'He would like you to come to Berlin – with your young daughter, of course – to be his personal fortune teller.'

'I . . . I don't know.' There were scores of reasons why

not, but I was too taken aback in that moment – and suddenly blurting them out would seem ungracious, rude even, in the face of what Strehl obviously saw as a golden invite.

'You would be generously rewarded, twice what your income is now, plus your own house fully paid for, a housemaid too.' Strehl glanced towards the music room. 'I daresay the garden that comes with that house would also be appreciated with the young girl you have.' He smiled. 'And of course, goes without saying, her own new grand piano.'

'But . . . but she's settled well in school here,' I meekly protested. 'Has many friends here now.'

'She will make new friends in Berlin,' Strehl said curtly. Then his expression softened again. 'Come now, we both know how easily young children can adapt. And she'll be going to one of the best schools in Berlin, also fully paid for. Her own private music tutor too.'

I felt trapped. Strehl was sugar-coating the package so heavily that any reluctance or refusal might come across as an insult, a slap in the face to the Führer. Europe's cities were littered with the corpses of those who had fallen out of favour with Hitler, let alone offered a direct insult. Hanussen himself had never slighted or insulted Hitler, yet still . . .

And, suddenly, I was seized by the image of Erik in that final week, his excitement like that of a schoolboy as he gripped my hand after he'd seen the Reichstag building in the speculum, flames leaping from its edges, a session I'd assisted in. '*I must warn the Führer straightaway. Perhaps with some added security, it can be avoided . . .*'

'I don't understand, though . . . with what happened to Hanussen in the end. With his . . .' With my heightened emotions, the words were suddenly tumbling out, though I stopped short of saying *murder*. That would have made the accusation too direct.

Strehl grimaced. 'The Führer feared this might come up, and so he shared this secret with me, which I'll now in turn share with you.' Strehl glanced towards the far window and the street outside for a moment, as if for inspiration. 'He said that he had regrets about what happened with Hanussen, but there were many pressures at the time. Not only the rumours that Hanussen might have had inside information about the fire, or even been in cahoots with its perpetrators, but also the fact that Hanussen was Jewish.' Strehl gestured towards me. 'A problem, of course, which you do not have. As a result, rumours were also starting to circulate of how it would look to the German public if the Führer was being guided and influenced by a Jewish fortune teller. The Führer thought his position was being compromised, and that is why he took the action he did. He felt he had no choice.' Strehl took a fresh breath. 'But, as I say, in the fullness of time, he later regretted that action, felt he might have been too hasty in listening to other voices close to him whose own influence with him was being threatened by Hanussen. Some indeed who also had financial debts owed to Hanussen that would be wiped out by his death. All of that started to prey on the Führer's mind, along with the fact that at heart he felt Hanussen's predictions had been accurate. After all, he was the man who'd accurately foretold the Führer's rise to power, along with a number of other vital forecasts.'

'I see.' I nodded slowly as the information sank in. 'But still, with what happened to Hanussen, I think you can appreciate my hesitance.'

'Yes, I can. Which is why I've shared this very private and personal story from the Führer with you now.'

I took a moment more weighing up the explanation. It couldn't have been easy for Hitler to bare his soul with such a story, if indeed it was true. I held a palm out. 'But why this approach to me now?'

Strehl ran a thumb down his jawline for a second, appearing to compose his thoughts. 'As I say, in retrospect, the Führer has found himself missing Hanussen's guiding hand, in particular what he saw as the accuracy of his forecasts and predictions. And there are many vital decisions the Führer is now facing which he feels would benefit from such added guidance.'

I said nothing, simply nodded my understanding. The explanation made sense, but then I daresay everything would have been carefully scripted in advance for Strehl.

Strehl observed my reaction for a moment, then: 'I understand also that your parents are still in Berlin. 'I'm sure they would be very happy to see you again, not to mention their granddaughter.'

And now, along with this heartfelt account shared from the Führer, some added personal pressure. 'Yes. I'm sure they would be.'

Strehl's eyes stayed on me a moment longer before, bracing his hands on his thighs, he stood up. 'Still, I expect you need a little time to think on all this, so I shall leave you to it.'

'Yes, of course,' I said numbly.

Strehl went into the hallway, turning as the younger officer fell into step behind him. 'I shall return in two days for your decision. Hopefully, that will give you enough time.'

'I daresay.' Though I knew already what my decision would be. Was there some bolt-hole I could disappear to with Louise in those two days?

As if half-reading my thoughts, Strehl turned again. 'I should add that the Führer is not someone you say no to lightly. And you have not only your own welfare to think of in this matter, but also your daughter's. So I'm sure that in the end, you will make the right decision.'

And there it was, the threat, and not even that subtle.

'I'm sure I will.' As I shut the door behind them, I rested with my back to it for a moment, eyes closed, trying to get my composure back through the turmoil of my thoughts.

6

Xavier and Teresa had heard enough of Strehl's conversation for Teresa to ask if I was OK when I gave them the 'all clear' from their hiding place in the larder. Or perhaps it was my burdened expression or the trembling of my hands, which seemed even more pronounced as I poured fresh coffee for us all and filled in the gaps they might have missed.

Teresa reached out and clasped my hand. Partly to comfort, partly as if to break me from my lost stupor. 'I'm so sorry, Edith. What do you plan to do?'

'I have no idea.' I stared emptily into space a second longer before looking back at Teresa, shaking my head. 'Or, rather, I do have a clear idea. But fear that refusing Hitler's offer would put myself and Louise in danger.'

Teresa pushed a tragicomic smile. 'Hell hath no fury like a dictator scorned.'

I returned her smile tamely after a second, appreciating her effort to lighten the mood.

Xavier's brow furrowed. 'Do you trust this explanation of why Hitler had Hanussen killed? And then his later regret?'

'It hardly matters either way if I do. I'd still be putting my and Louise's lives at the mercy of Hitler's fiery, unpredictable moods.' I sighed. 'His later regrets will mean little if he's already had us killed.'

Teresa took a sip of coffee, nodded sombrely. 'Not an easy decision you're facing. But at least you have two days to make it.'

It was evident that no hard-and-fast or sensible decisions would be made there and then – I was still too burdened with the enormity of the offer and its possible pitfalls and dangers. Though I did over the next thirty-six hours bounce off Teresa and Xavier my varying thoughts.

My first inclination the next day was to simply resign myself to accept the offer, ride along on whatever fate brought. At least Hitler would be initially pleased, so any problems in store would be delayed. Whereas if I rejected it, that fate would be instant. But when I aired it with my house guests, Teresa looked at me keenly.

'Are you sure? This Strehl might huff and puff and threaten initially – but in the end do nothing. And then the problem will be past, you'll be free. But if you accept the offer, you'll be living with the problems day to day when they come. You'll be trapped.'

'I don't know.' Suddenly uncertain again, I was wringing my hands without realizing. 'I don't know if I could take the risk of him just huffing and puffing and doing nothing else. And what if the later problems don't come?'

Teresa contemplated me steadily. 'I think you know in your heart that they will.'

I sighed, closed my eyes in acceptance after a moment. She was right. This was the man who'd ordered the murder of my beloved mentor; I doubted I could spend a minute in his company without my skin crawling, let alone months or years.

I noticed that Xavier had stayed silent throughout our exchange, hadn't offered an opinion either way, which was unlike him. But then he'd been out much of the day getting his new identity papers altered to match his new look. So perhaps he was still preoccupied with all that.

In my bedroom early the next morning, before anyone else was awake, I decided to run a speculum session on my own fate – given the two main options. With the first, refusing Hitler's offer, some dark swirling clouds appeared – yet there was a bright light beyond. Then those dark clouds moved back, that light obscured again for a while before a faint glimmer broke back through. And I seemed to read into that that any retribution might not be sudden, that Hitler would deal with the issue at leisure, my fate and Louise's uncertain for a while. With the second option, accepting his offer, the dark shifting images and bursts of intermittent light were even more confusing. I appeared to be confronting Hitler, going against him – which made no sense. If I accepted the offer, I'd be there purely as his fortune teller lackey, and pray that I did the job well enough to please him. The last thing I'd do is go against him and possibly draw his wrath, put myself and Louise in danger. As always with my clairvoyance, my own fate was never as clear as those of detached third parties.

But when I explained it later to Teresa and Xavier, while Teresa readily agreed it was odd and didn't make much sense, I noticed a faint flicker in Xavier's eyes when I mentioned 'conflict with Hitler'. Again, I was struck with the feeling that he was holding back on something.

I wasn't to discover what that 'something' might be until later that day, four or five hours before Strehl's planned return visit, when Xavier came to my door with another man. 'I'm sorry to confront you with this at the last hour, but time has been tight to arrange everything.' He introduced the other man as his Resistance unit leader, Pierre Meunier. 'And he has a proposition which he feels might help you turn your situation around.'

I was in a bit of a daze for the first part of Meunier's discourse, talking about his own background and his contacts in the Special Operations Executive, a branch of British Intelligence, and didn't see how it might relate to me. It was not until he said, 'And they've been looking to get someone close to Hitler, someone who might be able to influence him, for some while,' that I finally saw a possible connection. Meunier held a palm towards me. 'Of course, someone who was to become the Führer's personal fortune teller would present a unique opportunity for that.'

I looked from Meunier to Xavier. Suddenly the speculum images of conflict with Hitler made sense. 'You surely aren't serious. I'm worried sick as it is about going to Berlin with my daughter, fearful of doing the smallest thing wrong that might provoke Hitler's wrath. Why on earth would I want to make that situation worse by tricking him?'

'You would have the support of a whole team behind you,' Meunier offered. 'The best of British and French Intelligence to help guide you. The chances of Hitler finding out that he was being tricked are slight. And if in the end he did, that support would still be there to help you, get you and your daughter back out of Berlin.'

'I don't know.' I shook my head. 'He even suspected

that Hanussen was deceiving him when he wasn't. That vile man sees dark demons and shadows in every corner.'

'Exactly.' Meunier's tone brightened. 'And as his fortune teller, you can hopefully play on that, feed that.'

I sank in on myself for a moment, suddenly realizing how serious they were with this suggestion. They weren't going to let it go.

'You don't understand. I had a closer bond with Hanussen than any of his other protégés . . .' I bit at my lip. I couldn't let on just how close . . . the one secret I'd always held back and hadn't told anyone, let alone sharing it with this man I'd only just met. 'So his death affected me far more than the others. Which is why I left Berlin straight after. I couldn't bear being in the company of Hitler and his henchmen a second longer . . . so the thought of being back there now, so *close* to him, is pure anathema.' I shook my head again, a shudder running through me. 'Let alone what you are suggesting.'

'There are factors with Hanussen that put him at extra risk,' Meunier said, 'which won't apply to you. Such as him being Jewish.'

'Yes, I know. Strehl mentioned that the other day.' I shrugged. 'But that was all just a ruse. Hanussen being Jewish was an open secret among Hitler and his SA paramilitaries for some while. Hitler had him killed over the Reichstag fire prediction for his own personal aims and ambitions, then simply brought up him being Jewish as an excuse.'

Xavier interjected. 'Also some other voices close to Hitler influencing him. As Strehl described it the other day, that came across as very real.'

'Yes. But those voices of influence will still be there.' I looked at Xavier and Meunier levelly. 'Particularly if they feel someone else is getting close to the Führer and influencing him.'

Meunier exchanged a look with Xavier before turning back to me. 'But I understand that Strehl the other day said that Hitler had voiced some regret in that regard. So it could be a question of once bitten . . .'

Meunier left the sentence hanging and I nodded. 'Yes. *If* he was telling the truth about that.'

I could see they were both suddenly on the back foot, Meunier more subdued as he said, 'I fully appreciate the risks involved. I can't make light of those. But you would at the same time be doing a great service for the war effort.'

Xavier added, 'And thinking just of the shadow the Nazis have put over Paris these past weeks, any contributions that might help lift that would be greatly appreciated.' He smiled awkwardly. 'I suppose I'm also now something of an expert on taking risks to help the war effort.'

I felt a twinge of guilt in that instant. Here I was obsessing only over my own risk and the dangers, yet only a few days ago Xavier had risked his life to try and kill Hitler, and could be arrested any day or spend months or years in the shadows with a new identity and not able to live a normal life.

Meunier looked back at me, smiled warmly. 'So would you at least think about my offer in the few hours you have left before your meeting with Strehl?'

'Yes, I will.'

*

Revenge. The suggestion came initially from an unlikely source – Teresa – but perhaps it had been in my subconscious all along, because why else would I embrace it so readily rather than reject it outright?

It only struck me afterwards that Teresa had been out during my meeting with Xavier and Meunier. Perhaps a coincidence, but I wondered whether they might have purposely asked her to be absent. So, when she returned twenty minutes later, I asked her.

She flushed slightly – Teresa always was a hopeless liar or poker player. 'Yes, they did. They thought it was too private for me to overhear.'

'Did they tell you what it was?'

'Only the bones of it. Some personal request from the Resistance, no more than that.'

I nodded, sat Teresa down. My closest friend, I should share it with her; besides, I was interested in her reaction to it.

She lifted her eyes, whistling softly, as I finished. 'That's no small request. And what did you tell them?'

'That I'd think about it.' I sighed. 'But at heart, I already know I can't do it. Talking about what Hitler had done to Hanussen, having him killed despite Erik apparently being his favourite fortune teller – brought it home to me sharper. And I'd merely be putting myself in line for the same, trying to dupe Hitler like that.'

'Yes. I suppose on the face of it that makes sense.' Teresa took a fresh breath. 'And I don't want in any way to brush aside the gravity of what you'd be facing and its dangers, those would still be there – but have you thought of looking at it the other way?'

I knitted my brow. 'I'm sorry . . . I'm not following you.'

Teresa levelled her gaze on me. 'Let me ask you a question. You told me before that you felt particularly close to Erik Hanussen – closer than any of his other protégés.'

'Yes, I did.' I could almost hear the unspoken, *Yet you never told me why*. And if I was ever to share that secret with anyone, it would certainly be Teresa, my closest friend, second mother to Louise. But having harboured that secret for so long . . . 'We had a special affinity unlike the others.'

Teresa nodded understandingly. 'So when he died, you felt the shock and trauma of his death far more than the others – which was why you rushed from Berlin to be here in Paris.'

'Yes . . .' I wasn't sure where Teresa was headed with this. 'But there was also Christof's accident, happening not long before that. My baby had no father.'

'But the memory of Hanussen's death haunts you as much . . . and you miss him terribly too?'

'Yes, I do.' I looked down for a second in reluctant admission, nodded solemnly. 'He taught me everything I know. And he was still in his prime when Hitler had him killed, only forty-three.'

'So if anyone close to Hanussen was keen for revenge for what happened to him, it would be *you*.' Teresa gestured. 'And now this opportunity has landed in your lap.'

The room was deathly silent for a moment, Teresa looking at me intently as she watched the message sink home.

One hand went to my mouth, the audaciousness of Teresa's suggestion taking my breath away.

'*Yes*,' Teresa said, equally breathlessly, leaning forward and clasping my other hand, riding that rush of thought with me. 'Think about it. Duping Hitler, leading him a dance through fortune telling. A tailor-made karma. Erik would be laughing from his grave, willing you on. The perfect repayment for his early death.'

I had to sit back, eyes closed for a moment, as that feeling of euphoria washed fully through me. As if Erik's spirit was already guiding me. I shook my head. Perhaps that had been the problem all along. I'd always felt powerless over what had happened to Erik, and now faced a combination of fear and powerlessness at the thought of being thrown into the lion's den in Erik's place. But perhaps with Erik's spirit alongside me, driving me on, along with the back-up Meunier had mentioned – '*the best of British and French Intelligence to help guide you*' – I could brave it through.

But when I thought of little Louise and the danger I was putting her in, I was filled with doubt again. Another head-shake as I opened my eyes. 'I don't know.'

Teresa gripped my hand back tighter. 'I think you do.' And as her eyes searched mine intently again, I wondered whether she somehow knew or had guessed my long-held secret. Because certainly when I told myself that the revenge wouldn't just be for Erik and myself, those doubts quickly faded.

7

I looked out at the scenery rolling past our train carriage window. It had been flat most of the journey, but now there were some gently undulating hills and some long stretches of pine forest and the occasional lake to break up the patchwork of farm fields. I'd awoken with Louise in our sleeper compartment just as we were approaching the outskirts of Hanover, and we went to the dining car to have a breakfast of Danish pastries. Mine with coffee, chocolate milk for Louise. Travelling first class had its privileges.

Given my earlier hesitance, I'd made my acquiescence to Strehl's offer not too hasty and easy, in case he suspected something. I asked a few pertinent questions to get all the details clear and made a few minor requests, then after another weighted pause for thought, gently nodded. 'In that case, I would like to accept the Führer's kind offer.'

'That is good.' Strehl started to run through the final details and I commented that I'd need some time to settle affairs in Paris, notify Louise's school and say goodbye to friends.

'I'll probably need ten days for that, possibly even two weeks.'

Strehl looked at his watch as if checking the timing for an imminent appointment. 'You have eight days. A train will take you to Berlin. It's a day and a half journey, so there'll be a first-class sleeper compartment for you and your daughter.' He gestured towards the young SS officer to his side. 'Junker Hahn here will return with your tickets in two days' time.'

Louise looked up from the Marcel Aymé book she was reading. 'Will it be much longer now, Momma?'

'Not too much longer. We're most of the way through the journey.' I thought that better than saying another three or four hours. 'Then you'll be seeing Grandma Elsa, Grandpa Lukas and Uncle Tobias again. You haven't seen them in a while.'

Louise smiled and became absorbed in her book again.

I'd wanted the extra time in Paris not just to tie up affairs there but run through arrangements with Meunier and his SOE contact. So, in that eight days there'd been a lot of clandestine meetings while ensuring I wasn't followed to any of them. 'Good advance practice for what you'll be doing for much of your time in Berlin,' Meunier had commented with a dry smile as I'd turned up breathless for one meeting, having taken a particularly haphazard dog-leg route.

Strehl also had his fair share of advance instructions. 'You won't meet the Führer directly upon your arrival. The first time you'll see him will be a couple of days later, at a dinner at the Reich Chancellery. Eva Braun will be there with the Führer, Martin and Gerda Bormann and Joseph and Magda Goebbels, along with various other dignitaries with their wives – although Himmler and Göring and some others might be on their own. You'll be accompanied by a young SS officer not far from your own age, Stefan Hansel, so you could in fact appear as a couple – or at least it won't appear you're on your own in Berlin.'

'I understand.' Single women beyond their mid-twenties were often frowned upon or raised eyebrows: '*How on earth can they manage on their own without a man?*'

'You'll simply be introduced at that dinner as a personal adviser to the Führer.'

'*What?* Like a therapist or emotional adviser?'

'Goodness, no. That would raise as many if not more concerns than a clairvoyant.'

'So, my actual role will be kept secret?'

'Yes. At least for a while.' Strehl pushed an uneasy smile. 'We don't want a repeat of what happened with Hanussen, others close to the Führer getting concerned about you perhaps having undue influence over him, who start making noises about your removal.'

On the face of it, I realized, Strehl's earlier explanation about close associates of Hitler being partly responsible for Hanussen's death appeared to have substance.

'Stefan Hansel will help greatly in that regard. Nearly all of your sessions will take place directly with Hansel, who will then pass the end findings on to the Führer. The Führer will then in turn make his subsequent requests of what he wishes to know to Hansel. He will be your go-between, and much of your time will be spent with Stefan Hansel rather than the Führer.'

That pleased me no end, not having to spend time directly in Hitler's company, except for one practical element. 'But sometimes I need personal contact with a subject in order to get clear sightings, or at least a very personal object to connect with.'

'Rest assured, for vital issues the Führer wishes to know he will want personal contact too – but those might be at most once a month and will be accompanied by Hansel also, who will take notes. But in the interim, all contact and sessions will be with Hansel only – though I'm sure for many of those a personal object of the Führer's could be arranged.'

I was happy overall with the arrangement of this Stefan Hansel providing a buffer between myself and Hitler, and even more so when I met him not long before our arranged dinner two days later at the Reich Chancellery. He was strikingly good looking, with light golden-brown hair and warm grey-green eyes, and had an easy and comforting manner. But after a while talking at our dinner together, part of that unsettled me. I wondered whether Hansel might have been specifically chosen to put me at ease, take me into his confidence. With spending so much time in his company and meanwhile playing a double game, that could prove difficult.

The Reich Chancellery dining hall was resplendent with ornate chandeliers, fine crystal, porcelain and silver on the tables, liveried waiters and portraits of past noblemen, coats of arms and hunting trophies on the walls. Apart from the Nazi banners draped at intervals, it matched the splendour of most fine French restaurants or hotel dining rooms – albeit more masculine and Germanic in tone.

I noticed Hitler's eyes on me for a moment from the head of the table. Only the second time in the evening he'd looked my way and, as then, I returned an imperceptible nod of acknowledgement before looking away demurely.

But even those two brief looks had sent chills through me. Although the more intense private sessions with Hitler would only be once a month, how would I cope even with those?

I'd kept my working directly for Hitler secret from both Louise and my parents. Even at French primary-school level, playground talk circulated about Hitler being a 'monster', and I hadn't wanted to alarm Louise. While my parents might have a more benign viewpoint, I kept to a similar vaguely worded account with them of working for some government department in the Chancellery.

That first night's reunion with my parents and my younger brother Tobias had been emotional. Hugs and kisses all round, many tinged with joyful tears. At least, I thought, that was the silver lining to whatever fate had in store for me with Hitler. My mother had cooked an enormous chicken with apple sauce, and my father opened a bottle of aged Riesling in celebration – in part to emphasize how good life was under the Reich when in Paris rationing was already starting to bite. But halfway through the dinner I was hit with a terrible second-thoughts harbinger. If Hitler later discovered that I was duping him, would my parents and Tobias along with myself and Louise also be sent to death camps or face a firing squad?

My appetite half-went and from then I only picked at my food – though I made up the story of having already had a heavy meal on the train.

Among the advantages of being with my parents was

that they were able to take care of Louise when needed – with them not having seen their grandchild for so long, something they undertook with delight.

Before leaving Paris, Pierre Meunier had given me a list of Berlin bookshops that would be my main contact points for messages to the SOE. And after five days of settling into my new house with garden in Berlin's Scheunenviertel district, there was one bookshop on that list I was keen to check out. The person I was waiting for would be there by now.

On a narrow lane not far from Humboldt University, I looked up at the sign as I approached: Colmar Bücher.

In its front window, alongside mostly German classics with a sprinkling in French, were obligatory standfasts such as Hitler's *Mein Kampf*, Hans Grimm's *Volk ohne Raum* and Agnes Miegel's *Leben und Werk*.

A small brass bell tinkled above the door as I entered and approached the counter.

'May I help you?' A woman with corn-blonde hair in a bun looked up from the register she was checking, peering at me through pince-nez glasses.

Only a faint coy smile from her the giveaway – it took me a moment to in turn recognize her. The Resistance and SOE disguise operatives had outdone themselves. Though still I looked briefly to either side and behind to ensure nobody else was watching before reaching across and pulling my best friend into a hug.

'*Teresa!* So good to see you again.'

8

My main residual concern with accepting Meunier's suggestion had been, aside from upsetting my parents, not knowing anyone in Berlin; after seven years, I'd lost contact with past friends there. Before I'd left Paris, a last-minute urgent meeting had been arranged with Meunier just over an hour before Strehl was due to arrive. We met at a café two streets away, to avoid Strehl possibly seeing us together.

'My final decision to go to Berlin was largely guided by Teresa and Xavier,' I explained to Meunier. 'I don't know what I'd have done without their support.'

Meunier drew on his Gitane. 'You'll meet other new contacts in Berlin, have their support.'

'Yes. But when sharing personal details, some of which in this case might put myself and Louise in danger – it's very difficult to immediately trust people you've only just met.'

Meunier nodded through his smoke swirls, seemed to accept that. 'If you're suggesting that Teresa and Xavier go with you, you realize that would put them in danger too?' But as I'd looked away, biting at my lip at that dreadful drawback, Meunier shrugged. 'But, I suppose, probably no more than Xavier is in now, with half the SS and Gestapo in Paris hunting him down; and Teresa too, by association.' Meunier in turn looked aslant for a moment.

'Hundreds of kilometres away in Berlin might indeed be the last place they'd expect to find him. And having vital contacts there you already know would certainly help.'

Meunier's first suggestion was that the easiest way to arrange it would be to tell Strehl I had a couple of friends in Paris I'd like to go with me, 'One of whom in fact acts as a nanny to your daughter.'

But I was against that idea, felt it would put too much of a spotlight on Teresa and Xavier, 'And if my duplicity with Hitler was later uncovered, they'd likely go down in flames with me.'

'Sadly, a strong possibility.' Meunier started working on the idea of alternative identities for Teresa and Xavier. 'Teresa you say has very good German from her years at the Swiss music academy with you, but Xavier's is almost non-existent. So, we shall have to have good cover stories and identities for that.'

It was decided in the end that Teresa would hail originally from Colmar – thus the name chosen for her bookstore – eighty kilometres south of Strasbourg. 'Nearly everyone in Alsace-Lorraine speaks both French and German, given their chequered history shifting between French and German rule,' Meunier explained. 'And we'll have Xavier originate from Brittany, which would then explain his almost nil German.'

Teresa would be at the counter dealing with customers while Xavier stayed at the back dealing with stock and inventory, plus mending and rebinding damaged books. Because of the extra time necessary to arrange Xavier's identity, he would arrive slightly after her.

'When's Xavier due?' I asked her now.

'Three or four days' time. A bit of that delay is so that his train journey can start from Brittany, to add authenticity. Oh, and our new names are Odette and Luc Chastain.' She smiled tightly. 'We weren't married before, but we are now in our new identities. *Donc un avantage inattendu.*'

I talked for a while about my new house in Scheunenviertel and arrangements there. 'A housekeeper, Lara, who also doubles as a nanny. Four bedrooms, one of which Louise will also use as her music room – her new grand piano arrived just yesterday. A large office, and an almost fifty-metre garden out the back.'

'Sounds ideal. What's she like, this housekeeper?'

'Early forties, good cook – if a little standard and plain. They even found someone with passable French, so she can communicate with Louise. They get on well; Louise appears to like Lara.'

Teresa contemplated me. 'From your look, something seems to bother you about her.'

I shrugged. 'Just perhaps that I'm not used to having other people around me like that. Also, the feeling that she's been hand-picked and might be there partly to spy on me.'

'Perhaps she is. And that's to be expected – after all, you're new to the Hitler camp and staying in a place paid for by him.'

'I suppose.' Teresa-Odette could see that I was still troubled by something, so after a moment I started telling her about Stefan Hansel.

'Again, sounds ideal,' she said as I finished, then with a faint twinkle in her eye, 'Especially the bit about him being affable, charming and good looking. And your regular sessions taking place with him, so that you'll only have to face Hitler once a month, must come as a welcome relief.'

'Yes, it does.' I sighed, my earlier concerns about Hansel still weighing on me. 'It's just that he seems in many ways too affable, *too* perfect – as if he too has been hand-picked to win over my trust and confidence.'

'There might indeed be some of that with this Hansel – after all, they're hardly going to choose someone who will alienate you from the off.' She took a fresh breath. 'So, all I can advise is to remain wary and guarded with him – but not enough to raise concerns or suspicions.' She reached across and gently clasped my hands. 'You'll face enough dark demons these coming months without inventing or obsessing over still more in your mind.'

'Yes, I daresay you're right . . .' The shop bell went then, someone else walking in, '. . . Odette.'

So many things to remember.

The system of coded messages through bookshops had been devised between Meunier and his SOE contact before I left Paris, and was now explained to me fully by my main contact in Berlin, Gregor Lutz.

'Each time you visit a bookshop like this – five on a prescribed list that you'll have the rotation sequence of in advance – while browsing, you'll be pointed towards a book on one of the shelves by somebody close by. You'll in turn pick out a book and recommend it to your fellow browser. He'll slip a piece of paper with a sequence of numbers inside his book recommendation, and you'll slip one inside yours. Those numbers will relate to nothing in the books you each take – only to one of the thirty books sent from your Paris home along with other belongings in a few trunks.'

I nodded. 'The trunks in fact arrived just yesterday.'

'Very good. We have now the same thirty books in our collection too.' Lutz took a fresh breath. 'That series of numbers will relate to a page number, line down and word across. A full stop between each, then the next sequence of three numbers. But, as I said, if applied to that first book, they make no sense at all – only when applied to the second book. The purpose of this is that if found with that first book and numbers list, a message can't be worked out. But still try and keep that numbers list concealed, because it might raise suspicions.'

'Any ready or ideal answers if I am found with it?'

Lutz gestured. 'Perhaps say that it's reference notes for research. Applied to the book the code slip is in, nothing of any sense will be formed – so that explanation would stand up.'

'But won't that seem odd, references to just single words?'

'If you find yourself having to explain – then claim that the last reference is to when a certain passage starts. Three words, five or eight words in, for example.'

Lutz was in his early forties but looked almost ten years older, with grey peppered in his shock of wild dark-brown hair, round gold-rimmed glasses and an ill-fitting tweed jacket with elbow patches – perhaps all to support the appearance of a crusty bookworm rather than a spy.

We were in a private back room of the third bookshop on the list, Grunewald Bücher, the only one aside from

Teresa-Odette's new shop to also be run by an anti-Nazi sympathizer. At the other three, I'd simply be a casual visitor. No private meetings like this.

'That first book you pick up will be how we want Hitler guided,' Lutz said. 'The list of numbers you slip in your book recommendation days later will detail how you managed to guide him, his responses and any other areas of interest you pick up from him. The next book you pick up will be where we want him guided next, and so on.'

The idea of using books came initially from Meunier asking if I had any hobbies, 'Something that could take you out and about in Berlin without raising suspicions.' He went on to explain that meeting up with contacts there casually in cafés and restaurants could prove difficult, 'You'd be more in the open,' and it was then I hit on the vintage book-collecting hobby I'd had from a young age.

'My father, Lukas, was a leading bookbinder, and he brought home A. P. Schulz books when I was only four or five, then later a rare edition of Johanna Spyri's *Heidi* for my seventh birthday, with other vintage editions following for subsequent birthdays and Christmases. Then, not long after Louise was born, I decided to continue that, seeking out vintage editions for myself as well as for special presents for her.' We were in my Paris apartment at the time, and I held out one hand towards the far bookshelf. 'A number of them among my collection here.'

'Ideal! With your father being a bookbinder, that hobby will fit in well, shouldn't raise any concerns with the Nazis. But try, if you can, to mention it to Strehl before you leave for Berlin.'

That opportunity came when Strehl raised an eyebrow at the number of trunks I was shipping to Berlin.

'Half of them books, I'm afraid.'

'Yes, I noticed you had a fair collection.'

And I launched into the same account about how my book collecting had stemmed from my father buying me early rare editions as a young child. 'Hopefully, I might get a chance to add to my collection while in Berlin.'

'I'm sure you will. There are many fine bookshops in Berlin, and your sessions with Hansel and the Führer will likely take up no more than a few days a week.'

Perfect. The seed had been sown.

But six minutes later, as I was leaving the back room, I saw a man in profile at the far side of the bookshop whom I'd seen before. My breath caught in my throat and I quickly pushed the door shut again.

'What is it?' Lutz asked.

'A man on the far side of the shop – fairly young, dark-grey trilby. I think he's followed me here.'

'Are you sure?'

'Yes, pretty much. I stopped to look in a dress-shop window on the way here, and I saw him clearly in my side vision.' Part of my final briefing with Meunier had been relayed instructions from the SOE. '*You'll no doubt be followed in your first weeks in Berlin. That's to be expected. You're new to Hitler's circle, so no more than a standard precaution. So don't bother with any avoidance tactics that might raise suspicions, just act naturally. But try if you can to take note of who might be following you. A casual stop to look in a shop window and suchlike – but not too many. Try and not give away that you know you're being followed or appear anxious about it.*'

'With the delay, he obviously wondered what you might be doing in here,' Lutz said, taking a fresh breath. 'The important thing is that we're not seen together. So I'll go out into the main shop while you stay here. When I see that he's out of sight from the door here, I'll give it two light taps and you immediately come out and go to the back of the shop and browse there.'

'OK.'

'There are four or five rows of shelves grouped tight at the back – so hopefully he'll think you were browsing among those and that's why he hadn't immediately spotted you.' With a final perfunctory nod, Lutz headed out.

I waited by the door for what was probably only two minutes – though it felt like a lifetime – before those two light taps came.

I headed swiftly out and immediately away from Lutz, buried myself in the third row of books among the five at the back, started browsing through. And after just over another minute, I saw the man in the grey trilby look along my row. I thought for a minute he was coming into it – but he just peered towards the top two rows nearest in for a moment, then moved on. Not long after, I heard the shop doorbell, and seconds later Lutz appeared at the end of my row, nodding with a tight smile. 'He's gone.'

I nodded back my thanks and breathed out in relief, but again I was struck with the thought that had increasingly gripped me in the last two weeks of preparation: I don't know if I can do this.

9

The final part of Lutz's instructions had dealt with what I could expect in the early sessions.

'They'll try and trick you in those sessions – maybe more than once. Some of this you'll have to judge with your own intuition at the time – but probably best we run through a few possible scenarios now.'

I'd been three weeks in Berlin before our first session. Stefan Hansel had arrived four minutes late, which was unlike him and added to my nervousness. Perhaps on purpose, or possibly he was using that extra time to go over his prepared script from Hitler. The tricks they might try to play on me.

Lara's voice sailed from the hallway seconds after the doorbell went. 'It's Herr Hansel.' Adding with a faint smile as she walked into the main lounge, 'Stefan.'

I wondered whether unconsciously I might have betrayed some attraction to him, when in fact I'd told myself I felt just the opposite, had to remain guarded around him. Or whether it was just wishful thinking on Lara's part; that with someone as gracious and handsome, I *should* be attracted to him.

From the next room, Louise's piano playing stopped and she ran out to him. 'Stefan!'

'Oh, dear. I stopped the maestro playing.' He playfully ruffled her hair. 'You could have continued, you know. You know how much I enjoy your music.'

'Momma said that I have to stop for your meeting today.'

'Ah, Momma knows best.' He looked towards me with an endearing smile, shrugged.

On that first day he'd come to the house he'd stayed in Louise's room for a while, admiring her piano playing. But when he'd complimented her, it hadn't been in the same awkward way as Strehl had, but with sincere appreciation. Young children are particularly intuitive, and Louise had picked up on this, beaming in the light of his praise. From that day on, they'd been firm friends.

And perhaps Lara had noticed this too, could sense the warm approval a mother shows when a man gets on with her child. Though maybe that was also part of his plan to get more into my confidence, get close. I became more formal to put some distance back.

'Come on now, Louise. Let's get you moving.' I guided her away towards Lara. 'Lara has a story to read you while I'm with Stefan.'

Louise aimed a hurt pout back towards us as Lara led her towards her bedroom, and I had to suppress a smile as I turned to Stefan.

'Sorry about that.'

'Kids will be kids, I suppose.' He smiled gently. 'Even if they are young Mozarts in the making.'

The large downstairs office had been converted into my permanent clairvoyance room. Bookshelves filled one wall, where I had many of my vintage editions, and its desk had been moved out and a large circular table put at its centre for the speculum. The main light in the office was off, the only illumination now a stark spotlight suspended just above the speculum, casting a ghostly glow towards myself and Stefan Hansel as we sat on either side.

A combination of blackout shutters and curtains had been closed on the room's only window, but I noticed still a small shaft of light spilling through from the sunlight outside. Stefan went across and pulled the curtains tighter together, then returned to the table to commence his questions.

'The opposition you mentioned in Paris before. Do you see that presenting itself in a fiery, violent way?' Following on from the earlier questions posed through Albert Speer, I suppose that made sense: the need for more finite clarifications striking Hitler afterwards.

I peered into the speculum, but I knew the answer already from Meunier despite the calmer shadows there: '*After this recent attempt on Hitler's life, we won't be planning any more spectaculars or fightbacks for a while. Our numbers are too small, and we need to build those up before we attempt anything. We're too vulnerable right now.*'

'No. I don't see any strong agitation or violence for a while.'

'For how long?'

I peered back into the speculum. 'For two years at least, possibly three.'

Stefan nodded, made a note. 'But as you said before, you see the Reich prevailing in the end?'

'Yes, I do.'

My hand gripped tighter for a moment on the glove I was holding. I'd been given it at the outset by Stefan. '*You asked for a personal object of the Führer's to help make connections.*

This is a glove from one of his favourite pairs. He was wearing it just the other day.'

As I'd first gripped the glove, I'd seen again in the speculum the leaping flames of the Reichstag fire, then the image of Hanussen's body in the morgue. As if Erik was reaching from the grave now to confirm, '*It was Hitler himself who ordered my death. Not the SA or others close to him who he might want to shift the blame to.*'

Stefan took a fresh breath. 'We've been developing a new fighter aircraft at our factory in Fürth, the Köhler-8. We wondered if you see this as being a success?'

Looking into the speculum, I could see no clear images either way. Could this be one of the trick questions Lutz warned of? I felt my heart beating more rapidly. If I answered wrong, it could all be over right now . . . perhaps a similar fate to Hanussen awaiting me. But it hadn't been among any of the scenarios Lutz had run through. As he'd suggested, I would just have to go by intuition.

'I . . . I'm afraid I can't see anything clearly about this new aircraft,' I answered ambiguously, so that if indeed no such aircraft existed, I wouldn't be caught out.

'Perhaps because it's still in the development stage?'

'Possibly. But I can't see any indication one way or the other.'

'I see.'

I could feel Stefan's eyes still on me, and I was unsure whether I'd given the right answer or not as I peered into the speculum a moment longer. It was what I saw there in any case . . . murky images, indistinct.

Stefan then proceeded to ask more standard questions:

was there support or possible uprisings in Germany, Czechoslovakia and Poland?

In Germany, I saw few problems or turmoil in the speculum. 'I see support continuing strongly for the Führer in Germany, with little resistance.' I'd seen that for myself with the mass throngs of street rallies in Berlin; I hardly needed to judge that from the speculum.

'In Czechoslovakia, some continued opposition, but it will be quickly quashed and die down.'

But when I looked at Poland, I saw far darker, more ominous shades forming, like fast-shifting black clouds. As I started to become agitated, my breath falling short, Stefan reached across and clasped my hand.

'Are you OK?'

'Yes . . . *yes*. Just that I see many deaths there.'

'I'm sorry.' Stefan quickly pulled his hand back, as if only then realizing that he'd reached out and touched me. 'Renewed resistance and fighting? Do you see many German soldiers among the dead?'

'No . . . I . . .' It took a moment for the dark shifting images to settle back. 'It's somewhat in the future, a year or so or more. But I don't see them as German deaths – which I suppose must mean they are Polish deaths.'

I could see that Stefan looked puzzled by that for a moment, as I was: if there was not renewed fighting in Poland, why so many deaths just on one side? He made a longer note, then looked up.

'And the agreement we made last year with Stalin. Do you see that holding up? Can he be trusted?'

A longer, more intense study of the speculum this time – one of the key points on my guidance list from the

SOE. But I'd been instructed to go cautiously, stage by stage, so as not to raise any suspicions.

'For now it appears Stalin can be trusted – because the agreement suits him.'

'In what way?'

'He knows he doesn't have sufficient armaments yet to defeat the might of the German army – so he's playing for time.'

Stefan looked concerned, made another note. 'And do you see Stalin preparing those armaments now?'

Another considered study of the speculum and the shifting shadows there before I looked up again.

'Yes, I do.'

10

War Cabinet Room, London, September 1940

Calder Gibson's footsteps echoed hollowly off the long corridor three floors below Whitehall's pavement. Countless times he'd paced this long corridor; his nickname for it was 'The Cream Tunnel'. Not a window in sight, and while at intervals there were heavy wood beams and the occasional cabinet, chest or bench seat – they did little to break up the monotony of the cream-painted ceiling and brick walls each side.

The door he tapped on lightly was towards its end. A mid-sized briefing room rather than the full-sized conference room two doors along, because only a few of them would be present.

'Come in.' Churchill's gruff voice sounded from the other side.

Calder Gibson, head of SOE, took a seat two down from Winston Churchill at the head of the long table. To Churchill's side was Edward Bridges, War Cabinet Secretary, a dapper man with steel-rimmed glasses now in his late forties, and a young brunette stenographer sat opposite Calder.

Calder noticed that Churchill's cigar was already a quarter-way down, so some conversation must have taken place before he'd entered the room.

'So what news, Calder, from your man in Moscow?'

Quite early in their association, the Prime Minister had taken to calling him by his first name. Possibly because they were almost contemporaries – he was only six years younger than Churchill – though in appearance there was a stark contrast. Calder was slim and lanky with sharp, fine features, his hair at fifty-nine almost totally grey.

That familiar first-name usage wasn't one he felt he could reciprocate, though. 'Yes, Prime Minister, I have heard something from our man there. But it appears Stalin hasn't reacted to your note in the way we'd hoped.'

'In what way?'

Calder looked to Bridges and back to Churchill, swallowed imperceptibly. 'From what we've heard, he appears suspicious of it. Thinks that you might be trying to set him and Hitler against each other.'

Churchill's look was thunderous for a moment, then his expression softened. 'That much is true. So, Comrade Stalin isn't as foolish as we thought.'

Wry smiles were exchanged between Churchill and Bridges, but Calder joined in only fleetingly, his mouth suddenly dry. This next part was even more difficult.

'So much so that Stalin has sent a copy of your letter to Hitler, asking him what he thinks of it.'

Churchill's countenance became dark and brooding again, but this time tinged with disbelief. 'Incredible! I send General Stalin a polite note, informing him of what he should already be able to see with his own eyes – Hitler making troop movements where he shouldn't – and he reacts in this manner.' Churchill gestured with his cigar. 'Unless of course he's trying to play Hitler and me against each other.' He smiled wryly. 'As if he doesn't realize that ship has already sailed, that situation is now somewhat set in stone.'

'There could be something of that in it, Prime Minister,' Calder ventured.

Churchill's eyes settled on him: a weighted, more concerned look. 'You do appreciate that if we can't somehow split this alliance between Hitler and Stalin, our chances of winning the war are remote?'

'Yes, I appreciate that.' Calder took a deep breath. 'Which is where I think the person we've recently put in place close to Hitler might help.'

Churchill's gaze stayed on him steadily as he talked about the arrangements made with Edith Creutzen. 'It might be that Stalin sharing your letter with Hitler is something we could actually turn to our advantage. Hitler will already be nervous about contact between the two of you – so perhaps we can feed that, try and build his paranoia. Hopefully lead him towards making some unwise, premature moves.'

'Yes, certainly one ploy.' Churchill nodded pensively. 'I recall you briefly mentioning this woman before. So, what progress so far?'

'It's early days. We've put in the feeds of where we want Hitler led, but we're awaiting news from their first session. We'll know more later.' Calder gestured. 'Along with, of course, valuable insight on just where Hitler's thoughts are on the issue right now.'

'Of course.' Churchill took a long draw on his cigar. 'I must admit, I was sceptical at first when you mentioned this fortune teller. But I was thinking more of my own feelings on the issue rather than Hitler's. Desperate times call for desperate measures, and if Hitler's thoughts can be swayed even a fraction by this, then so be it. In this case, it could be that vital fraction needed.' Churchill stared the message home for a moment before easing into a gentle smile. 'And in future, I must be more selective of when and how I try to put myself in Hitler's shoes and read his mind.'

11

I knew it might take me a few hours to prepare the code list, especially as it was my first time, so just twenty minutes after putting Louise to bed I told Lara that I was having an early night – 'Busy day' – and headed to my bedroom with a copy of Hermann Hesse's *Siddhartha.*

I locked the door behind me, fearful that Lara might walk in on me halfway through the list – even though she'd never previously disturbed me in my bedroom unannounced. With the reminder that I might be spied on, I did a quick check again for any possible cameras.

'*Dolls or figures with glass eyes*,' Lutz had advised. '*Or any dark, polished surface or mirror that could carry a concealed lens.*'

No dolls or figures in sight. Only a dark onyx jewellery box and a wardrobe mirror. I put the onyx box into a dresser drawer and opened the mirrored wardrobe door so that it was angled away from me – then started on my list.

I made quicker work of it than I'd imagined. Most were standard words, which could be found on many pages, and for Stalin it was agreed I'd simply put 19 – signifying S in the alphabet. '*Few lines should have more than fifteen words in them, so it shouldn't become confused.*'

I'd become so absorbed in preparing the list that I jumped when Lara's voice sailed through the door forty minutes later.

'I'll be leaving now, Edith. I'll see you in the morning.' I'd told her to please drop the 'Fräulein Creutzen' on her third day here, '*Please just call me Edith.*'

'Yes . . . see you tomorrow, Lara.'

I found myself holding my breath until I heard the front door close and knew that she'd gone. I let the air out of my lungs and shut my eyes for a moment. *I don't know if I can do this.*

I finished the list just over an hour later, but looking back over it, it was spread out haphazardly, with the numbers at the bottom scrunched up tightly and almost illegible. I spent a further fifteen minutes rewriting the numbers on a fresh sheet of paper so that it fitted neatly and evenly on one page – then went down to the kitchen and set fire to the first list over the sink, running the tap to wash away every last trace of ash. *I don't know if I can do this.*

I went to bed soon after, but my sleep was fitful – images of that day's session replaying in my mind, the flickering flames of the Reichstag building in the speculum for a moment merging with the flames over the sink. Had I done enough? Had I answered some questions incorrectly? I knew that one question answered wrong could seal my fate. Words from *Siddhartha* and numbers from the list finally tipped me over the edge into sleep.

'Momma . . . *Momma!* You're not up yet!'

Louise was bouncing on the edge of my bed. Usually, I was up half an hour before her to prepare breakfast. I checked the time: 8.42 a.m. Lara would be here in just eighteen minutes!

'OK. Let's get you ready.'

I made quick work of my ablutions in the bathroom, and had Louise sat down at the kitchen table and half-way through her pastry and hot chocolate when Lara turned up.

'Who's been sleeping in a bit this morning?' Lara teased her.

'It wasn't me, it was –'

'We were both a bit restless last night,' I cut in. 'I could hear the drone of some aircraft not far away.' Only a few fleeting bombing raids so far, but German aircraft on manoeuvres or missions was a regular event.

Lara smiled tightly. Hopefully, I'd done enough to deflect any concerns. I checked my watch. 'Oh, Louise's music tutor, Frau Staedel, will be here in just under an hour.'

'OK.' Lara went over and started filling the sink, ready for Louise's dishes and cup to go in when she'd finished.

'I plan to go out to the shops shortly after.'

A brief smile of acceptance back at me. No point in going into detail that it was one of my bookshop visits. Set for 11 a.m. Fifty minutes should be more than enough to get there.

But I was held up a few minutes leaving. I'd carelessly left my numbers list on my bedside table. I must be more careful in future – Lara could have seen it if she'd walked in. On my last meeting with Lutz, he said they were looking into Lara's background, but so far nothing had come back from him. I spent another minute folding the list over repeatedly so it was ticket-sized and slipping it into a back pocket of my flat leather clutch purse usually used for tram and bus tickets, then with a quick goodbye to Louise, who was already in with Frau Staedel, I headed out.

The tram to Hegelplatz was on time, but the other thing I hadn't counted on were the crowds along Dorotheenstrasse. Hitler apparently had a planned speech at the Kroll Opera House, and a mass of people lined the pavements either side waiting for his motorized convoy.

I struggled to push past the throng. I realized too, as I threaded my way through, that the rest of the crowd were static, staring towards the road in expectation. I stood out. My breath falling short, I kept pushing through, a louder clamour from the crowd suddenly rising. Hitler's car was obviously approaching. And as I glanced back, I noticed a young man sixty metres behind me, also pushing his way through. *Was that the man tailing me today, or was he just someone else like me, eager to get somewhere?* Not the same man as last time, but then I'd been told they'd change each time.

Then suddenly the man stopped, staring towards the road, joining in with the chanting, '*Heil Hitler . . . Heil Hitler*', with a straight-armed salute as Hitler's car came into view. Against the bile and resentment I felt for Hitler and the Nazis in general, I paused and did the same, not wishing to appear unpatriotic or stand out even more in the crowd. I kept up with my chanting and salute until Hitler's car was eighty metres past, then continued on.

I checked my watch as the crowd started to thin. I was going to be late! Still half a kilometre to go to Zeughaus Bücher, and already it was three minutes to eleven.

Eight minutes past when I finally got there, breathless and agitated from the rush, and when I went to the back of the bookshop, I couldn't see anyone there. Perhaps they'd already left, tiring of the wait. When a middle-aged man in a beige trilby started browsing close to me I resisted the temptation to speak first, in case it wasn't my contact man.

When he finally spoke, he made no reference to my being late – that might have given away that it was an arranged meeting – only a fleeting frown before he picked a book from the shelf.

'You might find this one of interest. I read it just last week. Very informative!' As he passed the book to me, he deftly slipped a piece of paper into its middle pages.

'Thank you.' I in turn picked out a book from the shelves, took the piece of folded paper from my clutch purse and slipped it inside. 'Fair exchange is no robbery. You might like to try this one too.'

'Thank you.'

He made his way to the counter with the book I'd handed him, and I left it another three minutes – killing the time with more browsing – before I approached the assistant with my book. '*It's important that you're not seen leaving too close to your contact.*'

But on the way back, the fervour of the crowd that had delayed me earlier kept replaying in my mind. That level of mass adulation was quite frightening. And now, I reminded myself, I'd been away from my home for over an hour and a half, with no doubt two similarly ardent Hitler supporters left alone with my daughter – after all, both had been hired and paid for by the Führer. A sudden image of Lara and Frau Staedel teaming up to search through my every drawer and cupboard assaulted me. Had I left any incriminating clues? Had I left a copy of *Siddhartha*, the book the latest code sequence related to, by my bedside?

I hoped my agitation wasn't evident to Lara and Louise when I got back, but I found it difficult indulging in small talk and smiling at all the right moments, and I was sure there was an underlying tension in the remaining hours before the housekeeper left. Or was I just imagining it?

I breathed a sigh of relief when Lara finally said goodnight and I closed the front door behind her. I had moved *Siddhartha* from by bedside table – unless Lara in tidying up had put it back on my bookshelves – although I had forgotten to put back the onyx jewellery box I'd hidden in a drawer. I took it out and returned it to its place.

But when later that night I reached the part of the return deciphered message that read *Try if you can to build up Hitler's preoccupation and paranoia with Stalin*, I found myself closing my eyes as a shudder ran through me, as if trying to shed the last of the day's tensions. First, I had to face my own mounting paranoia.

12

By my fourth date with Stefan, I feared I was falling in love with him – which gave me the biggest conflict between heart and mind that I'd ever faced. My heart telling me it felt right, natural; my mind telling me it was wrong, dangerous.

A final element in my case was my clairvoyance, but when that too sided with my heart, telling me everything would be OK, I started doubting that also. One of the only times I'd gone against my own gifted insight.

I started falling for him, in fact, on our third date – a wonderful meal at Horcher, followed by a cabaret show at Quasimodo – but felt sure, guided by my mind, that I could hold my resolve by keeping back that last stage, that final intimacy.

The nights Stefan came round, I'd leave Louise with my parents for the night – they were glad of the extra time with their grandchild. Stefan had in part urged it. For some reason he didn't want Lara to know about our evenings out, and he always made sure to pick me up fifteen or twenty minutes after she'd left. Though the clue to his secrecy over Lara had been in what he'd said after my chaste goodnight kiss to his cheek after our third night out.

His lips hovered close to mine, and I didn't pull away, felt drawn in in that moment and unable to resist. Only a gently murmured, 'We shouldn't.' Repeated breathlessly, 'We *shouldn't* . . .' after that first, deep, seemingly endless kiss.

Stefan looked into my eyes then. 'I know. I shouldn't be doing this even more than you. It wasn't part of my instructions of being with you.' He shook his head as if shaking off the last of some unseen control.

At some time during the next kiss before we parted, he muttered, 'You're beautiful,' though he held short of saying 'I love you', as did I, that final admission still rattling uncertainly at the back of my mind as I felt myself sinking into his warmth and strength.

Later in my bed alone, I knew that after our next night out he'd probably expect to end up here with me, and so I delayed our next date, kept putting it off for the next two weeks. Create some distance, give me more time to think. But in that time gap, one phrase kept nagging at the back of my mind: '*I shouldn't be doing this even more than you. It wasn't part of my instructions* . . .' I sighed, shaking my head. My holding back from Stefan, keeping my distance, had been folly all along. I'd thought that his kindness and charm had been part of some ploy to get into my confidence, breach my defences. So that any secrets I was harbouring might be more easily uncovered. But now he was saying that courting and getting involved with me romantically wasn't part of his instructions. No wonder he'd wanted to keep our dinner dates secret from Lara.

I suppose I only had myself to blame, because in part I'd been using Stefan. His easy-going nature and affection were a welcome solace from the tension of the sessions and the coded-message bookshop visits. There had been only two sessions since, but the agendas had been fairly uniform: no trick questions, mostly clarifying details from that first session – the nature and extent of any uprisings in Germany, France, Czechoslovakia or Poland, any particular regions or groups indicated? I answered as best I could from what I saw, the only unclear region that of Poland again. '*I see a number of deaths in different regions there . . . but I can see few troop movements or deaths of German soldiers.*' Stalin wasn't raised again – perhaps Hitler was still ruminating over my first-session comments – and I felt it would appear unnatural to broach the issue, might raise brows.

So, in that time, we'd had as many dates as work sessions. I think I'd leaned on Stefan for that solace because there were few other people in Berlin I could turn to. I couldn't share any of my secrets with my parents, and while Teresa and Xavier were also here, I couldn't see them regularly, otherwise it might raise suspicions as to why I kept going repeatedly to the same bookshop, and they'd be investigated. So, I'd seen them only once in the last two weeks, spilling out my heart about how difficult the coded-message bookshop visits were proving.

'The sense that I'm being followed every time . . . and then when I get home, the feeling that Lara and Frau Staedel are spying on me too. No escape!'

'And Stefan?' Teresa probed.

'With him, it's different.' My easy smile already betraying my growing feelings for him. 'It doesn't feel like he's spying on me. I feel comfortable with him.'

Teresa shook her head. 'But maybe that "feeling comfortable" is what you should be most wary of. As you said before, using that to get under your skin. Let your barriers slip . . . and that's when secrets get revealed.'

That doubt lingered again for the first half-hour of our third date. But with his smiles as we clinked wine glasses over dinner – the grey flecks in his green eyes not only gave them warmth, but also made them more intriguing – I realized what it was. While I couldn't reveal to Stefan, as I could with Teresa and Xavier, any of my secrets, this now was one of the most natural things going on in my life – something I felt I desperately needed to balance out all the other madness – the attraction and affection between a man and a woman . . . something I hadn't had for years, not since . . . I tried to push the thought away, but it was quickly back again with the flickering candles between us on the table. *Flickering flames in the dark speculum . . . Erik's corpse in the morgue.*

I felt my eyes glistening, and Stefan reached across and wiped a stray tear from one cheek. 'I'm sorry. Have I made you sad over something?'

'No . . . *no.* I think it might be tears of happiness,' I covered quickly, though it was in part true. 'I haven't felt this happy in a while.' In the end, I managed to delay for a while my initial heart–mind dilemma of falling for Stefan. Though when on our first date after the forced delay period I left Stefan on my doorstep after our goodnight kiss, I noticed his brow rise quizzically for a second. And on the two necessary work sessions we'd had in the interim, I'd caught that same questioning air from him. Was my delay and keeping my distance starting to seem unnatural, so might actually create doubt and suspicion?

But when finally my heart prevailed, possibly aided by my clairvoyance insight, and we ended up in my bed after our next dinner date, Stefan did murmur, 'I love you,' in the middle of our lovemaking – though I waited for a while after my own summit of pleasure had abated before I said the same back to him. Was I also becoming calculating in my love life? Or was it my mind claiming one last vestige of control?

But then two days later I felt totally betrayed. In that time, I'd felt my spirits lifted, most of the burden of my inner tensions gone. And it felt somehow right, a sort of kinship in our relationship; after all, he was harbouring secrets too with our romance. '*It wasn't part of my instructions . . .*' What would happen if the commander of his unit or the Führer found out? A sudden worry that he'd suffer the same fate as Erik. *Was that to be my lot in life? Those close to me killed at Hitler's command?*

And perhaps that had been partly on my mind at our next session, because the trick question halfway through caught me unawares. And with the sudden turnaround, I felt foolish for accepting Stefan's claim of 'not being part of his instructions' at face value, purely because it sided with my heart and clairvoyance. I should have trusted my mind more.

'Some of our Luftwaffe aircraft have seen tanks, armaments and trucks massing on the East Anglian coast in England. Much of it camouflaged – but our aircraft observers have nevertheless seen through it. I wondered if you can see if this will build further, if an attack is imminent?'

I peered into the speculum, but it told me nothing. The shapes there were static, immobile. 'I'm not sure. The images are unclear, not moving. I . . .' And then I remembered one of the questions on Lutz's 'warning list'. That

SOE knew Luftwaffe aircraft had flown over East Anglia and seen what appeared as tanks and armaments being massed for an attack. '*But many of these are in fact broken-down tanks and trucks hauled from nearby armament graveyards put there to create that illusion. Many of them just shells with all vital engines and gearboxes removed. But we also know that the Abwehr have an agent on the ground in England who has viewed this site with binoculars, and seen through this subterfuge. So this might be a question they try and trick you with.*'

I felt abject fury in that moment: One day I let this man into my bed, then the next he's asking me trick questions that could lead to my death. I shifted my even stare from Stefan back to the speculum, calmed myself for my response.

'Not only do I see those images as static now, but I don't see them moving in the future, either.'

'So, you don't see those tanks and trucks moving in a later attack?'

'No, I don't. Don't ask me why.' I sighed, looking back up from the speculum. 'Perhaps they decided to call off such an attack – knowing that they'd been spotted by Luftwaffe planes.' I felt I'd done enough; indicating that I knew the tanks and trucks couldn't be moved might be going too far.

Stefan nodded his acceptance, made a note, and the session ended soon after.

But when Stefan phoned the next night asking for a date, I put him off; then the same the next two times. I think he got the message that something was wrong, because the next day he sent me a large bouquet of flowers with a small envelope attached. I palmed Lara off with the story that it was a secret admirer from my last bookshop visit, 'A fellow lover of vintage books,' then went into my bedroom to open the sealed note:

I'm sorry if something in my last visit somehow upset you. But please remember, I don't prepare the questions . . . I'm only the messenger.

I put my head in my hands. One day my lover; the next, the 'messenger' of my death. *I don't know if I can do this.*

13

Deià, Mallorca, October 1973

'. . . So, as you see, Edith falling in love with Stefan wasn't at all planned – quite the opposite. The *last* thing she wanted to do was fall in love with him, because of the associated dangers.' Teresa held a palm out. 'But, ironically, those same dangers and tensions with the sessions and running codes led her into his arms.'

Robert Graves nodded thoughtfully. 'She needed that love and affection in her life at that moment to balance all of that out. I can understand that.'

Jacob Bronowski sipped at his wine. 'I'm surprised that she was able to carry on after that. The thought that at any moment her lover could inadvertently sign her death warrant.'

'It wasn't easy, but I think in the end Edith became convinced that she might be better off in that situation with a lover, someone close to her, rather than just another random person with little care for her.'

'That couldn't have been an easy transition to make,' Bronowski commented. 'Getting to trust a lover in that situation, especially with all the connected dangers.'

'Well, she did have a little help with that.' Teresa took a sip of water, her expression taut. 'Edith came to see me at my bookshop shortly after all this happened and poured out her heart. After getting past the obvious that she'd perhaps been foolhardy given the risks involved, I started to look at the situation objectively: if she stopped her romance with Stefan but kept up the sessions, he could feel rebuffed and jilted, which could make things more tense and lead to a riskier situation if anything was later uncovered. And if she felt she needed to be *totally* apart from Stefan and stopped the sessions with him, they'd simply appoint someone else. I knew I had her swaying, but Xavier, more attuned to the harsh realities of the Nazis, helped with a final nudge when he said, "And that someone probably wouldn't care a jot for you, and certainly wouldn't try and protect you if things went wrong. At least with Stefan there's that possibility." '

Graves and Bronowski exchanged a look. 'Good thinking,' Graves said, gesturing. 'And obviously Edith accepted that?'

'Yes. Though reluctantly at first. To her, it just seemed the lesser of two evils. So, their relationship took a couple of weeks to warm up again. But then the session came where she'd be put to the test more than ever: Hitler had requested a personal visit at the Berghof, his mountain retreat. It appeared he had some issues of particular significance to him, and so he wanted to ask those questions directly. Stefan would be with her, but just taking notes.'

'I've seen photos of the Berghof,' Bronowski said. 'But what was it like for Edith actually being there – in the lion's den, so to speak?'

'Not too different from here.' Teresa waved a hand out. 'A remote mountain hideaway. Edith said that they actually went to the nearby Kehlsteinhaus for the session, which was like an eagle's nest in the sky, up among the clouds.' The timbre of Teresa's voice changed a fraction. '"The closest to God that I've ever felt . . . even though at that point I was sat opposite the devil."'

14

The pine forests of Southern Bavaria flashed by the window of Stefan's Mercedes 230 saloon. We said little on the first part of the journey, perhaps both fearful of what awaited at this personal session with Hitler. But Stefan did reach out and clasp my hand at intervals, as if in reassurance. That brief gap between us after the trick question of the last session was now firmly bridged.

I hadn't in fact broached the subject until our second dinner date after that brief respite, said simply that I didn't appreciate questions designed to catch me out, 'Especially now I've shared my bed with you.'

'I understand. But like I said, I'm just the messenger here . . . so don't shoot me.' His awkward smile had dropped as he became more serious. 'Do you want me to stop being the messenger?'

'No . . . no,' I'd said, recalling Teresa's advice. 'But perhaps you could notify me afterwards if I have at any time said the wrong thing.'

'I . . . I'm not sure they'd even tell me.' He held out a hand helplessly. 'I'm just a messenger to them too, not privy to all their secrets.'

I'd nodded. That made sense. He was just a pawn in this game. And I too was holding back as many secrets from him on my side. So, I'd aired the only thing I felt I was able to.

'If I did answer any questions wrong, displease the Führer in any way – what do you think they'd do with me? Simply send me back to Paris, or something more serious?'

'More serious?'

I explained about what had happened with Hanussen. In favour with the Führer one day, then killed the next. 'And I fear the same thing might happen to me.'

'I see.' Stefan stared emptily for a moment, as if seeking answers in the space between us, then: 'I'd try not to let that happen.'

Stefan hadn't elaborated on how he might do that, and I hadn't pressed the subject since.

One thing that began to intrigue me about Stefan was his lack of background. He knew much about me, but I knew little about him. He'd never volunteered anything and I'd never asked – perhaps thinking it was part of SS training to remain tight-lipped about personal details – though I did now.

When I asked him about his family his eyes stayed fixed for a moment on the road ahead before answering. 'My father died in the first war when I was only eight, and so I was raised mostly by my mother.'

'And is your mother still alive?'

'Yes, very much so. She lives in fact not far from here, in the small town of Rosenheim, seventy kilometres from Munich, where I was brought up.' He paused again then, as if this next part was difficult or he was unsure about sharing it. 'It wasn't easy for her, on her own, raising me and my two sisters after my father had died.' He fired me a quick, pained smile. 'Perhaps why I admire so much what you're doing with your little Louise. I know it's not easy.'

'Thank you.' I smiled tightly back. 'But I've had a lot of support. From my parents here, and some close friends in Paris.'

Stefan simply nodded, stared at the road again for a moment. Then, with a sigh, 'My mother had good support too, mainly from my uncle on her side. In fact, he was almost like a father to me – the only male figure I had around at that time to guide me.'

'And is your uncle still alive?'

'No . . . no, he's not.' Darker, pained shadows drifted behind his eyes. 'He died just six years ago.'

'That couldn't have been easy for your mother, either. Losing her husband at such a young age, then later her brother.'

'No, it wasn't easy at all.' His jaw set tight for a moment, then he waved one hand from the steering wheel, a dismissive motion. 'But by then I was twenty-six, a grown man, so it wasn't such an issue.'

I could tell that something else was troubling him about his uncle's death, but for whatever reason, he didn't want to elaborate.

'Ah, almost there,' Stefan announced soon after as a signpost appeared ahead: *Berchtesgaden.*

We spent only half an hour at the Berghof with Hitler – on a front terrace bathed in sunlight looking onto the surrounding mountains – before being plunged into the darkness of the long tunnel and elevator to the Kehlsteinhaus.

In fact, we'd been only fifteen minutes in Hitler's

company before he announced, 'I will leave now and go ahead of you to ensure everything is ready.' He gestured vaguely to some soldiers standing rigid, rifles at their side, five paces away. 'Some of my men will accompany you there shortly.'

My nerves were on a knife edge. In that brief time on the Berghof terrace with Hitler, he'd first of all commented on the marvellous view. 'I feel I can relax here like no other place.' Then he attempted polite conversation. 'I hope you're settling in well back in Berlin . . . Hopefully, SS-Hauptsturmführer Hansel is treating you well?' He spoke almost as if Stefan wasn't there, but I noticed a faint glimmer in his eyes, as if he knew or suspected something about our deeper relationship, or perhaps he had read it into the body language between us. *Or maybe Stefan had been lying all along and that* had *been part of his instructions.*

I kept to brief, compliant answers throughout, elaborating only when he inquired whether my daughter's music lessons were going well. 'Is the tutor we've assigned proficient?'

'Yes, very much so. Louise has progressed marvellously under her guidance these past few weeks.' I found myself swallowing back my nerves between comments, desperate to shield my clawing anxiety.

Then Hitler departed and we were left alone, the atmosphere as strained and awkward as in that brief exchange. What on earth could we talk about with the guards so close by within earshot?

So we filled that gap with comments again about the wonderful scenery, then next thing we were plunged into the darkness of the Kehlsteinhaus approach tunnel accompanied by three of those guards, who'd also been with us on the short drive there.

The air was cold and stagnant in the tunnel, only stark lights at intervals marking our progress. The ascent in the elevator seemed never-ending and was hardly better – stark brightness again assaulting our senses as its doors finally opened.

It was like rising from a tomb into life and light again – that contrast even more extreme because of the surrounding scenery: mountaintops and valleys spreading into the distance, clouds below us clinging to some mountainsides.

'And here I feel as if I am on top of the world,' Hitler commented as we admired the dramatic view. 'I think you can understand why I come up here.'

'Yes, I can,' I said, my breath half gone in awe at the view.

But I couldn't help thinking: he'd obviously chosen this spot to reflect what he saw increasingly as his 'overlord' status. But here he was far more remote from it, out of touch.

'Everything should be ready now,' Hitler said curtly, and led the way back into the heart of the Kehlsteinhaus.

Into the session room set up there. Into darkness again.

For the first fifteen minutes, Hitler let Stefan lead the questioning.

'I wish to observe how you conduct matters for a while, then I'll take over.'

The scrying room had been set up in a side chamber of the Kehlsteinhaus, a large study or bedroom five metres square, almost a carbon copy of my at-home session room in Berlin: a large round table at its centre carrying the speculum, a large spotlight suspended low over it, casting an eerie glow into the surrounding darkness. Three chairs around the central table, two against a back wall to one side, one of which Hitler took to observe Stefan and me at the speculum.

And I wondered for a moment if Hitler didn't just wish to see how the questions were conducted, but to observe the interaction between us; answer his curiosity as to whether there was anything deeper going on with us.

With my left hand, I gripped the glove Stefan held out, the first questions revolving around the possible groups behind the agitations and uprisings I'd previously mentioned.

I said that in Germany it appeared the actions of Bolsheviks and dissidents had been mostly quelled. 'Though I think at times the Führer has to be more cautious and wary about those close to him.' In part it was what I saw in the speculum, some clandestine plots, but also to ward off a possible repeat of Hanussen's fate, those close to him creating doubts about me.

'The minor agitations in the East I see waning as the communists lose their grip there.' The rapidly shifting images in the speculum washed over me. 'And any renewed rising resistance in France, I see now as mainly led by England . . . and so some time away.'

But then Stefan honed in on something specific. 'In regard to that resistance in France, there was an attempt on the Führer's life during his visit there. We are still looking for the perpetrator – but do you see us catching him?'

My nerves immediately tensed. Could they possibly know about my association with Xavier and Teresa, and this was another trick question? I looked into the speculum, tried to calm my nerves.

'I . . . I see that he is quite well hidden. So it might take some time.'

'Do you have an indication of where?'

My nerves tensed another notch. They knew something and were just playing with me. I peered into the speculum more intensely. 'It . . . it's not totally clear – but I don't see him in Paris.' My brow knitted as I concentrated, answering ambiguously, 'So perhaps another city or town in France.'

Stefan nodded after a second, then got up from his seat. Hitler, having indicated that he move without saying anything, strode across and sat in his place.

Was this the part where Hitler confronted me, declared that they knew about my past association with Xavier and Teresa? Knew that I was a fake planted to trick him, and ordered my execution?

But after a fresh breath, he broached the subject of the possible clandestine plots I'd mentioned earlier. 'You say that I have to be more wary of people close to me. Do you see any indications as to who?'

I stared into the speculum, saw some flashes of high-ranking insignia and badges among the shifting shadows. 'From what I see, it appears to be some high officials in the military. Or perhaps even your own SS.'

Hitler nodded pensively, but past him to the side I noticed Stefan flinch slightly at my comment. Hitler appeared to mull this over a moment longer, perhaps mentally sifting through possible suspects, before focusing on me sharply again.

'You also mentioned before seeing a number of deaths in Poland. I wondered if you see these deaths as of a particular ethnic group?'

I knew immediately what he was angling at, even aside from what the speculum showed me. His earlier obsession with the Jews, which hadn't been so prevalent the last two years, was coming to the forefront again. But I didn't want to openly say it, be responsible for possibly guiding him in that direction.

'I . . . I can't say with all clarity.' The speculum images weren't totally clear in any case. 'I see many ethnic groups. So all I can say with certainty is that none are true Aryans. Not pure.'

I'd used this last term to specifically please the Führer. I saw the faint trace of a smile, but then he did a strange thing. He reached out and gently clasped my hand across the table.

'Do you think you might be getting a stronger connection now, clearer images?'

'Yes . . . *yes*,' I answered breathlessly after a second, realizing he was referring to my preference for personal connection, his direct touch a step up from his glove. His hand was warm and clammy, in stark contrast to the icy shiver that ran down my spine.

But all I saw in the speculum again were the rising flames of the Reichstag fire, merging with the fires from ovens and crematoriums in Poland. Another shudder ran through me.

'And where do you see these large numbers of deaths in Poland?'

'In various places,' I answered shakily, drawn in by the flickering flames in the speculum. 'But mainly in the east. Many places not far from the Russian border.'

Hitler smiled tautly. 'Ah, Russia. Now there's a conundrum. Do you see these deaths in Poland as connected with Russia?'

'No, I don't . . .' The flames seemed to consume me for a moment. 'Not at the outset, at least.'

Hitler sat back, appearing to deliberate this for a moment, slot it into place with what he knew or had planned.

'And talking again of Russia now. You mentioned in one session that General Stalin was preparing armaments there, as if perhaps preparing for war?'

'Yes . . . that is what I saw.'

'But why would he do that? He knows that we have a pact together of non-aggression.'

'Be . . . because he fears that at some stage you will break that pact.' I felt uncertain telling Hitler directly about his likely errant actions; with the buffer of Stefan between us, it hadn't felt so perturbing. 'And if and when you do, he wants to be prepared.'

'I see.' Hitler looked across at me intently then. 'And is he preparing those armaments apace?'

I peered into the speculum, in part as a welcome release from Hitler's stare, lost myself in the shifting shadows and flames there. 'Yes, he is.'

Hitler sighed. 'So, the longer I leave it, the more prepared he will be for war. Is that what you see?'

But in that moment, the flames in the speculum moved from the ovens and crematoriums of Poland to the battlefields of Russia. Torn and bloodied bodies stretching into the distance. And as much as I knew that this is what my handlers wanted, I felt a sudden pang at what might be wrought on the Russian people. '*Hitler will break that pact in any case at some stage*,' Lutz had reassured me. '*All we're doing is trying to precipitate that action so that the war might be won*.' Hitler was staring at me intently, starting to ponder my uncertainty.

'Yes, it is,' I said at length, hoping I'd quelled any hesitance in my voice.

Hitler continued contemplating me steadily for a moment, then: 'So what you are saying is that if I am to take action, it should be sooner rather than later – if I hope to win such a war against Stalin?'

In the speculum, the flames were stronger now, all consuming. What on earth was I about to do?

'Yes . . . that is what I see,' I said with a final, resigned exhalation.

With a curt confirming nod from Hitler, the session ended then, and minutes later the overwhelming sinking sensation I felt was matched by the elevator taking us back down into the darkness of the Kehlsteinhaus tunnel, uncertain in that moment whether I was consumed more with the hope that I'd done enough to spark an invasion, or the prayer that I hadn't.

15

I knew the message I had to encode was a vitally important one, but this time I waited half an hour after Lara had left before starting on it. The chosen book this time was Paul Heyse's *Die Einsamen*.

I was getting more proficient. It took me only an hour and ten minutes this time, and the finished line of numbers was evenly spaced and fitted neatly onto one page; no need to rewrite it. No old list burned over the sink. And I made sure to put *Die Einsamen* neatly back in place on my downstairs bookshelves before I folded over the finished code sheet and tucked it into my bedside drawer, ready for the following morning.

Louise had her first day of summer school that day – a small local school just three streets away arranged for one month, including some music lessons. I slipped the coded note into the handbag I took with me for the short walk; didn't want to risk leaving it in the house with Lara there.

I'd left Louise with my parents again for the trip to the Berghof with Stefan, though didn't go into any detail with them about it. I'd spent more time too with Tobias before leaving. Though twenty-two now, after a while he seemed to gravitate more to Louise, converse and play with her more naturally than with me while I looked on with a bittersweet smile.

'Uncle Tobias says that he hates the Nazis and Hitler,' Louise said now on the way to school.

I looked at her with concern. 'Why's that?'

'He says he overheard Grandpa Lukas and Grandma Elsa talking about how the Nazis are trying to take him away, send him to an asylum and do bad things to him.'

A sudden pang hit my stomach. I stopped and crouched down to her height, clasped her shoulders. 'That might be so, but we will try and make sure not to let that happen. And you must *never* repeat that to anyone else.' I lightly shook her shoulders. 'You understand?'

'Yes.' Louise chewed at her bottom lip, looked shaken and perplexed by my firm insistence. 'But why?'

'Be . . . because some bad people might overhear you and then tell the Nazis. And then Tobias would be taken away with the excuse of trying to protect you.' I willed the message home as best I could with my eyes. How to explain Nazi policies to a seven-year-old? That the mentally ill or impeded were already on treacherous ground, and practically any excuse would be used to take them away, part of a Hitler speech echoing in my head: '*We cannot afford to have good, upright and healthy Aryan citizens infected by those who are mentally ill or have impure thoughts.*' 'And you wouldn't wish that to happen, would you?'

Louise was near tears now, her bottom lip trembling, as she murmured shakily, 'No, I wouldn't.'

'That's good,' I said with a tight smile of apology. I straightened and we carried on.

I was still rattled from the brief exchange when I got home. I checked my watch: fifty minutes left to get ready.

But just ten minutes before I was due to leave, Stefan turned up.

'Going shopping somewhere?' he asked, seeing that I was getting ready to go out.

'No. Just one of my boring bookshop trips to hunt out Berlin's vintage rarities.' Having already told Lara that I was going out 'book hunting' – she'd otherwise wonder on those occasions why I came back with just a book rather than dresses or lingerie – I couldn't shift my story.

'I should come with you,' Stefan ventured.

'No . . . *no*,' I said, perhaps a little too sharply. He'd suggested before that he accompany me on one of my bookshop visits and I'd put him off. 'Like I said, you'd just get bored waiting while I browsed.'

Stefan pouted. 'I could meanwhile busy myself reading Werner Beumelberg. Get my regular infusion of war stories.'

I looked back at him, my wire-taut nerves delaying the recognition that he was probably joking. I laughed uncomfortably. 'I get carried away so much at times that I stand there reading whole passages and muttering them to myself. Even the most exciting war stories wouldn't save you from that tedium.'

Stefan gave a wry smile back after a moment and nodded his acceptance. But I was aware of Lara picking up on our interchange in the background, hoping that I hadn't come across as too insistent, protesting too much, to either of them.

I blew a kiss to Stefan when Lara turned away, said my goodbyes and walked briskly to the nearest tram stop round the corner. Even that brief exchange had held me up a few minutes, and I didn't want to be late again.

With my rush to the tram stop and grabbing one that had just pulled up, I was in the end slightly early, so spent a moment looking in shop windows a few hundred metres from Nürnberger Buchhandlung to kill the time.

I saw what could have been my contact pass me and approach Nürnberger Buchhandlung, but couldn't be sure. Mid-thirties, dark-grey plaid jacket, black leather cap over dark-blond hair. But then I noticed something strange: a man in his late twenties, brown jacket and matching trilby, fairly nondescript, just fifty metres from me. I thought at first he was looking at me, but then noticed his gaze was fixed intently on the man in the leather cap approaching.

His eyes stayed fixed on the bookshop entrance as he drifted past me, hardly registering me, then he took up a position eighty metres along from me, turning into a shop doorway to light a cigarette. He was trying to act nonchalant, but I could see his eyes dart at intervals towards Nürnberger Buchhandlung.

I felt nervous for a moment going in there observed by him – but I was already one minute over the scheduled meeting time, and it wasn't until I saw a young couple enter the bookshop shortly after that I felt brave enough to walk the last few hundred metres and enter myself.

I hadn't looked towards the second man as I'd passed him, but feared my anxiety might be evident to anyone keenly observing me.

'I could strongly recommend this one.' The voice made me jump. The man with the black leather cap had drifted silently to my side without me noticing him.

'Yes . . . thank you,' I stuttered, taking the book from him. He must have already slipped the code-note inside without me seeing. I glanced past him and to one side before leaning in close. I knew I was disobeying instructions, but felt I had to warn him. 'As I approached, I noticed a man who appeared to be following you,' I muttered sotto-voce.

His voice was barely a whisper back. 'Did he appear to be watching you also?'

'No. He appeared to be focused solely on you, hardly noticed me.'

He cogitated this for a second. 'Then perhaps do me a favour. Leave only a minute after me, and try and notice if he's still following me – without drawing attention to yourself, of course. I'll try and lose him meanwhile.'

I nodded, and was about to ask how I might later get the message to him if he'd been followed, when an elderly man started browsing at the end of our row.

'Oh, and this one I can heartily recommend to you,' I said in a clearer voice, picking *Kunst und Macht* from the shelf. Now a dab-hand, I'd already palmed the folded code-note from my purse into my hand as I'd entered the row, and now slid it between the pages of the book.

'Thank you. I'll try it.'

I watched him approach the counter and pay, and I left it another minute before approaching myself – enough for him to get a few dozen metres away so I could observe if he was being followed.

At first, I couldn't see the second man at all, and by this stage the man in the black cap was a good distance ahead, walking at a steady pace along Nürnberger Strasse. But then I saw the man in the brown jacket and trilby emerge from a shop doorway and start following him.

He didn't seem to look back and spot me, his gaze intent on the man in the black leather cap ahead, and I followed for another two hundred metres or so until I was sure he was tailing the first man. And then, almost as if he sensed someone's eyes on him from behind, he half-turned to glance back. I ducked into the next right turn.

I was sure he hadn't fully seen me. I'd browse in some shops for a while, then circle back to the tram stop, by which time hopefully the man in the brown jacket would be out of sight.

But this still begged the question: how would I get a message to the man in the black cap that he'd been followed? And what would happen if he was apprehended with a code-note that I'd just prepared?

The man in the black leather cap, Felix Engelmann, was a veteran of Berlin's Resistance. It wasn't a particularly large or organized movement – almost by necessity in a nation where support of the Nazis encroached upon every corner. It helped to be small, discreet, mobile and ever-morphing.

The ex-SPD, FAUD and Rote Kapelle members who formed it had learned some harsh lessons from the fates of those who had been too vocal or visible in the past, many of whom had been rounded up by the Gestapo and SS and sent to camps or killed.

So now they operated quietly in the shadows, weren't part of any organized worker unions or groups and were never outspoken or drew attention to themselves. From a range of mostly unremarkable professions, the main thing bonding them was their abhorrence of Hitler and the Nazis.

Engelmann had been born with a club foot, hardly noticeable when he walked, but it had disqualified him from active service. He was now a night-watchman at a Krupp depot in north Berlin, which gave him the days free for any clandestine meetings. 'I spend my nights protecting one of the Reich's main arms manufacturers, then my days trying to destroy the Reich,' he'd jibed to Resistance colleagues.

But this reported sighting now from his bookshop contact was worrying, and as he walked rapidly back along Nürnberger Strasse he racked his brain for how it might have come about. He didn't think he'd been careless himself, so that meant one of his past recent contacts had been compromised or had tattled about him. He sifted back through for who that might be, taking a sharp left turn just ahead.

Then another right turn eighty metres on.

Then a left turn after seventy metres . . . glancing fleetingly back just before disappearing into the turn.

The man in the brown jacket and trilby was still following.

He realized he might have to take more drastic avoidance measures. The last thing he could let happen was to be caught with the code-note book on him, especially given the presumably vital nature of this particular message. But the man was closing the distance between them, and he couldn't walk much faster with his club foot, his breath already starting to fall short.

He could now see the Kaufhaus des Westens department

store two hundred metres ahead, and he picked up pace towards it. He caught a glimpse of the man following about ninety metres behind as he made his way into the store, then wended his way quickly towards the men's department at the back.

Picking trousers and a jacket off the racks, he approached the assistant to one side.

'I'd like to try these on.'

'Certainly, sir.' The assistant gestured towards the changing rooms.

On Engelmann's last glimpse back before going into them, the man in brown was standing uncertainly in the middle of the store, making out he was casually browsing. Engelmann knew that the man wouldn't try and apprehend him in the store, but he'd have to be quick before the assistant became suspicious.

The changing cubicle he sought was at the end. He pulled the curtain shut, hung his trousers and jacket on the hook to one side and donned the new ones. Then he stepped onto the bench seat and pushed open the high window above. A narrow window, it would be a squeeze – but he knew it was large enough to get through, having checked the cubicle before as a potential escape route on this busy main street. All part of their regular advance checks.

With *Kunst und Macht* tucked into his waistband, he levered up, squeezed through and eased down the far side, jumping the last two metres and crouching into a half-roll so that he didn't sprain his ankles, then brushed himself off as he started walking briskly away along the back alley. Two more dog-leg alley turns would take him into Ansbacher Strasse, and from there he was only half a kilometre from where the radio transmitter had been set up. The important thing was that he wasn't still being followed as he approached the transmitter rendezvous, and Engelmann felt sure he'd achieved that.

While they were tapping Morse-code messages to their SOE contacts in Paris and London, the man in brown would probably still be in Kaufhaus des Westens, scratching his head as to where he'd gone.

16

Tap, tap, tap . . . tap . . . tap, tap . . .

They always sent the messages as they were, just a series of numbers, so if picked up by chance on the airwaves en route, it would mean little or nothing to the interceptors and listeners.

Engelmann was so immersed in the message being sent that he barely discerned the faint sound beyond it. A creaking board on the staircase or in the corridor below.

There were only three of them in the room: Engelmann, the transmitter operator, nimble-fingered Reinhart Diener, and stocky Horst Friedberg at the far end of the room on lookout.

'I'll check it out,' Friedberg mumbled, moving from the side window to the door. He opened it a fraction, listening out.

Slightly more distinct now, the sound of faint shuffling feet, two people, maybe three.

'I'll be finished in under a minute,' Diener muttered under his breath.

Engelmann could see Diener's finger tracing frantically four-fifths of the way down the page of numbers.

They were in a small back office on the first floor of a derelict shoe factory. Nobody knew if the past owners were Jews who'd fled or Aryan-Germans whose business hadn't survived the depression. Just one of many handy abandoned sites they used throughout the city.

A slightly firmer step now, another floorboard creak. Someone was heading up the stairs.

Beads of sweat broke out on Diener's forehead as he desperately tapped out the last line of code.

Tap, tap . . . tap, tap, tap . . .

And possibly something was more insistent in those final taps because the footsteps below became firmer and more rapid.

'*Komm schon*. Here! They're up here!'

Diener threw the radio transmitter into a large rucksack, hoisted it over one shoulder and made his way out the side window onto the fire escape.

'I'll hold them off for a minute,' Friedberg said, drawing a pistol from his waistband as he looked anxiously through the gap in the door.

Rapid, frantic clattering of boots on the stairs now as Engelmann followed onto the fire escape and they started clambering hastily down towards the motorbike and sidecar in the alley below.

They were halfway down when they heard the first shot ring out above them, then a heavy volley of return fire.

For the second time that day Felix Engelmann found himself trying to escape. But at least the message had now been sent. As he knew all too well by now, the rest of them were subservient to that end. Expendable.

Tap, tap . . . tap, tap, tap . . .

'I don't know. Just looks like a series of numbers – could be just horseracing betting,' Gerhard Bachtel said, operating the 40cm-square HF/DF – high-frequency directional finder.

The man in the brown jacket and trilby standing to one side, Klaus Ziegler of the Gestapo, grimaced uncomfortably.

Two days ago, they'd received information from a Rote Kapelle member they'd captured and questioned that Felix Engelmann was a 'message sender' for SOE and the Allied forces. Ziegler had followed Engelmann the day before, but he'd gone nowhere of any consequence. Just to a working-man's café on his own, then in the evening to work. But with today's bookshop visit, Ziegler was sure he was onto something when he'd seen Engelmann leave with a book in his grasp.

That suspicion was then confirmed when Engelmann had gone to such lengths to elude him.

'I don't think so,' Ziegler said. 'Where I last saw him was not far from here. Try and triangulate a bit more from what they're picking up at Orpo central.'

They were sat in the back of an Ordnungspolizei Volkswagen van with a driver and two armed soldiers.

After losing Engelmann, Ziegler had circled around the block and got into the van. The main Orpo tracking centre in Berlin could only determine approximate coordinates of messages being sent, so the aim of the mobile vans with their own HF/DF units was to triangulate against that to pin down more precise locations.

But if and when a precise location *was* pinned down, there was little point if you didn't have at least a small armed group to apprehend whoever was transmitting.

'They'd probably been broadcasting for four or five

minutes before we even picked them up,' Bachtel said. 'So they might have only a few minutes left. You know these transmissions are usually short.'

'I *know*. But I'm sure we're close.'

Tap, tap, tap . . . tap . . . tap, tap.

Bachtel nodded, wrote some figures down, made a couple of arcs with a protractor on the map spread out before him, then called towards the driver.

'Take the next right, then turn left at the end and keep going until I tell you to stop.'

The drone of the engine half drowned out the high-pitched whine of the tapping, and Bachtel leaned in closer to the HF/DF, trying to pick up the strength of signal not only from his needle indicator, but from its sound.

At the point the needle dipped a fraction, the sound also weakening, he shouted, 'Stop!' He glanced out of the rear window of the van. 'Now back up and take the turning on the right.'

The driver reversed and swung into the turn, and as the signal rose in strength again: 'OK, here! *Stop!*' Bachtel looked through the front window this time, past the driver's shoulder. He turned to Ziegler, pointing. 'My guess is one of those two buildings on the right.'

Ziegler contemplated the two three-storey derelict-looking buildings, then nodded to the two soldiers. 'OK, let's go!'

The first building had a heavily rusted chain around its gate and didn't look like anyone had been in there in years. The door to the second was dusty and stiff, but opened. Ziegler beckoned the soldiers and they headed down a long corridor, moving as quietly and stealthily as they could.

As they approached the stairway, Ziegler held one hand up, listening out keenly. He thought he could hear some faint sounds from the floor above, but it could just be rats or mice scurrying. He started edging up the stairs cautiously, and as he reached the fifth step up, he heard it clearly then . . .

Tap, tap . . . tap, tap, tap . . .

'*Komm schon.* Here! They're up here!'

He urged on the two soldiers behind as he started rapidly up, the gunshot as he reached the top of the stairs catching him by surprise. He ducked back for a second, then fired at the gap in the door towards the end of the corridor, rifle fire from the soldiers behind him quickly following.

And as that gap closed under the heavy volley of fire, Ziegler ran towards it. He was determined that the man in the black cap wouldn't elude him for a second time that day.

17

Having dropped Louise off at summer school the next day, I was only a hundred metres down the road when the man seemed to come out of nowhere from behind and approach me. My breath caught in my throat until I realized at the last second that it was Gregor Lutz, whispering that we needed to meet urgently later that morning at eleven thirty at Grunewald Bücher.

Without elaborating, he went at a brisk pace ahead of me, walking away from the school.

My stomach was still in turmoil when I got back home. *What could it be?*

Lara was in the kitchen, halfway through washing up the plates and cups from breakfast.

'I have to go out again in just over an hour,' I said.

Lara half turned. 'Anywhere exciting?'

'Another bookshop visit. A book I was after is due in today, so I daren't leave it.'

'OK. Will you be back in time to pick Louise up from school?'

'I think so. But if I'm not back by two thirty, could you go and get her?'

'Of course.' Lara half turned again, smiling primly, then faced back to the sink as I left the kitchen.

After a moment, Lara heard the sound of Edith's footsteps heading up the stairs.

Lara finished washing up, then went into the lounge, her ears still attuned to Edith moving around upstairs.

The sound of the bathroom door opening and closing came after a couple of minutes, but Lara waited a moment more before reaching for the phone. *It should be safe now.* She took the piece of paper from her pocket and gave the operator the number on it.

The man at the other end answered after two rings.

'She's heading to another bookshop,' Lara muttered, one ear still attuned to the sounds upstairs. 'You asked me to call you if she did so.'

'Yes, *yes*. You did the right thing.' A faint sigh the other end. 'When is she going there?'

'In just over an hour.'

'That soon?' But it was said as a casual observation, not accusatory or doubting. 'Thank you for calling.'

'*My pleasure*' would seem odd, given the circumstances, so Lara simply responded, 'I'd better go,' and hung up.

The sound of water running had stopped upstairs, and usually the bathroom door opened a minute after.

For all the oddities of her profession, Edith Creutzen was at least a creature of habit.

Edith was still in a half-daze as she left the house, her worries mounting over her upcoming meeting with Gregor Lutz. One of the disadvantages of being a fortune teller that went beyond standard apprehension. *You already knew when the worst was coming.*

So that was perhaps why she didn't notice the Volkswagen 3 parked sixty metres back from the tram stop, nor spotted it following the tram all the way to Wilmersdorf.

Nor indeed noticed when it pulled in again behind her when she finally got off on Hohenzollerndamm and started heading towards Grunewald Bücher.

The Volkswagen 3 driver didn't edge closer until Edith was practically out of view, saw her go into Grunewald Bücher, then backed up again and parked a more discreet distance away, with the entrance of Grunewald Bücher just visible in the distance.

I shook my head in despair as Gregor Lutz finished talking.

One of Lutz's team followed. Part of the last coded message I'd delivered probably intercepted. Soldiers storming in and almost catching them transmitting. Another of the team shot. Could it get any worse?

'What happened to the man who was shot? Did he survive?' I inquired.

'Yes, he did. He reached the window uninjured but caught a bullet to one shoulder going down the fire escape.' Lutz made a moue. 'But I don't know if he'll be OK. We couldn't risk taking him to a hospital or listed doctor, and the only man we have with any experience is just a basic medic. He removed the bullet and cleaned the wound as best he could, but there's still the risk of gangrene or septicaemia.'

'And how much of that last message do you think was listened in to?'

'We don't know for sure. Might have been only the last minute, might have been as much as four or five minutes.' Lutz gestured. 'But I doubt more than that. It only took eight minutes to send the whole thing.'

I felt that despair sink deeper into my stomach. 'But they might have over half of my last message. That contained set phrases and comments from Hitler. They'll be able to work out from that that it's me.'

'No, you're very likely safe,' Lutz said. 'We send all the messages just in their original numbered code. And it's not like some Enigma deciphering, where they can piece a message together from the most common letters used. Each word is set and unique, and even if they work out it comes from a book, newspaper or magazine – unless they know the book concerned, the message will be gibberish. And they would also have to know the exact sequence of books used, because it changes each time.'

I nodded, sinking into thought. So, not as bad as I feared, but 'very likely' still didn't sound good enough when not only my own life was in the balance, but 'very likely' also my whole family's too. As with last time, we were sat in the back room at the bookstore Lutz's Resistance friend owned.

Lutz took a cigarette out of a packet of Boscos on his desk and lit it. I hadn't seen him smoke before, so maybe he did so infrequently, or only when tense and troubled. When things were going wrong.

'But with bookshops now possibly more in the spotlight, those visits will have to be lessened.' Lutz took a puff, looked to one side as if for inspiration. 'So, despite my earlier reservations about them, maybe we'll have to go mostly for café or shop meetings.'

'But if books are exchanged at those, surely that will be as bad?'

'No. Because my plan is that the books won't be visible.

A man or woman sitting at the next table to you with the same or similar shopping bag – or in a department store where the same bags would of course be expected.' Lutz exhaled, the words tumbling out with little pause for thought. He'd obviously worked all of this out beforehand. 'Then each of you picks up the wrong bag when you leave. Inside are books with messages in them, but they can't be seen by anyone. So, no possible giveaway.'

I nodded. A well-structured, workable plan; but then I expected no less from Gregor Lutz. I homed in on the only perceivable weakness. 'You say "lessened" for the bookshop visits. Why not stopped completely if they're now seen as a problem?'

'Because that might seem odd to the people around you – Stefan Hansel and your housekeeper, Lara. Regular bookshop visits, then suddenly they stop. So, you'd still visit bookshops regularly, but without dropping off or picking up coded messages. So, if you are apprehended at one of those, nothing possibly incriminating will be found on you.'

'I see.' Something worrying still niggled at the back of my mind about this, but I couldn't immediately pinpoint what it was.

Lutz held out a palm. 'We might, in fact, reintroduce the bookshop code-swap visits later, when everything's settled down. But with a changed and expanded rota of bookshops. After all, the man followed was only seen at *one* bookshop . . . and the Gestapo can't monitor *every* bookshop in the city. In fact, they'd be hard pushed to keep their eyes on more than a handful.'

'And this man who was followed – surely, they might be able to link everything through him, if they track him down?'

Lutz smiled tautly. 'Already thought of. He'll lie low for a while, probably in another town. And if and when he does return to Berlin, it'll be with a different appearance and changed identity.'

I suppose this was why Gregor Lutz was leader of this small Resistance group. The man most proficient at looking at every eventuality. But that niggling worry suddenly came to the forefront. 'If a bookshop link has now been picked up on, surely all my past bookshop visits might now be focused on?'

'And?' Lutz gestured, a swirl of smoke trailing in his hand's wake. 'If in future you're apprehended coming from a bookshop, there'll be no coded note on you, only a book. So nothing to worry about.' Lutz smiled more gently. 'And do you know how many book aficionados there are like you in Berlin? That would be a losing game for the Gestapo.'

Every eventuality. But despite all of Lutz's assurances, I still felt some disquiet worming in my stomach, a weight too now on my shoulders. As if some impending doom was pressing in on me. *Just the fortune teller's curse*, I told myself. Dealing regularly with the worries and demons of other people – often I found myself internalizing them.

Lutz slid the book at his side across the desktop towards me. 'In fact, this will be the last book with a coded message you carry from a bookshop for some while.'

I nodded numbly. I'd seen the book there, but hadn't attached any significance to it. Thought it was just a book he was reading; after all, we were in a bookshop.

'I didn't think they'd respond so quickly.'

Lutz looked at me keenly. 'Your last message was vitally

important, Edith. They didn't want to delay answering it. The return message came in just before midnight last night.'

'I thought with that last session, I'd done most of it.' My voice sounded strangely hollow, distant. 'Steered Hitler how they wanted.'

'Yes, you're doing well. But until such time as some direct actions are taken by Hitler, we can't be sure he's taken the bait.' Lutz tapped at the book with one hand. 'So some extra guidance on how to hopefully prod him that last stretch.'

I realized I was being naive. With all the talk of switching from bookshop to café and shop liaisons, I should have known that the sessions and code-message running would continue. In any case, Hitler would still demand ongoing sessions, so that would mean valuable information to pass on each time. It had just been wishful thinking on my part, no doubt spurred by my anxiety, that they would stop.

I breathed in. 'If we're to avoid bookshop visits in future, where will you and I meet?'

'Here once again, unless I designate somewhere else. But no coded messages inside books.' Lutz pushed the book a little closer my way, as if afraid that, without the prompt, I might not pick it up. 'This will be the last one.'

'*This will be the last one.*'

Lutz's parting words stayed with me as I walked away from Grunewald Bücher. On its own, it was a perfectly rational parting comment – after all, he'd explained in some detail how and why there'd be no more coded messages picked up and delivered via bookshops – but combined with my earlier anxiety, I couldn't shake off the feeling that it was an ominous premonition. That tightness again in my stomach, that weight once more pressing on my shoulders.

My step felt heavy, as if my body was telling me not to continue. Was something trying to pull me back? Something that was still worrying me about what Lutz had said, aside from his parting words? Something trying to make me return to Grunewald Bücher to discuss it further with him?

I was still trying to work it all out in my mind when the door opened on the Volkswagen 3 just ahead. I didn't see clearly the man getting out at first, or perhaps it didn't immediately register because this was the last place I expected to see him.

My hand went to my mouth. '*What?* What on earth are you doing here?'

But his expression was strange, somewhere between stern and quizzical. 'I might ask you the same question.'

Then next thing he was taking the book from my grasp. I tried to hold on to it, but as its pages opened during the tussle and the coded note fell out and fluttered to the pavement I knew that my life, what little might now remain of it, would never be the same again.

18

War Cabinet Room, London, October 1940

Winston Churchill would usually either puff determinedly on his cigar or rest it in the ashtray to his side. But now it seemed to hover uncertainly in mid-air, along with his thoughts, inches from his mouth.

'Are you saying this fortune teller influencer of yours might now be lost to us?'

'Unfortunately, yes, Prime Minister.' Calder Gibson couldn't help noting the subtle shift from 'ours' to 'yours' now that it looked like things had gone awry. 'Or, at least, that's how we fear it seems at the moment.'

'So explain to us how we might have arrived at this situation.' Churchill finally took a draw on his cigar.

'I'm not sure where to start,' Calder said hesitantly.

'The beginning is always a good place, I've found.' But it was said gently with no hint of sarcasm, and as War Cabinet Secretary Edward Bridges to his side started to smile, Churchill gave him a sharp glare, quickly dampening it. Churchill could sense that Calder was distressed. Losing an agent in the field was always a harrowing experience – especially as in this case it was a woman, with so much hanging in the balance – and he didn't want any extra salt rubbed into that wound.

But Calder knew that with such a convoluted account,

and after a long day of War Cabinet briefings, Churchill's patience would quickly wane. So, he made quick work of Engelmann earlier being followed and got to the part where the transmitting agents were raided by an Orpo team, 'Led by the same Gestapo man who'd earlier been following Engelmann, along with two soldiers.'

Part of this Bridges didn't seem to grasp. 'But we got the full message through, had it deciphered and sent our response late last night.'

'Yes. They got the last of the message out just in time.' Calder grimaced. 'But one of the transmitting team was shot and injured in the raid.'

'Anyone captured?' Churchill asked.

'Thankfully, they all got away.' Calder knew that was a main concern. One man forced to talk under torture could endanger the lives of many and bring down entire operations. 'And later Lutz also gave her our return coded message.'

Churchill nodded as he thought he'd slotted the pieces together. 'So, she baulked at hearing this and didn't wish to continue?'

Calder had asked for a glass of water at the start of the meeting and had taken a couple of mouthfuls, but his mouth felt dry again now. He took another sip.

'No, Prime Minister. Lutz very carefully laid out new plans by which they could proceed safely in the future, and she accepted these.'

Churchill's brow knitted. 'But I don't understand. I thought you stated at the outset that this woman was lost to us?'

'Yes, I did . . . and she probably is.' Calder swallowed

hard. 'But it was because of what happened *after* her meeting with Lutz.' Calder went on to describe Lutz seeing her being bundled into a Volkswagen by a man further along the road as he left the bookshop. 'I got a message about this from Lutz's team only two hours ago, which is why I called this urgent meeting now.'

'Gestapo?' Churchill quizzed.

'No, that was the strangest thing. It was the man who was acting as the conduit between her and Hitler on her clairvoyance sessions. SS Captain Stefan Hansel.'

19

Deià, Mallorca, October 1973

Robert Graves made a waving-pointing motion.

'Third door along on the kitchen cabinets. Rosa will help find it for you.'

The stocky, grey-haired man hovered by the kitchen door, still looking uncertain as he peered back at us on the terrace. 'Top or bottom row?'

'Top row, Horst.' Graves smiled. 'You never put something like sugar in easy reach when you have children in the house.'

'OK. Must remember.' A nod and smile back, and the man disappeared into the kitchen.

'That's Horst from Munich . . . or maybe Frankfurt,' Graves said, turning back to us. 'Used to be a journalist for some Springer newspaper before retiring a few years back. Often comes by to borrow a cup of sugar when he's just arrived back at his place.'

That was one of the problems with telling a story at the Graves villa, Teresa thought. It was a veritable 'open house' at times. The first visitor had been the middle-aged *Correos* man, seemingly too fat for the small moped he was on, a pile of envelopes strapped by a rubber band and three large packages – probably books and manuscripts – on the back. 'He likes to save me the walk up to the *correos* van to collect my post,' Graves explained. Then an hour later, a cocoa-trader in his mid-fifties from London, James, who lived just down the lane. Now Horst.

Graves's brow creased as he was struck with a thought. 'Does that German friend of yours in the village do the same with you – nip by to borrow a cup of sugar now and then?'

'What, Jannik?' Teresa smiled. 'Yes. He calls by regularly, especially when *Estudio 1* biographies and interviews are on TV, and we watch them together.'

'Ah, *Estudio 1*. That essential window on Spanish culture.' Graves twirled one hand theatrically, then looked at Teresa questioningly. 'How does that work? A French woman and a German socializing together. Are we all friends now?'

'Of course.' Teresa gave Graves a feigned 'behave' scowl. 'West Germany and France were two of the founder members of the Common Market. Britain didn't join until this year.'

'How easily we forget.' Graves sighed. 'Now where were we before Horst and his sugar panic interrupted?' His eyes settled back keenly on Teresa. 'Ah, yes. Edith's nightmare dilemma. Must have been horrendous for her. Were there any warning signs that this might happen?'

'No, nothing.' Teresa held a palm out. 'Except of course her earlier paranoia that in Stefan and her housekeeper, Lara, she had two people in Hitler's pay close to her.'

'But surely that must be the end of things right there,' Graves commented. 'No possible way that she could extricate herself from that situation.'

'On the face of it, yes. But we must remember, Stefan

actually loved her.' Teresa took a sip of water. 'And, as the old saying goes – love can conquer all.'

'In many cases,' Bronowski said, gesturing. 'But *this*?'

'Are you actually saying there might be hope?' Graves was quizzical. 'I don't see how, given the impossibility of the situation. After all, he's openly tricked her.'

Teresa smiled tightly. 'Let's leave the fortune telling to Edith, shall we?'

20

Berlin under a hazy sky was spread before us. The closest to a 'lover's leap' there was in Berlin, the car park on the slopes of the Viktoriapark. Stefan sat next to me in the Volkswagen as we looked out at the view.

This might be one of the last things I see, I thought, as I started on the bittersweet tale of what brought me to the point of a coded note fluttering to the pavement between us.

Sitting with Stefan in the car on Hohenzollerndamm, I tried at first to palm him off with the explanations suggested by Lutz – 'It's just general book references for research' – then followed that up by saying there was little I could tell him because the details hadn't been shared with me, but he was having none of it.

'I already half know or have guessed what's going on, so you might as well tell me the rest.' Although I didn't finally relent until he commented, 'Far better you tell me than some vicious Gestapo officer who will apply electrodes or pull your fingernails out to get to the truth.'

Teresa's and Xavier's advice resurged about others appointed not caring a jot for me, '*At least with Stefan there's that possibility*.' I could at least hopefully plead for a quicker, less painful death with him.

I started with Hitler's visit to Paris and Gustav Strehl's invitation for me to go to Berlin. Stefan nodded without comment through this – no doubt it had been part of his briefing.

'I was reluctant to go at first, couldn't forgive Hitler for ordering Erik Hanussen's murder. The last person I wanted to be working for was Hitler as some sort of Hanussen replacement. But then a friend introduced me to a Resistance member who said that SOE in London had wanted to get someone close to Hitler for some while to hopefully influence him. And I could be that person.'

'And that swayed you?'

'No, not at all. Quite the opposite.' I smiled ironically, but kept my gaze ahead at the city view, didn't look at Stefan. The man I'd trusted and who had now betrayed me – probably had planned to from the start. 'I was already in fear of falling out of favour with Hitler just from the danger of getting a forecast wrong – after all, look what happened with Hanussen. The last thing I'd want to do is put myself and my family more at risk by betraying Hitler.'

A slower, more contemplative nod this time. 'So, what changed your mind?'

'Revenge.'

That one word echoed between us for a moment, then seemed to sail down the hillside in the silence, so that I feared half of Berlin might hear it.

'For Hanussen?' Stefan said at length.

'Yes.' Don't you see? A tailor-made karma, duping Hitler through the same fortune telling, though I bit my tongue on adding that; it might have come across that I'd taken some satisfaction and glee in my actions now.

Another long pause, as if that didn't fully add up in Stefan's mind. 'You must have cared about him terribly to risk your own life and that of your family like this?'

'Yes, I did.' I could hear the doubt heavy in Stefan's voice. But I daren't tell him the rest, what also lay behind that revenge. Nor would I tell him that the woman who'd sparked the thought of revenge in my mind, my best friend Teresa, was now also in Berlin with me. I'd agreed at the outset that I'd come clean with him on what I'd done, but wouldn't tell him about any of the other people involved, wouldn't incriminate them. Stefan had nodded a reluctant acceptance, as if indicating he wasn't sure the hierarchy he answered to would also accept that. He made the short drive to the Viktoriapark shortly after I started on my account, feeling we were too conspicuous where we were on Hohenzollerndamm.

'Erik was still young at the time, only forty-three,' I said. 'And he was my first and main mentor, meant everything to me at the time.'

'I understand.' A slightly less reluctant affirmation this time.

'And Erik had trusted Hitler, had been the forecaster of his rise to power. So, with that trust, what Hitler had done to him was even more deplorable – like a master having an obedient pet dog put to death.'

Stefan's expression was solemn, muttering, 'Wouldn't be the first time he's done that.' Then, with a fresh breath, as if realizing he might have inadvertently said something out of place, 'And is that it? The full account of what led you to do this?'

'Yes, it is.' But as I looked out, the cityscape of Berlin

blurred in my vision. And it hit me that, while talking about Erik, I'd started crying. Or perhaps it was the understanding that, having shared my story, my fate was sealed, along with that of my family. My parents, my brother Tobias, little Louise. All I could ask for, *beg* for, was that my family should be spared. But duping Hitler like this, I realized the chances of that were slim. And I had a sudden anguishing vision of Louise and Tobias being led to their deaths, their faces filled with the same childlike bewilderment – the only saving grace being that, unlike adults, the portent of what was about to happen wouldn't fully hit them. The view ahead now a complete blur, my tears openly ran down my cheeks.

'What happens now?' I asked tremulously, my voice almost gone.

'I don't know.' Stefan joined me in staring emptily ahead at the view for a moment, then, with a resigned exhalation: 'I have something to tell you also. But I need a drink for that.'

I felt like laughing at the ludicrousness. I was sure I knew what was coming. He'd tell me he loved me, before sharing with me the various options of where and how I and my family would be killed. *Let me count the ways.* That there was only so much he could do, and if he withheld this duplicity from the Führer, he'd simply end up next to me in front of a firing squad. And now he needed Dutch courage to say all of that.

We drove to a nearby Bierkeller and sat at a table with our drinks. As Stefan turned to me, I was sure I saw his eyes glistening too. Unless it was a trick of the light through the blur of my own tears.

Stefan sighed, as if to ease the weight of what he had to say.

'You might recall I mentioned my uncle dying?'

'Yes.' I'd managed to get my tears under control, my breathing even again. But I still felt empty, detached, this beer-hall location now somehow surreal. 'I remember you saying how close you were, that he'd been almost like a father to you.'

'Yes, he was.' Stefan took a heavy swig. 'But his death held much in common with the way that Erik Hanussen died. My uncle's death was also ordered by the Führer.'

'I . . . I didn't realize.' The first hint that this conversation was going in a direction I hadn't expected.

'You've heard of the "Night of the Long Knives"?' Stefan looked at me keenly.

'Yes. I was already in Paris by then – but it was such a major event, I think half of Europe heard about it.'

Stefan nodded solemnly. 'Hitler's final purge to consolidate power. Get rid of all his perceived enemies and unify those remaining with unquestioning loyalty. Only two options left after that: support him or die.' Stefan looked down briefly; a momentary penance. 'My uncle was in fact loyal to the Führer, in the same way as Hanussen and many others, but it hardly helped. My uncle was a Generalleutnant at the time, but also the right-hand man to a leading general who Hitler saw as a threat – so the story was invented that the general and his key staff were disloyal, and they were all killed on Hitler's orders.'

'I'm sorry.' A numb, lame response. I had my answer now to what had so perturbed Stefan about his uncle's death, but I still couldn't see how it might relate to what he'd decide to do with me. After all, he was an SS officer in Hitler's command. No choice left for him, I thought. Though that thought did raise a contradiction. 'But after all that happened with your uncle, you decided to join the SS? And in a position working closely now with the Führer. I don't understand.'

'I was already an SS officer when my uncle was killed. I simply decided to stay and keep moving up the ranks. I thought that was the best way to deflect any suspicion.'

'*Suspicion?*'

'You still don't get it, do you?' Stefan looked at me intently, gave a jaded sigh. 'You and I are in much the same position. Both seeking revenge against Hitler. And preferably getting close to him in order to achieve that.'

The suddenness of the turnaround, the possible reprieve, took my breath away at first. But still some things didn't add up. I shook my head. 'But you conspired with Lara to follow me, catch me out? And the Volkswagen to shield that it was you?'

'The Volkswagen is just a staff unit car. And it wasn't to catch you out spying and running codes, I can assure you. I had no idea you were doing that.' Stefan smiled unevenly; reluctant admission. 'It was because I thought you were seeing someone else.'

'*Seeing someone else?*' My voice rose with the ridiculousness of the suggestion, a few workmen three tables away looked over, thinking a lovers' tiff was in full swing. 'I haven't been with anyone for years romantically before you – so why on earth would I suddenly want *two* men in my life?'

'I know. Forgive my foolishness.' Stefan held a hand out

helplessly. 'But all those times I said I wanted to go to bookshops with you and you rebuffed me – I didn't know what else to think. It certainly wasn't that you were a spy.'

I wanted to hit him for being such an oaf. But I felt drained of any emotion and strength, still coming to terms with the reprieve, as if I'd just been saved from a cliff drop, too numb for the euphoria to wash through me. And still one part didn't fully add up.

'But you kept our relationship from Lara all along. So how on earth did you get round that?'

'Of course, I didn't let on to Lara that we were having an affair.' Stefan smiled crookedly again, as if this was one part he was happy admitting. All's fair in love and war. 'I simply reminded her that you were newly arrived back in Berlin, so might be vulnerable. Hitler had ordered that we keep tabs on you, and all these bookshop visits were making me anxious. That you might unwittingly be lured into contact with some questionable or unsavoury characters – so could she inform me when you planned next to go to a bookshop?'

One last possible loose piece. 'And nobody made the connection between you and your uncle?'

'No. He was on my mother's side. And her maiden name was Lehmann – a fairly common surname.'

I nodded. 'And like me, you're obviously not working alone?'

'No, of course not.' Stefan grimaced. 'But also like you, I can't go into any detail as to who. All I can say is that it goes high into the German military and the Abwehr. Not everyone by any means is a Hitler supporter.'

I recalled Stefan looking uneasy when Hitler had

inquired about possible conspiracies against him. Now that part of the puzzle was also in place.

'What next for us both?' I asked, my voice sounding hollow, detached, as if this new reality still hadn't fully dawned on me.

'We could just continue on as before, I suppose. But with one proviso.' Stefan turned to me more fully, gently clasped my hand. 'What I just shared with you was something that took a lot of courage for me to do, something I haven't imparted to anyone outside of my tight circle before. And I daresay it was even more difficult for you – thinking you might be facing a terrible fate with what you shared.' He clasped my hand tighter, as if to lend reassurance. 'But I had to get you to do that to know for sure I could trust you before revealing my own account.'

'Yes, I . . . I see that now,' I said hesitantly.

'But having shared so many secrets tonight, we should make a pact.' That hand clasp still firm, as if forming a bond. 'Aside from giving away names and possibly incriminating others – *no more secrets* between us.'

I looked back directly into his eyes for one of the few times that night. '*No more secrets*,' I muttered back, like a mantra, closing my eyes briefly in final submission. Knowing even as I said it that there was one withheld secret I could never share with anyone.

21

Despite the unexpected reprieve from Stefan, I still felt my nerves in turmoil, so decided to spend the next two days at my parents' home – not least to be away from Lara for a spell. With her having gone along so willingly with Stefan to try and catch me out, I couldn't get rid of the thought that someone in my house was spying on me, ready to betray me at the first opportunity. But perhaps it was also the need to be with my family for a while, my fear of losing them, having got so close to the precipice edge.

My father, now in his early sixties, slim, tall and angular, with straggly grey hair – he was often lazy about getting it cut – had semi-retired from his bookbinding business, leaving the general running to a senior manager. This was due partly to him struggling more as the years advanced, but mainly to the downturn in business with the war on. There simply wasn't the same workload.

But he seemed at a loose end on those days off, our conversation quickly turning to books, as if he couldn't, at least contentedly, fully escape the business.

'Did you manage to track down any of the Johann Michael Hahn books I mentioned last time you were here? Because I think now with the war on, they're due to get increasingly rare.'

'No. I haven't managed to find any yet.'

My father looked across at me thoughtfully, took a deeper puff on his pipe. 'Seems that scarcity is already starting to have an effect.'

'Seems so.' I smiled tightly back. I could hardly admit to my father that I'd barely looked, my bookshop visits taken up with clandestine meetings and exchanging secret codes.

A shadow fell across us as my mother's voice came from behind me.

'Are you two ready? I'm serving up in a minute.'

Although it was still getting dark late, my mother always maintained her routine of drawing the blackout curtains at 7.15 p.m., just before serving dinner, so that she didn't get caught out having to draw them halfway through.

A number of homes in Berlin had their windows permanently blacked out. But I shared with my mother that yearning to have sunlight as long as possible, and thankfully had blackout shutters at my own house.

My mother put a side-lamp on, lit candles for the table – the lighting subdued, but with a touch of flickering magic – and called Louise and Tobias from the next room.

My parents sat beside each other. Five years younger than my father, my mother wasn't a small woman, but appeared so standing next to him. Also slim, she had a broad, expressive face and auburn hair – which she'd given up dying two months after the war started and which now had heavy strands of grey. My daughter Louise had never been able to work out the differing shades of my hazel eyes, but on my parents' visit to Paris when she was only five, she'd sat on their laps in turn and stared into their eyes. 'Now, I see,' she said, as if she'd worked out a grand puzzle. 'You get the green from Grandpa Lukas and the brown from Grandma Elsa.'

The topic of war was stoically avoided over dinner – too many reminders constantly on the radio and on the streets – so it was mostly mundane, day-to-day issues: How is Louise's music progressing? Settled in well in your new house now? Happy with your housekeeper?

'Most importantly – does Louise get on with her?' My mother elaborated. 'After all, she has to spend most time with her.'

'I like Lara,' Louise answered for herself.

'Yes. She gets on well with Louise.' *But not so well with me. She conspired to betray me just the other day.*

But the shadowy presence of war did nonetheless later intrude. The ominous rumble of some aircraft overhead.

'I wonder where they're headed?' my father aired to nobody in particular, glancing up.

Collective breath held listening out to whether the aircraft were moving closer, or for the sounds of bombs dropping or sirens wailing.

Slowly their drone receded into the distance.

Stefan called at mid-morning the next day. I met him by the front door, my father drifting back into the lounge.

'Sorry to come by like this, but another session has been called for tomorrow. I received a message about it just last night, and Lara said you were here.' He gestured apologetically. Was this another possible collaboration with Lara? 'I hope you don't mind.'

'No, it's OK . . . I –'

My mother came out at that point, appraising Stefan in

his uniform. 'You should ask your guest in. Otherwise, it seems impolite.'

'Yes, of course.' I dutifully held a hand out. 'This is a work colleague from the Chancellery, Stefan Hansel.' Then half-turning to Stefan. 'And this is my mother, Elsa. My father Lukas you've already met.'

'Pleased to meet you, Frau Creutzen.' Stefan gave a gracious smile, then a hearty handshake in greeting to my father when we went into the lounge. 'And you too, Herr Creutzen.'

My mother offered tea or coffee, which Stefan declined with thanks. 'Heavy day ahead, I'm afraid. I can't stay long.'

A nod in acceptance from my mother, then: 'Your work at the Chancellery with my daughter must be very important.'

Stefan shrugged. 'Quite boring, really. Just making sure that funds and arrangements for munitions and supply lines run smoothly.'

'You make light of it,' my father commented. 'But a vital factor in wartime, I would have thought.'

'Our daughter doesn't say much about it, you see,' my mother added.

'Yes, necessary secrecy and all that.' Stefan smiled tightly. 'Probably the same reason I don't like to make too much of it.'

My parents exchanged a brief look, and the conversation petered out shortly after, Stefan announcing that he must get going. 'The war effort awaits.'

I walked Stefan to the front door and out towards his car. Something on my mind I wanted to discuss privately.

'You know before when I had a few trick questions.' I turned to him more directly as we stood by his car. 'Now that we're working together more closely – *no more secrets* – I wondered if you might be able to forewarn me of those, if and when they come up again.'

'Like I said before – I'm just the messenger here.' Stefan exhaled softly. 'But I will if I can spot them.'

So that part was real – it hadn't just been an excuse. 'And if at any time it looks like my cover has been blown – can you warn me?' I looked at him imploringly. 'Give me time to get away to safety. Or at least get my family away.'

'Of course I will. Again, if they even let me know.' Stefan looked down for a second, pondering. 'The first indication might just be suspicion. The Führer voicing that he has some concerns, so to keep a closer eye on you and inform him of anything untoward.'

'And what would you tell him?'

'I'd tell him that you were an incorrigible spy working with British Intelligence, I was in cahoots with you . . . and we made passionate love together every night.'

I joined Stefan in a hearty chuckle, and would have leaned in to give him a hug and kiss, but I noticed at that moment my mother looking out the front window towards us.

'Louise says you have a dark crystal sphere in your house now in Berlin, same as the one you had in Paris.'

'Yes, I have.'

My attention half-gone for my last move, I watched as a beaming Tobias leapfrogged two of my pieces and took them.

He'd blurted it out suddenly in the middle of our draughts game that evening. Louise had spent much of the day with Tobias, playing games or the piano together, and I wanted to spend more time with him before I left. Draughts was his favourite game. I recalled when he was only twelve saying that soon we'd progress to playing chess, but he'd never fully grasped the complexity of the knight's move, so we were forever destined to remain playing draughts.

'Do you actually see things in it?' he asked. 'People and objects?'

'Not exactly. I see dark shapes moving, but not people or things clearly. It's just an indication, and I have to interpret the rest.'

'*Interpret?*' His rounded face, usually so full of wonder and light, looked troubled for a moment.

'Yes. Try and make out what those dark, shifting images *really* mean.'

He nodded after a second, smiling as he took another of my pieces. I smiled gently back, wondering if this talk now was merely a distraction tactic. Sometimes I let Tobias win, just to keep our scores even, but now he was winning of his own accord.

'And do you just see bad things in it?'

'No. I see good too.' I pondered some more after making my next move. 'But perhaps I see the bad things as more important to tell people – a sort of warning so that they might be able to avoid those bad things.'

'And do you see bad things for me?' Tobias asked, looking at me directly.

'No. Only good,' I said, biting at my bottom lip as at

length he looked back down at the board. Though I hadn't directly checked his fate, I was reminded how close I thought I'd been just the other day to condemning my whole family.

We played in silence for a moment. I captured one of Tobias's pieces and he took two more of mine.

'Louise says that you spend a lot of time in your room with the crystal sphere, looking into it with the man who was here earlier.'

Out of the mouths of babes. My composure completely gone for a moment, I lost another piece. And I thought back to that look exchanged between my parents earlier when Stefan had mentioned the 'secrecy' of our work, wondering whether Louise or Tobias might have inadvertently let something slip.

'Yes, we might do,' I answered evasively. 'But it's just harmless.'

'*What?* Games? Like this?'

'Yes, just games,' I latched onto his idea readily. One way of making light of sessions aimed at bringing down the Third Reich, I thought. *Just games.* 'They don't mean anything.'

But later in bed, my mind still active and sleep slow in coming, I thought: if I can't even successfully keep secrets from my backward brother, what chance did I have with Hitler?

22

Having worried about the upcoming session with Hitler, as I'd done with many of them, in the end it went smoothly, and that became the pattern for a number of sessions following. The months in the lead-up to Christmas were the most settled since I'd been back in Berlin.

But I should have realized that it couldn't last, that more troubling times lay ahead. Or in this case, my past catching up with me in a way that I never thought possible.

What had helped the sessions go smoothly was Stefan, now openly siding with me, guiding the way.

Most of the questions were quite straightforward, a number of them asking what I saw about the more minor campaigns Hitler hadn't mentioned before: Denmark, Norway and Holland. I answered honestly in each case, saw little resistance in each case.

But Stefan spotted in advance a possible trick question about a new tank being developed, the Krieger, 'Particularly good on snow and ice, so will help us if we decide to go to war with Russia.'

But Stefan had never heard of this make of tank, even from his friends high up in the military, so I answered ambiguously, 'I'm afraid I can see nothing clear about this make of tank, the Krieger. So, unfortunately, I can't offer anything worthwhile on that front.'

With the guidance and pointers easing the flow, I commented as we finished, 'Why couldn't we have done this before? It's taken so much of the pressure off. I've been a nervous wreck on many past sessions.'

Stefan arched a brow. 'And how would that have looked? I had no idea that you were playing a double game. So if I'd suddenly started forewarning you of trick questions, you might have simply advised the Führer about my disloyalty. That I wasn't acting on his behalf honestly.' A taut grimace as Stefan drew a finger across his throat.

'Sorry.' I playfully slapped my head. '*Dummkopf.* This spy game is all new to me.'

Stefan looked towards the speculum. 'And do you see yourself getting better at it?'

'Yes, I do.' I played along, staring wide-eyed into the speculum. 'But I see a tall man with golden hair in uniform helping me do so.'

We made light of what we were both doing, duping Hitler, as much as we could. Dark, gallows humour in an attempt to distract from the terrible consequences of what would happen if we were caught.

And, like his earlier jibe, we did make love every night; well, every other night. One night, as he was leaving my bedroom just after 2 a.m., Louise, on her way back from the bathroom, had seen Stefan heading down the stairs.

'Stefan left something here earlier,' I offered from my bedroom doorway, having kissed him goodbye just a moment before. 'He had to come back for it.'

Louise just nodded and gently smiled as she went back to her room. She obviously knew or had half-guessed, but didn't care. She liked Stefan.

That trick question about the Krieger tank had been the only oblique reference to possible war with Russia. There were no sessions for two weeks while Hitler had rounds of meetings with local and foreign dignitaries, catching up on current events, and the sessions afterwards were in the same vein: light, passing references to Stalin and Russia.

Having informed Lutz of the new situation with Stefan after one of my first café bag-swap rendezvous, Lutz later passed on from London that it was unlikely Hitler would launch a Russian campaign with winter on the horizon, 'But he might still want to prepare, ready for a spring offensive. So still gently guide and prompt, if and when the subject arises.'

We were still on a knife edge, though, as to whether Hitler would finally make that decision, and he played his cards close to his chest, gave nothing away.

Stefan had also suggested I try to steer Hitler away from any military hierarchy if he asked questions again about internal plots against him.

'Where would you suggest I steer him?'

Stefan pondered for a moment. 'Old SA members who are now part of the SS would be a good place. They couldn't be trusted then, and still can't now.' Then, as if struck with a bright afterthought, 'Many of the same people in fact who ordered Erik Hanussen's death. So you would be fine-toning your revenge even more acutely through that.'

I'd nodded a ready accord; just one more strand in our new working relationship.

Stefan had confided in me that he was working with two

small groups with threads that ran high into the German military and Abwehr, 'With the aim of bringing Hitler down through internal manoeuvres or assassination.'

I'd in turn shared SOE's aims for me to try and lead Hitler towards war with Russia. 'If he can be stretched on two fronts then his chances of winning the war would be diminished.' Though with no names or contacts shared on either side, no incrimination of others.

But Stefan voiced some concerns about this ploy, and the topic came back again when we finished our fourth session after the short break.

I held a palm out. 'The terrible loss of life you mentioned before?'

'Yes. My military contacts are particularly uneasy about it. Not just the loss of Russian lives, but the heavy toll on German soldiers too.'

I'd had the same concerns myself, so couldn't make light of it. In the end, I simply repeated one of Lutz's lines. 'You realize that Hitler would probably decide to invade Russia anyway?'

'That's an unknown.' Stefan shrugged. 'But it's one thing for Hitler to do it of his own volition, driven by his personal ambitions and madness. It's quite another to steer or urge him into it.'

'So do you think I should stop?'

A weighted pause for thought, then Stefan shook his head. 'No. In the end, it might be the only option.' A resigned sigh. 'But it has meant some plans have been pulled forward with my own people.'

I said nothing, waited for Stefan to tell me. If, indeed, it wasn't too secret for him to be able to share with me.

'It was something already on the table in any case – an assassination plan,' he said at length. 'Those above me wanted to go ahead with it now, before Hitler embarks on the madness of war with Russia. But I was uneasy about it. Unsure we had everything in place. Then a sudden flight with the Führer on board came up, and they wanted to seize the opportunity.'

'I see.' But I could sense Stefan's eyes on me keenly, as if he wanted something from me. Approval? Or was this him sharing his doubts?

'But I wondered if you might be able to foresee how it goes for one person in particular.' Stefan gestured to the glass sphere between us, its ghostly light still spilling out. We would usually turn on the main light at the end of a session, but hadn't done so yet.

'*What?*' This was something we'd never done before – a personal foretelling. Everything so far had been on Hitler's behalf. 'In the speculum?'

'If you could.' He reached across and gently clasped my right hand. 'His name's Unterscharführer Paulos Betzner. And I feel somehow responsible for him – because I was one of the three people guiding him on this mission.'

I looked into the speculum, saw shadows and shapes beginning to form. Stefan was staring at me keenly.

'Tell me what you see . . .'

23

Unterscharführer Paulos Betzner was average height, five-foot nine, and quite stocky, but not overly so, had light brown hair and was quite good looking, but again not overly so – not someone who would draw attention in a group by being too tall or short or strikingly attractive or ugly. Which was why he'd been seen as ideal for this mission: he could blend in among a group without catching the eye of the Führer or any of his Führerbegleitkommando key security staff. Somebody who later wouldn't easily be remembered.

But still Betzner felt anxious as he mingled with this small group of air crew getting the Führer's plane ready for his flight to Prague. A trip to see Reinhard Heydrich, Head Reich Protector, and give a morale-boosting speech to German troops stationed at the Karlin barracks.

'I have a friend of mine staying at Karlin,' Betzner said, approaching a young Junker busily loading suitcases and holdalls into the bowels of the FW 200-Condor plane at the start of the runway. 'And I'd like to get this to him, if I could. An early Christmas present of his favourite brandy.'

The Junker paused in his loading as Betzner opened the top of the wooden presentation box to show two Hine Brandy bottles nestled in crimson velvet.

The Junker raised an eyebrow. 'Very nice! He won't get

cold this Christmas.' He glanced towards the large aircraft hold, which was only half full. 'And I suppose there's room.'

'Thank you! It's really appreciated.' He closed and reclasped the wooden lid, tapped on the label where he'd written the recipient's name and *KARLIN BARRACKS, BY HAND*, and passed the box across.

'Carl Fischer,' read the Junker. 'And how will I recognize him or get this to him?' He waggled the box in his hand, and for a moment Betzner feared the delicate detonation mechanism, set for forty-five minutes' time, thirty minutes into the flight, would trigger prematurely.

'Just leave it in the Post Room at the barracks. He's expecting it, so he'll come and collect it there.'

The Junker nodded, leaned to one side and slid the box into the aircraft hold, almost as an afterthought asking, 'And what's your name?'

'Unterscharführer Ernst Schmidt.'

His rank the only thing evident by his uniform, Betzner had chosen a common name for himself. His handlers had also pre-checked that there were in fact two Carl Fischers among the three thousand men stationed at Karlin. Just in case anyone bothered to check now in the remaining minutes before the flight took off.

Betzner was eager to get away. Hitler would be arriving soon to board his plane, and he didn't want to be seen by either the Führer or his accompanying Führerbegleitkommando bodyguards.

'Thank you again.' He turned and half-waved back, the Junker giving an acknowledging wave as he threw in another holdall – Betzner again fearing that something hard landing on top of the box might set off the mechanism. However much he'd been assured by his handlers that the explosives packed in the false bottom were sensitive only to its timer, not motion.

He paced quickly away, a jolt of guilt closing his eyes for a second as he wondered if the young Junker would be among the twelve people designated for the flight, or whether he was just loading.

And as he opened them again, it seemed that the Führer, who had just got out of his Mercedes, was staring straight at him before he realized that Hitler's eyes were in fact fixed on his waiting personal aeroplane eighty metres past his shoulder. The plane about to take him to his doom.

Betzner's mouth felt suddenly dry, one of the Führerbegleitkommando group looking his way as they passed him. Though it was only fleeting, and then he was getting into his nondescript Volkswagen parked twenty metres past them, starting up and driving away.

Betzner's heart was still beating hard and fast, almost in step with his rapid pace, as he made his way up to his small first-floor apartment on Eitelstrasse.

Once inside, he switched on his Volksempfänger radio – which all good Germans possessed – already tuned to Rundfunk Berlin. Since the station played a mixture of military music, old classics, propaganda speeches and vital announcements from the Führer or Goebbels, he was sure Rundfunk would be among the first to announce the dire, tragic news of the Führer's death.

He was about to make coffee, then decided against it. His nerves were already jangling, so he decided on tea to help calm them. It hardly helped. His heart was still beating fast as he sipped from his cup.

He checked his watch. The device should be going off about now. He took another sip of tea, closing his eyes briefly as he got a picture in his mind of the aircraft exploding mid-air. The end of Hitler and all he stood for.

He found himself staring at the radio expectantly after ten minutes. Still military music interspersed with mundane public-service announcements, 'Don't forget to follow blackout tonight and every night. Local wardens will be checking in every neighbourhood and locality.'

Another half-hour gone with still no announcement, his nerves were shot. He got up and made himself another tea, but couldn't stay seated for more than another few minutes and took to pacing his small room. *Why no announcement by now?* Perhaps, as he tried to calm himself with long, slow breaths as he paced, it could be listed as just a delayed or missing aircraft – it could take some time to discover exactly what had happened.

That thought kept him going for another hour or so, but then his mounting anxiety started to grip him again. Surely, he'd have heard something by now? The constant military music and propaganda and public-service announcements were also beginning to grate on his nerves. He would have turned the radio off, but couldn't risk not listening to it for even a second.

By the time three hours had passed beyond the set explosion time, his nerves well past their tether. He felt he couldn't wait any longer. He had to know. He took from his pocket the number he'd written down earlier for Karlin barracks and picked up the phone.

A woman's voice answered. He asked to be put through to the Post Room.

'One minute please.'

A man's voice came on shortly after and Betzner explained his inquiry, 'A package that I had sent to the Post Room there for a friend. I wanted to check it had arrived.'

'I see. And what's your friend's name?'

'Carl Fischer.'

A heavy pause, then: 'And would his name have been marked clearly on the package?'

'Yes, it was.'

'OK.' The rustling of paper in the background. 'Packages are dealt with by my colleague here. I just deal with letters. One moment.'

The sound of him moving away, then what seemed an interminable wait, two minutes or more, Betzner hearing only his own beating heart with the more distant noises of rustling paper and movement. Then finally another man's voice came on the line.

'A package, you say?'

'Yes.'

A pause. 'For a Carl Fiesler?'

'No, Fischer.'

'OK. One moment. Just looking through here . . .'

The sound of more crinkling paper, some packages being moved around for a while. Another minute or so lost. 'And when would this have arrived?'

'About two and a half hours ago. A FW Condor flight from Berlin.'

A weightier pause, as if an inventory list was being checked. 'The Führer's flight?'

Betzner hadn't wanted to be the one to say it, attach any particular significance. He swallowed. 'Yes.'

'Hold on . . . I think I might be able to find it then.'

Another long gap, almost two more minutes, background sounds again of people shuffling around, packages being sorted through. And Betzner wondered whether to simply hang up. After all, they'd have mentioned straightaway if something had happened, if the flight hadn't arrived safely.

The man was finally back. 'There was a problem with that flight, though.'

Betzner's heart was in his throat. '*Oh*. What was that?'

'Some bad weather.' Another long pause. 'They had to divert slightly, so were delayed.'

'I see.' Betzner felt his breath falling slow and heavy. So, the plane had arrived safely after all. For whatever reason, the device hadn't gone off.

'Think I've got it here now . . .' Brief delay with more package shuffling. 'Carl Fischer, you say?'

'Yes.'

'Wooden box, quite heavy?'

'Yes . . .'

Betzner felt numb, and was still trying to work out what might have happened, toying again with the idea of just hanging up – after all, he had what he wanted, but that might seem odd and just raise suspicions – when he heard the thundering of boots heading up the stairs towards his flat.

And he realized what they'd done. They'd purposely kept him on the line long enough to trace his call.

He dropped the phone back in its cradle as if it was a

hot potato as the heavy banging came on his door. He looked frantically around. Where had he left his holster and pistol when he came in?

But it was too late. They'd splintered through the door with their rifle butts and were bursting in when he was only halfway towards lunging for his pistol on a side table.

24

'It went pretty much as you forecast. No plane destroyed or end to Hitler, and Paulos Betzner unfortunately caught. But it gets worse than that . . .'

I leaned up on one elbow, looked pointedly at Stefan. 'How on earth can it get worse than that?'

'Because now they're going to question him to get to the truth. No doubt the most unimaginable torture . . . and the Führer wants me to sit in and watch it, take notes.'

We were in my bed in the afterglow of having made love. Stefan had come back and we'd sneaked up to my bedroom two hours after Louise had gone to bed, as we'd done on so many nights now. But it had been an awkward, stilted lovemaking from Stefan. I could tell he was still troubled by my earlier forecast and what had finally happened to Paulos Betzner, and the shadows of that were still etched on his face now.

My brow knitted. 'Why would the Führer want you to do that?'

'He says he wants an accurate record of all that Betzner says and admits.' Stefan held out a palm. 'But he claims it's also to prevent any possible excesses from the man questioning him, Kurt Schneider.'

'Excesses?'

'Yes. SS-Obersturmbannführer Kurt Schneider has a reputation of being one of the most efficient interrogators, but also the most brutal. As if he takes a delight in the pain and suffering he's inflicting during questioning. The Führer says he wants me there to "temper Schneider's possible enthusiasm. Ensure he doesn't get too carried away."' Stefan eased a tired breath. 'But I fear something else might be going on, that it's all a trap.'

'In what way?'

'That they somehow know I'm one of Betzner's handlers who put him up to this, and Schneider will expose me in the middle of questioning.'

I nodded slowly, saw the dark shadows in Stefan's eyes, like shifting clouds in the speculum, and could tell this was a real concern. Not something to try and dispel simply with trite assurances.

Stefan grimaced tautly. 'Or perhaps Betzner will break halfway through the interrogation, and simply point my way when Schneider presses for who put him up to it?'

I said nothing, simply laid one hand on his shoulder, gently stroking; part consolation, part calming.

Stefan shook his head. 'Do you know how difficult it is to watch someone getting tortured during questioning, have the power to stop it – yet you just sit by and watch and let it happen? Because you're afraid for not only your own life, but those of others too. The many more who would be tortured and killed. Do you know how difficult that is?'

I could see Stefan's eyes glistening, near tears. I felt my throat tighten, could see too clear an image of it all for my own good. 'I'm so sorry.' Banal consolation in the end all that I could manage.

As if half-reading my thoughts, Stefan looked at me

directly after a moment. 'So, do you think you might be able to see whether it's a trap? Warn me?'

I met his gaze, saw the fear and dark clouds still there, but knew from past experience that not only was this my main failing, but also that of many fortune tellers. I admitted lamentably that I didn't think I could, that with my own future or that of someone so close, I was often unable to face something so personal and terrible. 'That's why, however much fortune tellers might be good at seeing the fate of those detached from us, with those close we develop something of a blind spot. That fate too terrible for us to take on board . . . so we blot it out, don't foresee it. After all, Erik wasn't able to foresee his own demise.'

I watched Stefan nod after a second with a faint wry smile. Bittersweet acceptance: pleased that he was now considered 'so close' but disappointed that our love might now preclude any clear vision.

But there was one thing I could sense clearly. 'This Schneider. Something seems to particularly worry you about him.'

'You mean apart from him being a merciless brute who'll now be torturing Paulos Betzner, whom I feel responsible for?' A crooked downturn to that wry smile, but I said nothing, let Stefan get there in his own time. Stefan looked up at the ceiling after a moment, unseeing. 'We were in the same SS training camp together years ago, so of course I got the measure of him more than most. He'd just come from the SA – one of those who successfully made the transition, despite the havoc they'd caused – but I never trusted the SA.' He waved one hand in a discarding motion. 'Hitler's "Storm Troopers" were never truly loyal to him, later just made out they were in order to save their own necks, ratting on other SA members in the process. That's why I don't trust them one jot: they've got where they are on the blood of their colleagues, and Schneider is one of the worst examples.'

'Responsible for quite a bit, it seems,' I said resignedly. 'Not just Erik Hanussen's murder.'

'Yes. They were Hitler's main henchmen back then. Before Röhm started to get more ambitious and the Führer decided to cull them.'

'Do you think this Schneider might have been one of those actually responsible for Erik's death?'

'A possibility, I suppose. Schneider has been Berlin-based all along.' Stefan shifted his brief glance at me back to staring unseeing at the ceiling; sighed. 'But unlikely. They were quite a large force at the time.'

In the following silence, I felt bereft that I hadn't been able to give any insight on his upcoming questioning session, which clearly still worried him deeply. But I did in that moment get some brief flash images.

I gently stroked his shoulder again, soothing, *calming*. 'I know I haven't been much help in being able to see how it might go with this Schneider, whether it's a trap or not. And the horror of it, especially with Paulos Betzner being a friend you feel responsible for, will be terribly difficult to face. But there might be some things you could do . . .'

25

Stefan observed Paulos Betzner being hauled into the interrogation room by three guards and forced to sit in one of two metal chairs facing each other at its centre. SS-Obersturmbannführer Kurt Schneider and a young Junker – stockier, heavy-muscled and wearing only his khaki uniform trousers and a grey T-shirt, as if he'd just finished a gym exercise – entered a moment after.

Stefan bit at his lip. He knew that the 'exercise' was about to start, and what form it would take. He'd managed to get a few minutes in private with Betzner before the interrogation started on the pretext of completing formalities for the interview: 'Name? Date of birth? Next of kin? Are you aware what will happen in the interview now . . . that you'll be asked questions about your alleged involvement in an attempted assassination of the Führer? Do you have anything to say now on the matter?' The guards had waited outside the cell meanwhile, and Stefan had managed between the formalities to mumble some advice to Betzner.

He wasn't sure how much of it Betzner had taken in. Numb nods and brief mumbled responses. They'd kept a radio playing in his cell all night long with military music and Hitler's rousing speeches – not only to weaken his resolve but remind him of the loyalty and devotion to the Führer he should have observed all along.

Paulos Betzner still looked out of it now, head lolling towards sleep, hardly paying attention as the T-shirted Junker strapped his arms and ankles to the chair.

Stefan was sat to one side at a trestle table, a tape recorder and notepad in front of him. Schneider placed a half-metre-long oblong wooden box he'd been carrying at the end of the bench table, then took up the seat opposite Betzner with a sly smile.

Mid-thirties with wavy flax-blond hair and pale-blue eyes, Schneider might have been considered good looking if it weren't for that smile, which seemed almost constantly evident and pulled his features down on his left side, making his face appear slightly lopsided. His reputation as one of the most brutal SS officers and interrogators preceded him.

Stefan was dreading the hour or so ahead, found his hands clammy as he started the tape recorder.

'Let us cut to the chase on why you are here,' Schneider said pointedly. 'Who put you up to this attempted assassination of the Führer? The names of your associates?'

'I don't know what you're talking about.'

'You most certainly do.' Schneider tapped a finger impatiently on his right thigh. 'And you'll tell me now!'

'No . . . I don't know anything.'

This game of question and refusal tennis continued for a while, then Schneider with a huff beckoned over T-shirt Junker.

'I feared as much. Some persuasion is obviously required.'

Stefan found himself looking slightly away, cringing with each blow – four heavy punches to Betzner's stomach, two to his face and jaw, breaking his nose and knocking two teeth loose. But he noted that Schneider kept his gaze steadily on Betzner, his smile seeming to take on an extra lopsided slant of satisfaction.

'So. Are you feeling more pliant to tell me now?'

Betzner coughed and spat out some blood. 'What . . . what good would it do?'

'Now you're making no sense.' Schneider glanced at his watch. 'It would mean at least we would finish early today, and with less pain caused to you.'

'Be . . . because you know it would implicate you as well.' Betzner met Schneider's gaze directly for the first time since the interrogation started. 'You know the people involved as much as me.'

Schneider glared back, then quickly stood, slapping Betzner with a hard backhand across the face.

'What nonsense you utter! You know I have no idea of your accomplices. You'll tell me now, or else . . .'

Schneider glanced towards the oblong box, Stefan pondering once again what was inside it. The ploys he'd cooked up with Edith the night before about Schneider's 'accomplices' were appearing to work. Schneider was starting to lose his composure.

Then, as if realizing the image he'd just cut – not his normal detached, ice-cold persona – Schneider sat back down, took a measured breath.

'I suppose you're wondering why your little box of tricks with the brandy didn't work?'

Betzner looked back with feigned disinterest; even in his sleep-deprived state, he knew he shouldn't rise to Schneider's bait.

'Everything was going well,' Schneider continued, 'until

the Führer's plane got to five thousand metres. At which altitude the air was so cold that the timer mechanism and the ignition fuses froze, and so the bomb was *kaput*. You could say that the Führer had a guardian angel, perhaps God even, protecting him.' Schneider's faint smile purposely slipped. 'But I doubt that same God is here protecting you now.'

Betzner held a constant look of disinterest throughout – even though so much had ridden on hopes of the bomb succeeding. But Stefan noticed a faint twinge of alarm in Betzner's eyes as Schneider strode across, picked up the wooden oblong box and opened it. Inside was a small hammer, a pair of pliers and ten small pieces of triangular-shaped metal.

'Have you ever played the guitar, Betzner?'

Noncommittal mumble from Betzner, though slightly more alarm in his eyes now. Schneider continued.

'Everyone thinks that these metal plectrums are only good for playing guitars. A favourite in fact with guitar supremos like Django Reinhardt and Eddie Lang, especially when they're playing steel-stringed or Hawaiian guitars.' He contemplated Betzner steadily, drinking in each faint eye-flicker of emotion and fear. 'But they overlook their other areas of usefulness. That when pulling out fingernails, they're often hard to detach. Some degree of separation and easing is required beforehand. And this is where these plectrums also serve to great purpose.'

Now the fear in Betzner's eyes was absolute.

'Are you ready now to tell me who your associates are?' Schneider raised the hammer. 'Before I drive home the first plectrum.'

Betzner scrunched his hands into tight fists and shook his head. T-shirt Junker came across and held flat the fingers of his right hand as Schneider positioned the first plectrum.

'No, I . . . *uuuggghh!*' Betzner's scream of agony filled the room as the plectrum was hammered beneath his index fingernail.

Stefan had to look slightly away again, and did so too for the next few steel plectrums hammered beneath Betzner's fingernails – Schneider asking each time, 'Are you ready to tell me now?' The same garbled, grunting refusals punctuated now by groans and screams of pain.

Stefan's gaze fixed instead on the warped satisfaction on Schneider's face, rising in turn with his own loathing for the man. Or was he avoiding looking at Betzner – not only because he was getting all too clear a picture of what was happening from the groans and screams of pain, but because he feared seeing a plea in Betzner's eyes. *Please stop this . . . you know you can!* Or perhaps even a tell-tale look between them that would give away his own involvement.

But as Schneider was halfway through hammering in the fingernail plectrums on Betzner's left hand, Stefan felt he'd heard and not-seen enough.

He stood up. 'This is outrageous! I've been asked to monitor this interrogation on behalf of the Führer. And what on earth would he think of such excesses?'

Schneider glared back defiantly. 'I think he'd no doubt approve. Give me a badge of honour. After all, I feel we're close now to uncovering the truth.'

'*Close?*' Stefan looked disdainfully at Betzner's broken

body. 'You're as far away now as ever. He clearly either doesn't know anything or isn't about to say.'

'I beg to disagree.' Schneider raised a brow challengingly. 'Or are you for some reason now eager to halt proceedings?'

Stefan wondered if this was the moment the trap would be sprung on him. His mouth felt dry, a faint shudder running through him. A frozen moment, then he sat back down.

His bluff called, he felt strangely empty and powerless as the gut-rending torture continued, was even inclined at one point to put a stop to it by shouting, '*It was me! I put him up to it!* . . .' before thinking of all the other lives he would then put in danger. His own handlers and overlords in the German military, Edith and her family, *little Louise* . . .

So he bit at his lip and tried to weather it, dutifully made notes at intervals.

To Betzner's credit, just after his third fingernail had been pulled out with pliers – perhaps because he'd already gone beyond a pain threshold or was past caring – his defiance resurged.

'Like I said . . . you know as much as I do,' Betzner spluttered, 'if not more, who was involved.'

'Again – what nonsense!' Schneider glared back, brutally yanked out another fingernail. 'Now tell me who is behind it!'

On the back of a low, guttural groan: 'It . . . it goes all the way to the top of the old SA, and you know it. Röhm's old pals. You're far closer to them than me . . .'

'Wild fantasy! I have no patience for this,' Schneider

snarled, his face flushing. The raw tension of the session combined with Betzner's reluctance to speak – Schneider was used to getting his way far more easily – had pushed him to the edge. He pulled his pistol from its holster, pointed it close to Betzner's face. 'If you're going to persist with such lies.'

'Yes, go on,' Betzner goaded, blood specks spraying down his shirt front as he spat the words out. 'You know you want to . . . so that the truth implicating you doesn't come out!'

Stefan watched Schneider's jaw set tight, his finger itching on the trigger. Stefan was quickly on his feet.

'If you shoot him now, it will look like what the suspect has said has some substance. So I strongly recommend you desist.'

Schneider glared at him, then back at Betzner, as if undecided which one of them to shoot, or perhaps *both*, before, his taut jawline slowly easing, he finally reholstered his pistol, nodding curtly.

And in that moment, for one of the first times in the session, Betzner looked Stefan's way, this time with a worn, sorrowful plea, as if to say, '*Why did you stop him? I wanted it ended now . . . I can't take any more.*'

But Stefan had one more card up his sleeve to help Paulos Betzner that he prayed he might be able to play.

One thing was clear. The momentum seemed to have gone from the interrogation in that instant. Though it was another forty minutes of repeated questioning after the last fingernail had been pulled out and a last brutal pummelling from T-shirt Junker before Schneider finally conceded that

Betzner wasn't going to say anything worthwhile – aside perhaps from more defiance and casting suspicion his way – and threw in the towel.

'Take him away!' He beckoned to the two armed guards by the door. 'I'm done with him. Dispose of him at the usual place.'

Stefan rode with Paulos Betzner in the back of a Kübelwagen jeep while two soldiers sat in the front. The 'usual place' was a woodland just four kilometres away where suspects were shot.

Schneider had raised a brow when Stefan had said he'd be accompanying them. 'Why would that be necessary?'

'I've been tasked by the Führer to monitor both his interrogation and execution. To ensure it's not only done, but done correctly. Two or three clean shots, not hacked to pieces with knives or bayonets.'

Schneider shrugged, as if not wishing to acknowledge some past messy executions, but didn't protest.

Stefan had a few minutes again in private in the cell with Betzner, telling the two soldiers it was for final preparations or any confession Betzner might make.

Now he informed them, 'Herr Betzner has expressed the last wish to be executed in a particular woodland – apparently it holds special significance for him because he used to play there as a child.' Stefan gestured meekly, as if it was neither here nor there to him. 'And I have granted this final request. It's not far from the usual spot you've mentioned – barely two kilometres further on. I'll direct you.'

The soldiers exchanged a look, but they knew better

than to question a senior officer who was getting his orders directly from the Führer.

The soldier driving nodded numbly. 'OK.'

Stefan gave directions for much of the rest of the journey. They parked at the edge of the woodland and stepped out. Their breath showed on the damp, frosty air as they walked.

Stefan noticed that Betzner didn't have too much trouble walking, but his upper body was slightly hunched over, as if he might have some internal injuries. Two hundred metres into the woodland, Stefan held a hand up.

'This will be fine. Herr Betzner has also asked that in the absence of a priest I give him the last rites, which I have agreed to. So, if you two would like to hold back here for a moment, so that we have some privacy . . .' Stefan took a few steps forward with Betzner, then paused, looked back at the two guards. 'In fact, to save too much shuffling back and forth, I might as well take care of the final execution once I've finished saying his rites.' He smiled tightly. 'At least then I can report to the Führer that it has been done according to his wishes.'

Their initial hesitance was quickly overridden by the fact that they'd be spared this final, unpleasant duty.

The soldier who'd been driving simply nodded, while his colleague tamely asked, 'Are you sure?'

'Quite sure.'

Stefan strode firmly away from them with Betzner, stopping about twenty-five metres ahead in a small clearing, in sight but out of earshot of the two soldiers.

He started muttering the last rites, but in between he gave Betzner directions on what would happen next. The final part of the plan he'd conceived with Edith the night before.

'In a minute, I'll stand back from you and fire just past your shoulder. You instantly slump to the ground as if dead.'

Muted nod from Betzner.

'. . . *May the Lord in his love and mercy help you* . . . Then I'll move over you and fire two more shots – one by your back, another by your head. Jolt on each, but don't move. Stay as if dead.'

Another brief nod.

'*With the grace of the Holy Spirit. May the Lord* . . . Stay prone on the ground, unmoving, until after you hear our jeep is gone. Then go towards that large fir tree directly ahead. Three hundred metres beyond that, you'll see the lights of a small cabin. A man named Otto will be waiting for you there.'

'But . . . but I don't think I can make it. I'm too weak . . . my body feels broken.'

'*Who frees you from sin to save you and raise you up* . . . Don't worry, you'll make it, and Otto will take care of you. If it's only organs bruised, he will be able to save you.'

A final, more uncertain nod.

Stefan unholstered his pistol, took two steps back and fired just past Betzner's shoulder, saw him slump forward to the ground. He moved closer and fired two more shots close to his back and head, watched him dutifully jolt each time.

Then he reholstered and strode back to the two soldiers.

'Let's get moving,' he said with a resigned sigh. 'These duties are never pleasant.'

They drove in silence, Stefan saying a quiet prayer beneath the drone of the engine that Paulos Betzner – however much the odds might be against it – would make it to Otto's cabin and survive.

26

The clatter of footsteps echoed heavily as we crossed the cavernous reception hall. My own and Stefan's footfalls almost lost among the heavier bootsteps of the two soldiers ahead of us, the Führer between them, with three more soldiers bringing up the rear.

The large reception hall adjoined the old Reich Chancellery and was used for state banquets and conferences as well as a ballroom. Now, late morning, one end had been allocated for clerks and Reich army personnel, four rows of desks, six in each row, piled with papers and files, from which the steady clatter of typewriters rose as we passed and went through a door at the end.

Descending into semi-darkness. Stark, intermittent wall lights guided the way down a stone staircase, the walk seeming never ending – reminding me in that moment of the approach tunnel to the Kehlsteinhaus, another of Hitler's private lairs – as we made our way down into the Vorbunker.

We were both carrying bags. Stefan had his tape recorder and notepad in his, and I had my glass speculum in mine. Stefan had informed me that the Führer had insisted in particular that the speculum not be seen by anyone. 'Keeping up his secrecy with your role, it seems,' Stefan had added. 'Perhaps keen to avoid the same problems he had with Hanussen from some quarters.'

Hitler had summoned Stefan to his private office in the Vorbunker to hear his report and taped interview with Betzner, and for some reason had also requested that I be there. 'Don't ask me why,' Stefan had added with a shrug as he'd informed me.

'Do you think this might be the trap you were worried about?'

'I don't know.' Stefan shook his head, a blend of concern and puzzlement in his face. 'You're the fortune teller.'

Now, descending the endless steps into the Vorbunker, that concern was heavy again on our shoulders.

Hitler instructed one of the soldiers to take our bags, and we were left alone for twenty minutes in a small room with single bed and chair, hardly bigger than a cell – which did little for our anxiety.

Then we were finally led down a short corridor by another soldier to a much larger office. Oil paintings, coats of arms, hunting trophies and a two-metre gold-plated Swastika adorned the walls. Hitler sat behind a large walnut desk with red-leather inlay and held a hand towards the trestle table opposite.

'Everything's been prepared as best it could.'

Stefan nodded. His tape recorder was at one end of the table, my speculum the other, the spotlight of an Anglepoise lamp hovering just above. We took our obvious respective seats behind them.

'Let us start with the recording of yesterday's interview,' Hitler said.

'Of course, Mein Führer,' Stefan responded promptly, pressing 'Play'.

Hitler looked towards me as the tape started. 'I may

invite you later to consult your speculum. But let us see how we progress.'

I couldn't help noticing Hitler's eyes staying on me more than Stefan as the tape played, as if far more curious about my reaction. Was he intrigued by the sensitivity of a woman hearing such horrors, or something else?

Stefan had already shared with me the worst of the interrogation, and of course I'd foreseen some of it – but it was nothing compared to listening to it live. I found myself cringing and closing my eyes at intervals – the Führer's gaze on me even more intent as I opened them again. Relishing my discomfort, or just a detached, curious observation?

Hitler held a hand up and Stefan stopped the tape.

'I see that when Betzner starts talking about the SA, Schneider is ready to finish him off there and then, as if afraid he might be incriminated.'

'Yes, Mein Führer. I could see that Schneider became very agitated at that point.'

'Until you stopped him, that is . . .'

Hitler was staring across sharply, and I heard Stefan swallow faintly. We both knew that Hitler's moods could turn in a heartbeat from calm to blood-curdling rage.

'Yes, well. I felt Betzner had much more to say, and I was keen to hear it. As I'm sure you are now.'

A curt nod after a second from Hitler, one hand gesturing to continue.

He let the rest of the tape run without comment, then sat back, tapping two fingers on his desk. A metronome beat to his settling thoughts.

'Interesting too that only a short while ago in the

fortune-telling sessions, the issue of past SA involvement came up when we talked about possible plots against me. And now Betzner is also mentioning them.'

'Yes. I had noted that, Mein Führer.'

I had already started to feel uncomfortable with the conversation continuing in part as if I wasn't there, but the feeling became more acute with Hitler's next comment.

'Though, of course, some of that might have been guided by the loss of her past mentor, Hanussen, with the SA directly involved in his death.'

My nerves tensed, unease worming in my stomach. Stefan's suspicions had probably been right. It was a trap! Could they know of Stefan's association with Betzner? Or perhaps my intercepted code-note had been deciphered? Or, despite us painstakingly searching, my bedroom had been bugged? Did they know of my Hanussen-linked revenge plot? So many possibilities of us being found out . . .

'That could be a partial factor,' Stefan conceded, a brief grimace my way – perhaps in apology for also speaking as if I wasn't there, or: *Don't worry, I can cope with this.* 'But I think as you are well aware, Mein Führer, the SA has quite a long history of plots against you, of seeking glory in their own right. So there might be something in what has been foretold, and what Betzner revealed.'

We both watched Hitler chew this over, fearful that the coup de grâce would now come, if he knew more than he was letting on.

But after a moment, he changed tack. Or was he just building up towards that coup de grâce? He looked at Stefan tersely.

'Did you happen to know Unterscharführer Betzner personally?'

'I . . . I've met him maybe once or twice before.' Stefan held a hand out. 'But, no, not well at all.'

The Führer contemplated Stefan steadily for a moment, the mood in the room stiflingly tense. 'Because Obersturmbannführer Schneider said that he thought there was some personal connection between the two of you. That you seemed protective of him for some reason.'

The shock on Stefan's face was only fleeting, though could have been read as affront. Then he quickly eased into a dry smile.

'SS-Obersturmbannführer Schneider thinks and says many things. Few of them by any means correct.' That smile shared faintly by the Führer before Stefan became more serious. 'But I was there primarily to do your bidding, Mein Führer. To get to the truth. I was not there to revel in the torture – which I suspect might have been the case with Schneider and would have precluded us getting to the truth if Betzner had passed out or expired.' Stefan held out one palm. 'And, of course, any opportunity of unearthing the truth would have also gone if I hadn't stopped Schneider from shooting Betzner there and then.'

We watched these comments settle with Hitler, everything balancing on a knife-edge. How many paranoias and personal demons was he juggling? I was only seeing the tip of the iceberg in my sessions with him – at the same time steering and feeding those paranoias.

There was a heavy pause. 'Let us see what Fräulein Creutzen has to say on the matter directly, shall we?' Hitler looked pointedly towards me. 'What are your thoughts?

Do you see Betzner's comments about old Sturmabteilung connections possibly having some substance?'

I was cautious as I looked into the speculum, conscious that I had to walk a tightrope between what I knew, Hitler's reference to my possible past Hanussen allegiance, and what I could conceivably see.

'It's not totally clear . . . because he's held many things back. And, indeed, I should also try to separate from my own personal feelings about the SA not being my favourites . . . even though that's not easy at times.' I took a fresh breath, saw a brief nod of accord from Hitler beyond the speculum, as if to say: *Nor mine. After all, look what I had done to them.* 'But, yes, I do overall see some substance in what Betzner said. Some connection.'

Hitler considered this for a moment, then: 'And as for Obersturmbannführer Schneider. Do you see some possible allegiances to the old SA that he's not revealing and might be troublesome for me?'

Again, that tightrope. If Hitler knew more than he was letting on, then I could be pulling the noose tighter round our necks with my answer.

I looked more intensely into the speculum. 'Again, he's not revealing all, keeping some things to himself – though whether that might be worrying or directly threatening to you isn't clear.' I sighed. 'And I must also try and separate what I've just heard with him on the recording, not let that colour my view . . .'

The Führer smiled tamely and held out one hand, as if in appreciation of my honesty and diplomacy, if nothing else. 'But your overall feeling?'

A more laboured sigh as I looked up from the speculum. 'He certainly can't be trusted . . . but whether that equals a direct threat, I can't be sure. Though others he's connected with might well be. It appears some past SA still hold resentment for you ordering Röhm's death.'

At the mention of Röhm, Hitler's eyes glared, seeming to bore right through me. Getting rid of what Hitler had come to see as a key adversary in Röhm had been highly controversial within the party. Stefan too glanced worriedly my way, and I wondered whether I might have overstepped the mark – sealed our fate, if he knew or suspected something.

The Führer looked aslant after a moment, eyes darting, mentally slotting the information into his filing cabinet of possible enemies and clandestine plots.

Then with a tired breath, he swept his right arm partially to one side, as if clearing the air of talk about Betzner and Schneider. He leaned forward, looked at me intently.

'Let us return now to a subject we discussed at some length before. That of my old friend and adversary, General Stalin . . .'

27

That tightrope walk continued. We weren't sure whether Hitler's clarifications regarding Stalin and how that influenced his own next moves were to seal his decision to proceed with an invasion of Russia, or the opposite, because he'd uncovered – either through an exposed connection with Betzner, a coded message deciphered, or perhaps a Berlin Resistance member turning traitor and ratting – that we'd been duping him all along.

And we knew there'd be little or no warning of this. There had been no warning for Hanussen, none for Stefan's uncle or others in the Night of the Long Knives, nor for the SA. Hitler was a master of the poker face and concealing his hand. His decisions invariably made in private, a final thread of information slotting into place in his jigsaw mind, by turn both methodical and haphazard, or sometimes just on a whim. The only warning a squad of soldiers breaking down your door in the dead of night or early hours and dragging you away.

That tightrope in the end stretched for another week, the Führer cancelling his next planned session at the last minute, 'I have too many official matters and affairs to see to before Christmas.'

I could see that Stefan was anxious, wasn't totally convinced by the postponement.

And when the next night in bed, he asked me whether

I might be able to see something, some indication of Hitler's intentions, I looked at him curiously.

'Not an easy task I have, is it? Trying to predict one of the most unpredictable men on earth.' I smiled crookedly. 'Besides, I thought it was my job just to guide him through foretelling, not predict what he might do next.'

Nevertheless, I did the next morning consult the speculum, once again gripping one of the Führer's gloves. Dark shadows swirling rather than shifting, and when a sudden brighter light broke through, I wasn't sure if it was some blinding, final destruction or fresh hope.

It did little to lift my own cloud of anxiety, or Stefan's – but then three days later he turned up with a wider smile.

'Come on. I'm taking you somewhere.'

I glanced at my watch, perplexed. Lunchtime, when usually he took me out in the evening.

He said little on the drive, but I could tell that he was pleased about something. It wasn't until the last few hundred metres that I realized where we were going: the Bierkeller in Reinickendorf where he'd bared his soul and we'd become partners in crime plotting Hitler's downfall.

'You were probably wondering why I brought you here before. It was one of my uncle's favourite beer halls as a young man. He was stationed at a barracks not far away. And I thought it particularly fitting to return here now.'

A few more soldiers were present today, and I noticed Stefan glance around as he chose a table – far enough to be out of earshot of others, particularly military men, but close by one of its speakers, used to ensure important announcements or nearby air-raid sirens were heard through the expansive hall.

Stefan ordered a half-bottle of champagne from the waitress, enough for a large glass each, holding one hand up at my increasingly quizzical expression.

'All will become clear soon enough.'

I didn't have to wait long. Only a quarter of my champagne flute gone before the speaker crackled to life. Brief preamble from an announcer that an important message from the Reich Führer would follow. Three seconds' silence punctuated by static, then Hitler's strident voice came over:

'*I have today made the decision with my military commanders that an invasion of Russia will take place. We are no longer prepared to stand by as General Stalin manufactures armaments at an alarming rate, having already moved in and occupied Bessarabia and Northern Bukovina. Actions which effectively break the non-aggression pact signed between us last year. The order I have signed today is Directive 21 and the final battle plan will be known as Operation Barbarossa, after the great German emperor who was part of Rome's empire.*' Marked pause and new breath. '*Today is a proud day for the German Reich. The furtherance of our* Lebensraum *and an end to the Slavic hordes and their Jewish-Bolshevik conspirators to our east . . .*'

A cheer rose from some of the soldiers and workmen in the beer hall, and Stefan chose that moment to raise his champagne glass and clink it against mine.

'You did it. He's finally made the move that you and your people in London were hoping for.'

'Yes,' I said. Though as I sipped my champagne, part of me still felt numb – a painful mixture of emotions. While the Sword of Damocles we'd feared these past days was no longer hanging over us – with the main aim of my sessions now fulfilled, my concern about the terrible loss of life resurfaced, something I knew Stefan and a number of his military handlers also shared. Stark contrast to his brighter mood now. 'You already knew this announcement was going to be made, didn't you?'

'Yes. The Führer told me this morning that he was going to make it public. So that's when I decided to come by and pick you up.'

I pushed a smile. 'Thank you. It's much appreciated.'

'What's the worry?' he asked, detecting my tempered enthusiasm. 'I thought you'd be elated.'

I glanced towards the soldiers in the room, some now clinking beer steins and singing 'Es zittern die morschen Knochen'. 'Now that it's a reality, that loss of life you mentioned before is starting to hit me harder.'

Stefan forced a pained smile. 'If it's any consolation, it's far from over. An actual invasion of Russia won't take place during winter, so the earliest would be spring. Stalin, meanwhile, will probably consider it just a bluff. And if those early invasion moves aren't successful, Hitler might well just pull out and we'll be back to square one.'

I wasn't sure if that made me feel any easier. It would mean that much of my cat-and-mouse game with guiding Hitler in those sessions would continue – the Führer asking me to see the likely success or failure of each stage in his battle plans.

I managed to put on a brighter face as I finished my champagne with Stefan, aided by him lifting my spirits when he said I should feel more positive about what I'd done.

'After all, it's quite an accomplishment – especially for a girl with no previous spying experience.'

I playfully punched his arm, and that night our lovemaking – perhaps the main litmus test that the recent worries hanging over us had been lifted – was more heartfelt and abandoned than it had been in a while.

The next morning, five days before Christmas, I went out and bought a Christmas tree in the Mauerpark market, and some decorations at Kaufhaus des Westens, and spent the afternoon dressing it with Lara and a joyful Louise, who clapped in excitement as a porcelain St Nicholas was finally put on top.

Apart from buying presents and preparations for Christmas, I had some catching up to do. I hadn't seen Teresa in a while, hadn't brought her up to date about Stefan.

I'd left Louise with my parents while I went out Christmas shopping, and to be discreet called by Colmar Bücher just as they were closing. Teresa hastily locked up and hustled me into a back room, both she and Xavier giving me a hearty hug in greeting.

'It's been too long,' Teresa said.

'Yes, I'm sorry.' I quickly explained about having to cut back on bookshop visits after Engelmann had been followed and the fact that for the past few weeks I'd also feared I might have been uncovered. 'Well, we *both* did actually . . .'

Teresa's brow knitted, and after handing over their early Christmas presents – a large box of Rausch chocolates for Teresa and a bottle of Calvados for Xavier – I embarked on the dramatic turn of events with Stefan.

Teresa reached across and clasped my hand, her expression taut as I got to the part where I feared Stefan had trapped me – 'That must have been terrifying for you' – quickly lifting into a smile of relief as the unexpected turnaround came, breaking off only to direct Xavier to pour us some drinks, 'It is Christmas, after all . . . and we haven't seen Edith in a while.' Xavier held up a bottle of peach schnapps for approval before pouring a glass each for us.

'So now you're like two musketeers working together,' Teresa commented as I finished.

'Well, *three*, if you count Churchill.' I smiled with a mock 'oops' and a hand to my mouth. 'That's the only rule between us. No names of our contacts shared either side.'

Teresa nodded in understanding, and we talked for a moment about café visits replacing bookshops for the coded-note exchanges. 'Only half a dozen so far, but still feels strange seeing someone I've never met fleetingly at a café, and minutes later they walk off with my identical bag and I with theirs.' I sipped at my schnapps. 'I sometimes worry that one of them might be a Gestapo agent – a handy way for them to get my coded note and catch me out.'

Teresa grimaced her acceptance of my concern, but Xavier largely dispelled it. 'Unlikely. They'd have to know you were there and carrying a coded note in advance, as well as which shopping bag to intercept. And if they knew all of that, they'd simply march in and arrest you.'

I ended up staying for two glasses of schnapps as we exchanged stories and reminisced, and I resolved to cut back the next few days until Christmas.

It was planned that I would go with Louise to my parents' house for Christmas Day, then they'd come with Tobias to my place the following day.

Surrounded by the warm cocoon of *all* my family, that Christmas was one of the most restful and joyous I could remember for some while, and I should have known it couldn't last – after all, isn't that what I did? *Warned of perils to come.*

But I hadn't suspected it would come so soon, at the New Year's Eve Ball Stefan had invited me to. Because the presence of half of the Reich hierarchy and elite of Berlin society at what on the surface promised to be a jubilant, glittering occasion made it a minefield of dangers and adversaries.

Held in the large baroque hall adjoining the old Chancellery we'd crossed only weeks before on the way to the Vorbunker – chandelier-light now filling the room while heavy steel shutters blacked out every window and protected against bomb blasts – the evening had started well.

After greeting dignitaries and some exchanges with Himmler and Goebbels, the Führer even came over to greet us. I was unknown to most people in the room, and I could feel a number of eyes drift our way as Hitler approached. An endorsement of sorts, though they knew better than to delve into the Führer's many personal alliances.

'Good that you were able to make it. You look a fine couple, if I may say.'

Stefan smiled uncomfortably. 'Sadly, Mein Führer, we're not attached in that way. But Fräulein Creutzen doesn't have a husband or partner, and I felt I couldn't leave her sitting at home alone on New Year's Eve.'

Hitler appraised us a moment longer. 'Your devotion to duty is admirable. And probably the best thing in wartime – no romantic ties. Too many secrets slip out.' Then, with a curt nod and an 'Excuse me', he was as quickly gone to greet other guests.

I caught her eye in that moment across the far side of the room, and my heart skipped a beat: *Ingrid Bittner, a ghost from my past.*

I had in fact noticed her not long after walking into the ballroom, even though it had taken me a moment to adjust for the eight years since I'd last seen her: broader and slightly heavier now, her mousy brown hair cut shorter. But she hadn't noticed me, and I'd hoped the rest of the evening would pass without her doing so.

But with the Führer having spoken to us, her attention had been drawn our way. And I saw now a spark of recognition in her eyes.

Stefan picked up on my agitation. 'What is it?'

I turned away from her. 'Someone from my past that I was hoping I wouldn't see again. So don't look over there, possibly draw her attention.'

Stefan leaned closer, barely a whisper as he looked at me with concern. 'Who is she?'

I tried not to appear visibly troubled, aware that she was probably still looking towards me. I smiled tamely. 'Someone who used to also work with Hanussen. One of his other protégés.'

'I see,' Stefan said, starting to weigh up the implications.

'If she comes over, don't mention anything about my continuing fortune telling.'

Stefan nodded. 'That's understood in any case, with the Führer's insistence on secrecy.'

'And don't tell her or let on that I have a daughter.'

But this Stefan seemed to struggle to comprehend. 'Why?'

I closed my eyes for a moment. Even harder for me to explain. The secret that I'd withheld from everyone for so long. That if revealed would mean the end of me and Louise. 'Just don't,' I said flatly. 'I have my reasons.'

In my side vision I noticed Ingrid Bittner now talking with a fresh group of people, and I began to hope that she'd become distracted and would forget about me. But moments later she broke away from them and started heading my way.

28

'I wasn't sure it was you at first,' Ingrid Bittner said with a strained smile.

'Nor I you. Your hair looks different – shorter than it used to be.' I avoided mentioning her more rounded face and stockier build. Enough bad history between us in the past to start on the wrong foot now. I held out one hand. 'This is my friend, Stefan Hansel.'

'Pleased to meet you, I'm sure.' Stefan held Ingrid's hand lightly and made a small bow in greeting. Then with a brief smile, 'I'll leave you two ladies to it. Some colleagues to catch up with.'

Obviously keen to avoid any possible questions or slip-ups about my daughter, Stefan drifted over to a man in SS uniform in his early forties across the room, who had acknowledged him with a half-raised hand.

Ingrid looked back at me. 'How long is it since we last saw each other?'

'Oh, must be eight or nine years,' I said, eager to mask the time-gap as much as possible.

'Yes. I certainly thought it was approaching that.'

I was sure Ingrid knew the exact time before she'd even crossed the room to me. Erik Hanussen's death was set in stone, 25 March 1933, and everyone knew I left Berlin only two weeks after.

Ingrid looked to one side for a moment, her expression

darkening. 'It was a difficult time for us. I think we *both* cared about him deeply in our own way.'

She could have been talking about Hanussen, but I knew she meant Christof, my boyfriend who'd died in a motorcycle accident only two weeks before we'd lost Erik.

I simply nodded, my throat suddenly tight. Words were difficult in that moment, even if I could have found the right ones.

'Did you continue with the fortune telling?' she asked.

'Only for a short while. Gave it up long ago.'

Her mouth skewed. 'Strange. I thought I heard somewhere that you'd set up in Paris and continued with it.'

'First few years, yes.' I'd had enough with questions from Hitler where the answers might already be known, without now also fending them off from Ingrid Bittner. I pushed a smile. 'Old news.'

We were distracted for a second by a band moving into position on a small rostrum in the corner, getting behind their instruments.

'And what are you doing now?' she asked.

'Working at the Reich Chancellery with the man you just met.' I gestured towards Stefan talking to two men eight paces away. 'You? Did you continue with the fortune telling?'

I knew she hadn't, had given it up almost straightaway, but it would be nice to see her in turn on the back foot, if only for a second.

'Goodness, no,' she said with a half-guffaw, as if the suggestion was ridiculous. She pointed towards the far end of the room and the small group she'd just come from. 'I work in the motor pool doing inventory and helping Carl, who makes sure the Reich's Berlin fleet runs smoothly. You might remember him?'

I looked towards the group and, in the same way I had with her, adjusting for the years in between, finally picked out a man I vaguely recognized: Carl Voltner, a second-hand-car salesman I recalled Ingrid having an on–off relationship with before our fateful love triangle with Christof. But I noticed in that moment Stefan returning the half-salute of a uniformed SS officer in that same group. 'Yes, now you mention it.'

Ingrid smiled tightly. 'Anyway, must get going. Nice to see you again.'

Even though we both knew it wasn't.

As she got back to Carl and his group at the end of the room, Stefan drifted back over.

'How did it go?'

'Better than I expected. When she asked what I was doing these days, I told her I worked with you and had left fortune telling years ago, and she seemed to accept that.' I eased a strained breath. 'But mark what I said before. Don't trust her, and certainly don't tell her I have a daughter.'

'You never explained to me why.'

'*Later*. It's complicated.' I was already starting to think how I might tiptoe around it. 'And now's not the time,' I added, as the hubbub in the room rose with the band tuning up.

Halfway through their rendition of 'Stern von Rio', Stefan leaned in closer as he noticed Ingrid talking to the SS officer he'd just half-saluted. 'Seems like our two adversaries know each other?'

'*Two* adversaries?'

'Yes, of course. You've only heard his voice on tape . . . never met him in person.' A strained grimace. 'That officer over there is Obersturmbannführer Kurt Schneider. Master of the plectrums and pliers.'

A chill ran through me. I tried to tell myself it was nothing; a chance, casual meeting and conversation that had nothing to do with me. But as Ingrid deftly pointed and looked our way, Schneider joining her with a few brief nods as she spoke, I began to fear the worst.

Towards the end of the evening I went to the ladies' powder room. As I came out, I was alarmed to see Kurt Schneider talking to Stefan. I hung back in the shadows out of sight and waited for Schneider to walk away before I returned to Stefan.

'What was that about?'

Stefan looked around awkwardly for a second before nodding towards the exit. 'Not here.'

We made our way round the corner to the café in Hotel Kaiserhof, one of the few places still open. I ordered coffee and Stefan a brandy; a sign perhaps, especially after a night of wine and champagne, that what he had to tell me required something stronger than coffee.

'Schneider said that he'd been talking to Fräulein Bittner and she'd informed him that she used to be a protégée of Erik Hanussen's along with yourself. Bittner said that she moved onto other things long ago, but felt sure that you'd remained with fortune telling.'

'My God.' My heart sank at our two potential adversaries possibly in league together. 'What did you tell him?'

'I said it was ludicrous, of course. I said that you and I were simply working on something in the Reich Chancellery, but the Führer has insisted that it remains private. Not to be shared with anyone.' Stefan took another slug of brandy. 'Then when he started pushing, I warned him off by saying that he could ask the Führer directly, though he wouldn't be pleased when I told him someone had been snooping around about his private affairs.'

I nodded with a gentle smile. 'Do you think it worked?'

'Hopefully it's defused his suspicions, *for now.*' Stefan returned a more pained smile. 'But I know Schneider of old. He's like a dog with a bone once he feels he's got hold of something. He might well return to the subject, start digging. We must be prepared for that.' Stefan looked at me evenly. 'So best you tell me everything you know. Perhaps starting with why it's so important that Ingrid Bittner doesn't know you have a daughter.'

I took a sip of coffee, looked down for a moment. The long years of avoiding the subject and still I was delaying.

'You recall I mentioned Louise's father dying in a motorbike accident before she was even born?'

Stefan nodded. 'Yes. I recall you said you'd been together for a while, but weren't married.'

'Twenty months, to be precise. His name was Christof.' I looked aslant briefly, my eyes moistening as the memories flooded back. 'But in fact he wasn't with me all of that time – for the last three months before he died, he had an affair with Ingrid Bittner.' I bit at my lip. 'Well, *almost* three months – for the last two weeks of Christof's life, he came back to me, and that's when Louise was conceived. But Ingrid never knew.'

I watched Stefan slotting the pieces together. 'I see. And if she saw Louise or knew you had her, she might work out she was Christof's?'

'Yes. When Christof died, Ingrid said he was the love of her life, and of course I did too – despite the hurt of that almost-three-month affair. And it would break her heart to know.' I shook my head. 'Particularly because on the night he died, he said he was on his way to let her know it was over, that we were back together. She thought he was just away at his parents' house in Eberswalde in that two weeks he was with me, and had died on his way from his parents back to her.'

'Oh, what a tangled web we weave . . .'

Stefan left the sentence hanging and I prickled for a moment thinking he was referring to me, before realizing it was aimed more at Christof.

'Yes, it was complicated. I suspected Christof had been seeing her even before that three months, and it was me that broke it off then. But he kept begging to come back to me, said that he and Ingrid weren't really suited and that I was the *real* love of his life. And in that last two weeks, I finally relented.'

Stefan took a swig of brandy, his look one of understanding more than recrimination. He reached across and gently clasped my hand as I continued.

'Then when, just two weeks later, Erik was killed, it was all too much for me and I left Berlin, only realizing not long after I arrived in Paris that I was actually pregnant.'

Stefan spent a moment letting his thoughts settle, that hand now gently stroking, *consoling*. He took a deep breath. 'I can see how Ingrid Bittner finding out about Louise would be a worry, might hurt her and make her vindictive.' He held out a palm. 'But if she's already done the worst by sharing her suspicions with Schneider, it becomes less of a concern.'

'I suppose,' I said, a tame concession. 'But I know Ingrid. She too can be like a dog with a bone. Right now, it's only a suspicion, but if it becomes a *conviction* in her mind, she won't let it go either. She'll either dig herself or bend Schneider's ear about it again.'

Stefan nodded, his expression mirroring my concern. He sighed. 'Either way, clinging to Hitler's secrecy on the matter is our best defence. That will deter *both* of them from digging.'

What Stefan said made sense, but I found myself shaking my head. The problem with not telling long-held secrets in full was that the gaps inevitably began to show. 'But it could so easily be uncovered. Through Lara, or the soldiers who set up my speculum at the Kehlsteinhaus and the Vorbunker.' *Let me count the ways.*

Stefan grimaced, but his hand was now patting, reassuring. 'I'm sure Lara would have been sworn to secrecy when she was hired, and those few disconnected soldiers as well.' He gestured. 'Besides, the soldiers might not even know what the speculum is for or make the connection with you. The only person who has been in the room with you during a session besides the Führer has been myself.'

I nodded numbly. I wasn't sure if that made me feel any easier. The only thing protecting me was Hitler and his insistence on secrecy. Yet at the same time he held in his power both my life and Stefan's.

Our fates now rested entirely in his hands.

29

War Cabinet Room, London, March 1941

'It appears that Hitler has delayed,' Calder Gibson said. 'It was all set for this week, but now it could be another month or so.'

'Do we know this just from our contacts in Berlin?' Churchill looked towards the other two men in the room: War Cabinet Secretary Edward Bridges and Chiefs of Staff Committee member General Hastings Ismay. 'Or also from activities on the ground?'

It was Ismay who answered. Appointed by Churchill to be Chief Co-ordinator of all the armed forces, his knowledge of ground operations was second to none.

'No final thrust yet from troops gathered on the eastern front with Russia. But more regiments have joined that contingent in the past few weeks alone – so it appears imminent.'

'Do you think he might be bluffing?' Churchill pressed.

'Unlikely. There are more German troops now massed on the Russian border than in any previous campaigns.' Ismay eased a tight-lipped smile. 'So if it's a bluff, it's one hell of a big one.'

Edward Bridges joined in briefly with a wry smile. 'I think it's General Stalin who thinks Hitler's been bluffing all along more than us.'

Churchill nodded knowingly, his own smile more tempered. 'The number of messages we've sent telling him so. And he surely must be able to see it for himself from his own troop dispatches from the border with Germany.' Churchill puffed at his cigar, looked again to Ismay. 'Have the Russians made many defence preparations? Perhaps their actions on the ground belie their diplomatic responses.'

'Minimal. Especially considering the forces massed the other side of the Russian border.'

Churchill turned to Calder Gibson. 'And do our contacts in Berlin say the same? That it looks inevitable that Hitler will now go ahead?'

'Yes, they do.' Gibson's expression clouded. 'But that presents another problem.'

'Oh, what's that?'

With the first major assault on Russia now appearing imminent, Calder Gibson thought it an apt time to raise the issue; there might not be the opportunity later. But now with Churchill staring at him directly, he wasn't so sure.

'It was something we touched on before, Prime Minister. That when our contact in Berlin made forecasts that ended up wrong, her days were numbered. And it would be time then to make good on our initial promises to get her and her family out of Germany to safety.'

Churchill tapped his cigar in the ashtray. 'And on the same subject of safety – has the issue we discussed last time now been resolved?'

'Yes. Our contact in the Abwehr confirmed that Hansel is in fact one of their men.' Gibson let out a laboured breath. 'Only problem now is that if we lose one asset, we risk losing *both*.'

'I see.' Churchill's expression was heavier as he exchanged a look with Ismay. 'But on that impending battle front – from what I'm hearing today, those initial manoeuvres will be something of a rout.'

Ismay nodded, turned to Gibson. 'Yes. But what you mention might be something we have to look at more closely on future advances and battles.'

Calder Gibson looked from Ismay back to Churchill. 'So is that your final word on the subject, gentlemen? What should be passed on to her if and when Hitler asks her how she sees this first major assault going?' Gibson held up a cautionary hand. 'Keeping in mind that if she gets it wrong, not only are her and her family's lives in danger, but our mission too. Because once she's lost credibility by getting such a crucial forecast wrong, our overall game plan collapses.'

Churchill sank into deeper deliberation for a moment. 'Far be it for me or anyone else here to tell her directly what she must say. All we can do is inform her how we see it from troop activities on the ground. But if through her skills she sees something different, then she should also take that into account. After all, they seem to have guided her well so far.'

Calder Gibson nodded his acceptance, reminded again why Winston Churchill was considered such a great statesman. Although he wasn't sure he felt entirely comfortable with the fate of Edith Creutzen and her family and the outcome of the Second World War hingeing solely on a diplomatic response.

30

I felt more anxious today than on previous café visits, because I knew that the message from London was a crucial one – if I hadn't already known from Hitler's ordering of another personal meeting at the Kehlsteinhaus the next day. I'd pick Louise up after school and take her to my parents' house, then set off early the next morning with Stefan for the meeting.

I glanced casually around the café, as if I had little interest in others there, but at the same time was taking everything in. Someone who might look my way a second too long, or a face that I thought I'd seen before; or perhaps just someone like me, looking around nonchalantly, but at the same time absorbing everything.

That was what I didn't like about cafés, I realized. As Lutz had said initially, '*They're far too open*.' Whereas in a bookstore there were lots of hidden nooks and crannies behind the bookshelf rows. Here, anyone among the many in the café could be a Gestapo agent or SD in plain clothes.

After five minutes a slim woman with light-brown hair whom I hadn't seen before walked in and put a Kaufhaus des Westens shopping bag right next to mine – the café was only a hundred metres from the department store – then went past the serving counter to the washrooms beyond. She obviously didn't want to stay long, as when she came out, she didn't order anything, simply picked up my bag and headed off.

I got a glimpse of a book inside the bag she'd left, my eyes tracking her for a moment through the café's front window – another thing suggested by Lutz. '*Try and pick up if anyone might be tailing your contacts.*'

Nothing. Nobody getting up soon after and following her.

With a limited number of people in Lutz's network, every so often I'd see a familiar face. Which in a way was reassuring. At least then I knew they weren't Gestapo agents.

I finished my coffee and pastry soon after, paid and left.

I took my first look at the coded note in the book only once I was home, in the privacy of my bedroom. Yes, decidedly my assigned contact, *not a Gestapo agent.*

I released a faint breath of relief. Practically the same now after every book swap; despite the repetition, it didn't get any easier.

I didn't want to leave the coded note at home with Lara still there, so having pushed it deep into my pocket, I slid the book in among the many on the shelves downstairs before going to pick up Louise from school.

I was five or six minutes earlier than usual approaching the school gates. I wanted to make sure to get away with her as soon as she came out and get on the first tram to my parents' house.

Then suddenly I froze as I looked ahead: Ingrid Bittner was coming out of the school gates! She turned left on the road ahead, walking away from me. She hadn't seen me, and within seconds had gone from sight.

The knot in my stomach eased a fraction since at least

she hadn't seen me with Louise. But what on earth had she been doing here?

'Momma . . . Momma. Are you OK?'

My thoughts still lost among the screeching of children leaving the school, I hadn't immediately registered Louise.

'Yes . . . yes. Of course.' I patted her shoulder affectionately. 'Let's go.'

But a short distance away, it suddenly hit me why Ingrid Bittner might have gone into the school and who she might have seen there. I turned back with Louise.

'One moment, *Liebling*. Something I must check with your school.'

'She's been at Louise's school asking about her.'

'Who?'

'Ingrid Bittner.'

A nod of recognition after a moment from Stefan. With Ingrid Bittner's name hardly coming up in the past few months, I shouldn't have been surprised at Stefan's pause for thought. I too had been lulled into a false sense of security.

I'd waited forty minutes into our drive before raising the issue. I was still so het-up and troubled by what I'd discovered at Louise's school that I'd had difficulty deciphering the coded message the night before. Three goes at it before I got it right; three pieces of paper burned over the sink in the early hours.

I don't know if I can do this.

So now I was tired and tried to close my eyes and unwind or sleep for the first part of the drive. But I found it impossible: too many burning thoughts I needed to unburden before I could relax.

'She went in to see the secretary at the school. Found out Louise's birth date.'

Stefan glanced across briefly, brow creasing. 'How did she manage that?'

'Said she was a friend of mine and wanted to get a surprise birthday present for my daughter, but didn't know when it was.'

'I see.' Stefan looked straight ahead for a moment, jaw clenching. 'So now she's probably worked out that Louise is Christof's, her old boyfriend.'

'Yes.'

A weighted silence for a moment as the scenery rolled by. Stefan no doubt working out the ramifications as I had the night before; except for *one* area.

'And did she actually see you with Louise?'

'No.' Laboured exhalation. One link I'd worked out not long after leaving the school secretary's office: 'Though she obviously had done before and I hadn't noticed her, or someone told her I had a child there.'

Stefan's eyes flickered, assimilating thoughts, as he stared at the road ahead. 'And she hasn't confronted you?'

'No. Not yet.' The admission now open that I knew she would, and for far more than Stefan suspected. I felt everything pressing in. *How much longer could I cling on to the last shreds of my secret?* 'It only happened yesterday afternoon, so there probably hasn't been the time.'

Getting back from my parents' house last night, with Lara having already left, I dreaded hearing that knock on my door and seeing Ingrid there. Or even worse, in those early hours while I was fumbling to decode the note and burning the wasted attempts over the sink.

Stefan glanced across at me, no doubt caught my troubled expression. 'Probably a good idea that you're away for a day or so now.'

'Yes, I suppose.' I smiled awkwardly. 'Never thought I'd find myself admitting that I looked upon a direct session with Hitler as a welcome break.'

Stefan mirrored my smile ruefully for a moment. 'At least we have this time now to talk and get your own thoughts clear before you have to see her again.' Stefan tapped one finger on the steering wheel, as if tamping down his final thoughts, then turned towards me. 'Much of this we touched on before . . . and could be that you're overthinking it now, over-worrying. Because while your having a child with an old boyfriend of hers might be a reason for personal upset between the two of you, it isn't a crime. And I don't think anything that's happened now changes what I said last time, necessarily makes it any worse . . .'

I nodded lamely as Stefan emphasized again his previous points. That while Ingrid Bittner might now be spiteful and vindictive, she'd already done her worst by confiding her suspicions in Kurt Schneider.

'And while the Führer insists on the whole matter of your fortune telling being kept secret, that remains our ace card. Because if she delves too deep and oversteps that line, she could find herself in hot water.'

I felt totally empty inside, bereft. The gap between Stefan's advice and my real fears was becoming a chasm. Yet until I let go from my grip the last part of my long-held secret, he could never fully understand those fears. *No more secrets.* I would certainly have to tell him once Ingrid Bittner finally confronted me – which I suspected would be within days. Eight long years holding back that secret, and still I was begging for more time.

The session room had been set up as before at the Kehlsteinhaus, although this time we'd had longer to ourselves on the terrace admiring the dramatic view, almost thirty minutes, before finally going in.

And in that time, I appreciated why the Führer liked to come up here, separated from the front lines and various plots against him, real or imagined. Though in my case that separation – that feeling of those troubles being suddenly distant as I drank in the mountain air and breathtaking view – was from what awaited me back in Berlin with Ingrid Bittner and my continuing spy game; or, more immediately, in the next room with Hitler.

As before, Stefan started the questioning while the Führer observed from the side of the room. Most of those questions followed on from earlier sessions, about rising resistance in Czechoslovakia and Poland, which I still didn't foresee as becoming strong enough to be of any particular threat 'to the might of the German Reich'.

I noticed Hitler smile faintly. I'd purposely chosen the words, knew by now that flattery often helped soften his mood.

'But now we've been forced to develop separate communities for many of the people there, particularly Jews. Do you see these communities as becoming troublesome?'

I knew that 'communities' referred to what were already being termed 'ghettos' in the foreign press. The shifting shadows in the speculum were darker and deeper now, and I saw Stefan look concerned at the rapid flinching in my eyes as I took in the pain and suffering I saw there.

'I . . . I see there will be some hardship and difficulties,' I said as steadily as I could. 'But not sufficient to ignite rebellions that will cause the Reich any problems. What few there are will be quickly quashed.'

A faint nod of satisfaction from Hitler, then he waved an arm to one side, a clear indication that he wished to take over. Stefan shifted to the edge of the room, and for the first moment in front of me the Führer simply observed me steadily. Then he reached across and clasped my hand for his first question.

'And in Germany? Indeed in Berlin itself. Do we have dissident activity here too?'

My throat felt tight under his steady, penetrating stare. I averted my eyes to the speculum. 'Yes . . . as mentioned before. But once again these are not strong enough to pose any threat to the might of the German Reich.' But this time his smile in appreciation of the flattery and reassurance died quickly.

'Do you see any particular group who might in the future pose a threat?'

I swallowed back my palpitations as I looked again into the speculum. Of the many dissidents, I knew I was being foolish to think it might relate to me. I was letting my personal worries overlap. *Detach yourself . . . divert!*

'I see one of the most active groups continuing to hand out anti-Reich propaganda . . . much of it about activities in the eastern territories and Poland that we previously touched on.' A ready nod from Hitler, so he'd picked up that I was talking about the Baum group. But in the speculum, I saw flames now too. 'And I see them also starting some fires.'

Hitler looked momentarily alarmed. 'What? As in the Reichstag?'

'No . . . no. Nothing on that scale. Maybe just burning Reich posters and hoardings . . . or perhaps a small building.'

'And is that the most worrying activity you see?'

I looked back into the speculum, saw now the glint of crosses reflecting the flickering flames. 'I also see tensions with the Catholic Church that if not handled correctly could lead to more open revolt.'

'Any particular regions?'

Misty shapes of mountains and pine forests emerged from the flickering flames. 'I'm not sure . . . but looks like Westphalia . . . possibly Bavaria too.'

'I see.' Hitler leaned forward, one finger held on a specific point on his question sheet. 'On the subject of Bavaria, we do in fact have a new secret manufacturing plant at Jachenau, in the Bavarian foothills, vital to the success now of the overall war effort. Can you see if this will remain free from bombing raids from our enemies?'

I felt suddenly adrift. The speculum told me nothing. Before the session, knowing that with Hitler present, Stefan couldn't overtly warn me, we'd agreed a signal: he'd touch his right ear if he thought it was a real question, his left if he thought it a trick. But in my side vision, I saw his hand drift towards his left ear, then change and go to his right, followed by the hand wavering. *Unsure.*

I lost myself again in the speculum, but the shadows there just swirled steadily. *Nothing*. 'I'm not sure I see anything there clearly,' I started, reading solely what the speculum related. Then I had sudden recall of something Lutz told me a while ago: '*Sometimes you might be fed information in what's known as a "barium meal test". If you in turn pass that information on to London and they act on it, then they know here in Berlin that you're a spy.*' So that meant this particular manufacturing plant was false, because they wouldn't risk a real plant being bombed. But did it also mean they suspected I might be a spy?

A faint tremble gripped me, and I feared it might be picked up by Hitler still clasping my left hand. Hopefully, he thought the troubling images in the speculum were the cause. 'Perhaps my clear vision of this plant is obscured by its heavy camouflage.' I closed my eyes for a second, nodding slowly as I looked back more intently into the speculum. 'But I do sense you might be worried about other hidden plants close to hillside and forest areas, if not this one . . . and my answer is *no*, I don't see the secrecy of those being breached and those plants bombed.'

Stefan's expression was stolid, still unsure whether I'd answered correctly. I thought I detected a trace of a satisfied smile on the Führer's face – but again it was as quickly gone, his expression grave.

'We've touched on this subject before over the past months, but now I have many of my regiments by the Russian border poised for attack. Do you still see great success for the Reich, or are there any surprises General Stalin might have in store for me?'

I saw those countless thousands of men lined up in the speculum . . . then next saw the bodies spread over the battlefields. *Broken and bloodied among dying flames.* And from that last note from London, yet another issue in today's session where I was getting little guidance. I was on my own.

31

On the drive back to Berlin, Stefan tried to put my mind at ease about the possible 'barium meal' spy test.

'I don't know if it was that. I think just some false information that might have been part of a barium spy test used with others – but in this case was simply used to once again test if your forecasts are accurate.'

'What makes you say that?'

'Think about it. The Führer's very next question was about his impending Russian invasion – a crucial action. So it makes sense that at that juncture he might once again want to test the substance of your foretelling.' Stefan held one hand from the steering wheel. 'Whereas a spy test involving bombing raids on a fictitous factory would take several weeks to know about with the planning involved at the British end.'

Stefan's suggestion made sense, except for one other factor. 'But all those questions beforehand about dissident activity.'

'You've been asked those before.'

'Yes, but this time he specifically mentioned Berlin.'

Stefan shrugged. 'Most German dissident activity would be in Berlin, because that's the centre of everything.'

I nodded slowly after a moment. Stefan was probably right. I was once again letting my personal fears infringe. I lifted a challenging eyebrow across at him with a half-smile.

'But you didn't seem to know either about this Jachenau plant, which didn't help.'

'I must admit, I wasn't sure. I know we have a couple of secret plants in Bavaria, but in the heat of the moment their names escaped me. The problem with questions asked directly by the Führer.' Stefan pushed a tight smile. 'Alone and with the time, I'd have been able to check with my military superiors.'

'So, do you think I gave the right answer?'

Stefan thought for a moment. 'In the end there are no right or wrong answers. In the same way as I can't say for sure that it wasn't a barium-meal spy test. Just that it's unlikely, and your answer was certainly ambiguous and diplomatic enough. So, you're learning.' A pained grimace. 'But we won't know for sure until there's a knock on our doors in the dead of night.'

Silence for a while as the scenery rolled by, that portent we lived with every day back on our shoulders.

'I certainly think you gave the right answer with the Russian invasion,' Stefan said at last, trying to lift my spirits again. 'All the indicators are on your side.'

I nodded numbly. But even with that there was no certainty. And meanwhile, during the next few weeks we'd be reading and hearing news of those initial battles with bated breath. Knowing that if at any time they took a turn for the worse, our gazes should move to the door, waiting for that knock.

It was late, just past 10 p.m., when we got back to my place in Berlin. Louise was staying over at my parents' house another night, and I'd pick her up from school tomorrow.

Stefan came in only for a quick coffee. He had an early start the next day and was tired after the long drive, and I was too from the stress of the session.

So with a quick hug and parting kiss by the front door, 'See you tomorrow,' he headed off.

The knock came only minutes later, and I thought at first Stefan might have forgotten something.

But when I opened the door, Ingrid Bittner stood there.

'Tell me . . . What is it? What's wrong?' Teresa asked concernedly, clasping my hands across the table.

My knuckles were red-raw from knocking at her bookstore door. I knew she and Xavier lived in a small apartment above the shop. But, past midnight, it had taken ten minutes of knocking to wake them before they came downstairs and let me in.

Xavier sat one side of the table, a bottle of brandy between us. He'd already poured a glass for me and I'd taken a first sip with shaking hands.

'Sorry . . . someone came by my place earlier, and I had to come . . .' I was still fighting to catch my breath, having run full pelt from the nearest tram stop. 'You were the first person I thought of.'

Teresa's brow knitted. 'What? Gestapo . . . SS?'

'No.' I shook my head, eyes closed for a second. 'A ghost from my past. And now she's caught up with me.'

Teresa was looking at me expectantly. So many years withholding this secret, spinning the right words in my mind of how I might finally reveal it, but now they seemed to catch in my throat. I started tremulously.

'You recall I used to have a boyfriend in Berlin . . . who died in a motorbike accident not long before I left there.'

'Yes. Louise's father. A terrible tragedy. I remember that you didn't know you were pregnant with his child until you were already in Paris.'

Hopefully, Teresa hadn't picked up on my faint flinch. I quickly masked it by taking another sip of brandy.

'Christof . . . Christof Lange was his name. And I made sure at least his name was put on Louise's birth certificate when she was born.'

Teresa nodded. 'I was there with you at the time. Actually held little Louise in my arms while you signed the register.'

Tight smile in acknowledgement. Teresa had done much more than that. I'd been a wreck at the time, my French still limited, and Teresa had arranged everything and helped raise Louise. That's why I thought I must share this secret with her first – my best friend and Louise's second mother.

I looked at Teresa directly. 'But there was one thing I never told you about my relationship with Christof, or anyone else for that matter . . . I'm sorry.' I again closed my eyes for a second as I tried to calm my still ragged breath. 'But the last few months of Christof's life, except for two weeks – well, that's the story I clung to if anyone asked – he had an affair with another girl, also a Hanussen protégée. And she's turned up again now.' Deflated sigh. 'I first saw her at a New Year's Eve party – but she's been digging since at Louise's school and found out her actual birth date. And earlier tonight she finally confronted me with it all.'

Teresa's eyes flickered as she put the pieces together. 'So, you're saying that Louise was conceived in that two weeks, and now this other woman has found out that she might be Christof's?'

'Yes, as I said, that's the account I clung to if pressed.' I watched Teresa's brow furrow deeper. This was proving even harder than I'd first thought. 'The only person I've so far shared that curtailed account with has been Stefan, when I saw this woman at the party, and he wondered why I was so perturbed.'

'Curtailed?'

'Yes. I told Stefan that Christof had come back to me in that last two weeks, and that's when Louise was conceived – while Ingrid thought he was simply away at his parents' house in Eberswalde. But most of that wasn't true.'

'*Most?*'

Impatience now in Teresa's tone, her stare cutting, half-curiosity, half-hurt that I hadn't trusted her enough to share this before.

'Christof did in fact beg to come back to me, even before that two-week period – said that I was the *real* love of his life, not Ingrid – and I always said no. The last time was at the end of that two weeks, on the way back from his parents' house, and I said *no* then too.' I closed my eyes again as I got an image of Christof pleading with me, the tears starting to run down my cheeks. 'He rode away from my place on his bike that same night, and that was the last I saw of him. He died in a collision with a truck on his way back to Ingrid Bittner's.' I shook my head. 'That's why I've always partly blamed myself for his death. If only I'd said *yes* that night, that I'd take him back, it might have been different . . .'

Teresa was clasping my hand more firmly now, consoling, 'You shouldn't blame yourself.' But I could see her thoughts still turning. 'Are you saying that you and Christof never got back together in all of those three months?'

'Yes, that's what I'm saying.'

I said it simply, straightforwardly, belying the portent of those few words, watched the shifting shadows in Teresa's eyes as the rest fell into place.

'But if Louise isn't Christof's child, then whose?'

Maybe it was the years of holding the secret back, but just blurting it out seemed wrong, so I started with a preamble. 'You recall my mentioning how close I was to Erik Hanussen, how we had a special affinity together . . .' But Teresa got there ahead of me, cut in.

'*Hanussen's?*' Half-question, half-exclamation, said on the back of a hissed breath, as if she was afraid others might hear it. 'And he was Jewish . . .'

I just nodded, held her eyes as I watched the rest of her realization trickle down: why I'd kept it secret all along, the drastic fate that Louise and I would face if it was discovered. But now, seeing Teresa still struggling to make sense of it all, it was my turn to fill in the gaps. I clasped her hand back.

'You recall in Paris when you finally convinced me to work with SOE and the Resistance. That it would be the perfect revenge for what Hitler had done to Hanussen . . . duping him through the same fortune telling.' I gently rocked her hand. 'But I don't think you realized why that resonated so strongly with me. Because I'd not only be seeking revenge for Hitler killing my lover and the father of my daughter, but for Louise also. Retribution against the man who killed her father. Otherwise, I doubt I'd have taken the risk.'

Xavier looked from Teresa to me, as if my desire for revenge was a motive he was hearing for the first time. 'Whatever the reasoning, it's much appreciated,' he said, once again wearing his Resistance hat. He raised the brandy bottle. 'More?'

I indicated with my thumb and forefinger close, *just a little bit*.

Xavier poured a finger of brandy into my glass, and with a few more questions from Teresa, the rest was filled in: Yes, my relationship with Hanussen started at the time of Christof's affair with Ingrid Bittner. But, no, it wasn't simply on the rebound. 'Something had been growing between us for a while, and it became a full and heartfelt relationship. We truly loved each other, and then . . .' I left hanging the one thing I had mentioned many times before: the unfairness and ruthlessness of Hitler ordering Erik's death.

Teresa sighed with the weight of it all, held a palm out. 'And what's this Bittner woman going to do? Report what she's uncovered to the Gestapo or SS?'

'That's what she's *threatening* to do. But she's after money from me to stop her telling all. She's blackmailing me.'

'How much?' Xavier asked.

'Ten thousand Marks.'

Xavier exchanged a look with Teresa and whistled softly. You could buy a fair-sized house with that.

'Have you got anything like that sort of money?' Teresa asked.

I shook my head. 'I could raise maybe seven or eight thousand from my parents – but it would be practically all their savings from my father's bookbinding business. And I could perhaps scrape together the rest from my own savings. But it would leave all of us penniless.'

'How can she be sure Louise isn't Christof's?' asked Teresa. 'After all, he did his best to get back with you.'

'She made him swear on his mother's life that he hadn't slept with me. We both know Christof wouldn't have taken that oath lightly.'

'Even so, could you try and call her bluff?' Teresa suggested. 'After all, Louise is only half Jewish.'

'Too risky. There were rumours about Erik and me at the time, and with what she now knows there'd remain little doubt.' I shook my head. 'And I've checked the status of people who are part-Jewish. As a *Mischling*, Louise would be taken to a camp, with little chance of survival. I've heard that many such children are killed on arrival.'

Teresa closed her eyes as the horror settled on her shoulders, as it had on mine these past months and years.

'And I would almost certainly be joining her. Misleading Hitler with something like this.' The Führer had in fact dedicated part of a recent speech to the topic: '*Those who attempt to hide Jews among good upstanding Aryans will be dealt with particularly harshly*.' 'Especially given Hanussen's past status and what happened to him.' I attempted a laconic smile. 'Then no doubt the rest of my double game with Hitler would also be uncovered. No, there's no other choice. I'll have to pay her.'

Teresa's eyes continued darting, as if seeking other

options, before she let out a resigned breath. 'OK. But you need help with this. You can't face it on your own.'

I shook my head when I realized what Teresa was suggesting. 'I came to tell you this because I felt it was something I should have shared with you long ago, not for any help. You'd both be too much at risk if you got involved.'

Teresa slowly nodded in acceptance. 'What about Stefan? He's in a far more powerful, less compromised position – and you've already confided much of it to him.'

'Yes. But the rest might be problematical, especially since I made a pact with Stefan a while back of *no more secrets*.' Laboured exhalation. 'And this might seem a secret too far for him.'

Teresa was staring at me incredulously, as if to say: *There isn't anybody else. And this isn't the time for petty sensitivities between lovers*. 'Perhaps,' she said. 'But from what you've told me about Stefan's uncle, Stefan would relate to your revenge motive better than anyone, especially now that it's far more personal. And, with the threat to Louise, also understand why you've kept this secret for so long.'

32

'I realize all of that, and why you had to keep it secret. The terrible burden on you all these years. But you should have told me before.' Stefan shook his head. 'And not just because we agreed, *no more secrets*, but because you should have felt you could trust me with this – especially after all we've been through.'

I looked at Stefan tersely. 'But this isn't just about me, is it? It's more about Louise. It's *her* life that's mainly in danger by this secret being known.'

Stefan nodded sombrely. 'You don't think I care about Louise equally? You could have trusted me with this, rather than only tell me half the story when you let me know about Christof and Ingrid Bittner.'

I looked straight ahead at the view. We'd gone again to the car park halfway up the slope of the Viktoriapark, the panorama of Berlin spread before us. Except now it was night-time, sparse lights dotted into the distance with the blackout. I took a fresh breath.

'When I was young, my parents used to have a maid who stole from them. But she didn't steal the items straightaway. If she saw something she took a shine to, a little jewelled box of my mother's, for instance, she'd move it from my parents' bedroom to the back of the lounge. Then next time she was there, she'd move it to the front of the lounge. Then next time, the hallway. Only then would it finally make its way out of the front door. As if she was testing – if they hadn't noticed those previous moves of the item, then they obviously didn't care about it.' I sighed. 'And I think it's been the same way with me with this secret. I could only take it in stages – either because I felt it might soften the impact, or I felt it was too terrible a secret to reveal all at once.'

I'd already shared a veiled version of the saga earlier with my parents – leaving aside that Erik Hanussen was actually Louise's father, keeping it just to an intense 'love triangle' drama over Christof and some past awkward secrets being revealed – while Louise played with Tobias in another room, then later left Louise with them to see Stefan. A story withheld for so many years, then told three times in as many days – I should be proficient at it by now. With that softened account, my parents had been very understanding, but my father only had six thousand Marks to help out, which with my three thousand still left me a thousand short.

Stefan looked unseeing at the view for a moment, his thoughts elsewhere, then with a deflated sigh, 'I'll help out with that remaining thousand. It's part of the money my uncle left me years ago, and I think he'd approve of this particular cause.'

I looked across poignantly, clasped Stefan's hand and said that he didn't have to, but he insisted, 'I'm doing this for myself as much as you and Louise,' and we sat in silence again.

'Without that revenge motive being more personal,' he said eventually, 'do you think you might have still gone ahead with what you're doing now with Hitler?'

'I'm not sure.' I thought back to Gustav Strehl's visits.

'Pressure was being put on me in any case by a senior SS officer in Paris to accept Hitler's invitation. But that revenge motive made my decision more ready rather than just reluctant. Swayed things heavily and so outweighed the terrible risks to myself and my family.'

Stefan nodded. 'Then I can only admire your fortitude and bravery, walking closer to the lion's mouth like this.'

I saw immediately what Stefan was suggesting. 'They're rounding up Jews in Paris now too. Louise wouldn't have been safe there either.'

'True.' A strained grimace as Stefan looked at me pointedly. 'But this payment now to this Bittner woman is the first and last one. If she comes back for more later, then we'll have to think of something else.'

'Something else?'

Stefan didn't answer directly, simply stared the message home. And as much as I knew Stefan was right – I couldn't risk letting Ingrid Bittner bleed me dry indefinitely with that threat still hanging over me and Louise – that look still made me feel uncomfortable.

'Is that it there?'

Ingrid Bittner pointed at the shopping bag between us on the lounge floor. I'd wrapped the money in plain brown paper and put it in an AWAG bag. Kaufhaus des Westens would have been too grand for such a tawdry exchange.

'Yes, that's it.' Between my parents and Stefan, three days to get it all together. I watched her pick up the bag, tear off one end of the brown paper and thumb the notes inside. 'I think you'll find it's all there.'

She flicked through a moment more before looking at me with a crooked smile. 'Don't worry. If it's not, I'll be back later to tell you how much you're short.'

I was anxious, my nerves on a tripwire, not only because of what this monetary exchange represented, but because I could hardly bear to be in Ingrid Bittner's presence a moment longer. If I'd had my way, I'd have just handed her the money at the front door and got rid of her. But Stefan had insisted that I ask her in and press the point that with this money now, *that's it*! 'Because we can't afford her trying to come back later for more.'

Stefan had also insisted on being present for the exchange, listening in. The door from the lounge to the hallway I'd purposely left open, and he was just the other side of the hall in Louise's music room, the door left slightly ajar. Another turn of the ratchet on my nerves: any faint movement or shuffling heard from the room and Bittner would know someone else was here.

She looked at me with a faint leer. 'You know, it's strange. I heard some of the rumours at the time about you and Hanussen, but always pooh-poohed them. Not only because he was so much older, but because he was a Jew.' A downturn to her mouth as she said it, as if she'd encountered a bad taste. 'I also didn't put much stock in the other rumour going around at the time, no doubt initiated by you, that Christof had begged to come back to you.'

'He did ask to come back to me, several times, in fact,' I said flatly, 'but I always said no. Because I was with Erik then.'

Her leer broadened. 'That makes your account even more preposterous. That if Christof had asked to come back, you'd have said *no*. Meanwhile settling for a Jew like Hanussen.'

I glared back stonily. 'Look. You've got your money, so just go.' I gestured towards the shopping bag. 'But let me make one thing crystal clear between us. This money now is the only and last payment you'll see from me. I don't want to ever see you again!'

Bittner met my stare evenly. 'If you hadn't realized, you're not exactly in a position to dictate the terms. So, I'll think about it.' She half-smiled. 'But if later I need more money, don't be surprised to see me back again in six months or a year. After all, this is too juicy a secret to let go for just this money now.'

'Are you trying to tell me you might well come back later for more?' I pressed.

Ingrid Bittner shrugged. 'You catch on quickly.'

Acid return stare. 'You never were a nice person, were you? And it seems the rise of Nazism has made you even more despicable.' I shook my head. 'But you don't understand. There isn't *any* more money. This now was difficult enough to scrape together from my parents and my own savings.'

'I'm sure you'll find a way when the time comes.' Bittner arched a brow cynically. 'If not, you'll just have to face the consequences.'

'The *consequences*?' I hissed back. 'But those would mainly be against my daughter, not me. She'd be taken to a camp and killed straightaway . . . and she's only eight years old! I know you and I have had our differences and grievances in the past, but *this*.' My voice rising with my anger, I held a hand helplessly towards the shopping bag, towards the money that, in the end, might not be enough to buy my daughter's life. 'Have some mercy, for God's sake!'

'*Mercy?* Perhaps you should have thought about that before deciding to have your half-Jewish runt with Hanussen,' she sneered. 'And *really*? Invoking God's name while expecting me to bury your illicit tryst with a Jew. Do you have no shame?' She lifted the shopping bag. 'And to add insult – to expect my full compliance for ever for just this money now.'

'I've told you . . . there is *no* more money.' A final exasperated plea through my burning anger.

Bittner smiled lopsidedly. 'You know, I was glad when they killed him. Building his fortune-telling name on the back of the Führer, yet all the time he was little more than a despicable Jew. And now you're no doubt doing the same, and pathetically trying to –'

My rage boiling over, I'd lunged towards her on the words *despicable Jew*, pushing her over and tumbling her to the floor. Striking out in blind fury to her chest and face, I didn't see the flick-knife she slid out of her pocket until it was too late. I felt it enter my left shoulder, and as most of the strength went from that arm, she got the advantage and rolled me over, the knife now little more than a blur through my dizzying vision, raised above me.

I held my hands up desperately and gripped her knife arm. I could feel her breath on me, hot and sour with the exertion, eyes gleaming as the blade hovered above my neck – unsure if she intended to plunge the knife down or just threaten me with it – when I heard the two shots from behind and her body slumped against me.

33

The chatter on the street was vibrant, constant. The German Reich was at the height of its power and that triumphant mood ran through its people like an electric current. Talk of successes on this battle front or that, the Reich seemed unstoppable and that largesse soothed the wounds of the humiliation the German people had felt from the Treaty of Versailles imposed upon them after the First World War – as Hitler had promised all along. Restoring German national pride and putting the German race back in its rightful position in the world.

But I felt numb to it all. I should have been paying heed to the latest news broadcasts about the great Reich army successes on the Russian front, Operation Barbarossa, because if those offensives did take a turn for the worse, I could expect that knock on my door in the dead of night that Stefan had warned of.

Though Stefan had also rightly commented that there would be little of value in those regular broadcasts announcing successes in the East. Because even if things had started going badly, it wouldn't be broadcast to the German people on the pretext of 'possibly lowering morale', tempering that national pride and fervour.

So the only news I could trust about the matter came directly from Stefan, who in turn gained his information from his contacts high up in the German military.

'You can rest easy. It's going well, as you predicted. You have nothing to worry about.'

I smiled up at him meekly as he soothed my brow with one hand, calming. The first couple of nights, at the height of my fever, that soothing had been given with a damp cloth, either by my parents or by Stefan. Beyond my numbness, I still felt shivers run through me now and then – though I wasn't sure if it was from the cold and fever I'd developed that night from being out in the damp forest, or the shock of what had happened.

We'd wrapped Ingrid Bittner's body in my heavily bloodstained lounge rug and dumped it into the boot of Stefan's Mercedes 230. We'd cleaned any remaining stains from my floor with bleach, then put my bloodstained blouse and skirt and all the cleaning rags in a bag alongside her body in the boot. I then put on fresh clothes and Stefan drove to a forest area ten kilometres away – but I'd already started to shiver with the shock of it all before the damp night air of the forest got to me.

'This is the perfect spot,' Stefan had said. 'It's where the SS and the Gestapo take many traitors and informers to be shot. Hopefully, they'll think she's been one of those and that will muddy the investigation for a while.'

Laying Ingrid Bittner on her back, Stefan had shot her once more in the chest, then rolled her over and dragged her back two metres. 'This will help make it appear that she's been shot once from the front, then started to run and got shot twice more in the back.'

It was at that point I threw up, trembling now gripping my whole body. Stefan looked at me with concern.

'Are you OK?' He came in close as I straightened up

again, bracing my shoulders. 'You're shivering! Look. Just one more thing to do, and then I'll get you home for some hot chocolate or soup.'

'Oh . . . OK.' My voice sounded distant, uncertain.

We drove two kilometres to another forest area, then walked with the bloodied rug and bag a further kilometre to a cabin in the woods where a man named Otto said he'd burn them on his bonfire the next day. But my legs already felt weak, and I had to half-lean against Stefan for the walk to his car.

I passed out on the drive back to my house, awaking hours later to find myself at my parents' home. Realizing how ill I was, Stefan had solicited their help. He had work the next day, so couldn't care for me round the clock – though he did come by the next few evenings to sit with me and soothe my brow through the worst of my fever as my knife wound healed.

'We should give the money back to your parents, since we still have it.' One of the first things he muttered to me when I was more lucid.

I readily agreed and we made a plan. Stefan would tell them he'd complained to a Reich Chancellery contact about a work colleague being blackmailed, and in the end the woman hadn't shown up. 'So perhaps my contact warned her off.' I hadn't mentioned Ingrid Bittner's name to my parents, and hopefully they wouldn't connect newspaper reports about a body being found in woodland far away. Stefan hadn't seen any reports yet, 'But if they think it's a traitor or informant shot by the SS or Gestapo, nothing will appear in any case.'

He'd already deflected questions about my injured

shoulder by saying I'd slipped and fallen on the sharp corner of a coffee table. He'd also phoned Lara to advise her I was recovering from flu at my parents' house for a couple of days.

The only remaining worry was if Ingrid Bittner had shared her blackmail plans with anyone: her on–off boyfriend, Carl Voltner, or worse still, Obersturmbannführer Kurt Schneider.

So in those days after my recovery, we got news of activity on the Russian front from the radio or Stefan's military contacts, and meanwhile read the local newspapers for 'Woman's Body Found in Woodland' reports – wondering from which direction, if any, a knock might come at my door.

34

The knock was heavy, insistent, on my parents' door early the next morning. My father had only left to take Louise to school ten minutes ago – I was well enough to be out of bed, '*but not well enough yet to make the long trek to school*', my father had insisted – and my mother was in the kitchen, washing up after breakfast. So with only myself and Tobias left, I went to answer it.

A stiff-backed man in his early forties in olive-green uniform with bristle-cut dark hair stood there, looked like SD or local police. He flashed me a badge, which hardly registered.

'Oberwachtmeister Hermann Gessner.' He appraised me coolly. 'And you are?'

'Uh, Edith . . . Edith Creutzen.'

He nodded curtly. 'And is this your house?'

'No, it's my parents' house. I've been staying here for a few days.'

'I see.' He mulled this over for a second, then with a firmer tone: 'I am part of a special Ordnungspolizei attachment dealing with *undesirables*.' His mouth skewed slightly with the word. 'Jews, dissidents, Gypsies, and the mentally unfit.'

I just nodded lamely, any words catching in my throat. While this wasn't about Ingrid Bittner's body being found, it looked like she'd somehow reported me about Louise.

One of those 'from the grave' notes: '*In the event of my death, I'd like to inform you . . .*'

'And it has been brought to our attention by neighbours that you and your parents are harbouring one such person here.'

'*Neighbours?* . . . I don't understand.' I felt light-headed, dizzy, still hadn't fully recovered from my illness. What on earth would they have to do with Bittner and Louise? The only thing I could think of was that neighbours had seen Louise, so Gessner knew she was here rather than at my own house.

'Yes. Your neighbours have reported that there's a mongoloid individual here. He's been seen playing in the garden with a young girl.'

'That would be my younger brother.' My relief that this visit now wasn't about Louise was quickly followed by self-reproach: Tobias being the focus here should be no less cause for concern.

'And the little girl?'

'It's my daughter.'

Gessner raised a brow sharply, as if I'd broken some cardinal sin – then looked past my shoulder as my mother, drawn by our voices, approached.

'What's this all about?'

Gessner started repeating the reason for his visit, to which my mother huffed halfway through, 'Not this again. We had Tobias assigned to our care years ago by a specialist doctor.'

'Do you have papers to support that?'

'Yes, I do,' my mother said firmly, and turned back into the house to get them.

After a strained smile to fill the awkward gap, Gessner asked, 'Do you come here often with your daughter?'

'Yes, quite often. And sometimes my parents take care of my daughter while I'm working or away.'

'I see.' That eyebrow arching again. 'So, your daughter would be alone with your brother for some periods of time and –'

'Here it is!' My mother's voice cut in as she handed across some papers.

A two-page document, Gessner started reading, then tapped brusquely at its top. 'This now is over seven years old. I'm afraid it's out of date, no longer valid.'

'Then I'll get a new one.' My mother attempted an assertive tone to mask the underlying tremble in her voice. 'If necessary, from the very same doctor.'

Gessner looked at my mother condescendingly. 'I think you fail to understand. Far more stringent regulations have come in since then. A document like this would no longer pass muster. Your son will need to go to a safe and secure place with proper medical care from now on.'

My mother's look towards me was desperate, imploring. *Please do something!* We'd both known about the Aktion T4 programme for some years now – numerous 'homes' and sanatoriums set up for the mentally infirm. We'd also heard alarmingly that these had increasingly become a cover for a staged euthanasia programme – Tobias would be lucky to last two months in such a place before being put quietly to death with an injection 'for his own good and welfare'. But we hadn't heard that the medical rules regarding family 'home care' options had also changed.

'Surely, there's another solution . . . a better way?' I pleaded.

Gessner looked up briefly from a form he'd started filling in, smiled tightly. 'I'm sorry, but these rules have been put in place for your safety as much as his.'

My mother shook her head, tears now filling her eyes. 'But Tobias has been with us his whole life. He'd be completely lost in such a place.'

That smile was even tighter now. Losing patience. 'I'm afraid I don't make the rules.' Then he looked at me as he finished the form and signed it with a flourish. 'In the meantime, you should be more careful, letting your young daughter be with him. He's a fully grown man now, could easily rape or harm her.'

My mother glared at him through teary eyes. 'Then it appears you completely misunderstand those affected by Down's.'

'Are you questioning my judgement?' Gessner looked back sternly. 'I've given you one month to make your own arrangement to move him – only to a state-approved establishment, mind you – before he's taken away and the Reich Ministry make their own arrangements. But I can easily change that to just two weeks, if you wish.'

I saw my mother was tempted to bite back with something, so I held her arm and interjected. 'Thank you. I'm sure your advice was made in good faith. But in this case, I know my brother. He's quite a gentle soul, and so I know he would never harm my daughter.'

Gessner looked at me doubtfully, gave a '*your funeral*' shrug as he handed the form to my mother. 'One month, then we'll be back to collect him.'

I hugged my mother tight after I closed the door on Gessner, unsure if it was reassurance or consolation. My eyes had started filling on the words *gentle soul*, but now my tears ran freely. My dear, beloved brother . . . now a 'gentle soul' with a death sentence hanging over him.

35

Hans Diestler was considered one of the more efficient inspectors in the Kriminalpolizei. The Kripo dealt with all criminal matters that fell outside state security, and the investigation into the killing of Ingrid Bittner had landed on his desk two weeks ago.

The term 'killing' was being used for now, because her death hadn't yet been designated as a 'murder'. The woodland area in which she'd been found, and the bullets having been fired by an SS service pistol, a Walther P38, indicated that it might well have been an internal matter. So, until Diestler had checked whether the SS or Gestapo had been responsible, no press announcements or wider bulletins would be made.

In his early thirties, stocky with sandy hair and wearing a light-grey suit – he favoured lighter tones rather than the more sombre colours of his Kripo colleagues – Diestler was finishing his Bierwurst sausages with potatoes in his favourite lunch-time restaurant, Das Aschinger, when he saw Obersturmbannführer Kurt Schneider on the far side. Schneider spotted him, lifted one hand in acknowledgement and made his way over.

'Ah, I thought I might find you here.' Schneider folded his gloves and put them on the table as he took a seat, then lifted one hand and ordered a tea from the nearest waiter before looking back at Diestler. 'I hear that you've been making inquiries internally about the death of this Bittner woman?'

Diestler swilled down the last of some sausage with a mouthful of beer. 'Come to inform me that your unit might have been responsible, have you?'

Schneider returned Diestler's dry smile. 'No such luck, I'm afraid. As much as I'm sure you'd have liked a quickly closed file so that you could move on to the next case.' Schneider briefly cast a disdainful eye at the restaurant. Half-full of working men and the down-at-heel, it was a place that he wouldn't visit under normal circumstances. 'Just that I have some information that might be useful to you. But I wondered if we could make an exchange of sorts – if you could fill me in on progress to date?'

Diestler looked across levelly. Schneider was not one of his favourite people. While Diestler accepted that a certain amount of force and brutality was often necessary to get their jobs done effectively, Schneider took it to a level he found distasteful. He also wouldn't usually share such information, but Schneider outranked him, so could force his hand. And the thought of useful extra information in return was tempting.

Diestler dabbed at his mouth with his napkin as he finished. 'Obviously, since it's not yet officially a murder investigation until I've heard back from every department, things haven't progressed that much. But there were some oddities about the crime scene.'

'Such as?'

'Of the three shots to Ingrid Bittner, only one was from the front, the other two from the back.' Diestler gestured. 'But from blood lividity, the forensic examiner thinks the two shots to the back came first.'

'Very odd.' Schneider sank into thought for a moment, thanked the waiter as his tea arrived. 'Certainly, something none of my unit would do, shoot someone in the back – especially a woman.'

'Well, the thinking is that she turned and attempted to run before they could get off their first shot.' And, of course, your own suspects would already be half-dead from your interrogation to be able to attempt an escape.

'And the last shot to her front?'

Diestler held out a palm. 'Perhaps she was still alive when they turned her over, so that was to finish her off.'

Schneider nodded his acceptance and took a sip of tea. Diestler continued.

'The main thing I've done so far is visit her boyfriend, Carl Voltner, and his neighbours, because, as with many murder cases, partners and family are the first suspects.'

'Of course. Much forthcoming from him?'

'Very little. He said the last time he saw her was two nights before she was killed, though he didn't realize something might be wrong until much later – they don't live together, you see,' Diestler added as Schneider appeared quizzical. 'No problems, he claimed, between them, but one neighbour reported hearing raised voices at times.'

'Any other suspects?'

'None as yet.' Diestler took a slug of beer. 'Thing is, the girl Bittner shared a flat in Heinersdorf with is a nurse who has been away on field duty in Poland, and is now on the Russian front. So I haven't had a chance to see her yet and find out who else Ingrid Bittner might have known or had contact with.'

'I see.' A more measured tea sip. 'And did Voltner at any time mention a woman named Edith Creutzen?'

'No, he didn't.' Diestler looked at Schneider expectantly. Obviously the hopefully 'useful information' Schneider had gone out of his way to tell him about.

Schneider started with the New Year's Eve party where he first met Ingrid Bittner. 'And she shared with me that she had some "bad history" with this Edith Creutzen. Something about an old boyfriend they were wrangling over – but she didn't go into detail. The two of them apparently used to work together as protégées of Erik Hanussen.'

Diestler's brow creased. 'Now there's a name from the past.'

'Yes, well. Bittner stopped all that clairvoyance nonsense shortly after his death – but felt sure that Edith Creutzen had continued.' Schneider gestured. 'Along with the fact Creutzen and her colleague, Hauptsturmführer Stefan Hansel, are doing some hush-hush work directly for the Führer. But when I confronted Hansel about this, that Creutzen might be continuing with her fortune telling, he got quite high-handed about it. Rebuked me that the Führer might take exception if he knew I was delving into the issue.'

Diestler sank into thought, the noise of the busy restaurant imposing for a moment. 'So, if Ingrid Bittner had gone digging into the matter, that might have invoked a sudden Gestapo or internal security action to silence her – which of course would also be kept secret.'

'Yes, I . . . I hadn't thought of that.' Although Schneider certainly had. His nose had been put out of joint by Hansel's thinly veiled warning. But if he could get Diestler digging into Creutzen while pursuing an official investigation, it was a different matter.

'And tell me, when you had this conversation with Fräulein Bittner about this bad history with Edith Creutzen and her suspicions about her continuing fortune telling, was her boyfriend Carl Voltner also present at the time?'

'Very much so. In fact, they were in conversation about it first – I just came in on the tail end of it.' As he saw Diestler become pensive: 'Why do you ask?'

'Oh, it might be nothing.' Diestler exhaled tiredly. 'As I said, in interviewing Voltner, he mentioned nothing about this situation with Creutzen. When I would have thought – given that right now he's the prime suspect – he'd be eager to divert attention to other possible suspects.'

36

War Cabinet Room, London, July 1941

'Quite impressive advances so far,' General Hastings Ismay commented, running one finger down the report before him. 'Within the first few weeks, the Luftwaffe has managed to gain air dominance over much of the Western Soviet Union and the main battlefields. Strong inroads into Belorussia, Moldavia and the Ukraine. They've even managed to have success on the northwestern front by convincing Finland – who had previously said they wished to remain neutral – that the Soviets were about to attack them, so have gained Finnish support on advances there.'

Winston Churchill raised a brow. 'Probably not too difficult to achieve through fear-mongering, given that Stalin not long ago attacked Finland. And the major cities?'

'Grodno, Vilnius, Minsk and Smolensk have already fallen to German and Axis troops, and Kiev is under heavy threat.' Ismay prodded his finger at his report. 'But the move on Leningrad appears to have stalled for now.'

The room was stifling. Three floors above them the building's ventilation system was struggling to cope on what was one of the hottest days of the year. Whether from the heat or the weight of decisions that now needed to be made, Churchill looked more hangdog than usual as he considered the various advances, moving them around on a mental map of Russia for a moment.

'Might this be the right opportunity for us to push for a move on Moscow?'

'Still too early,' Ismay said. 'We need our contacts in Berlin to try and urge a delay for six weeks or more, if possible. So that German troops hopefully get bogged down in the Russian winter. Although they've had great successes so far, we're getting reports that their supply lines are severely stretched.'

Seeing Churchill weighing up the advice, his War Cabinet Secretary, Edward Bridges, supported him. 'I daresay there would be little point in this whole exercise if Hitler ends up winning the war with Russia. He'd then not only have the benefit of their resources, including their extensive oil fields – but be terribly emboldened for his continued attacks on the West. Probably feel by that stage he's invincible.'

'Yes, you have a point,' Churchill said at length. He looked back at Hastings Ismay. 'But what appears the best diversionary tactic to delay his advance on Moscow?'

Ismay held a hand towards Bridges. 'The very oil fields in the Caucasus that Bridges mentions could be one of them, perhaps also the Donbas coal mines and industrial centres like Kharkov – if Hitler could be convinced to try and strangle Russia via the supply and economics route. But I fear there are strong voices now in the German military pushing for a speedy advance on Moscow.'

'So, a difficult line for us to tread,' Churchill aired thoughtfully. 'And thus in turn our contacts in Berlin.'

Calder Gibson had so far observed the proceedings

without comment. Indeed, the nature of the meeting appeared to mainly be a summary of the German advances on the Russian front to date, then he'd simply be advised at the end of it how his SOE contacts should be guided for their next meeting with Hitler. But now he felt he had to intervene.

'Surely, though, we've already achieved our main objectives. Our directive was to steer Hitler towards a war we felt sure he'd lose – but to become far enough entrenched that Stalin would then counter-sue that war. Not just a quick retreat and all forgiven and forgotten.' Calder gestured. 'And surely we are well past that stage now.'

Hastings Ismay nodded. 'We most certainly are. The Soviet army has already lost over four hundred thousand men, and as many Russian civilians have also perished. Stalin will now pursue this war to its bitter end.' Ismay's eyes shifted to Churchill, away from Calder Gibson's expectant gaze. His role was simply to advise, not make final decisions.

Churchill huffed a disgruntled sigh. 'I'm afraid, gentlemen, we find ourselves aboard this for the duration too. The wrong advice given at this delicate juncture could endanger the whole operation.' Churchill held out a palm. 'Hitler will surely still be asking critical questions – especially at such a crucial battle-decision juncture – and those will require answering. So, best those are answered in a way that benefits us, wouldn't you agree?'

'Yes, of course, Prime Minister,' Calder said. Then, hoping he'd kept any edge out of his voice, 'Though that does put focus back firmly on the issue I raised before. That the moment Edith Creutzen gives advice which is seen as false – especially if it results in a calamitous battle – she and her family are immediately at risk.'

'I'm quite aware of that, and shall take that into account when I finally decide in which direction Hitler should be steered next.' Churchill looked at Calder keenly. 'When is her next session scheduled for?'

'Two days from now.'

'Very well. There is much to consider here.' Churchill gestured with his cigar – which throughout had remained unlit – towards Hasting Ismay's report. 'But I will have decided how she should proceed by first light tomorrow.'

37

I felt as if everything was closing in on me from all sides: Tobias being taken away to a home, increasing worries about Ingrid Bittner's murder – the first newspaper reports about her death had appeared that morning – and now another direct speculum session with the Führer.

We'd gone again to the Vorbunker, probably my least favourite place, trapped in a cellar several floors down. Half a dozen rows of desks with clerks and typists busy again at the end of the large reception hall – where the New Year's Eve party had also been held and I'd first seen Ingrid Bittner again – before we made our way down the endless steps.

Ingrid's trite smile as she'd greeted me that night replayed in my mind, but as I stared into the dark shadows of the speculum during those first questions, it transposed to Stefan firing that final shot in the woods. *Ingrid's dead eyes staring back up at me.*

'Are you all right?' A firmer squeeze of my hand as Hitler looked on curiously.

'Yes . . . yes, fine. Just that these war images can be quite disturbing.'

Rows of bodies, many bloodied and mangled with limbs askew, spread towards the horizon. And what I've guided has been responsible for much of this. I took a deep breath, tried to gain some clarity among the dark, shifting shadows and horrendous images.

'I . . . I see further advances in the northwest with the help of Finnish troops.' One point of clarity had been differentiating between the various uniforms. 'I see another town being taken shortly.'

'Leningrad?' Hitler asked hopefully.

I looked back into the speculum, saw only three onion-domed churches, not very high, through the shifting shadows. 'No, this appears to be a smaller town.'

'Valday or Ostashkov,' he surmised. 'So, my ploy of involving Finnish troops you see as aiding our overall efforts?'

'Very much so.' Apart from it being what I saw in the speculum, I'd learned that it always paid to flatter the Führer's decisions, bolster his pride. Helped balance out his darker, more tempestuous moods.

'And of the two larger cities that now concern me, Leningrad and Kiev, which do you see as being taken more easily?'

A more intense study of the speculum before I looked across. 'I see both being difficult, but Leningrad appears the far harder-fought battle.'

'So, if I were to attack Leningrad first, my forces would be more depleted for their assault on Kiev . . .' But the Führer was looking slightly aslant as he spoke, as if airing the question as much to himself.

'Russian forces would be equally depleted.' I held a hand towards the speculum. 'Or even more so proportionately, from what I see.'

'Yes, of course.' He seemed to calculate something in his mind before looking back at me directly. 'And what of Moscow? What do you see there?'

The key question had come up sooner than I'd expected.

I looked back into the speculum more to gather my thoughts than anything else; because I knew that regardless of what I saw – in this case a far broader landscape of bloodied and torn bodies among smoking ruins – my answer had already been decided in London. I tried to steer a cautious line between the two.

'I see an even more intense, hard-fought battle there. More so than even Leningrad.'

'But you see the German Reich prevailing in the end?'

Hitler's eyes settled on me intently, and I could see Stefan too looking at me anxiously from the side of the room – having stepped aside after only the first two perfunctory questions. I was keenly aware that I'd stated this from the outset, so needed to remain consistent.

'Yes, I do. But the correct strategy is also vitally important. If a wrong move is made that I can't have foreseen, it can change the outcome.' I swallowed imperceptibly as Hitler held his stare on me. Had I steered an even course?

'That's why I have you here now,' he said curtly. 'To be able to guide the right moves from what you foresee. So that the correct outcome is finally attained.'

A faint tremble gripped me under the intensity of his gaze. I'd been too ambiguous for his liking. 'I appreciate that, Mein Führer. But the images I see here are disturbing in the extreme, and the last thing I'd want to do is suggest a choice that could lead to more German troops lost. Though I'm sure that regardless of what I foresee, you will make the right decision.'

The tame compliment appeared to assuage him slightly; or perhaps it was my attempt at diplomacy. His intense stare slipped into a dry smile after a second.

'I have the very same problem with many of my commanders. I often cannot get a firm answer from them – although right now a number of them are urging an advance on Moscow, no doubt because they see a swift victory there. But this is where I have a distinct advantage over them. Because from what you see, the battle there would not be so easy.'

'Yes, that is what I see.'

'With Leningrad to a lesser degree, and Kiev the lightest battle?'

'Yes.'

Hitler was pensive for a moment. 'Another option would be to now strike at Russian resources. At their oil fields in the Caucasus and industrial centres like Kharkov and Donetz. What do you foresee on those fronts?'

Even though the names had been mentioned in my last coded message from London and I'd done a trial run last night on my speculum at home, I looked again now, brow creasing for a moment before looking back up.

'I see hard conflicts there too, but a far less fraught situation than the other options. And with fewer military losses.'

Hitler nodded slowly as he sat back, weighing everything up.

Had I done enough? Steered Hitler's attack on Moscow closer to winter and impending doom? A strange wish in a way, because it also equalled my own doom. As soon as the war on the Russian front took such a drastic turn for the worse, my fate would be sealed. The one thing I didn't even need to look into the speculum to see.

*

Stefan was concerned about Edith. She'd put on a competent performance with the Führer, but it had been like watching a swan swim. Graceful gliding on the surface, but frantic paddling beneath.

He could see it in every nuance on her face, every taut muscle or faint flinch as she'd looked into the speculum – trying desperately to balance what she saw with what she needed to say. She'd covered well by claiming it was the horror of the war images, but Stefan wondered how much of it had been from the horrors going on in her own life. In short, he feared she was simply too mentally frail right now to be playing these sorts of mind games with Hitler.

The sessions combined with her gauntlet-running with coded messages already had her nerves on a tripwire, and Stefan worried these new threats against her brother Tobias and from Ingrid Bittner's murder would push her over the edge.

He'd felt frustrated that he hadn't been able to help much with her brother's plight. He had hardly any contact with the T4 mental-care programme, 'And if I did openly show my hand by intervening, I could come under scrutiny for everything else. Which would put me at risk and, by extension, you as well. Other things we're now involved in could be exposed.'

'What if we simply refused to let Tobias go to an asylum?'

'Then those obstructing, you and your parents, would likely be sent to a concentration camp.' The one thing he'd been able to check about the process.

Stefan had seen those 'lack of options' still weighing heavy on her on the drive to the Vorbunker, the only respite, paradoxically, the more pressing issue of Hitler's Russian-front manoeuvres.

But now on the return journey he offered, 'The only thing we might be able to do is play for time.'

'In what way?'

'Choose an asylum where their T4 euthanasia programme is slow or delayed, then make sure to get Tobias out of there beforehand.'

'But surely that's too risky. What if they go ahead earlier?' Edith raised a brow. 'And where would we take Tobias?'

'It reduces the risk, that's all. And probably to outside of Germany.' Stefan exhaled wearily. 'Don't forget, with what you've just told Hitler, that's a journey you and your family will have to be making soon in any case.'

Edith stared emptily ahead before making a slow nod in acceptance, and Stefan felt immediately guilty. What was he doing, trying to rationalize the situation with Tobias by reminding her of her own and her family's drastic plight?

They were silent for much of the rest of the short drive back, though Edith did thank him as he pulled up at her house.

'I know you have my interests at heart, and at least now with Tobias we have one option, where before we had none. Much to think about.'

They said their goodbyes, but three hundred metres along the road, Stefan passed a parked grey DKW saloon car with two men in suits looking towards Edith's house. Just the sort of discreet distance that the police might observe – though it could be nothing: a couple of salesmen or local officials visiting someone. But as a precaution, Stefan waited until he was over a low hill out of sight, then did a three-point-turn and edged back, tucking in behind two parked cars.

He tapped one finger on his steering wheel. And, sure enough, after another minute he saw the grey DKW pull out and head along the road. He still hoped his suspicions might be wrong, but those hopes were dashed when he saw it turn into Edith's small driveway.

His finger-tapping now more insistent, he'd wait two more minutes, then go back. Edith was too frail right now to face an interview like this on her own.

38

'Yes, Ingrid Bittner did come by my house a while ago,' I said after applying brief thought. What Stefan had advised from the outset: *Keep close to the truth. Otherwise checks with neighbours and other sightings could catch us out.* 'But I think it might have been a day or so before you say she disappeared.'

'And what was the purpose of her visit?' Hans Diestler asked.

I glanced briefly at Stefan before looking back at Diestler. *Keep close to the truth.* Stefan coming back only minutes later – 'I left some of my papers here' – had startled me almost as much as the two men rapping at my door. The older man, early thirties and wearing a tan suit, had introduced himself as Inspector Hans Diestler of the Kripo, with the name of his younger assistant partly obscured by the rising buzzing in my head. Something 'Schulte', if I recalled correctly. Diestler's gaze had shifted expectantly to Lara, so I'd sent her to the shops and asked her to pick up Louise later from school. Whether feigned or not, Diestler appeared to welcome Stefan's arrival. 'I'm pleased you're here, because I have a question or two to ask you also. And so it saves me another visit.'

Stefan had nodded his accord, and Diestler started asking his questions as Schulte made notes.

'Ingrid came by to talk about my daughter, Louise. Said

that she'd found out Louise's birthdate from her school, and felt sure she was the daughter of a boyfriend we shared at the time, Christof Lange.'

'And was her claim true?'

'Yes, it was.' Keep close to the truth: '*The police could have checked with the school. Also, Christof's name is on Louise's birth certificate – so no avoiding that.*'

'That must have been very upsetting for her.'

I shrugged. 'Not particularly. There were rumours about this when Christof was alive, that he was seeing us both at the same time. In fact, Christof was my boyfriend before he went off with Ingrid.'

'So, some upset for you too?'

'*Some*, admittedly.' I gave a bittersweet smile. 'But we're talking many years ago, Inspector, and time has mellowed many things on the issue. Particularly after Christof's death.'

Diestler nodded thoughtfully. 'But perhaps Fräulein Bittner didn't feel quite the same way, bore a grudge?'

'Yes, possibly. But a minor grudge years after the event . . . ? Not something you'd harm anyone over. And that harm would have been to *me* rather than Ingrid.'

Diestler held a palm out. 'But if you'd argued and she'd attacked you, and you'd defended . . .'

I prayed I'd kept the faint flinch from my face: images of wrestling on the floor with Ingrid only two paces from where he was now . . . the knife going into my shoulder. But his hand held out seemed tentative, *conjecturing*.

I smiled disarmingly. 'Certainly not, Inspector. I read also that she was shot, and I don't even have a gun in the house . . . nor know how to use one.'

His eyes stayed on me for a moment. Perhaps not only juggling with me not having a gun, but wondering how I could have possibly shot Ingrid from behind.

'And how long did Fräulein Bittner stay here overall?'

'Twenty . . . twenty-five minutes, no more.'

'And she left unharmed?'

Diestler's cool green eyes again on me searchingly. Perhaps psychosomatic, but I felt a twinge and stiffness come back to my arm. I'd got full movement back within days, and the bandage had been removed within a week. But it felt almost as if Diestler's eyes boring through me could see the scar still there.

'Yes . . . yes, she did.' Stark images arose of us wrapping Ingrid's bloodied body in my rug. Stefan's final shot to her body in the woods.

Diestler's gaze was slow in moving from me to Stefan.

'And were you here at any time during Fräulein Bittner's visit?'

'No, I wasn't,' Stefan said firmly. He'd parked his car some way along the road so that Ingrid wouldn't know he was already here. And it had taken only a few minutes to dump Ingrid's body in its rug-wrapping and her clothes into his boot when he did finally pull up – so, hopefully, no neighbours would have seen either. 'But Fräulein Creutzen did tell me about her visit later.'

'I see.' Diestler looked back at me. 'And while she was here, did Ingrid Bittner raise another issue with you – that of your possible continued fortune telling?'

'No, she didn't.' I sighed. 'Though it was something she broached when I met her before at a New Year's Eve dance, and –'

'That was a topic raised more with me,' Stefan interjected, 'and not by Fräulein Bittner directly, but by another SS officer at the same dance who had been talking to her. I told him clearly that Fräulein Creutzen had left all that behind her years ago. And, besides, the work we were doing directly with the Führer was a matter of extreme secrecy, so I couldn't go into any detail.'

'On the same issue of *secrecy*' – strained grimace from Diestler – 'I wondered whether, as a result of that, you might have shared concerns about Bittner possibly digging into this sensitive area with any fellow officers?'

'I . . . I'm not sure.' Stefan's brow knitted. Uncertain where Diestler was headed.

'Because, of course, something like that shared internally could lead to a drastic action with something so sensitive.' Diestler gestured. 'Particularly because, from the manner of Bittner's death and with an SS-issue gun being used, our first assumption was that this was an internal SS or Gestapo action.'

I saw the pieces settling in Stefan's mind before he leapt for the possible escape route. 'Yes, I . . . I might have unwittingly done so.'

But I wondered if the comment had also been aimed obliquely at Stefan, for he too had a regulation SS gun, of course.

The interview wound down then, but I could see something still on Stefan's mind as he accompanied Diestler and Schulte to the front door.

'By the way, Inspector, was it Fräulein Bittner's boyfriend, Carl Voltner, who told you about her possible concerns with continued fortune telling?'

'No, strangely enough, he didn't mention that when we questioned him – nor indeed anything about her visit here. That came from another source.'

'I see.' Stefan's face clouded briefly. 'Just one last thing I'd like to mention before you go, Inspector.'

Stefan held one hand towards me, making it clear this should be private, before going outside with Diestler and standing by his car talking for a while.

'What was it?' I asked with concern as Stefan came back inside and Diestler's car had driven away.

'I said that, given the sensitive nature of this and my close work with the Führer, could he inform me immediately if anything untoward came up regarding you in the investigation. Because I would need to inform the Führer straightaway, couldn't afford to have him tainted by it.'

My brow creased. 'Why on earth do that?'

Stefan clasped my hands. 'Think about it, Edith. If anything bad does come up, we need to know about it immediately, have some warning.'

I nodded emptily, but could see Stefan was still concerned about something. It took him a moment to get it fully clear as we sat back down in the lounge.

'Diestler said the mention of your continued fortune telling came from "another source", not Voltner. But the only person I can think of that would know about it is Obersturmbannführer Kurt Schneider.'

'Oh, my,' I uttered, my breath almost gone.

'But worse than that . . .'

I looked at Stefan strangely, as if anything could be worse than that hammer-blow news.

'. . . Why didn't Voltner mention it or anything about

Ingrid's visit here? Family and those close are always the first suspects – so he should have been keen to shift suspicion elsewhere. It's almost as if he's keeping his powder dry for something else.'

'*Something else?*' The realization hit me then, another hammer blow. 'You think he knows more than he's letting on, and might approach me about it?'

Stefan closed his eyes briefly in submission. 'Yes, I fear so.'

39

With nothing heard from Carl Voltner and no visit from him over the next couple of weeks, we began to think that our initial suppositions about him had been wrong.

'Perhaps Ingrid was more cautious in sharing information with him than we thought,' Stefan had aired. 'Or, following on from Diestler's suggestion, if she had fallen victim to an internal action, Voltner wishes to stay well clear for fear of the same.'

But while things had settled on that front – no return visits from Hans Diestler, either – we were only one week away from Gessner returning to take Tobias. Stefan had so far found two asylums – he had access to Aktion T4 internal records that I didn't have – where the average life expectancy was ten to eleven weeks rather than the usual seven or eight.

'OK. That's the average. But what's the shortest time at those?'

'Eight days at one. Fifteen days at the other.'

I'd closed my eyes and shaken my head at that news. It would be like playing Russian roulette with Tobias's life.

'But one of them has a three-day notice of any final action, and an appeal period, which generally gives another five or six days,' Stefan added, trying to lift me from my gloom.

The three latest speculum sessions had all been handled

by Stefan, and thankfully no trick questions. Most of them were focused on minor troop movements on the Russian front.

'As we make our final advances on Kiev, we have a choice between concentrating extra forces on the more obvious northwest approach, or trying to encircle from the northeast in a pincer movement . . .'

'Our advances in Leningrad have so far met with stiff resistance. Might we have more success in making a strong push from the north combined with Finnish troops? What do you see?'

Hitler was of a mind to push again on Leningrad as part of his combined assault on Russian oil and resources – Leningrad was also a major manufacturing centre – and London were keen to encourage that inclination because it pushed his assault on Moscow even further away and closer to a Russian winter.

And so now I was sitting in another café with my coded message of how that last session had gone tucked inside a book in one of two shopping bags. AWAG bags this time – the café was only eighty metres from their most prestigious store in Leipziger Platz. Café Holbein was quite illustrious too, with a lot of women in silk scarfs and furs, and busy: a fair flow of people back and forth, though I hadn't seen my likely contact approach so far.

I'd also done some shopping for myself today – a new hat, a necklace and a bracelet – but had made sure to put those in a separate bag, the bag carrying the book slightly open, so my contact could see clearly which one to pick up.

A few people had walked in so far with AWAG shopping bags, but they'd all gone to different parts of the café, hadn't put their bags close to mine.

And as the minutes ticked by and still nobody had shown up, I began to get anxious. Though when they finally did, I had to hide my shock. As Xavier Achard appeared at the entrance of Café Holbein, he touched one finger to his right eyebrow, as if to say, '*Don't show any recognition of me.*'

Given the history and associated risks, Xavier should have turned his back strongly on the proposal. But he'd in fact leapt at the opportunity. Stuck in a room at the back of the shop studying books and doing occasional surface binding and mending, he'd started to go stir-crazy, missed his previous front-line involvement as part of the Resistance. So when Gregor Lutz told him that they'd been let down at the last minute by their contact, he'd sold himself as best he could. His German had improved tenfold since first arriving in Berlin, mainly from listening in on shop conversations, and he'd even been out on a couple of recent book deliveries. At Xavier's signal, I looked down slightly, drank another sip of coffee. Xavier took a seat at the next table and put his AWAG bag down a metre from mine. But perhaps I was still slightly in shock, because I didn't notice the young man two tables behind me eyeing my bags until the last moment.

Then he was suddenly up, a deft lean down to grab both bags, and he was running full pelt out of the café.

I almost shouted after him, '*You forgot to leave your own . . .*' before the realization of what had happened hit me, and I was on my feet bolting after him, shouting '*Thief!* . . . Please, stop him!' Xavier had been quicker to notice and was on his feet a couple of metres ahead of me.

Bolder shouts of 'Thief, thief! . . . *Stop him*!' as I was

outside on Leipziger Strasse running after him, by which time he'd already gained twenty metres on Xavier and thirty on me.

A middle-aged couple and a soldier looked around with alarm, but he was already half past them. A police whistle sounded from somewhere to my side, and then another policeman in olive-green uniform came out of a shop-doorway recess just ahead of the young man and swung his baton at his legs. The thief stumbled and sprawled onto the pavement, the contents of my bags spilling out.

A second policeman appeared from across the road and yanked the young thief to his feet, pulling his hands behind him and handcuffing him. The first policeman, his baton now back in its holster, was leaning down and starting to put my things back in the bags. He looked up towards Xavier, who was just ahead of me.

'Is this your bag?'

'No, no. It belongs to this lady here.' Xavier gestured towards me as I stepped forward, still slightly breathless.

'Thank you . . . *thank you so much*!'

But as he reached for the book, my heart was in my mouth. The folded sheet of paper with my coded message had half-slipped out from its pages.

As he straightened up with my book, he held the folded paper between his thumb and forefinger. The blood raged through my head as I feared he was going to pull the note out, unfold it and see the lines of numbers. But with a tight smile, he just tapped the folded paper back in and handed over the book.

'Your bookmark almost came out.'

*

'It was terrible. I had to make the excuse of not being able to give a statement there and then, because I had some friends I was planning to meet back in the café. So, I'd come by the police station in an hour or so and do it.'

Stefan nodded. 'And what happened with Xavier?'

'With a brief nod my way, he drifted off, I think realized that with the police presence, it was too risky for him. But as I headed back towards the café, I noticed Gregor Lutz across the road, who held a hand towards me as if to say, "Hold on." I think Lutz was a bit nervous about involving Xavier, so wanted to monitor the situation. And sure enough, a little while later, somebody did show up – a young man not much older than the earlier thief – and we made the exchange.'

I'd phoned Stefan as soon as I'd got back from the police station: 'Some other things have just struck me after our last session' – our code for 'problems' that we didn't want to discuss over the phone with lines possibly being tapped. He'd called by later and we'd dropped Louise with my parents before going to dinner at a small bistro on Behrenstrasse. Stefan felt that somewhere with a mellow ambience would be preferable with all the pressures on me right now.

It had an entrance that reminded me of an American speakeasy, a small door with a doorman sliding across a narrow viewing slit to check who was there before letting us in. Then down two flights of stairs, which reminded me unsettlingly of the Vorbunker.

Stefan smiled reassuringly. 'One of the few places in Berlin where we won't have to shift if we hear sirens going off. It's as secure down here as any shelter. That's why it's so popular – and the food is excellent.'

Stefan was right about the food; it matched the best I'd found in Paris, and a backlit lifelike mural of a bacchanalian feast elevated the place from a basement feel.

A number of men in uniform were in the restaurant, one of whom Stefan acknowledged with a brief wave, and we did in fact hear sirens going off towards the end of our meal – slightly distant, though Stefan was right, nobody here seemed to be paying any attention to them.

That was in stark contrast to my reaction at home. Only three times so far I'd heard sirens directly in our neighbourhood, and I'd had to rush for the shelter with Louise. But even when I'd heard sirens in the distance, I found myself listening out for a while for whether the drone of aircraft and the sound of bombing would move closer; which, in the dead of night, might keep me awake for an hour or more.

'You're stronger than you appreciate.' Stefan reached across and gently clasped my hands. 'Many others would have crumbled long ago with all you have going on in your life right now. But you need to remain steadfast for yourself and Louise, and now Tobias.' A slight squeeze of reassurance. 'I'm sure in the end we'll find a good solution for him.'

'I pray so.' But my mind suddenly leapt back to Erik clasping my hand on one of our first dinner dates. He'd already told me that part of his act involved holding subjects' hands and 'muscle reading' as a guide to what they might do next, and I'd teased him, '*Is that how you first sensed I was attracted to you?*'

He'd smiled gently. '*I think as the more natural clairvoyant of the two of us, you probably know that answer better than I.*'

Now I muttered to Stefan, 'I think it was also recalling the death of a past love he felt devoted to.'

'What?'

'What you asked me last time – how and why the change might have come with Erik?' Only days ago, we'd touched on the thorny subject of Erik Hanussen's rumoured womanizing – as if Stefan was being retrospectively defensive of my honour – and I'd answered that, while that had been true when he was younger, it had changed as he approached his forties. Stefan had asked what brought about that change, and I'd answered that he'd probably just got tired of the chase, but still there seemed something missing. Only now did it strike me. 'He in fact foresaw her death, rushed to the hospital mid-performance, but he was too late. I think he lamented in that moment not respecting her more in life, so vowed to do so if he ever got the chance of true love again. They also lost their child together, a baby boy, so I know he'd have been delighted with Louise.'

'I think any man with half a soul would be delighted with Louise, father or not.' Stefan nodded summarily, but I could see that something else was on his mind. 'You mentioned before that Hanussen remarked you didn't get drained in the same way that he did in sessions – but you do with the Führer.'

Stefan had looked around briefly to ensure we couldn't be overheard, but still kept his voice low, as I did now in answering. 'Yes, when I'm dealing with forecasts honestly, it doesn't tire me. It's all the subterfuge that does that, plus the worrying burden of the risks involved to me and my family.'

Stefan grimaced tautly, clasped my hand back. 'As I said before, you're stronger than you realize. Many others couldn't cope with it all.'

The blackout slowed our passage home. With no street-lights, Stefan crawled along. As we approached my house, Stefan flicked his headlamps on only briefly to ensure he had the right driveway. That brief glare illuminated a large Mercedes 320 saloon parked ten metres past my house.

'Do you know who that car belongs to?' Stefan asked as he swung into my driveway.

'No. Don't think I've ever seen it here before.'

We watched the Mercedes' own headlamps come on as it turned into the driveway only a moment after us; but its headlamps stayed on, so we couldn't see clearly the person behind the wheel.

'Look. You go into the house ahead of me,' Stefan said anxiously. 'I just need to get something out of my car, then I'll be with you.'

40

'I wasn't sure at first it was you,' Stefan said. He nodded towards their cars outside. 'I thought that model was reserved for senior officials.'

'One of the benefits of running the motor pool.' Carl Voltner smiled smugly, answering why, despite being an SS rank below Stefan, he had such a high-end model.

'Yes, I'm sure.' Stefan's return smile slipped quickly. 'So, state what you've come for, then leave. Fräulein Creutzen has had a busy day and I'm sure would appreciate an early night.'

I hadn't offered Voltner a seat, and we stood as an awkward triangle in my lounge. Stefan had been getting something from the boot of his car as Voltner approached my door. But as Stefan joined us, he wasn't carrying a bag, and the only thing different I noticed was that he was wearing tan leather gloves. Voltner was only slightly shorter than Stefan and had the same golden hair colour, though his was straight rather than wavy, but there the similarity ended. Voltner's face was more rounded with practically no eyelids, his eyes an insipid pale blue rather than Stefan's warmer grey-green.

Voltner stared back stonily. 'But not as early a night as you gave Ingrid, eh?'

Stefan stared back equally stonily, said nothing.

'You know, it took me a while to work out what had happened.'

'To no purpose, no doubt. But explains the delay.'

'Yes, that and making sure it wasn't an internal SS squad action, which some factors pointed to. But having now made my own inquiries, that looks unlikely.' Voltner held out a hand. 'Though, of course, having an SS-issue gun yourself, you'd be in a perfect position to make it look like an internal action. So, it struck me that you must have been in on it as well – which is why I've made sure to return now when you're both together.'

'Your surmising is very interesting, but I'm afraid holds no substance.'

'You see, that was one thing I couldn't initially work out.' As if restless standing in one position, Voltner started pacing to one side, across the very patch where we'd cleaned up the spilled blood and rolled Ingrid's body in my rug. 'Those two shots to the back. Would a woman on her own have done that?' He looked my way. 'If you'd had a gun, you'd have shot Ingrid from the front. I then realized someone else must have been here, even though Ingrid indicated she was coming to see you alone.'

'So, Ingrid told you she was coming to see Edith?' Stefan aired. 'Which you didn't tell Inspector Diestler. That won't look particularly good, will it?'

'Ah, but far worse for you two, if I have to finally share everything with him. I'm sure my minor lapse of not telling him beforehand will be overlooked.'

Stefan nodded pensively. 'Did your girlfriend also share with you just *why* she was coming to see Edith?'

'Most of it, but not *all*.' He turned to me again. 'She told me that she'd discovered a big secret about your daughter, Louise, that you'd be keen to keep under wraps.

And if her plan worked, she'd bag a big windfall – she'd tell me everything when she returned.' Voltner's expression dropped. 'But, of course, she never did return.'

Silence settled over the three of us for a second. I exchanged a quick look with Stefan: at least Voltner hadn't got the full account from Ingrid. Stefan raised a brow as he looked back at Voltner.

'Has it ever struck you that the reason your girlfriend didn't share the details with you is because it was all fantasy? That no such big secret existed?'

'Yes, Louise's father is known,' I said, hoping my voice didn't betray my body's trembling. 'Christof Lange – his name is on her birth certificate.'

Stefan supported me. 'And while that might have been reason for upset when your girlfriend discovered this – because Christof was also Ingrid's boyfriend at the time – it was certainly no big secret that you could hold over anyone.'

'That's what I might have thought initially, but then I started doing some digging – the other reason for my delaying until now. And I discovered from Ingrid's friends that Christof was with her all the time during those last few months of his life. But there were rumours about Edith and Erik Hanussen, which would then make more sense.' Voltner smiled smugly, as if particularly pleased with his discovery; turned to me more directly. 'Hanussen was Jewish, which would then make your daughter a half-Jewish *Mischling*. Certainly something you'd wish to keep secret at any cost.'

Stefan could see that I was flustered, in danger of taking Voltner's bait. He smiled incredulously. 'Ludicrous!

And it's all just supposition built on little more than loose rumours. Certainly not nearly enough to counter who is actually on Louise's birth certificate as the legal father.'

'We shall see, shall we?' Voltner's smug smile became more resolute. 'I'm sure if I went to Inspector Diestler with all of this, it wouldn't take him long to put it all together. A forensic team perhaps called in that would find blood residues here. Unless, of course, we could come to the same arrangement I imagine Ingrid was making with you two – in which case there'd be no need for me to go to the police.'

I looked at Stefan with concern, but his gaze was steadfastly on Voltner.

'So, your intention is to blackmail us? In the same way that you believe your girlfriend did?'

'Yes,' Voltner said firmly, trying to mask any uncertainty under Stefan's intense gaze.

Stefan's eyes shifted momentarily as he weighed up the situation, the silence in the room stifling.

'I don't think so,' he said at length. A calm, cold statement as he pulled a gun out from inside his jacket.

Voltner sucked in his breath sharply at the sight of the gun. He started to tremble, wondering whether he'd been foolish to confront us. He could pull his own gun, but that might prompt Stefan to simply shoot him as he drew it out. He held up one hand. 'Don't even think about it! You think I'm stupid?' He leered uncertainly. 'I told a friend exactly where I was going before I left. *Two* bodies from the same last known location would really give Diestler something to get his teeth into.'

I looked towards Stefan imploringly, *Don't do anything*

rash, and noticed that the gun was held loosely, pointing down. But Voltner's eyes were still fixed on it worriedly.

'So, you really think that I shot your girlfriend?' Stefan asked flatly.

'Yes, I do,' Voltner answered after a faint swallow, still mesmerized by the gun.

Stefan nodded thoughtfully. 'In that case, if it was me, I'd be keen to do something about that. Avenge her death, rather than come here with some pathetic blackmail attempt.' Stefan smiled lopsidedly. 'And to be frank, I'd rather you did that too, *shoot me*, rather than have to sit around waiting for the police to knock on my door.'

Stefan held the gun out by the barrel and took a step forward, offering its grip to Voltner.

'Go on, *take it*!'

'*What?* You're mad!'

'What's wrong? Don't you have the guts?' Stefan taunted. 'This is your girlfriend we're talking about. The love of your life. Be a man for once . . . *take it*!' Voltner's eyes darted between Stefan and the gun. 'If you don't, then maybe I'll change my mind about letting you have it . . . simply turn it around and shoot you for being so pathetic.'

Voltner did take the gun then, but uncertainly, its barrel pointing down slightly, his hand shaking.

'So . . . raise the gun and pull the trigger,' Stefan urged, but as Voltner still held it slanting down, 'Or aren't you man enough?'

My heart was in my throat as Voltner raised the gun slightly. This game had gone far enough.

'No . . . no! *Stop it!*' I shouted. I looked searchingly at Stefan. 'Let's just pay him and get rid of him!'

But Stefan ignored me, continued to taunt Voltner. 'Go on . . . pull the trigger, if you're man enough. You know that's what Ingrid would have wanted. You proving your love for her by avenging her death.'

'You're mad!' Voltner said again, half-hissed this time. 'Completely mad.'

'But maybe not as mad as Ingrid's spirit will be if you don't do it,' Stefan jeered. 'Or maybe the rumours I've heard about you are true – you simply don't have the balls for it.'

Voltner's jaw set tighter, the gun rising another few centimetres, now pointed at Stefan's thigh.

'No . . . for God's sake no!' I screamed. '*Stop it!*'

But Stefan's gaze was held resolutely on Voltner, with no acknowledgement my way.

'I'll make it easier for you. More of a challenge,' Stefan said, and pulled another gun from inside his jacket and pointed it at Voltner. 'If you don't shoot me first, then I'll shoot you.'

Voltner's eyes rose in alarm, and his gun in turn rose to almost match Stefan's weapon pointed straight at his chest.

'My God. Mad as a hatter,' Voltner muttered under his breath, almost to himself, the trembling in his hand getting worse.

'This is how all matters of honour used to be settled,' Stefan said distantly, as if half lost in reverie. 'Pistols at dawn. But instead of ten paces, I shall merely count down. And if you haven't shot me before I get to zero . . . I will shoot you.'

'No, no . . . *stop it*!' I implored, slapping Stefan's shoulder.

Stefan started his count and had reached EIGHT before Voltner had hardly gathered his thoughts, his gun dropping slightly before rising again to point straight at Stefan only three paces away.

'No, Stefan . . . *no*!' I screamed again as he hit SEVEN. 'Pay him!'

SIX . . . FIVE . . .

I lunged at Stefan hard with another frantic '*No*, for God's sake *stop*!' as he hit FOUR, but he wavered only slightly, then swung one arm out and knocked me over onto the sofa.

THREE . . .

I was half up again, the room seeming to tilt with my sudden movement, blood pounding through my head as he hit TWO – but I was too late. I saw Voltner pulling his trigger . . .

My final screech of '*Nooooo!*' so loud that it drowned out everything else.

41

Teresa always felt that she and Edith were reflections of each other. She'd see strengths and traits in Edith that Edith herself wasn't aware of and Edith would in turn see the same in her.

That was why, when Edith had first been offered to join a team in Berlin secretly duping Hitler, Teresa felt sure she'd accept. But always the more cautious and guarded of the two, Teresa had also advised Edith about possibly being too naive over Stefan's involvement, which had at least led Edith to make a more cautious, balanced decision.

Teresa had also been keenly aware of Xavier's core traits. And while it made perfect sense for Xavier to be hiding in plain sight in the city where the Nazis would least expect to find him, at the same time Teresa knew that, as a true Resistance man, Xavier would be chomping at the bit for front-line involvement. Being stuck in a back room binding books simply wasn't cutting it for him.

So, when at the last minute one of Gregor Lutz's go-betweens had let him down, Teresa wasn't that surprised when Xavier offered to step in.

Lutz had been nervous about Xavier's last-minute involvement, so tailed him to observe. After the attempted theft was thwarted, he'd motioned for Edith to return to the café and wait for a replacement . . .

*

At twenty-four, Timo Kretzler was one of the youngest on Gregor Lutz's Resistance team. Lutz had few under thirty, because most able-bodied men were by necessity fighting in the war. As a result, Lutz's team was made up heavily of the over-forties, women, or young men with physical impediments. In Timo's case, it was severe asthma, so he was kept mainly to backroom duties or short-distance message running. But he'd been called upon suddenly that day because of a 'problem' with the previous stand-in.

'What sort of problem?' he'd asked Lutz.

'He was seen at the last minute by some police apprehending a thief outside the café.'

'I see.' He perhaps should have seen that as some sort of omen.

'Don't worry. It's a simple enough duty. You're to meet a woman – blonde hair, early thirties, quite pretty – in Café Holbein, eighty metres from the Leipziger Platz AWAG store,' Lutz instructed. He pointed to an AWAG shopping bag on his desk with a book inside. 'You're to leave this bag with her and pick up a similar AWAG bag also with a book inside it.'

'What do I say to her? Is there a message?'

'No. No words spoken between you. Just pick up the bag and leave, then head straight to this address where a transmitter has been set up.' Lutz passed across a slip of paper.

'And that's it?' Timo held a hand out.

'Yes. Simple enough on the face of it.' Lutz eased a worn exhalation. 'But inside that book is a vitally important message. So if you think at any time you're being followed, particularly on the last leg towards the transmitting team, then divert and lose them and return there later.'

Yes, *simple enough*, Timo thought, except it involved trailing across half the city, which he wasn't used to. He was already out of breath after the three-hundred-metre walk from the nearest tram stop to the café.

He made sure too, as instructed, that he wasn't followed as he walked from the café or headed towards the transmission address in Haselhorst.

That was an even longer walk from the nearest tram stop. He had to stop halfway to get his breath back, then was out of breath again as he finally approached the building: a partly bombed three-storey house, one corner and some of its roof completely gone.

It looked deserted, its remaining intact windows all painted black. Seven hard knocks on its front door – Timo began to think he'd got the wrong address – before it was finally opened to him.

A stocky man with a grey cloth cap pulled sharply down peered at him, then past his shoulder for anyone possibly looking on – as Timo had done in the last hundred metres of his approach.

Nobody in sight.

Both of them had been looking at street-level. If they'd looked up, they might have caught the brief glint of binoculars from the third-floor attic window of a similarly ramshackle house sixty metres away on the opposite side.

As soon as he saw the two figures go inside the house, the man put down his binoculars and picked up the phone to his side. It was answered after only two rings by Klaus Ziegler in an Orpo signal-tracking van four hundred metres away.

'Another man has just arrived, early twenties, and carrying an AWAG bag with a book poking out.'

'Anyone on lookout, and which position?' the Gestapo officer asked.

'All the windows appear blacked out. There's only a small clear patch, possibly recently scratched out, on the first-floor window furthest from me.'

'Thanks. We'll move in now.' Ziegler hung up his SCR radio phone and directed the driver: 'First right ahead, house partly bombed two hundred metres down – but park fifty metres short.'

The three armed Orpo guards with him sat up more alertly, one of them checking his rifle. Ziegler looked at his watch. If his assumptions were right, they'd start transmitting any second, then anything from three to five minutes to send the message. But his team would be upon them in only two or three minutes.

After his failure chasing Engelmann, Ziegler had felt frustrated, and even more so when the following weeks of staking out the key bookshops on his list had yielded nothing. So he'd decided to change tack and devise another plan.

Triangulation signal tracking between Orpo central and mobile vans had brought them close on at least three occasions, but the transmissions had stopped before they arrived – sometimes within only seconds of them pinning down the *exact* location. Then it struck him that there couldn't be an endless source of locations to transmit from, so they'd likely have to return to the same ones now and then.

So Ziegler had decided to stake out those near-miss

locations with lookouts. He knew that the set-ups each time would invariably be the same – two or three men appearing in advance with rucksacks with the transmitter, then shortly after another man or woman appearing with a book carrying the message to be sent. If Ziegler got a call as soon as that first team had arrived, they'd have time to move in closer before the final signal was sent.

Ziegler looked up from checking his pistol and taking off the safety catch. The van had stopped.

'Is this close enough?' the driver asked.

Tap, tap . . . tap, tap, tap . . .

Timo found the sound strangely mesmerizing, his breath falling fast and short with its rhythm. Even though it was minutes after his long walk to get here, and he'd only had to climb one flight of stairs since.

Sudden bedlam. The man with the cloth cap, Leo, burst in and bolted the door behind him top and bottom only seconds before they heard the clattering of boots coming up the stairs.

'Orpo squad!' Leo said breathlessly. 'We might have only a minute more before they're upon us.'

'Two-thirds through,' Reinhart Diener said, eyes not shifting from the sheet of paper before him as he kept tapping.

They heard the barging against the door across the hallway – Leo had used that for lookout rather than the transmitting room – then three shots before that door crashed open.

'Two lines more!' Diener said anxiously, the banging against their own door coming only a second after.

Leo nervously watched the rivets on the door bolts, saw them start to loosen. He took the pistol from his waistband.

'The bolts might hold them twenty seconds longer, no more!'

The man at the far end, wiry and in his mid-forties – Timo had been introduced to him briefly as Rudi – had already taken a thick rope with grappling hook from his rucksack. Pushing open the blacked-out window there, he fed the rope down and tested the grappling hook's tension against the windowsill.

'All done!' Diener shouted, grabbing the transmitter and putting it in his own rucksack.

Three shots came through the door then, and Leo saw that the door's hinge bolts would burst open any second. Leo desperately fired back through the door from an angle to hopefully gain some extra seconds.

Diener and Rudi clambered out the window and started frantically shinning down the rope, rucksacks on their backs.

Timo, waved off sharply by Leo – 'You get going too, I'll hold them off' – followed, seeing that the rope snaked down to an overgrown garden thirty metres long, a battered grey Henschel van the same distance from its back gate.

A split-second pause in rifle fire before a heavier volley in return through the door. Leo fired back twice more, then as the last bolt on the door was giving way, he ran towards the window and the rope. But gunfire from the first soldier bursting through caught him in the back, slumping him to the ground a metre short.

Diener and Rudi were already at the end of the garden, Timo halfway along, as one soldier was at the open window firing their way while another frantically slid down the rope to chase them.

But Timo felt as if an anvil was suddenly in his chest, a dizzy, spinning sensation as his legs turned to jelly and he gasped for breath. The soldier was already at the bottom of the rope and catching up with him.

He was desperate for his inhaler to ignite some breath back into his lungs. He reached the bottom of the garden gasping for air, and the last thirty metres towards the van – its back doors open and Diener and Rudi already inside, frantically beckoning him – felt like a lifetime away.

He was also aware that the rifle fire had stopped. And as he heard the pounding step and fractured breathing of the soldier close behind, he realized why: the men in the house were either afraid of shooting their colleague or felt sure he'd catch him.

42

Deià, Mallorca, October 1973

Robert Graves squinted at the three men as they approached, one of them holding a Rolleiflex camera.

'To what do I owe this pleasure?' Graves turned to Teresa and Bronowski, muttering under his breath, 'Excuse the loose terminology, because I'm not sure this will be a pleasure at all. On the face of it, quite the opposite.' Then in a louder voice as he looked back at the three men, 'Come back for some sugar for your two friends as well, Horst?'

Horst offered a strained smile. 'No. This is the young reporter I mentioned before. We arranged that as soon as I got back, he'd do a story on you for *Die Welt*, and you agreed to it, what, about six weeks ago.'

Graves looked befuddled for a moment, then snorted and waved an arm out theatrically. 'Six weeks? You might as well be talking six months or six years ago, for all I remember.' Then he broke into a smile and winked towards Bronowski. 'Now thirty or forty years ago is a different matter. I remember all of that very clearly – as indeed it appears does our guest here today.' Graves held a hand towards Teresa, who nodded and smiled graciously.

'We . . . we can come back another day,' Horst said hesitantly, 'if it's not convenient now.'

Graves looked undecided, took a sip of wine. 'And have your two friends come all the way from Munich as well?'

'Berlin,' Horst corrected. He pointed. 'Only Dieter here has come from Berlin, but is now staying in Palma, and . . .'

'And I'm a local based permanently near Palma,' the young man with the camera interjected in perfect English, and gave a half-nod, half-bow. 'Steven Wetherell, at your service.'

'Yes. It was seen as too unwieldy to send a photographer all the way from Berlin as well,' Horst explained. 'So our mutual friend, James, recommended a good freelancer who also works sometimes for local newspapers here.'

'So, a true international delegation today.' Graves grimaced. 'And how long will all this take?'

Horst looked at Dieter, who answered, 'Half an hour, no more.'

Seeing Graves still undecided, Bronowski got to his feet, 'We'll go for a quick walk, leave you to it.' He held a hand in invitation towards Teresa. 'I think we could all do with a break in any case.'

'OK. See you shortly.' Graves smiled begrudgingly and returned their brief waves as they headed off.

As they started walking, Teresa realized they were headed to the amphitheatre on the ridge. They didn't speak for the first hundred metres or so.

'I think he was more upset at the interruption than

anything else,' Bronowski said at length. 'Normally, he's quite pleased to get visitors, even if they are journalists sticking a camera in his face.' He smiled laconically. 'Helps sell more books, I suppose – so a necessary evil.'

'I daresay.'

Another brief silence, then he looked at Teresa keenly. 'I must say, though, part of that is down to you – keeping Robert and me so enrapt like that. And Horst and his little entourage did show up at a particularly delicate moment.'

'They did at that.' Teresa chuckled lightly.

As they reached the amphitheatre, Teresa felt her breath pulling in with the rugged mountain and coastline vista spread before them, even though it was a view she'd seen many times before.

'Wonderful, isn't it?' Bronowski commented. 'Not too different, I would imagine, to how Edith described the view from Hitler's Kehlsteinhaus. I felt I was practically there myself in those moments you described it. Almost as if it was Edith herself talking . . .'

Teresa could feel his eyes on her searchingly, almost as if he sensed something wasn't quite right.

'Yes, well,' she said, turning to him. 'We did know each other very well all those years. And I feel the only way to do her story justice is to relate it exactly as she told me . . . from her point of view.'

'Probably the only way,' Bronowski agreed, turning back to enjoy the view. 'And, as with the vista here, quite breathtaking.' His brief smile held a sweet-and-sour quality. 'Let us only hope, as we are reminded of with the amphitheatre here, that it doesn't end up as yet another Greek tragedy.'

43

Click . . . !

Click . . . !

Click . . . Click . . . Click!

My scream seemed to echo in the room, masking all but the last couple of *clicks*, so I then realized what had happened. A combined wave of shock and relief swept through me, leaving me slightly breathless.

Stefan stepped forward and gripped the barrel of the gun, took it from Voltner's grasp.

'What now?' Voltner asked tremulously, shell-shocked at the gun not firing. 'Having tricked me with the gun, you shoot me?'

'I suppose I should. Seeing as I'm dealing with a man quite prepared to shoot *me*.' Stefan teased Voltner a second longer with a faint smile, then took a bag from his inside pocket and slipped the gun held by its barrel inside, his own weapon still trained on Voltner. 'But no need. I have what I want. Your prints are now on the gun that shot your girlfriend – the *only* prints to now appear on the gun. All other times I've handled it wearing gloves.'

Voltner's gaze went incredulously from Stefan to the gun, and I found myself doing the same, though my own expression was tempered with a faint smile at the audacity of Stefan's little ruse. I also felt in equal measure like slapping him silly for not telling me in advance, giving me such a fright, but now wasn't the time.

'So, what do you expect me to do now?' Voltner asked uncertainly.

'I expect you to go away from here like a good boy and forget that anything happened. Forget your far-fetched tales about Edith and Erik Hanussen, or your girlfriend's intended blackmail.' Stefan's expression dropped, became more stern. 'And most certainly forget your own planned blackmail, or that you've even been here tonight.'

'And if I don't?' But it was said without conviction, a last-ditch challenge.

'Then this gun here will turn up where you least expect it.' Stefan patted the bag. 'Under a floorboard at your house or perhaps concealed in the lining of one of your cars in the motor pool. Diestler's team directed to exactly where it is by someone anonymous.'

Voltner's eyes darted anxiously for a second before settling. 'But I could equally tell Diestler about the blackmail over Hanussen and Ingrid coming here, and you then shooting her.'

'Except for a few small problems.' Stefan smiled dryly. 'You've already made the mistake of not mentioning previously to Diestler that Ingrid came here. So you coming up with it now, combined with some wild story about Edith and Hanussen – especially when Christof Lange's name is firmly on Louise's birth certificate – will just come across as a ridiculous invention to divert suspicion from yourself.'

As Voltner's eyes started darting again, looking for possible escape routes, Stefan continued.

'But against you, we have a far clearer path. Arguments overheard by neighbours between you and Ingrid. Your fingerprints now on the gun that shot her. That gun concealed at your home or workplace. Case closed!'

Voltner looked desperately from me to Stefan.

'But I could tell Diestler about what happened tonight,' he spluttered. He felt abject anger at being trapped, fired back with the only thing left that he could. 'You tricking me to get my fingerprints on the gun.'

'Good luck with that one,' Stefan said slyly. 'That will come across as an even more ludicrous story than Edith and Hanussen and Ingrid's blackmail. Will just appear to Diestler as more wild invention to divert suspicion away from yourself, the main suspect.'

The main suspect.

That term seemed to sit heavy on Voltner's shoulders for the first time, make him fully aware of the perilous situation he was in.

'We shall see,' Voltner said as he started towards the front door; but it was a last-shot defiance, held no strength.

'No, we won't,' Stefan said flatly, patting the bag with the gun again as he opened the door for Voltner. 'Not unless you wish to see yourself quickly behind bars and facing a death sentence.'

We watched a disgruntled Voltner stride back towards his car. And as Stefan closed the front door, I gave him a big hug, feeling the last of my tension wash away. Though I did pull back halfway through to give him the shoulder slap I felt he deserved.

'You should have told me! You scared the hell out of me!'

'*Sorry.*' Stefan grimaced uncomfortably. 'But if I had told you in advance, something in your expression might have given away that it was a trick, and he wouldn't have taken the gun. I needed it to appear real.'

I nodded after a second, rested my head back against his shoulder. 'Do you think he'll be back or say anything to the police?'

'I don't think so.' Stefan held me tight, comforting, his warm breath close by my face as he gently smiled. 'But as I keep reminding you, you're the fortune teller – you tell me.'

44

'Sometimes, I think it's a curse – my being able to tell fortunes, get a glimpse of the future.'

'You shouldn't think that way. Many people would look at it as a gift.'

'Some gift! More a curse. Sometimes the images I see in the speculum stay with me, haunt me, keep me awake at night. As if I didn't have enough with night-time bombing raids.'

'Every gift has its other side, its curse, I suppose. The yin and yang, the rough with the smooth.'

'I often wonder whether people asking me to look in the speculum for them is the right thing to do.'

'In what way?'

'Well, if I give advice on what I see – as I did earlier tonight about Timo Kretzler – that will make you react a certain way. But if I'd said nothing, you might handle it differently.'

'But then I'd be going in blind.'

'As is everyone else.'

'Yes. But I have an advantage from what you've seen and told me.'

'Advantage? Or another curse? Think about it. You suddenly acting differently might change the outcome I see – because my foresight is based on you acting naturally, with no prior knowledge.'

'I hadn't thought of it like that . . . but now you've got me worried. And you know it's vital I get everything right tomorrow with Timo Kretzler. Too much depends on it.'

'Do you want me to look again?'

My earlier conversation with Stefan replayed in my mind as I stared up blankly at the ceiling, his breath falling slow and shallow beside me. He was still asleep.

Too much depends on it.

The first sign that something was drastically wrong was when Gregor Lutz approached me – seeming to come out of nowhere by my side – as I was on the way to pick up Louise from school.

'One of our team has been apprehended by the Gestapo – the young man who picked up your book yesterday, Timo Kretzler.'

'Does he know much about me, know my involvement?'

'He's fairly new to the team, so hopefully not. I certainly haven't said anything to him, but others might have let things slip. But he knows about me and others in the team, which could then lead to you. That's why I'm telling you everything now rather than at the bookshop. I'll have to lie low for a while, as will others.'

The school gates loomed three hundred metres away, so I slowed my pace.

'How will I get in touch with you or liaise for future messages?'

'I or someone else will make contact somehow, I'm just not sure how.' Lutz held a hand out desperately. 'I simply don't know how much of our network will remain intact if Kretzler talks. You might want to think about moving or lying low too. *I'm sorry.*'

Lutz peeled off with a strained grimace and disappeared into the next side street.

I was still numb when later I explained the situation to

Stefan. We sat in the speculum room, our voices low, while outside Lara took care of Louise.

Then we convened there again that evening after Lara had left, by which time Stefan had made a frantic series of phone calls.

'OK. The interrogation of Timo Kretzler will take place tomorrow with a young Gestapo officer, Klaus Ziegler. Hopefully not as brutal as Schneider, but I have managed to convince the Führer that I should sit in on the interrogation and record it – because with messages being passed to London, it could involve quite delicate state secrets.'

'How does Ziegler feel about this?'

Stefan shrugged. 'He has little choice. I outrank him, and this directive has now come straight from the Führer.'

'And how might it help – you sitting in and recording it?'

Stefan sighed. 'I don't have the same close contact I had with Betzner, so of course can't guide this Kretzler in any way. But if he breaks and talks, I will at least know straightaway what he's said, how much danger you and Lutz's network might be in – plus I do have a couple of other ideas.' He gestured towards the speculum. 'If perhaps you can see how effective these might be?'

I nodded numbly. Hardly different from Hitler, I thought: asking which advances on the Russian front might be better. I could sense this was a struggle for Stefan, having to sit in, but knew how vital it was. If Kretzler talked, I was probably sunk.

So, I'd looked into the speculum, but some things had remained unclear; possibly because it did affect me and my family so directly – the fortune teller's curse – and Stefan in turn remained unsettled, unsure about what he should do the next day.

We didn't make love that night, both of us too weighed down with the turmoil of thoughts in our heads, but we did cling together and gain solace from the warmth of each other's bodies – like two lone survivors adrift on a life-raft – and I gently soothed Stefan's brow with one hand as he finally fell asleep.

I looked at the clock: 4.15 a.m. Something had suddenly awoken me again now. One of the options Stefan had put forward earlier. I wondered if with a slight adjustment, it might actually work . . . or, at least, have more chance of working.

Slipping quietly out of bed so that I didn't wake Stefan, I went downstairs to the speculum to check.

45

Timo Kretzler's breath was still gently rasping a minute after he'd been dragged into the room by two guards and strapped into an upright metal chair. No leg straps. The two guards then promptly left the room.

One of Stefan's first stipulations with Klaus Ziegler: 'Because of the sensitive nature of what might come out during the interrogation, the Führer has insisted that nobody else be present but you and I. No possible loose talk by guards or others.'

Ziegler was no more than five-foot seven with dark hair and dark eyes; a compact, sharp-featured hatchet of a man, his movements also sharp and economical, his gaze intense.

Ziegler had nodded his accord, but then forty minutes into his increasingly insistent and impatient questioning, with Timo shaking his head and still saying he didn't know anything, 'I'm little more than a messenger boy' – Ziegler turned to Stefan running his tape recorder at a side table.

'At this point, I'd normally welcome a muscle-man to soften him up a bit – but since I now have to do that myself, I've always had a hankering to use these.' Ziegler smiled slyly as he took a set of knuckledusters out of his pocket and slipped them on. 'Cuts down on the exertion required.'

Timo's rasping breath became more rapid, sinking into

guttural groans as Ziegler swung two punches onto his stomach, then another to the left side of his mouth, splitting his lip.

'Are you ready to tell me more now?' Ziegler demanded.

'I told you . . . I . . . I don't know what's on what I'm carrying,' Timo spluttered, his mouth filling with blood. 'Could be betting slips for all I know.'

'And what's the significance of the books?'

'I . . . I'm not sure. I think jus' to shield the notes we're carrying, ss . . . so they don't fall out.'

Ziegler swung and hit him with another body blow. A heavy grunt from Timo, frantically gasping for breath as blood spilled down his shirt front.

'So, let us turn to these people you meet at the transmission location . . .'

'It . . . it was the first time I met them, so I don' know their names.'

Ziegler shrugged. 'But whoever gives you these messages to carry – you most certainly would know them.'

A brief tell-tale look in Timo's eyes before he glanced away and shook his head.

Ziegler turned towards the small black box with a handle at its side he'd brought in at the outset, which Stefan recognized as a dynamo.

'I've always found these quite effective for low-voltage shocks.' Ziegler gestured at the bucket of water and ladle the guard had left to one side. 'Even more so when combined with a metal chair and some water.'

Timo's breath fell faster and more ragged. Stefan saw the rising fear in his eyes, and began to revise his opinion on Ziegler being less brutal than Schneider. At least it would make easier what he might have to do later. Despite his inner anger, Stefan observed as if nonplussed. After all, he was a hardened SS officer; he should revel in such things, or, at least, not be affected by them.

'And even more effective in your case,' Ziegler continued, 'because I understand you have asthma.'

Timo's breathing lapsed into a tortured wheezing.

Stefan bit at his lip, could hardly bear it. But he wondered whether part of his anger was because he felt so powerless. He had no influence over Timo's destiny, couldn't guide him in the same way he had Paulos Betzner, so regardless of whether Timo talked or not, the young man's fate was sealed.

The next hour was one of the worst that Stefan had ever endured. Screams of agony punctuated by rasping, laboured breathing, and all the time Stefan having to observe emptily, deadpan as the tape spool steadily turned.

He wished he could rescue Timo in the same way he had Paulos Betzner. As instructed, Paulos had found his way through to the cabin of the backwoodsman Otto, who even with just one arm was quite adept at firing a Sten gun. When he'd visited Paulos there six months later, he was stir-crazy from the cramped surroundings and having rabbit stew and goulash every day, but alive and mostly recovered. Stefan had arranged his new papers and identity as Nils Hartmann from Stuttgart.

But there was little hope for Timo. At one point, Timo's body writhing against the chair under a strong electric shock, his head lolling forward – Ziegler broke off, fearing he was unconscious or dead.

Ziegler splashed some water on Timo's face with the

ladle, and as his eyes slowly flickered open again, his head lifting a fraction, Ziegler moved to just behind him.

'That's the beauty with asthma. You don't always have to apply shock treatment for maximum effect.' Then, cradling Timo's head, he firmly clasped one hand over his mouth, rocking with Timo as he writhed, eyes bulging, his face turning almost blue from lack of air – before Ziegler finally released his hand.

That first gasp of air a desperate sucked-in vortex before verging into rapid-fire shorter gasps.

Ziegler alternated between the electric shock treatment and stopping Timo breathing – Stefan's stomach churning with it, desperately wanting to stop it, but knowing he couldn't, especially with everything being recorded on tape – so that when Timo finally said, 'Ss . . . stop . . . *stop*! I . . . I'll talk . . . tell you what I know,' it was like a welcome relief. Even though now it would set in motion a far more difficult stage in Stefan's planning. His hand covering the motion, he gently eased the microphone plug a few millimetres from its socket, the tape spool still rolling.

Ziegler's gaze was locked too intently on Timo Kretzler – the prize he'd been aiming for the last two hours now hopefully at hand. He hadn't noticed.

'So, let us start with your main contact man – who is that?'

'Hi . . . his name is Gregor . . . Gregor Lutz.'

'And where do you normally meet him?'

'At . . . at a bookshop on Hohenzollerndamm. Grunewald Bücher. Sometimes at a café or safe house.'

'And the addresses of these safe houses?'

'I . . . I don't remember.' Timo's breath caught and he

coughed out another spurt of blood. 'They . . . they change each time in any case . . . ss . . . so it wouldn't help.'

Ziegler looked at Timo intently, nodded his acceptance after a moment. 'Who else do you know in this network . . . their names?'

Timo acted vague, started shaking his head, and Ziegler went behind him and stiffled his breath again for a moment before he finally stuttered out a couple of names while gasping to get his breath back.

Stefan hadn't heard of either, but made a note of them on a pad.

Ziegler glanced down, assessed for a moment. 'And was it this Gregor Lutz who gave you the book that day to take to the transmission location?'

'Nn . . . no. It was a woman I met at Café Holbein on Leipziger Strasse . . . ww . . . we exchanged books.'

Stefan tensed at the mention of Edith.

'What was her name?'

'I . . . I don't know. I was never given it by Lutz.'

'And what part did this woman play in all of this?'

A pause this time from Timo, his head lolling slightly, and Stefan's hand clenched below his table.

'I . . . I'm not sure. I . . . I was never told her role.' Another cough broke through Timo's rapid, fractured breathing. 'Per . . . perhaps just another messenger like me.'

Stefan swallowed back his own faint gasp of relief. But still much to do. Ziegler could easily get to Edith through Lutz or these other two names given.

The interrogation wound down then, Ziegler going back over some minor points before calling the two guards in to haul Timo away.

'I have no more use for him . . . you know what to do with him,' Ziegler mumbled to the guards, and Stefan knew what would now happen to Timo: he'd be taken to the nearest woodland and shot.

Stefan felt sick to his stomach that he could do nothing to help Timo – he couldn't even risk a look of sorrow or regret his way – he now had to concentrate on those he might still be able to save.

46

'Where does this Voltner character live?' Ziegler asked as Stefan swung into Charlottenstrasse.

'On the edge of Schillerkiez, only eight or nine minutes away now.' Stefan lifted one hand from the wheel, glanced at his watch. 'I'm sure he'll be back home now from the motor pool. It wouldn't have been a good idea to confront him over a delicate matter like this with others around.'

Ziegler gave a perfunctory nod. Stefan fixed his eyes on the road ahead, but he could feel his hands sweating inside his leather gloves gripping the wheel. Still so much could go wrong if Voltner wasn't there or had someone with him, or Ziegler started to smell a rat.

As soon as the guards had taken Timo away, Stefan had become more animated: 'I thought as much. Ties into work I've already been doing for the Führer – which is why he asked me to sit in now.'

He then spun a story about the man heading the Berlin motor pool, Carl Voltner, and how they'd suspected him of passing secrets. 'And you've done some admirable work here – the Führer will be delighted at you now tying up the loose ends. Because Voltner has been followed to Grunewald Bücher on a few past occasions.'

Ziegler raised a brow. 'So, Lutz is probably his contact man?'

'It would appear so.' Stefan had tapped his watch. 'But we'd better be quick – because I fear he'll have got wind of Kretzler being questioned and might hightail it. And you should certainly be there when we confront him, because it's *your* investigation. I think the Führer would insist upon it.'

Stefan suspected the combination of praise and the Führer's name would sway Ziegler, and a minute later they were speeding away.

Now Ziegler asked, 'How is Voltner getting this important information to pass on?'

'He's a hale-and-hearty fellow, and over a few drinks with military high-ups, he appears able to prise information from them.' Stefan tilted a gloved hand from the wheel. 'Perhaps also from the Führer's security staff and advisers.'

Another curt nod from Ziegler. Stefan found the tension stifling, a faint ringing now in one ear. Was there doubt or suspicion from Ziegler? Stefan couldn't discern any. Though like most Gestapo, Ziegler was a master of the poker-face.

'And how long do you suspect he's been passing secrets?'

'Five or six months, maybe longer. But we've only started closing in on him the last few weeks.' Stefan sighed. 'We even suspect a woman in the motor pool, Ingrid Bittner, found out about him sending secret messages, so he got rid of her. She was found shot in woodland, made to look like an internal action.'

A faint twitch pulled at Ziegler's jawline. 'So, we should be cautious.'

'Yes, we should,' Stefan said, patting the gun inside his

jacket. He knew that Ziegler would also be armed. 'That's why also it's best there are two of us.'

A moment later, Stefan pulled his car up in front of Voltner's place: a small bungalow with an A-frame roof in a short row of similar properties. A light was on in a front window, so somebody was in.

As Stefan approached and knocked on the door, he noticed Ziegler hung back in his shadow. Perhaps hearing that Voltner might have killed Ingrid Bittner, Ziegler didn't want to be first to catch a bullet.

Voltner, his uniform jacket off, looked surprised to see them, and Stefan knew he'd have to push the initiative quickly.

'Are you alone? We need to come in and speak to you.' Stefan stepped inside as Voltner had hardly finished nodding, Ziegler close behind.

'What's this all about?' Voltner asked as he led them down a short hallway into the lounge.

'May I introduce Klaus Ziegler of the Gestapo.' Stefan held a hand towards Ziegler as he quickly glanced around: Voltner's SS uniform jacket over a chair, his service pistol in its holster on a side table. The buzzing was like a mosquito in his ear, getting stronger as the blood pounded through his head. 'And he's come here to ask you some questions about your meetings with a certain Gregor Lutz.'

Voltner's brow creased. 'Gregor Lutz? . . . never heard of him.'

Strained smile from Ziegler, as if he half-expected such a response. 'More specifically, the messages you've been passing through Lutz.'

'*Messages?* Don't know what you're talking about.' He

turned to Stefan. 'And just why you're here about this is beyond me. Especially after –'

Stefan drew the gun out while both Voltner and Ziegler were off balance – the buzzing almost deafening with the pounding rush of blood – and put a bullet through Ziegler's head.

But Voltner's aghast expression lasted only a split-second before he was in motion towards his own pistol and holster two metres away on the side table. Stefan drew out a second pistol and fired, caught Voltner in his side. Voltner slumped to the ground and Stefan moved around and shot him more squarely in the chest.

Stefan's breath fell short and ragged, the buzzing in his head drowning out much of it as he checked angles of fire between the two bodies three metres apart. Then he took the pistol he'd used to shoot Ziegler – he'd removed it from its bag earlier and handled it since only with gloves on, so it still had Voltner's prints on it – and, after removing two bullets, slipped it loosely into Voltner's right hand.

After one last check of relative body positions, he reholstered his service pistol and left, taking Voltner's gun with him for later disposal.

'It was terrible. In particular, because there was nothing I could do for Timo. And he was so young . . .' Stefan looked across the table with haunted eyes, as if Timo's agonizing screams and fractured breathing still replayed in his head.

I bit at my lip as I met Stefan's gaze, trying to offer some solace. Having met Timo that day in the café, I didn't need reminding of how young he was.

'He had asthma . . . and Ziegler played on that when he tortured him in the interrogation.'

'*Oh, God.*' I clasped Stefan's hand across the table.

'But at least it made easier what I had to do later . . .' Stefan went on to explain how he'd duped Ziegler into suspecting Voltner and made it appear as if they'd shot each other. 'Especially with what was at stake. Lutz's network, your and your family's survival.'

'The end justifies the means,' I said, closing my eyes for a second as I clasped his hand tighter in reassurance. I sighed. 'I've been using that phrase a lot myself with what I've been doing in the sessions with Hitler. Trying to justify all those deaths I see if it means in the end the war will be won.'

Stefan nodded hollowly. It had been a long night.

Stefan had reported the incident from the nearest phone box to a local Orpo unit. 'I have a report to make tonight directly to the Führer on all of this, so I'll come by the station tomorrow morning and make a full statement.'

But his begging off for the extra time that night was to fill in all the details to suit on the stretch of blank tape that had run from halfway through Timo's interrogation. Working from a set script, it took his contact from a Berlin radio station – a master of impressions and voiceovers – almost four hours to get the timbre and pitch of Ziegler's and Timo's voices right and the dialogue to run smoothly.

No references to Gregor Lutz or Grunewald Bücher, these were all replaced with meetings with Carl Voltner in various cafés. For the sake of keeping close to the truth, Café Holbein was left as where Timo had his final meeting with Carl Voltner.

It had been past 1 a.m. when Stefan finally arrived at

my house, and I made strong coffee for us both while he related the nightmare chain of events.

'And do you think you've covered everything?'

'I think so. I've played the tape through twice – it sounds natural. And everything at the crime scene should hopefully fit – especially after I've given my statement tomorrow.'

I gently squeezed his hand. 'Let's pray so.'

Stefan nodded slowly, his gaze lost for a moment, then he suddenly blurted out, 'Sergey Nechayev.'

'Who?'

'The man who coined that phrase, "The end justifies the means."'

'I think Machiavelli said something similar . . . but I didn't know you were up on your Russian literature.'

'I'm not. But with political history, I'm better. And Nechayev was a real figure in the Russian revolution, not from literature.' Stefan's gaze slightly lost focus again. 'It was my uncle who first told me about him – because that expression was being used a lot by the SS to justify their own actions, and still is.' Stefan's sombre gaze settled back on me directly, resolutely. 'And now you and I are doing exactly the same.'

47

'And how far away is this place I have to go?' Tobias asked.

'About twenty kilometres away to the west of Berlin. A small town called Nikolassee.' I could see Tobias trying to work out what twenty kilometres meant in his terms. Hardly surprising for someone who'd hardly been outside the garden gate all his life. I added, 'About thirty minutes' drive away.'

A slow nod after a moment. 'So you and Momma and Pappa could see me more often than once a week?'

I pursed my lips. This was proving more difficult than I'd imagined. My parents were due to run Tobias to the institute near Nikolassee late tomorrow morning. Louise had already spent an hour with Tobias playing and saying goodbye, and I'd had to instruct her beforehand, '*Try and be strong, no tears, as we don't want to upset Tobias, make him worry too much. Everything will be fine where he's going.*' Now it was my turn to say my last goodbye to Tobias.

'The people there have a lot of others to care for. They wouldn't be able to cope if they had visits from all these families at all hours of the day.' It had been a miracle to even gain these once-a-week visits. Most were once a month or never. Some families didn't even take advantage of the monthly visits; with most 'terminations' taking place within two months, they were too distraught to face their child and tell them this was the last time they'd see them.

'What will happen there?'

'They'll take care of you.'

'But Momma and Pappa do that.'

'They do. But with the medications you take, you have to be observed by doctors and trained staff from now on.'

'Who says?'

'The Party. The government.'

'The *government*,' Tobias echoed emptily, his expression slightly lost.

Though he was probably no less bewildered than I and many others about Reich diktats and actions now. One of the few times that Tobias was actually in tune with much of the German populace.

And maybe that cloud of bewilderment and mystery was best. I could hide behind that; saved me from telling Tobias the appalling horror that it was part of a programme to eradicate all those like him. Anyone the Nazi Party deemed not to be a 'perfect Aryan'.

'There'll be others there like you,' I said, then quickly turned it to a positive. 'So you'll make friends.'

'Others like me . . . *friends*?'

Tobias appeared even more lost, and I realized that with him hardly ever venturing out from the family home, both concepts were difficult for him to grasp. While my parents' protective cocoon around Tobias was understandable, at the same time it had impeded his development.

'Yes. People you like. In the same way you like Momma, Pappa, Louise and me.'

Tobias thought about this for a moment. 'I'll never like anyone else the same way I like all of you.'

'I know. But these are *extra* people you'll like, not

replacements. And those extra friends will hopefully make you feel better about being there.'

But even that had a sting in the tail, I realized. Tobias making friends, then the next week they were gone, had been 'terminated'. How long before he worked out what they had planned for him?

'I suppose.' Tobias chewed at his lip, looked up anxiously. 'You won't all just leave me there?'

'No, of course not.' I hugged Tobias tight as his eyes filled, and I felt my own eyes stinging with tears. I closed them briefly leaning over his shoulder. 'We'll always love you, always be there for you.'

Not even knowing as I said it whether it was true. Whether we'd be able to save Tobias at the eleventh hour.

The next day, returning from dropping Louise at school, I was confronted by Kurt Schneider waiting for me in my lounge. The only warning from Lara, 'Someone here to see you,' as I walked into the house.

Schneider's back was to me, one hand tracing absently along a line of books on my shelves. Some of the very same books used to send messages. A faint shudder ran through me.

'Marvellous collection you have here.' Schneider half-turned to acknowledge me. 'Some classics among them, I see.'

A younger SS man stood to one side, trying to appear alert yet at the same time not invested in our conversation. Simply an observer or perhaps Schneider's driver.

'Yes, I've always had a good collection of books. And have kept that up now for the sake of my daughter.'

'Of course.' Schneider turned to me more fully, took a fresh breath. 'I think I owe you an apology.'

I raised an inquiring eyebrow, said nothing.

'You see, I might have been misled by Ingrid Bittner probing into your possible fortune telling.' He held a palm out. 'And as Hauptsturmführer Hansel rightly pointed out, if indeed that was continuing, that was a private matter between you and the Führer. None of her business – or mine, for that matter.' Schneider's eyes settled on me. 'But it appears now it might have been a smokescreen for something else.'

'In what way?' I asked hesitantly, concerned where Schneider might be heading.

'There has been another death – Ingrid Bittner's boyfriend, Carl Voltner. As we see from this investigation now with her and Voltner's deaths – it appears he was passing on secrets, and got rid of her because she was on to him.' Schneider pursed his lips for a moment. 'But what if they were in on it together? And then he disposed of her because he feared her cover had been broken and so she might implicate him under questioning. That would also provide strong motive.'

'I suppose,' I said, shrugging. Noncommittal.

'In which case, as she felt things closing in on her, she'd have been keen on a diversion. Which would then explain her sudden obsession with your continuing fortune telling. And then all that nonsense with that old boyfriend you shared.' Schneider looked at me keenly. 'That would make perfect sense, don't you think?'

Another brief shrug. 'I must admit, it did mystify me a bit. All of it with Christof happened so long ago.'

'Yes, of course.' Schneider's eyes stayed on me for a

moment, then he started pacing. 'The only thing that doesn't fit in with all of this is *books* being used to pass these messages. You'd have thought that using automotive components would have suited him better.'

'Perhaps too close to home,' I muttered.

'Yes. But he didn't seem a particularly bookish person to me, nor Bittner for that matter.' He traced one finger back along a bookshelf. 'Whereas you have quite a collection here.'

'As do many in Berlin. And Ingrid was a keen booklover too.' I said it plainly, matter-of-factly, but inside my nerves were galloping.

'Yes, well. We can hardly ask her now, can we?'

With Schneider's gently rising smile – challenging, *disbelieving?* – all that hit me in that moment was Betzner's cries and groans of pain. I imagined Schneider saying to me now, '*I think you know more than you're letting on. I'm taking you in for questioning . . .*'

'Of course, the other scenario is that *you* and Voltner were working together. Voltner collecting the information, you passing it on with your books.' Schneider gestured. 'And you do have a track record with playing a double game with Bittner's boyfriends. And then when she found out about the messages and the two of you, he had to get rid of her.'

I let out a half-gasp, half-laugh at the ludicrousness of the suggestion. '*What?* Me and Carl Voltner?'

'I've seen more unlikely associations.' Schneider's smile tempered only slightly. 'And you have to admit, that scenario fits much better: Voltner gathering secrets among high-ranking generals and Reich staff; you with your books for the messages.'

I felt suddenly dizzy, unsteady. However tenuous, Schneider seemed to be clinging to these suggestions. I still felt as if he was only a sentence away from saying, '*Come with me* . . .' And then the steel plectrums and hammer would come out. I wished now I hadn't listened to that tape with Betzner, didn't know what horrific fate I might be facing.

'I'd rather have my fingernails pulled out than have been associated with Carl Voltner,' I said cuttingly, my thoughts leaching into my words. But it had the same effect as saying *I'd rather die*. Schneider nodded his acceptance, became pensive.

'The main reason I'm thinking of these scenarios is that I feel it needs *two* people to make them work. I don't see Voltner working on his own. So, Voltner with Bittner or you? But if you say you couldn't have possibly worked with Voltner, then who?' Schneider held a hand out helplessly. 'Who would you be working with?'

Stefan? I felt my breath gone for a moment with how Schneider had worked his way around to us. Had some extra information come to light that pointed to the two of us? '*Come with me.*' I clenched my hands, a cold tingle running up my spine. I could almost feel those steel plectrums being driven beneath my fingernails. I steeled myself as I met his penetrating gaze.

'I think you already have your two people, Herr Schneider, in Ingrid Bittner and Carl Voltner. Which I understand from my colleague is borne out by the facts and forensic findings of the case – so wouldn't involve me or anyone else.'

'And no doubt you got these facts and forensic findings from Hauptsturmführer Stefan Hansel?'

'Yes. As you know, we work closely together.'

'Work closely together,' Schneider repeated thoughtfully under his breath, as if to himself, and I could almost hear the unspoken, '*But we don't know on what, and daren't ask. Führer's secrecy.*' He raised a brow. 'Though of course, with you working closely with the Führer, you'd also be privy to secrets. So maybe there were *three* of you all along: you and Voltner gathering information, then you and Bittner both passing it on.'

A shiver ran through me. No doubt now remained that he knew or suspected something. Perhaps a stronger warning off was needed. He'd either say, '*Enough, come with me*,' or take a step back. I shook my head. 'Might make sense, *if* you ignore all the facts of this case. Which I'm sure in the Führer's eyes isn't what a good investigator should do.'

A faint flinch at the veiled insult-threat, then his eyes fixed back on me. 'Somewhat ironic that you should raise that point – as indeed it was the facts and forensics of this case which have led me to stray elsewhere. Because in many ways those *facts* seem more unlikely than my alternative suggestions.' Schneider smiled primly and nodded. 'But you're right – those facts can't be ignored. So please forgive my ramblings here this morning. Good day.'

'Of course.' I gave a polite nod in return, caught as much by surprise by his sudden about-turn as by his rambling suggestions.

But a minute after Lara had shown Schneider and his assistant out, the full wave of nerves hit me. I went into the bathroom, gripping tight to the edge of the sink to steady myself as I caught my haunted reflection in the mirror above. *I can't do this any more.*

48

'OK. Tell me the rest now,' Stefan said as soon as he'd stopped the car and put the handbrake on.

I nodded, closed my eyes for a second to gather my thoughts before continuing about Schneider's nightmare visit.

Stefan hadn't wanted to have this conversation at my house with Lara present, so after telling her, 'We're heading to the Reich Chancellery for a couple of hours,' we drove to the Volkspark Wuhlheide. Gardens and playing fields stretched out ahead, a children's playground to one side. It was oddly peaceful for a city in the midst of war, no sentry boxes or barbed wire in sight, the only hint of conflict from the number of men in uniform among the couples strolling in the park.

Stefan had shown up at my house only five minutes after Schneider left, and I'd taken him through to the speculum room to tell him he'd just visited. 'God, it was awful, Stefan. I'm sure Schneider knows something.'

Stefan had gripped my shoulders lightly; calming, reassuring. 'I thought it might have been him here. I saw the Gestapo staff car as I approached, so drove past two hundred metres and waited. Saw him leave minutes ago in my rear-view mirror. But let's go somewhere private so you can tell me what happened.'

I didn't start speaking until we were a kilometre away

from my house. The spectre, the shadow of Schneider's visit still too close; or perhaps I needed that gap to coalesce my thoughts, get them clear. And now, more calmly, Schneider's words related more sequentially, I told Stefan the rest as we gazed unseeing at people enjoying a sunny morning in the park.

Stefan nodded at intervals in uncomfortable acknowledgement, conflicting shadows playing in his eyes.

'I think he's just fishing,' he said on the back of a sigh as I finished. 'I'm fairly sure he doesn't know anything, otherwise he wouldn't just ramble through those various scenarios. But he's obviously suspicious, isn't satisfied the details with Bittner and Voltner fully add up, so we'll have to be careful.'

'But what can I do if he just shows up out of the blue, confronts me like he did now?'

'Mentioning the Führer was a good move, so could be used again. Aside from that, give him short shrift. Say that if he's unhappy with the findings of the investigation, then he should bring it up with Hans Diestler, not you.' Stefan could see that I was still unsettled and reached across and stroked my hair, calming, soothing. Then he gently tapped my forehead. 'The important thing is not to let Schneider in here. That's the game he's playing, what he's depending on.'

I grimaced meekly. 'I'll do my best.'

But perhaps my expression gave away that I hadn't fully grasped his intent. He looked at me steadily for a moment, as if willing the message home, before lowering his hand and staring ahead at the park. He sighed.

'You know I mentioned before about Schneider being like a dog with a bone once he felt he was onto something?'

'Yes. But that was about my possible continuing clairvoyance.'

'Hopefully, on that front I've warned him off. But look what he does now. He starts with an apology about that, knowing it's forbidden territory, then starts probing about everything else. Looking for possible cracks.'

'I see.'

'I'm not sure you do.' Stefan looked at me meaningfully. A more measured sigh. 'Because Schneider hasn't gained his reputation just from being a brutal interrogator, but also because of the mind games he plays with people. That thing with the hammer and steel plectrums he used on Betzner. Most people no doubt start talking as soon as he takes them out of that box – picturing what's about to happen too clearly for them to take. And Schneider knows that, plays on it.'

I nodded numbly. Nightmare thoughts about the hammer and plectrums had plagued me within minutes of Schneider's arrival. 'Half the time he was with me, I felt he was only a sentence away from saying, "Come with me," and hauling me in for questioning. Surely, if I'm off-hand or abrupt with him, he might lose patience and do just that.'

'Doubtful. You're doing private work for the Führer which he doesn't know any details about – even though he has his suspicions. And while he might outrank me, I'm a personal adjutant to the Führer.' Stefan grimaced. 'Schneider wouldn't risk crossing that line without firm proof.'

I held a hand out. 'That was part of the problem. In the midst of his rambling, I feared he *had* found out something incriminating.'

'Believe me, if he had, he'd have just hauled you straight in for questioning. Wouldn't have troubled with all that roundabout speculation.'

I hoped Stefan wasn't saying it just to make me feel more settled – we were too close, knew each other too well for that now – and it certainly sounded right. But I was probably still too rattled after Schneider's visit for balanced judgement. My thoughts spun back to something Stefan had said at the start of our conversation.

'When you saw Schneider's staff car in front of my house, what were you coming to see me about?'

'Certainly nothing to do with Schneider – his visit was as much of a surprise to me as to you.' He grimaced awkwardly. 'It was to do with Tobias and this clinic he's going to. Another possible option I've thought of.'

I checked my watch: 11.20 a.m. 'But my parents will be running him there now.'

Stefan held up a hand. 'It's OK. I've already phoned them. Told them to hold on until three or four, so there was time for us to talk first. You mentioned that Tobias was anxious about going to this clinic.'

'Beyond that, I'm afraid. He's absolutely dreading it. I tried to put his mind at ease, saying that we'll see him every week and he'll make friends there, but none of it helped. He looked so lost, Stefan, like a little child about to be taken from his parents – which in his psyche he still is. Possibly even worse.'

Stefan's brow creased. 'In what way?'

'A child at least will have been to school, made friends. Had some sort of life outside of his parents and family. Tobias has had none of that. My parents and then myself and Louise on and off are all he's ever known. Yanking him away from that would be terribly cruel – even aside from the fear of him being put down in a month or two, like some sort of sick dog.'

My voice had a bitter edge to it as I finished, my eyes misting with tears.

Stefan reached across and gently clasped my left hand. 'We've done all we can in finding the best clinic, one where we'll at least get some warning. But this other option has its risks too, and I'm not sure yet it will even work.' He took a breath. 'I recall you mentioning that your father was originally from Switzerland, is that right?'

'Yes. From Basel. He came to Berlin when he was in his late twenties.'

'And does he have any relatives still in Basel?'

'Only a younger brother now. His elder sister passed away four years ago.'

Stefan nodded thoughtfully. 'Has your father kept in touch with his brother?'

'Yes. Mostly letters, the occasional phone call. Though with the war the last few years, it's been more difficult.'

Stefan sank into thought again for a moment. 'And this Orpo man's next visit about Tobias is tomorrow?'

'Yes. Which is why we'd planned to get Tobias to the clinic today. To avoid Gessner possibly taking him away to an assigned T4 clinic.'

A longer pause. And as Stefan finally shared this alternative option with me, I could see why he'd been cautious and asked his questions. In many ways, it carried more risk than Tobias being at the Nikolassee clinic.

49

Kurt Schneider sat having afternoon coffee and cake in his favourite café in the luxurious Hotel Adlon. A resplendent room over twenty-five metres square with a wealth of palms in brass pots, an eleven-piece orchestra in one corner playing a variety of classics by German and Austrian composers.

A creature of habit, he always took the same table to one side so that he could look through a large picture window towards Pariser Platz with the Brandenburg Gate flanking it behind. He felt at the very centre of German culture and power – its rightful place, and *his*. Even the shadow of the war outside felt remote here, the number of men in uniform fewer – most of his fellow officers preferred the nearby Hotel Kaiserhof – the café almost unchanged since his parents had first brought him here as a treat when he was only twelve years old.

As he sipped at his coffee, he recalled his meetings of the past few days and made intermittent notes on a pad. His first meeting had been with Hans Diestler, finding him at his usual lunchtime restaurant, Das Aschinger. Diestler had been quite open and forthcoming.

'After our last conversation, I went to see this Edith Creutzen you mentioned, also spoke to Hauptsturmführer Hansel, but found nothing untoward or suspicious.'

'Did she say that Bittner had paid her a visit? Perhaps broached the subject of their past shared boyfriend?'

'Yes, she did. But as she rightly pointed out, it was a boyfriend of many moons ago – hardly worth a heated fight, let alone killing someone over it.'

'And her possible continuing clairvoyance?'

'She said that she'd told Bittner that it wasn't continuing and, as with you, Hansel had already warned me that whatever work Creutzen was doing with the Führer was a matter of state secrecy. So, for obvious reasons, I didn't push the issue.'

'Obviously,' Diestler agreed.

'And are you happy with this culmination now – how the case has ended up?'

'I must admit, some of it was a surprise at first, didn't seem to fit. But then the same calibre of gun and bullet-groove striations for both Bittner and Ziegler – hard to ignore that. It also answered that first anomaly I faced with Bittner being shot in the back. Shooting your girlfriend to protect yourself – you'd probably do it from the back. Then the frontal shot to make it look like something else, possibly an internal SS execution.'

'I suppose . . .' Schneider hadn't thought of that.

'And, of course, I've listened to the tape, which then ties everything together.'

'The tape?'

'Yes. Ziegler was conducting an interrogation of a suspect, and all the details about Voltner being involved in passing secrets came out in that.'

'And who made the recording?'

'Hauptsturmführer Hansel, sitting in and making it

personally for the Führer.' Diestler held a palm out. 'Which isn't unusual, given that it involved quite delicate state security matters.'

'One way of viewing it,' allowed Schneider.

'That's why, when the facts came out on that tape, Hansel went with Ziegler to see Voltner, and that final unfortunate confrontation took place. The shooting was initially reported to a local Orpo unit, and I had to get security clearance to hear the tape. But having done so, it all makes sense and fits together quite neatly.'

'Don't you think perhaps *too* neatly?'

'In what way?'

'Think about it. All the main witnesses are now gone – including Ziegler, who conducted that last crucial interrogation. Only Hansel and Creutzen now remain.'

A faint shadow of doubt crossed Diestler's face, the first since they'd started talking. The policeman shrugged. 'I have enough on my plate with cases where the pieces don't fall together – or where I can't even find the pieces – without concerning myself with cases where they do.'

In the days following his meeting with Diestler, Schneider did more digging. He got hold of the various records of Ziegler's investigation, which included following a certain Felix Engelmann and later Timo Kretzler to message-transmission addresses, then the final interrogation of Kretzler. He noted that the earlier meetings in bookshops were later relocated to cafés, but books remained the common denominator throughout.

Looking into Edith Creutzen's background was more difficult. The only point of contact he could find was a high-ranking SS officer, Gustav Strehl, who had handled Creutzen's move from Paris to Berlin. He knew he'd have to be careful with Strehl, because no doubt the same code of secrecy had been applied with him too. But luckily the events with Bittner had given him a valid excuse.

Schneider phoned Paris and told Strehl about Ingrid Bittner and her being exposed as part of a secret message-passing network. 'And it has come to our attention that she was also a past friend of Edith Creutzen's, when they both worked as protégées of Erik Hanussen.'

'I see.'

'Nothing alarming, just routine. But we need to check any and all associates of anyone involved in something like that.'

'Of course.'

As they talked, Schneider noted that Strehl made no reference to her clairvoyance, or indeed what work she might be doing with the Führer, and Schneider didn't ask directly – that would have been too clumsy. So he merely asked whether any other friends or associates travelled from Paris with her at the time, 'Or was there anything she had sent on which might have been unusual?'

Of course, the mention of a speculum or other clairvoyance paraphernalia would immediately have given the game away, but Strehl answered simply that no friends or associates had accompanied her, 'Only her young daughter. And nothing particularly unusual – unless you count a grand piano and a large collection of books.'

'I see. Thank you.'

The next day he'd made his impromptu visit to Edith Creutzen's home.

Schneider brought his attention back to his surroundings, waving one finger in the air in time with the orchestra's strident rendition of Mozart's *Eine kleine Nachtmusik*. He looked down at his brief notes on his pad:

Bookshops ... later cafés. Kretzler. Engelmann. Books. Creutzen and Hansel. Secrecy.

He thought he'd worked out why there was such an insistence on secrecy, if indeed Creutzen was involved with clairvoyance for the Führer. The whole debacle with Hanussen had ended up an embarrassment: the Führer consulting a Jewish fortune teller, questions raised about his soundness of mind, others vying for power within the Reich using it as an excuse to possibly unseat him. The Führer would want to avoid a repeat of that at any cost.

But what Schneider couldn't work out was what secrets a clairvoyant could possibly be privy to. In his experience, exchanges with clairvoyants would usually involve a range of quite standard questions. In the Führer's case, this would no doubt be what was foreseen on various campaigns or battlefronts. *Which areas of the Reich's expanded territory might be more troublesome?* How would any of that involve the passing of secrets?

'And when did your uncle come to take your brother?'

'Just yesterday afternoon.'

'That's rather last minute.' Gessner's brow furrowed, the first doubt creeping in.

'We were looking at a clinic in nearby Nikolassee to take Tobias,' I said. '*Keep close to the truth*,' Stefan had advised, '*in case Gessner checks*.' 'Meanwhile, my father had been in touch with his family in Basel, and his brother agreed to take care of Tobias for a while.'

'And that's where your brother is now – in Basel?'

'Yes.' I said it calmly, matter-of-factly, but Gessner's eyes stayed on me keenly, weighing up the veracity.

'This is most irregular,' Gessner huffed at length. 'You are aware that if your brother was born here, he is a German citizen, so subject to Reich laws.'

'That's open to debate, according to the Swiss lawyer my uncle was in touch with. Under Swiss law, those with Down's carry the same rights as minors, so are subject to care orders, which can include family.' I took a piece of paper and handed it across. 'This is my uncle's address and telephone number in Switzerland, where indeed Tobias is now staying. You can check with him, if you wish.'

Slightly flushed, obviously not used to being challenged, Gessner gave the slip of paper a cursory glance before putting it in his pocket. 'And where are your parents now?'

'My mother is in the kitchen and my father is at work.'

Gessner peered past my shoulder. 'I will need to check.'

'Is that necessary?'

Gessner looked at me sharply. 'Are you questioning my authority?'

'No. It . . . it's just that now you have my uncle's address and phone number, you could check with him.'

'Due to the unusual nature of your brother leaving, I need to check directly.' Gessner stepped over the threshold and sidled past me as I stepped aside without waiting for my response.

I followed him down the hallway, my mother giving him a tight smile as we came by the half-open kitchen door. We'd agreed that I would handle Gessner's visit in case she said something untoward, as had happened last time.

With a perfunctory nod, Gessner walked past my mother and opened the larder door to check inside, then crossed the hallway to check the lounge and dining room before coming to stand at the bottom of the stairs.

'I will need to check the bedrooms as well. You can remain here.'

It was more of an order than a request, so I stayed where I was as I heard Gessner moving around upstairs checking the three bedrooms and the bathroom, his purposeful stride thudding ominously on the floorboards, cupboard doors opening and closing. As I heard him pause, I wondered whether he might have found something. We'd left Tobias's room neat and tidy, as if he had gone away for a while, but I began to fear we might have missed something. I caught my mother's eye as she stood by the kitchen doorway, her expression worried, haunted.

My eyes shifted to the low door with bookshelves to one side, then through and down the steps, picturing my father and Tobias down there with the same haunted expressions, eyes wide as they heard the footsteps above. Stefan had warned us: '*It's high risk. If Tobias is discovered still in your house, you'll all face going to a camp for misleading an Orpo officer. So consider carefully before finally deciding.*'

Gessner came back down the stairs, his step steady, a portentous countdown to our demise. He glanced back up the stairs, as if he might have overlooked something, then his eyes rested back on me briefly in the hallway before shifting to the low door.

'What is through here?'

'That . . . that's the coal cellar.'

'And do you have an air-raid shelter?'

'There's a communal one at the end of next-door's garden. But we often use the cellar as well.'

Gessner nodded and reached to open the cellar door, my heart in my mouth as he ducked through the portal and started making his way down. I followed two steps behind, saw Gessner take a torch from his belt as he was two-thirds of the way down, swinging its beam around the cellar walls and floor: a metre-high stack of coal to one side, a two-metre stretch of narrow, empty concrete floor straight ahead.

'A bit cramped for you all down here during a raid,' Gessner commented.

'Well, it's just my parents and Tobias . . . now just my parents. I have my own place.'

As Gessner nodded, we heard a faint muffled thud through the wall to one side.

'What's that noise?'

I froze, my heart pounding.

'Er . . . just the water pipes,' I covered quickly; the first thing to come to mind. 'They rattle and knock sometimes when my mother is emptying the kitchen sink, or when someone's had a bath.'

Gessner's eyes fixed on the wall to our side, listening intently. My breath felt trapped, my heart's pounding now in my eardrums, getting an image again of my father and Tobias just the other side of that wall: eyes wider now, perhaps my father's hand over Tobias's mouth, fearful of him making any more noise. Obviously one of them had bumped against something.

At length a faint exhalation, as if Gessner too had been holding his breath as he listened, then he turned to make his way back up.

I was still nervous as he closed the cellar door, hoping he didn't pay too much attention to the bookcase to one side: a little higher than the door with a potted plant on the top, a small latch behind a top-shelf book would release it to swing open, revealing the steps beyond. A small storage area, one side had wine racks, the back wall stacked high with boxes of books.

My father had become fascinated by a film in which a bookcase swung open to reveal a secret room, and when he planned to use half of the large coal store as a wine cellar and stockroom, he'd included his own makeshift version. The plant pot above had its base glued down, so moved with the bookcase.

'Ah, someone appears to appreciate their books,' Gessner said.

My heart was in my mouth again as Gessner reached out towards the bookshelf, but he chose one from the second row down, Hermann Broch's *Die Schlafwandler*, flicking through its pages absently.

'My father is a bookbinder. So we often get much of the overspill here.' I was sure that Gessner would have noticed one wall in the lounge taken up with shelves full of books, so hopefully this addition in the hallway wouldn't seem strange.

Gessner nodded curtly, replaced the book and started

back down the hallway. He turned to me by the front door.

'Please get your uncle to send ticket stubs of his train journey with your brother, so that I have final proof. I will return in four or five days for those. Good day to you.'

With a final curt nod, Gessner headed away. After closing the front door, I stayed for a moment by it with my eyes closed, catching my breath as my hammering nerves started to settle.

50

Richmond, Surrey, October 1941

Calder Gibson sat in his favourite pub, The Cricketers, only a half-mile from his Richmond home, as he finished the last of his pint of ale and looked towards the green opposite. Mid autumn, now there were only a few stragglers, some walking dogs, some strollers, a lone cyclist; whereas in the summer there would be a cricket game in full flow and the fringes of the green teeming with people playing ball, walking, running or cycling, war on or not.

His view was partially blocked as a long black Humber Pullman stopped in front. He got up sharply; the Prime Minister wasn't someone you kept waiting. In the front passenger seat an armed adjutant in khaki uniform sat by a similarly dressed and armed chauffeur. Winston Churchill sat in the back.

Calder Gibson slid into the back alongside him. One of two army outriders on Norton motorbikes fifty yards ahead, Sten guns strapped around their backs, waved the all-clear and they started moving. Calder didn't need to look back to know that two similar outriders were fifty yards behind them and another single rider a hundred yards ahead: the 'early warning' lookout. It was his department's job to know every detail of the Prime Minister's security arrangements.

'How is His Majesty?' Calder inquired. It had been arranged that Churchill would pick him up in Richmond on his way back into London from Windsor Castle, where the King and Queen often spent the weekend.

'As well as can be expected, under the circumstances.' Churchill tapped his cigar. It wasn't lit; he never smoked while he had close company in his car, it was more of a prop, a comforter. 'Now that we face uncertain times again.'

Calder nodded knowingly. Their last conversation about the monarch had been in the glory days after the Battle of Britain, Churchill talking about how gratified he was to have been able to sway King George from a lukewarm Hitler appeaser, like his predecessor Edward VIII, to a full-blown anti-Hitler advocate. But now with Hitler gaining such strength in Europe, the tide of the war was turning again. Unless they could get Hitler stretched more on the Russian front.

'Hastings Ismay thinks we might have done enough,' Churchill told him. 'That the German army is already too far entrenched, and that Stalin, having suffered such heavy losses, would pursue a continuing war in any case, even if the Wehrmacht withdrew. But Bridges disagrees, feels we need five or six weeks more, possibly even two months, to get the German army to take Moscow, or even beyond – before Hitler is fully committed and can't go back.' Churchill looked at Calder directly. 'Thus, our private meeting now. I didn't want to get you in the middle of that. You obviously have your own thoughts on how much more your own people can safely accomplish. I wanted to avoid a possible three-way discord. That would have headed nowhere.'

'I doubt my people could last two more months. In fact, everything almost came to a head recently.' Calder talked about the problems faced by Edith Creutzen and Hansel, and their network falling apart after the interrogation of Timo Kretzler. 'As a result, the last session had to run blind, without any instructions, and it will take a few more weeks for the network to regroup safely.'

'And in the interim?'

Calder read Churchill's tone. Things couldn't be left to chance in guiding Hitler at such a crucial juncture, and Churchill fully expected him to have made contingency plans.

'The only option until the network regroups has been to use Hansel's network to pass messages.'

Churchill raised a brow. '*What?* Grey Wolf?'

'Yes.' Grey Wolf was their code name for a group of high-ranking generals and Abwehr officers, including Wilhelm Canaris, Hans Oster and Karl Sack, who were secretly opposed to Hitler. They preferred a singular code name, so if one of their number was ever uncovered, the Nazis would think they'd caught Grey Wolf, his days numbered. As Calder observed Churchill's troubled countenance he added, 'If there was any other feasible option, I'd have taken it.'

'But surely the risks of continuing that way are too great?'

'Since Hansel got involved with Creutzen, we've risked losing both assets for some while. But I doubt it would reach the upper echelons of Grey Wolf – unless Hansel was captured and talked. Another good reason for his involvement to end at the same time as Edith Creutzen's.'

Calder held out a hand. 'And it is only for a matter of a few more weeks.'

'I suppose.' Churchill looked out absently for a moment at trees flashing past, the last of Surrey's greenery starting to give way to the outskirts of London. 'But tell me more about how you see this continuing to work with Grey Wolf and Hansel.' With a decision of this magnitude, one of the toughest he'd yet had to make over the whole saga, he needed to be doubly sure.

51

I didn't need the regular radio broadcasts to let me know the progress on the Russian front; I knew from what I'd seen in the speculum these past two months. And, as Stefan had pointed out, those broadcasts were strictly controlled and always painted a positive or hopeful picture, so as to boost morale. '*We are making strong progress on the Russian front, and while some advances are taking longer than initially planned, final victory on all fronts is assured.*'

But the background comments from generals and senior Abwehr figures that Stefan was privy to were more sceptical, especially in the past few weeks as the Russian winter bit deeper and Reich troop movements had got bogged down. Then the queries from Hitler himself, passed directly to Stefan or his close advisers, or clear from the different tone of his questions related through Stefan, '*You said last time that you foresaw higher chances of success on the southwestern flanks of Moscow – but now we find ourselves held up there for several weeks. What do you see now?*'

The last few sessions had been with only Stefan present, so I'd had the benefit of his guidance, but the change in tone of Hitler's questions began to concern me.

'We're living on borrowed time, aren't we?' I remarked to Stefan after the last session.

'We always have been.'

'Perhaps.' I shook my head. 'But now it seems he might have caught on that I've misled him.'

'I don't think it's reached that stage. More a question that you might have been mistaken in some areas – or that other developments have changed the direction of what you foresaw. That's why we've answered as we have the last two sessions.'

I nodded. It had been a daunting tightrope to walk. Part guided from London, part from our own intuition of what might be acceptable to the Führer given known facts, and the best path steered to fit in with past predictions.

'At least you've always maintained that the battle for Moscow would be long and hard fought,' Stefan said. 'So many of these minor setbacks could be viewed through that lens. And, of course, you've always maintained the forecast that in the end the Reich would be victorious.'

'The main prize the Führer is no doubt clinging to,' I ventured hollowly. But how long before he realized that victory was slipping from his grasp? How long before I fell from that tightrope?

'You're right to be anxious that if the Führer ever uncovered he was being purposely misled – that would be the end of it. But you're allowed to make a few mistakes.'

'Some might argue that a fortune teller who makes mistakes is hardly any use at all.' I smiled lopsidedly. 'And look what happened with Erik. He didn't make any mistakes, and Hitler still got rid of him.'

'The main mistake Erik Hanussen made was being Jewish. You don't have that same problem.'

But in the uncomfortable silence that followed, it struck

me as simply an offhand comment to dismiss the topic. We both knew that often the Führer had people killed on just a whim or a vague suspicion. Stefan's uncle had suffered the same fate, and now that portent was possibly close for both of us, we didn't want to face it.

I could see that something else was on Stefan's mind. 'What is it?'

'This past session message. It's the last one I can handle directly.'

We'd discussed before that Stefan using his own network contacts for guidance was only short term, the risks of him continuing to do so too great.

'So, what now?'

I listened as he laid out his plans: my old contacts from Paris, Teresa and Xavier, involved more as contacts; bookbinding used as the main cover . . . *Bookbinding?*

I should have guessed then where he was headed, but still I looked at him incredulously as he came around to it, my breath slightly gone as I confirmed, 'My *father*?'

I hadn't been shocked by any other part of the plan. All of that made sense, the elements slotting neatly into place: Xavier would deliver books to my father's workplace for final binding – the messages folded over and slipped into the spine, its end then sealed with glue. I'd then slit that end-piece again, take out the message, and replace it with my return message two days later, gluing that end section back.

My return to my father would be during a family visit, as would my handover of fresh messages, so nothing would seem untoward.

Stefan felt it likely that I was now being followed, fearing that at some stage he would be too – thus his reluctance to continue running messages directly. Whereas Xavier, now that we'd had access to Ziegler's past file notes, wasn't a suspect, nor had Colmar Bücher, Teresa and Xavier's bookshop at any time been under surveillance.

Xavier had a roster of bookbinders he'd regularly visit. He'd do basic gluing, stitching and mending, but for more detailed work or elaborate covers, he'd visit the bookbinders on his list. My father's establishment would be just one of five or six Xavier would visit on any given day, and the message would be sealed within the book's spine in any case. The chances of discovery were slim.

All the component parts of Stefan's plan slotted neatly together. Except that my father had throughout been a supporter of Hitler. How on earth was I going to talk him into being a betrayer, or even broach the subject?

'I'm not sure I should answer that,' my father said uncertainly.

'Why not?'

'Well, with you working so close to the Führer with Stefan.'

'I wouldn't have asked the question if I, or indeed many others, didn't feel the same.' Stefan had suggested I start with a tame question, '*Have your views about Hitler changed over the past two years? Do you harbour any doubts?*'

My father raised a brow, said nothing. Then he looked blankly ahead at the view, his uncertainty worming deeper.

I'd wanted this to be private, so we'd gone to the nearest park from his home: a hundred-metre-square patch of green with some children's swings and a see-saw in one corner. A shallow blanket of snow was still on the ground from overnight, hadn't yet melted. But this was nothing to the sixty-centimetres-deep covering that German troops were trudging through on the surrounds of Moscow.

'*What?* You don't think it's possible to work closely with the Führer, yet still hold strong doubts about him?' I could see the cogs working in his mind, but still some clinging uncertainty. I needed something to jar him. 'Surely even you saw that before it was brought personally to our door with the brutal, unfair policies against Tobias.'

I saw my father flinch; perhaps too hard a jar. A step too far.

He looked at me levelly. 'Of course I saw it. But what good would saying anything do? It would just make matters worse.'

A tame admission, but a start. The door was beginning to open. I nudged against it harder. 'And look how you've seen many of your favourite authors disappear these past years: Kafka, Hermann Hesse, Proust, Remarque . . .'

'Zweig, Ossietzky, Werfel, Thomas Mann, Orwell,' my father continued wistfully. He shook his head. 'One of the publishers I worked closely with, Isaac Keller, was Jewish, and was forced to close a year ago. Then just two months ago, I heard that he and his wife and young family had been sent to Dachau, never to be heard from again.' He looked at me harrowingly. 'Yet I felt I could never mention any of that at home. Not to your mother or to you.'

I nodded sombrely. I wondered how many in Germany felt the same way now. Disagreed with or felt aggrieved at Nazi policies, but daren't say anything for fear of appearing to sway from the 'party line'. Stray too far and you'd be labelled a dissident and would also disappear.

'Did you know that Erik Hanussen was Jewish?'

'Yes, I did,' he said softly.

'I never forgave Hitler for killing Erik, in the same way that I hate him for his policies now against Tobias. That's part of the reason why I returned to Berlin. To get my revenge.'

'*Revenge?*'

A sharp, disbelieving tone, and again I wondered whether I'd gone too far, too quickly. It was one thing to disagree with Hitler's policies, quite another to be an active traitor – even though I'd used the stepping-stones of *I'll never forgive* and *I hate him* in between.

'I'm not sure it would have been enough for Erik's sake alone, even though we were close . . . *very* close.' The emphasis perhaps gave my father some warning, but still his eyes widened as I finished. 'But being little Louise's father gave it a whole different perspective. For the father she'd lost, killed by Hitler, revenge seemed suddenly worthwhile.'

My father stammered, 'But . . . but I thought Christof was Louise's father.'

'That's what was put on the birth certificate. Because, of course, Hitler's purge isn't just against Jews, but half-Jews, *Mischlinge* like Louise.'

My father appeared totally lost, looked at me incredulously for a moment before staring blankly ahead at the snow-covered playing field. And I felt terribly guilty in that moment. Already he was burdened with Tobias's survival, ensuring he was hidden away every time someone came to the house; now I'd added the crushing weight that little Louise was also in danger. But I'd been juggling with the other guilt for some while – that having already shared Louise's true paternity with my best friend, Teresa, and my lover, Stefan, I should have also told my parents.

And while my father was still shell-shocked, in a half-stupor, I told him the rest: my invitation to Berlin from the Führer through Gustav Strehl. SOE approaching me through the Resistance in Paris. The network with book-shops and café liaisons to pass messages. Stefan finding out and his later involvement.

My father's expression ranged from incredulity to numb, resigned acceptance. He shook his head as I finished.

'You're either very brave or very foolish.'

'Probably a bit of both.'

He nodded slowly, some residual pieces also seeming to fall into place. 'And that was what was behind that earlier blackmail attempt?'

'Yes.'

He grimaced tautly. 'I must admit, something about that earlier love-triangle confrontation didn't sit fully right with me.'

I said nothing, chewed at my lip, my earlier concern resurging that a connection with Bittner might be made from the newspaper reports of her body being found.

Stagnant silence between us for a moment, our breath showing on the cold air as we contemplated the empty park.

With a fresh exhalation he commented, 'At the outset, before you suggested we go somewhere private for our discussion, you said you had a favour to ask?'

'Yes, and I'd perfectly understand if you felt you couldn't help.' I told my father the rest about the network falling apart temporarily, and Stefan's suggestion to get messages passed through his bookbinding business. 'A book passed during a family visit, nothing would seem untoward.'

'I can see the perfect sense in the plan,' my father said at length, sighing. 'But I'm not sure I'd feel comfortable with this . . .' He stumbled to find the right word, or perhaps feared it might come across as an accusation. 'This *betrayal*.'

I nodded slowly, looked across at him. I could see that this was a difficult line for him, a loyal citizen for most of his life, to cross. 'You shouldn't look upon it as a betrayal of the German people. Many feel that Hitler has already betrayed the German population with this war and his policies. They feel aggrieved at his persecution of Jews and innocents like Tobias – but, like you, are afraid to say anything. Let alone take a stand against him.' I held a hand out. 'Many of Stefan's contacts are indeed high-ranking Reich officers, loyal to Germany their entire lives. They would not take these actions now if they thought it was not for the good of Germany.'

'I . . . I didn't realize.'

Perhaps, as I had initially, he thought all Reich officers were in accord. I could see his resolve weakening. One last push. 'And your help now would only be for a matter of a few weeks – until the network was back in place.'

My father stared ahead again for a long moment, as if trying to read messages on the blank page of the whited-out grass merging into the pale skyline above.

'OK, I'll do it. I'll help,' he said with a final, resigned sigh. Then gave a pained, crooked smile. 'Though God knows how I'm going to explain all of this to your mother.'

'Are you sure?' I said, mirroring his smile meekly. 'I don't want you doing this purely because you feel some indebtedness to me, or believe you have no choice.'

'If I was just thinking of myself, it still wouldn't sit right.' My father looked at me steadily. 'But when I think of Tobias and what Nazi policies have brought to bear on him, that shadow of death constantly hanging over him, it does.'

I nodded sombrely. 'I understand.' My father's eyes were heavy, dark half-circles below. Even just the last few weeks of hiding in the basement with Tobias every time someone came to the door had taken their toll, but we both knew that couldn't continue indefinitely. His gaze fixed for a moment on a young boy who'd just come into the park playing with his mother at the far end.

'Also, something else. You recall the author A. P. Schulz?'

'Yes, of course. One of my favourites as a child.'

'Well, he was widely known as a Lutheran, but a select few people in the trade, including myself, knew that he was originally Jewish. There was in fact an on–off history of antisemitism in Germany and Schulz saw the writing on the wall and changed his religion early. But Hitler appointed a special unit to look into the background of "hidden Jews" and he was later sent to a death camp.'

'I had no idea.'

'Well, I didn't want to unnecessarily spoil childhood

memories.' He took a new breath. 'But in the same way that for you it feels right doing this for Hanussen and Louise, I feel the same about Tobias and writers such as A. P. Schulz.' My father grimaced awkwardly. 'My own small contribution.'

52

I'd shared with Stefan before that at times my clairvoyance was a curse, that while it gave me a glimpse of the future, at the same time I'd see things I'd rather not see. This was particularly true with the horrific images of the Russian battlefront, on which most of the past few sessions had focused. But when those images related to my family or me personally, a defensive mechanism would often blot them out. Though sometimes they broke through, and when Stefan told me that the Führer had requested another personal session at the Vorbunker, a shiver ran through me.

'I . . . I fear this might be the one.' I closed my eyes fleetingly in penance. 'I don't think we're going to make it out.'

Stefan looked at me steadily for a moment, took in that this wasn't just mild agitation. 'I know that the Vorbunker is one of your least favourite places for meetings, and I appreciate too that the Führer's questions have become more pointed and edgy the past two sessions – but I still think you're overthinking, over-worrying. I don't think he openly suspects anything.'

'But now with German troops bogged down in a Russian winter, he might partly blame me for giving the wrong advice.'

'Not exactly *wrong*. The alternative battlefronts you steered him towards with your predictions were mostly successful. The Führer can't be sure that if he'd attacked Moscow earlier, he'd have had any more success than now. And the Russian winter would have hit in any case, whichever fronts were advanced upon.' Stefan gestured. 'Besides, now that the troops are bogged down, he needs your insight more than ever. He can't risk getting rid of you at such a delicate juncture.'

I met Stefan's steady gaze, unsure if he was being straight and forthright or just trying to placate me, ease my concerns.

'I saw something in the speculum,' I said flatly. 'And I don't think I should ignore it.'

'What did you see?' The first twinge of concern from Stefan.

I'd looked into the speculum to gain some foresight on this new involvement of my father and Xavier. I knew that Xavier was particularly keen to be more active, but I still had reservations whether I was doing the right thing involving my father and a friend like this. But when I looked into the speculum, other images quickly superimposed themselves.

'Much the same as I've seen before: broken and bloodied bodies stretching into the distance. But this time I could see that they were German soldiers, and Hitler was to one side, angry, pointing: "*You see. This is what you have caused!*" '

Stefan sank into thought, his expression heavier. We spent half our time together dealing with my predictions and their implications; he knew they should be given due consideration.

'I daresay that could be a glimpse of something further

on. But from what I read in Hitler's current mood, I don't see it happening now.'

'To me, this seemed to be something happening imminently. Not sometime in the future.'

Stefan nodded his acceptance, his concern worming deeper; now torn between what he felt and my worrying prediction. And I was the same, the reverse side of that coin.

The short time before the next session did little to change our respective uneasy thoughts. And so, two days later, with heavy steps and equally heavy hearts, we made our way down the five flights of stairs to Hitler's Vorbunker, uncertain whether we would make our way out again.

'You explained two sessions ago that you saw many women and children digging.' Hitler looked at me steadily. Stefan had started with a few questions clarifying past comments about troop movements on the approaches to Moscow, then the Führer had taken over.

'Yes, but I couldn't see clearly their purpose in digging like that.' Truth was, some images following had shown the same women and children, along with some soldiers, lying inert and dead in ditches. So I feared they'd been forced to dig their own graves, as I'd heard had happened in many instances in Poland and other eastern front territories, particularly with Jews, Gypsies and so-called subversives – but didn't want to openly say it, betray that I knew something the Nazis were unwilling to admit.

'Well, as we advanced closer upon Moscow, our fine troops discovered what they were up to.' Hitler's intense stare now had a faint glimmer to it. 'The Red Army had dug numerous trenches and also built some makeshift wooden barriers to try and impede our advance.'

'I see, yes. That would correlate with what I saw.'

'You have to admire that level of dedication. But of no matter, we prevailed in the end.' His mouth took a slight downturn at one corner; a condescending grimace. 'And partly thanks to your prediction, our troops questioned what they might be doing, and so came around those trenches and barriers in a pincer movement.'

'I . . . I'm glad my prediction helped.' I noticed Stefan's eyes on me keenly. It was our job to impede German troop advances, not aid them. My throat felt suddenly tight. I didn't need to ask what happened to those women and children or the Russian soldiers behind the trenches and barricades. In the speculum, I'd seen their bodies lining the very same ditches.

'You were also correct in seeing large flows of water – although initially it wasn't clear either what this meant.' Hitler took a fresh breath. 'Red Army troops opened up or partly destroyed several reservoirs in and around Moscow, and those artificial floods impeded our crossing of the Volga.'

I simply nodded. Hitler didn't usually offer such unconditional praise. I sensed something else was coming.

The Führer's expression darkened, became sterner. 'But that hasn't been the case with a number of your other predictions.'

I met the Führer's intense stare calmly, without strong reaction or reproach, as he ranted about German troops getting bogged down in a severe Russian winter, with snowfall heavier than in many recent years and their lack of winter clothing and blocked supply lines frustrating their advance. Hitler's face was a mask of fury as he finished.

'. . . As a result, we now face the ignominy of Red Army troops regaining some positions on the Kalinin front.'

'I always said that the battle for Moscow would be difficult, hard fought,' I asserted.

'In that regard, you have been painfully correct,' he said sharply. His expression was stormy, volatile. 'Have you any idea of the losses we have incurred?'

And suddenly the image was before me again: masses of prone, bloodied bodies stretching into the distance, with Hitler to one side pointing accusingly, '*See what you have done.*'

'There have been heavy losses too on the Russian side,' I offered. 'All of which I also forecast – the losses heavy for *both* armies.'

Hitler waved an arm to one side, as if that was hardly relevant. 'Regardless, I would be foolhardy not to question some of the things you have foreseen – in particular guiding me towards delaying the advance on Moscow, so that now we see our fine troops bogged down in a Russian winter.' His voice rose as he slapped one hand against his desk. 'An impossible dilemma that would have been avoided if we'd gone in earlier!'

With the sudden about-turn, I was reminded of my recent prediction: *This would be our last visit with the Führer, we weren't going to make it out.* As we'd made our way down to the Vorbunker we'd passed some small cells on the final corridor towards Hitler's office. Is that where Stefan and I would now be held before being executed? Stefan, sitting to one side, looked uneasy, uncertain, and I felt a sudden pang as I thought of Louise and Tobias. I hadn't even had a chance to say goodbye or give any warning that they might not see me again. Would they and my parents also now be taken? My heart felt heavy, *crushed.* I swallowed, started to stutter out a defence.

'With all due respect, Mein Führer, you yourself preferred a delayed attack on Moscow, seeing assaults first on resources and industry in the Caucasus and Kharkov as more advantageous.' His anger sparking that I had the temerity to challenge or partly blame him, I followed on quickly with a compliment before it spilled over. 'And from what I foresaw, that decision was correct. The same heavy snowfalls would have been faced also in those industrial regions, or indeed Leningrad. And so a heavy blow to Russian resources would not have been effected at a vital time.'

Hitler nodded slowly as he eased out a tired breath, looked aslant for a moment before his eyes rested back on me.

'And what advice do you have now? Given the drastic situation faced in Moscow, some of my commanders have ordered troop withdrawals without my permission. Do I leave those commanders in place or dismiss them and take control myself?'

I sensed that he'd already half made up his mind, but I still looked for a moment into the speculum to give it due credence.

'I see that following your heart in this instance would be the right decision. And if you feel some commanders have betrayed you and gone against your orders, you should take personal control.'

Hitler's eyes flickered briefly. 'From what you see, you are certain this is the right way forward?'

'Yes, I . . . I am.' More hesitant now. From his tone, it was almost as if he was testing that this wasn't another possibly errant foresight. Or perhaps, as in some past sessions, it was a trick question? His commanders hadn't ordered withdrawals at all, and this was a final test.

The Führer's eyes settled on me more heavily, his gaze penetrating. 'You stand also by your past predictions? Maintain they are correct?'

And this now had an ominous ring to it. As if the Führer had already reached a decision about me, but wanted a final admission before acting on it.

My mouth felt suddenly dry, my breath laboured. Buried deep below Berlin's pavements, the Vorbunker always felt hot, even in the depths of winter – the air-conditioning struggling to bring fresh air to such depths – but now it felt stifling. The heat of the room and Hitler's penetrating stare seemed to be pressing in on me. We weren't going to make it out! But for whatever reason, reckless or simply misguided, I felt I had to remain steadfast.

'Yes, I do,' I said firmly, then sweetened this with another compliment. 'As I'm sure you do also with your own brave and bold decisions, Mein Führer.'

He continued to contemplate me steadily. Had I done enough? Or would my own most recent predictions come true?

53

It wasn't until the third excursion from Colmar Bücher that Xavier Achard sensed he was being followed.

Xavier felt good being back at the forefront. While he was aware of the vital importance of the message network that he and Teresa had been part of since arriving in Berlin, being just in the background at the bookshop had never sat that comfortably with him. Even though he understood the reasons: his initial lack of German and the fact that, given his recent failed attempt on the Führer in Paris, he should be keeping a low profile in any case.

He'd enjoyed stepping in briefly when Gregor Lutz had been let down at the last minute, and was glad to be called upon again now.

The first sign of trouble was seeing a black Mercedes 320 parked two hundred metres from Colmar Bücher when he went past on his bicycle. Always the same routine for his runs: he'd have a large rucksack on his back for all his deliveries and pick-ups. Today's were three bookbinders, two other bookshops and four private addresses. But among that list was Lichten Buchbinder, Edith's father's establishment, and one of the private addresses was where the radio transmission would be sent using the coded message in the book he was picking up from Lukas. So he was particularly cautious today.

Xavier thought he saw the black Mercedes 320 again

when he was halfway through his runs for the day, just after his second private-address delivery, but it was a common make of car, so could be just a coincidence. He made a note of the registration number this time.

He didn't see the Mercedes again for the next hour, a bookshop and private-address delivery on the west side of Marzhan. Next on his list was Lichten Buchbinder.

He handled reverently the book that Lukas Creutzen gave to him. A 110-year-old edition of Adelbert von Chamisso's *Peter Schlemihl.*

'My, you've done a fine job with this,' Xavier remarked. 'It was in tatters when the customer brought it to us. The front cover half off and many of the pages loose and falling out.'

'Yes, I was pleased with how it turned out.' Lukas smiled amiably. 'The cover in particular required a delicate touch to bring the original embossing to its former glory. So I handled this one personally.'

Only the second time he'd met Lukas Creutzen, they'd had a brief and pleasant exchange the first time too. Partly for the benefit of anyone listening in, but Xavier anyway thought it would be odd if they just had silent meetings. Their brief discourse lent assurance that they both knew and were comfortable with what was happening.

Xavier tucked *Peter Schlemihl* into his rucksack, bade Lukas Creutzen a pleasant day and headed out to his bicycle.

But a hundred metres from Lichten Buchbinder, his pedalling paused. The same black Mercedes 320 was parked at the kerb. No mistaking it this time, he recognized the number plate straightaway. And had he been seen leaving Lichten Buchbinder? He picked up a steady cycling pace again as if he hadn't noticed anything – but he was aware of the Mercedes pulling out behind him.

His nerves tightened. His next port of call was meant to be the transmission location, but he couldn't risk it while being followed, so he changed the next intended location to the last private-address drop-off on his roster.

But he should try and lose the Mercedes meanwhile, and put on an extra spurt to his pedalling. The Mercedes kept pace for a while a few hundred metres behind, then sped up and drifted past him. But he saw it pull in six hundred metres ahead, perhaps the driver thinking he'd be out of sight and no doubt would pull out again when he passed.

Xavier took the next right turn a hundred metres ahead, pedalling fast to hopefully get out of sight before the Mercedes driver realized what had happened and doubled back.

Then he saw an alleyway ahead – too narrow to take a car – and swung into it, his legs pumping.

And suddenly it felt as if he was back in Paris again, pedalling frantically to get away from the SS and Führerbegleitkommando, desperately trying to catch Hitler's would-be assassin.

Another alleyway to the right. He took it, swinging in sharply. At the next major road – no sign of the black Mercedes in either direction – he again sought the next alleyway turn-off.

Despite the fear of being caught – or perhaps because of it – Xavier felt a tremendous adrenaline rush, felt suddenly *alive*. As if this was where he was always meant to be, at the forefront of Resistance actions. Xavier took alleyways for most of the way to the next customer drop-off, then again looked keenly each way as he dismounted from his bike. No black Mercedes in sight.

Heading away minutes later, he dog-legged through alleyways again wherever possible, and took a longer, harder look around as he finally approached the transmission location – a second-floor apartment in a run-down building in Hellersdorf.

Xavier was still out of breath from the frantic cycling, the burly early thirties cloth-capped man who opened the door asking him if he was OK.

'Yes, fine. Bit of a rush getting here, that's all.' He handed over *Peter Schlemihl* from his rucksack and the man peered past him briefly.

'And you made sure you weren't followed?'

'Yes. Checked a kilometre or so back and again as I approached.' Xavier didn't see any point in mentioning that he might have been seen leaving Lichten Buchbinder. He'd lost the black Mercedes long ago.

Kurt Schneider was reminded as he went back through Klaus Ziegler's file on the case: all too convenient.

Ingrid Bittner starts making uncomfortable noises about Edith Creutzen, and next thing she's killed. Her boyfriend Carl Voltner is then the only person remaining who might know the truth, and suddenly he's gone too, along with Ziegler, who was hot on the heels of a vital message-sending network.

No other links remaining. All leads dead. *Too convenient.*

Schneider sighed as he looked back at the transcript of Ziegler's final interrogation with Timo Kretzler . . .

'And was it Carl Voltner who gave you the book that day to take to the transmission location?'

'Ye . . . es. We met that day at Café Holbein on Leipziger Strasse . . . and ww . . . we exchanged books.'

Schneider pondered again the main sea change from bookshop to café meetings. That appeared to have come shortly after Ziegler had followed suspect Felix Engelmann from a bookshop on Nürnberger Strasse. Engelmann had since gone to ground, hadn't reappeared, and the bookshop, Nürnberger Buchhandlung, was now closed. But despite bookshops no longer being used, books were still the main link for exchanges.

Something that had struck a chord with him when he'd heard from Gustav Strehl that Edith Creutzen had several boxes of books sent from Paris, then seen for himself the large collection on her shelves.

But, surely, if Creutzen was somehow involved, she might have felt uncomfortable diving in at the deep end, having bookshop rendezvous with people she'd never met before. She might wish for at least one familiar contact.

He started searching for bookshops that had opened in Berlin about the time of Edith Creutzen's arrival. Only two names came up: Colmar Bücher and Strasserism Bücher. He quickly discounted the latter. Strasserism Bücher was mainly a Reich-party propaganda bookshop. While that might be an ideal cover to deflect suspicion, they were strictly run by Reich-appointed staff. It wouldn't be an option.

Whereas Colmar Bücher with its new owners, Odette and Luc Chastain, was the ideal cover for someone who spoke German and French equally, or whose German might have a strong French inflection.

Schneider leafed further through the file, until he came to the name of the Gestapo officer who'd taken over from Ziegler – Nikolaus Strohm. Schneider tapped on the page thoughtfully.

'This is the café where the main suspect in this message-sending network, SS-Unterscharführer Carl Voltner, had his rendezvous with Timo Kretzler,' Schneider said to Strohm when they met two days later. 'Not long before Kretzler's interrogation and the unfortunate demise of your predecessor, Klaus Ziegler.'

'Yes, I realize.' Strohm smiled primly. 'I know that many officers might not pay attention to the finer details of the cases they take over. I do.'

'Very good.' Schneider nodded curtly.

Strohm was young, no more than twenty-six, medium height but painfully thin, with white-blond hair cropped so tight that in some lights he looked bald. Schneider had decided against meeting Strohm in his favourite Hotel Adlon café, its grandeur and orchestra possibly too distracting. Meeting at Café Holbein was more functional, gave a starting point to their conversation.

'But there are elements of what is recorded on file that I don't feel entirely comfortable with.' As Schneider explained his suspicions, Strohm nodded at intervals, sipped at his coffee. A more thoughtful countenance as he finished. Neither accepting nor dismissing Schneider's doubts. Playing Devil's advocate.

'Are you saying all of this perhaps to defend the honour of a fellow SS member?' Strohm commented after a moment. 'That you might find Voltner's role in this hard to accept?'

'Not at all.' Schneider smiled disarmingly, held a hand out. 'If that was the case, I'd find it hard to harbour any suspicions about Stefan Hansel, also a fellow SS officer.'

'Carl Voltner wasn't a friend or close associate of yours?'

'No. Nothing of the sort,' Schneider said firmly, suddenly wary. Strohm was far sharper than his young age might indicate. Strohm's suggestion, if indeed Voltner was guilty, could hint that he himself was implicated as well. 'A passing acquaintance at best – no more or less than SS officer Stefan Hansel.'

A slower, accepting nod from Strohm. 'OK. Tell me more.'

Strohm listened carefully as Schneider continued with his suspicions and possible leads, taking out a pad halfway through and making some notes.

'Colmar Bücher?' Strohm queried as Schneider finished.

'Yes.' Schneider gestured. 'Might be nothing. But in the absence of any other leads, might be worth following up.'

Four days later, Nikolaus Strohm phoned him with his initial findings.

'Only one person appeared to be going on regular excursions from Colmar Bücher: Luc Chastain. I followed him the past few days, but nothing untoward.' Strohm drew a breath on the other end of the line. 'Until yesterday, that is.'

'What happened?'

'Chastain's routine was deliveries and pick-ups by bicycle to various bookbinders, other bookshops and some private customers.'

'Could one of those private customers perhaps have been a transmission location?'

'No. I don't think so. They were mostly established residences in and around Berlin. At one, a woman and child came to the door, and others I checked out afterwards. Nothing.'

'So what changed yesterday?' Schneider prompted.

'After his fifth or sixth call, he started pedalling with more purpose. I wasn't sure if he'd spotted me, but I went ahead of him and pulled in out of sight, just in case. But he must have taken a turn-off in between. And by the time I'd tracked back, I could no longer see him. Then I noticed a side street halfway down. He must have taken that and cut through.'

'Has he done that before?'

'Only once. But that time, I caught up with him again at the next intersection. This time, there was no sign of him. So he must have zig-zagged through quite determinedly – perhaps on purpose to lose me. Although I can't be a hundred per cent sure.'

'Of course.' Schneider sighed. 'But the end result is that you lost sight of him – so he could have visited a transmission location on one of his next calls.'

'Yes, he could have.'

Schneider's shoulders slumped. It had been a long shot from the outset. But one thing nagged at the back of his mind: what had made Luc Chastain more watchful or put on a sudden spurt at that point?

'What was the last place that Chastain called at before you lost him?'

Flicking of paper on the other end of the line as Strohm checked his notes.

'A workshop in north-east Berlin. Lichten Buchbinder.'

54

By the time Ingrid Bittner's flatmate, Katrin Seidel, was given leave from her military nursing duties on the eastern front, Inspector Hans Diestler had half forgotten about the case.

He had a body, in fact *two* bodies, matching bullet calibres, and motive. To him, the case was firmly closed, despite SS-Obersturmbannführer Kurt Schneider trying to prise at its edges. And besides, he'd had a slew of other files meanwhile land on his desk, was too busy to bother with pursuing an already closed case based on just vague suspicions.

So when, as the doubts Schneider had raised began to nag at him, he went to see Katrin Seidel at the small flat she'd shared with Bittner, he wasn't expecting much. She hadn't even been there when Bittner disappeared, and the building porter had already let Diestler into the flat to look around. Some old love letters to Bittner from her boyfriend, Carl Voltner – obviously no longer necessary once they were together more steadily – some bills, official correspondence. Nothing exceptional or hinting at what might have led to her demise.

'It came as something of a shock,' Seidel said, 'when I heard about Ingrid's death.' Early thirties and slim, almost gaunt, she twirled uneasily a strand of her light-brown hair.

'And you were already on the Polish front at the time?'

'Yes. I'd been there almost a month by then.'

'Before you left, did she share with you anything she was concerned about? Any problems with her boyfriend, Carl Voltner?' Diestler gestured. 'Or with anyone else for that matter?'

'No, she didn't. Everything seemed OK between them. And no other problems I was aware of.' Seidel shook her head softly, eyes downcast, as if only now fully grasping the reality that her friend and flatmate was gone. 'But then it was some time after I left. So perhaps something came up in the meantime.'

'Yes, a possibility.'

'I suppose you've already checked through her things?' Katrin Seidel pointed towards the chest of drawers to one side.

'Yes.' Ingrid Bittner's clothes had filled the bottom four drawers. Letters and documents had been in the top two.

'And did you also go through Ingrid's diary?'

'*Diary?*'

'Yes. Ingrid made entries regularly. But sometimes, for whatever reason, she'd keep it hidden under the bottom drawer.'

'I see.' Diestler nodded. 'Perhaps when she wished to be more secretive.'

'I daresay.' Seidel flushed slightly. She might have imparted something she wasn't meant to know.

'You do the honours.' Diestler gestured. There might be a special knack to lifting the drawer out.

Katrin Seidel went across and made quick work of it – tilting up the drawer from its runner, then out. She fished inside and lifted out a small burgundy book.

'There you are – Ingrid's diary.' She passed it to Diestler. 'Hopefully, that will be more revealing.'

'Hopefully.' Though Diestler wasn't sure if that was what he wished for. A closed case suddenly reopened to add to the pile on his desk.

'"*I saw Edith Creutzen the other night for the first time in years. I'm sure she's still active with clairvoyancy, but for some reason she's keeping it secret. And I think there's more to her past association with Christof than meets the eye. Something she's not telling me.*"'

Stefan's palm sweated on the receiver as he listened. At the other end of the line Hans Diestler took a fresh breath.

'Then the next entry on the same topic a few weeks later: "*Found out that Edith has a daughter. Her age means she was conceived in Berlin. Another big secret she's hiding, but I'm sure she's not Christof's.*"

'Then ten days later: "*Discovered finally who fathered Edith's daughter. No less than Erik Hanussen! No wonder she ran off suddenly and all the secrecy. But something big like this would surely be worth a lot to her to keep quiet. Harbouring Hanussen's daughter, a half-Jew! Especially with her now working in the Reich Chancellery and close to the Führer.*"'

Stefan clenched a fist as he listened. Obviously, from her birthdate, Bittner had worked out that Louise was Hanussen's rather than Christof's, and now Diestler had the final shreds in his grasp.

'Finally, the last entry, just the day before she died: "*Have confronted Edith over it all already and expect to pick up the money from her tomorrow. All I've told Carl so far is that I've uncovered a big secret about Edith Creutzen that could lead to a windfall. Not sure yet I'll tell him about the whole amount, he might have his hands out too quickly. Probably admit only half – my own little remaining secret!*" '

Stefan exhaled heavily on his end of the line. 'Thanks for informing me. I know that the Führer has insisted on secrecy about his work with Edith Creutzen – but I simply don't know whether this was part of it as well. That he was aware of her past association with Hanussen, beyond simply being his protégée. I need now to speak to Creutzen and the Führer to ascertain all of that.'

'I understand. That's why I informed you first – given the sensitive nature of the situation.' Diestler took a fresh breath. 'But you are aware that this changes the entire nature of the investigation – so I will need to question Creutzen straight after you speak to her and the Führer.'

'Yes, of course.' Stefan's head was boiling. He'd pulled a rabbit out the hat a couple of times before, but there was no escaping this time. Once the secret was out that Edith had a half-Jewish daughter, the rest would quickly unravel: his own complicity in getting rid of Ingrid Bittner, then Voltner and Ziegler, Edith's involvement with the message-sending network. Only one option remaining: *play for time.*

'I'll talk to Creutzen straightaway and get her account, but the Führer is busy in meetings with commanders and chiefs of staff regarding the eastern front – so I'm not due to see him until after midday tomorrow. Can you hold off until then?'

'I . . . I suppose so.'

Stefan read the uncertainty in Diestler's voice. 'Given the sensitive nature of the issue, I wondered if you could also delay sharing anything interdepartmentally until then. If the Führer has been duped by Creutzen withholding information about having Hanussen's child, he won't relish others knowing about it before him.'

'Yes, of course.'

Stefan noted the moment's pause that indicated once again this stepped outside of Diestler's normal protocol. But how many cases came up that were so close to the Führer?

'One other thing that struck me as odd,' Diestler said, 'is that Bittner made no mention in her diary of Carl Voltner passing secret messages.'

Stefan's temples throbbed. Think. *Think!* 'Perhaps that was an entry too far for her. Knowing that if her boyfriend read it, it would mean her death sentence.'

'I suppose.' Diestler's tone one of residual doubt. 'Also, the question that if Voltner knew about Bittner's blackmail of Creutzen, why didn't he mention any of that when I questioned him?'

'Yes, quite a conundrum,' Stefan said, his mouth suddenly dry. He thanked Diestler again for informing him straightaway. 'I'll get back to you soon after midday tomorrow.'

He closed his eyes as he ended the call, his head still throbbing. Twenty-six hours to get himself, Edith and her whole family out of Germany to safety.

55

I saw the surprise on little Louise's face as I crossed the school playground towards her. I'd never before come to see her in the middle of a school day. This was the early break, so she'd been in school less than two hours.

I crouched down so that I was at her height and gently clasped one of her hands. 'An appointment I forgot about, *Liebling*. We have to go now.'

'Where to?'

'The dentist.' I needed to keep to that story for the time being. Only medical appointments would give a good enough reason to take a child out of school halfway through the day. Already I could see Louise's class teacher, Frau Busch – her brown hair tight in a bun and her stern appearance making her look older than her thirty-five years – looking our way, starting towards us. 'Sorry, I forgot to tell you earlier.'

Louise's brow creased. 'But I went to the dentist only four months ago.'

'I know. But this is only a check-up – nothing to worry about.'

Frau Busch approached then, heard the last part. I straightened up and smiled tightly towards her.

'A dental appointment I appear to have overlooked. Louise will be back in school first thing tomorrow.'

'Somewhat irregular . . . but I suppose if it can't be

avoided.' She smiled back equally tersely and gave Louise a half-wave as we turned and headed off.

My heart pounded double-time to my step as we went out through the school gates and away. Had Frau Busch suspected anything? Was I already perhaps on a Gestapo or SS watch list for the school to notify them of any unusual activity?

We had the same to go through with Lara at home so that no suspicions were raised. She was directly in the Führer's pay, so would pick up the phone the instant she thought something was wrong.

I was still slightly out of breath from the fast walk as I repeated the same to Lara about Louse's forgotten dental appointment. 'Then she's staying with her grandparents tonight. They'll take her to school tomorrow.'

'I see.'

Lara looked at me blandly, and I wondered whether some suspicion was beginning to brew. First, Stefan had swung into the driveway just over an hour ago and beeped his horn frantically, as if we were late for some Reich Chancellery appointment. We drove off and, after a kilometre, he pulled in and explained the drastic situation. But he seemed to have it all mapped out, as if he knew this was coming and so had pre-planned everything.

'Your parents should leave immediately by train with Tobias and Louise. Train passages can be made only with three border passes. They're strictly checked for any Jews or subversives, but your father is a Swiss national. If he says he's visiting relatives with his family, everything should be fine. Xavier and Teresa will come by to pick you up by car. I'll lead the way, then I'll change into civilian clothes and we'll switch over as we approach the Swiss border – so I can make sure you get through OK before following you.'

'You don't think it's safe for Teresa and Xavier to stay in Berlin?'

'The rest of the network can regroup and continue, but they're too close to you. Also, no point in them staying once you're gone.'

But now I needed to get rid of Lara for when Xavier and Teresa came to pick me up. I took from my pocket the shopping list I'd prepared before leaving for Louise's school and handed it to Lara.

'I wondered if you could meanwhile get these things from the shops for me?'

'Yes . . . yes, of course.'

But it was said uncertainly as Lara studied the list. Three changes in quick succession to the day's normal routine. Were her suspicions worming deeper, or was she just off-kilter from those sudden changes?

'I'll see you later tonight or tomorrow.' I handed Lara twenty Marks from my purse for the shopping. 'I'll already have left with Louise for the dentist and then on to my parents by the time you get back.'

I felt Lara's eyes on me for a moment as I went up the stairs with Louise, then heard some rustling in the kitchen with bags and her wheeling out the shopping trolley. I felt as if I was suddenly back in those first weeks in Berlin: everyone spying on me, ready to report me. *The Creutzen woman is doing some strange, different things today. You asked me to phone you to let you know.*

Finally, Lara's footsteps in the hallway and the front door closing. I eased a sigh of relief. Xavier and Teresa's instructions were to wait eight minutes after they saw Lara leave, then pull in. Lara should be gone just over an hour, more than enough time to pack two suitcases and a dozen treasured books to take – then rearrange the remaining books on the shelves so that the gaps didn't show. Any more than that and Lara would immediately suspect we'd gone for good when she returned.

Louise looked at me curiously as I started packing the first suitcase with some of our things.

'I thought we were just going to the dentist?'

'No, we're not.' Mixture of relief and confusion on her face. My heart felt suddenly heavy. How best to explain the situation to her? Would any of us make it? And if only one group of us did, would I ever see her again? I crouched down, gently braced her shoulders. 'We're going straight to Grandma and Grandpa's. Then we're going on a great adventure.'

56

As the fir trees became taller and denser each side, Lukas Creutzen lightly gripped his granddaughter Louise's arm and pointed through the train window.

'We're going through the Black Forest now. The largest forest in Germany.'

'Do they have bears there?'

'Yes.'

'And wolves?'

'Yes. And wild boars and reindeers.'

Great adventure.

That is what his daughter had told Louise about this trip, to distract from any worry and anxiety, so that is what Lukas now tried to keep to. Besides, Louise had gone straight by train from Paris to Berlin, so hadn't seen much of Germany outside of that city, and this now might be her last chance to see it. He swallowed. Might be the last chance for *all* of them, but he'd kept that fact from his wife. Born and bred German, Elsa had hardly ever left Germany, apart from their trip to Paris to see Edith and Louise. So telling her now that she might never see her beloved Fatherland again would be too much for her to accept, let alone the reasons *why*.

So, he'd stoically avoided any mention of their daughter being a spy and passing messages to the British and Allied forces. Apart from the length and complexity of such an explanation when they were in so great a rush to leave, Elsa might find it hard to accept, and it would only make her more anxious on the journey now, especially when they approached the Swiss border.

'How long will we be staying with your brother in Zurich?' she'd asked halfway through their packing.

'A few weeks, a month at most.' He'd told her simply that he'd got advance news from Stefan that the Orpo had received information – perhaps from neighbours – that they were harbouring Tobias at home and would call imminently to search the house again and possibly arrest them. 'At least until we're sure the coast is clear.'

'You think we'll later still be in trouble, even though Tobias will by then be safely ensconced in Switzerland?'

'I don't know. If he's not at home then, how will they know for sure we were harbouring him earlier and had deceived them?' He'd sighed tiredly, even the exertion of packing and the anxiety of what lay ahead telling on his nerves, leaving him slightly out of breath. 'That's why the delay – for us to be able to find all of that out.'

Playing for time. Then as the days and weeks passed at his brother's house, he'd bit by bit feed her the rest of the reasons they'd left.

Our daughter is a spy, has been for some while, ever since she arrived back in Berlin. And her partner, Stefan, is in with her too. Her betrayal of the Führer so extreme that not only would she be put to death, but very likely her whole family as well. Or, at least, we'd all be sent to a concentration camp . . . which often means the same thing, only slower.

He couldn't tell Elsa all of that now. The only way would be a slow drip, give her time to accept it.

For himself, a Swiss-born national, that acceptance had been far easier. He'd never had an unshakeable attachment to the Fatherland. His love for Elsa had come first, an affection for Germany had been secondary. Most of that in any case had been built on his burgeoning book trade in Germany, but when Hitler had started to ban one by one some of his favourite authors, much of that shine went with it. Then Hitler's ludicrous edicts had reached their tentacles to his own family, *to Tobias.*

No, enough was enough.

At some stage in the journey, with Louise reading a book and the gentle click-clack of the train, he fell asleep. A sudden jolt and shunting, then the opening and slamming of train doors awoke him. Two sets of boots marching down the corridor towards them.

'Papers, please.'

They'd arrived at the last German border post with Switzerland. Lukas fished into his inside pocket for their papers.

Would his excuse of his family visiting relatives in Zurich be accepted? Would their new, false identity papers pass muster? With them travelling with a Down's syndrome child, they'd even had fresh false medical papers prepared – hopefully enough to fool border guards. But might there be an alert out for them already which would override their false papers? Or what if the guard asked where was Louise's mother? 'Why isn't she with her now?'

So many things that could go wrong.

Weak sunlight flickered through the trees above as the young soldier ran, desperately seeking cover from the rifle-fire behind. Fresh-faced, no more than nineteen, there was a light sweat on his brow, despite the intense cold. His fellow platoon colleagues ran alongside him, but with each fresh volley of rifle fire, more of them would fall. Five of them, then three . . . and finally he was the only one left, his heart beating hard, a silent plea on his lips, '*Please, I'm too young to die.*'

I felt my heart clench along with him, and suddenly there were piles of bodies before him, blocking his way. He couldn't run any further. But I couldn't see clearly if they were German or Russian soldiers.

A final rifle crack and he fell. Nothing but deathly silence in the forest, and I could see clearly Hitler now holding an arm out towards the mounds of bodies, his face a mask of fury.

'*See what you have been responsible for. All these lives lost. You think you can escape me, but you can't. I will find you and make you pay for all this . . .*'

I awoke with a jolt, my breath catching in my throat, weak sunlight flickering through the trees as Stefan drove.

It had been important we weren't seen together leaving Berlin, but halfway through rural Germany, there seemed little point keeping to that. Just past Erfurt, I'd moved from Xavier and Teresa's car to Stefan's. Some things I wanted to discuss with Stefan in any case, and we'd agreed that fifty kilometres from the Swiss border, I'd go back with Xavier and Teresa and he'd change into plain clothes. German soldiers were not allowed into Switzerland, so he'd be crossing as a civilian under a false name. Stefan looked over at me now.

'Are you OK?'

'Yes . . . *no*.' I and my family were desperately fleeing for our lives, so I was far from OK. But I knew that's not what Stefan meant. This burden was heavy on his shoulders too. 'Just a bad dream. I'll be all right in a minute.'

Stefan glanced back at me with an understanding grimace.

I rubbed at my forehead. 'You know, one of the last things to hit me when I said goodbye to Louise, Tobias and my parents, was whether I'd ever see them again. Do you think their paperwork will pass muster?'

'I think so. Your father being a Swiss national will help, along with that travel permit I gave them from their local municipal office.'

'You don't think it might be picked up as a forgery?'

'I don't think so. We've had scores of others prepared by my contacts before with no problem.'

We too were carrying similar forged papers, so it hit me we would also face the same life-or-death acid test when we reached the border. I'd tried to get a clear picture of what would happen, but there was nothing. Just a vague, unsettling feeling. But that might have just been nerves. I shook my head.

'What's the use in fortune telling, when I can't foresee the things that matter?'

'As you said before, you're perhaps too close.'

I nodded slowly. 'Or sometimes I just get a very general feeling or impression, but the images aren't clear. Such as the feeling I had that something portentous was imminent – but I misread it as that last meeting with Hitler, because it was only two days away. That we wouldn't make it out.' I gestured. 'But in the end it was this diary of Ingrid's, discovered just after.'

'I don't think anyone could have foreseen that. It came so much out of the blue.'

I smiled tightly back at Stefan. Always trying to make me feel good, more sure of myself. I didn't think I or my family would have been able to get through half of this without his help. He'd also in that time secured a place in my heart like no other man before, and I had the same sudden pang now that I'd had earlier with Louise and my family. We would be approaching the last German checkpoint before the Swiss border crossing in separate cars. Would we ever see each other again?

A thought that was given sudden immediacy when I noticed his jaw tighten as he looked ahead. I saw it then myself: the Schweinfurt checkpoint six hundred metres ahead. We let two other vehicles go first, to take the guards' attention.

'Leave all the talking to Teresa,' Stefan said as we stopped for me to switch back to their car. A lead guard with a machine gun, two others at his side, another behind. 'I'm sure it will be OK.'

But this time it came across as empty reassurance. I knew that if an alert had already been put out from Berlin, we were sunk.

57

London, December, 1941

When Calder Gibson walked into The Red Lion, Winston Churchill had already been there almost an hour.

It was the nearest pub to Downing Street, and Churchill liked to visit it occasionally for impromptu meetings or simply to sit alone making notes. He by no means trusted every civil servant at No. 10, and calling for another secure meeting at the War Cabinet Room might have seemed overkill with just the two of them.

But the rush to put in place the necessary protective measures drove the security services to distraction. Those measures were now evidenced by the policeman and two soldiers with Sten guns by the entrance, whom Calder nodded to as he approached. Another policeman and a soldier guarded the rear of the pub, and inside what appeared to be a mild-mannered accountant sat in one corner doing the *Times* crossword. He was in fact one of the Secret Service's best crack shots, and could put a bullet through someone's eye at thirty paces before they'd got their gun halfway out of their jacket.

Churchill sat in a side alcove twenty feet back from the entrance. A front position would have been too difficult to monitor and guard.

'I took the liberty,' Churchill said as Calder sat down,

and Calder wasn't sure what he meant until the barmaid approached with a pint of Watney's Burton strong ale on a small tray. 'I know it's one of your favourites.'

'Thank you.' Calder raised his beer mug and Churchill did the same with his balloon of brandy – though they stopped short of clinking glasses. Perhaps because there wasn't much to celebrate. More a consolation, drowning-sorrows drinks meeting. 'I'm afraid we've finally lost her. There won't be any more messages back and forth with Hitler.'

'The Nazis have actually caught her?'

'No. She got away before that could happen. But she and her family are desperately trying to escape Germany as we speak. So whether indeed she might be caught is still very much in question.'

'I see.' Churchill mulled over the situation, took a steady draw on his cigar. 'And does Hitler know that we've duped him?'

'Not as yet. But in the weeks to come as the pieces fall into place – especially with Hansel also hightailing it at the same time – I'm sure he'll work that out.'

'Not the best of situations,' Churchill said glumly.

'Indeed.' Calder became thoughtful for a second. 'Though there is one saving grace. Hitler has maintained strict secrecy about his dealings with Edith Creutzen – mainly because of the past debacle with Hanussen. Only a handful of people know. So he would not be keen on it becoming common knowledge that he'd used a fortune teller, let alone that he'd been so openly duped by her. Again, I think he'll be keen to keep that under wraps.'

'One silver lining from this mess, I suppose.' Churchill

nodded slowly, tamped his cigar. 'And is there anything we can do from our end to aid her?'

'No. I don't think so. Although we knew it was inevitable at some stage, in the end it blew up quite suddenly.' Calder took a mouthful of beer, held a hand out. 'Though at least it appears she's got the help of her colleague, Stefan Hansel, preparing papers and everything to get them all out safely.'

'The man we discussed before, who's part of Grey Wolf's cell?'

'Yes.'

Churchill took a sip of his brandy. 'And as we also discussed previously, now it looks likely we'll lose *two* valuable assets at the same time?'

'Unfortunately, yes, Prime Minister.'

Churchill looked into the mid-distance for a moment before bringing his gaze back keenly on Calder Gibson.

'One consolation, at least. I spoke to Hastings Ismay the other day, and he feels we've already done enough. Even if Hitler pulls back at this stage, Russian losses have been so heavy that Stalin would pursue German forces all the way back to Berlin.' Churchill smiled crookedly. 'In fact, Hitler is now in a "damned if I do, damned if I don't" situation. He needs to keep pushing to keep the Red Army at bay and away from Berlin.'

Calder took another swig of beer, nodded thoughtfully. 'I'll obviously inform you the moment I have news that they've crossed safely into Switzerland.'

'Of course.' Churchill breathed in deeply. 'And we can but pray meanwhile that they make it safely out. My thoughts are with them.'

Calder grimaced his accord. But he wondered whether Churchill's primary concern was for Edith Creutzen and her family, or for the fallout and possible damage to their wider security network if she was captured and questioned.

58

SS-Obersturmbannführer Kurt Schneider was in the Hotel Adlon café when the thought hit.

Lichten Buchbinder.

The name had initially rung a bell, but he couldn't remember from where. He recalled that Creutzen's father was a bookbinder, could that be it? But then quickly dismissed it. *Too close to home.*

Now it hit him that the name had only come up recently, had never featured earlier. And if books were still being used to pass messages and Creutzen was no longer able to risk visiting bookshops, or now even cafés, what better place than through her father's business? She wouldn't even need to visit his place of work, the exchanges could all be done at family gatherings.

But first he needed to check if Lichten was her father's company.

Twenty minutes later – still slightly breathless from the kilometre walk – he was prodding a finger at the entry in his files. Only one mention among Gustav Strehl's report filling in Edith Creutzen's family background.

He picked up the phone and made two quick calls – one to Nikolaus Strohm, the other to Hans Diestler – informing them of his findings. Strohm thanked him for the information, 'At least something of a possible breakthrough,' but Diestler was more circumspect.

'I'm not sure how that would help me with the Bittner investigation.'

'Don't you see?' Schneider exclaimed. 'If it's been Creutzen all along passing secret messages rather than Voltner, and she'd been found out by Bittner, then the same motive would stand. Creutzen would have been the one keen to get rid of Bittner, not Voltner.'

A slow exhalation at the other end of the line. 'I have actually received some fresh information on the case through Bittner's diary. But it doesn't mention or relate to any of that. More an intended confrontation with Edith Creutzen on another issue.'

'*What?* The old boyfriend they shared at one stage?'

'I'm afraid I can't say.' A curt, clipped tone. 'With a case like this involving someone close to the Führer, I have to proceed cautiously – as indeed you were warned when delving into Creutzen's possible clairvoyancy. But Stefan Hansel has promised to come back to me by early tomorrow afternoon, after which I can speak more openly about this new turn of events.'

'You told Hauptsturmführer Hansel?' Schneider's tone was edgy, incredulous.

'Of course. He's the Führer's adjutant. And with something delicate like this, it's perfectly understandable that the Führer would wish to know about it first before it was shared with other internal departments.'

'Don't you realize that Hansel is probably in on it with Creutzen?'

'Now you're just being ridiculous,' Diestler huffed, his patience half gone. 'I know your nose was put out of joint by Hansel when you first started probing about Creutzen, but –'

'That quickly became irrelevant,' Schneider cut in sharply. 'Do you really think that Creutzen shot Bittner? I never thought so. I always favoured Hansel more for that.'

Brief silence the other end, as if some things were shifting in Diestler's mind, others slotting into place.

'One factor which can't be overlooked,' Diestler said at length, his tone calmer. 'It was Voltner's prints on the gun that shot Ziegler, not anyone else's. And the bullet grooves matched precisely those found in Bittner's body.'

Schneider had no ready answer to that, so simply sidestepped it. 'You realize that if I'm correct, they could be using this delay now to escape.'

'If you have proof that they've run off, rather than just supposition, by all means come back to me.' Diestler sighed tiredly. 'Otherwise, it's my intention to wait until tomorrow, when Hansel will have spoken to the Führer.'

After making a few quick phone calls, Schneider drove like a man possessed to get to Lichten Buchbinder before they closed. Dusk light, he thought he could just about get away with sidelights without breaking blackout rules.

Diestler had made his closing comment offhandedly, as if to simply get him off the line. But what if he was right about the delay being used by them to escape? A few phone calls should ascertain that. His first was to Edith Creutzen's house. Her housekeeper, Lara, answered.

'No, Fräulein Creutzen isn't here. She left with her

daughter to go to the dentist late morning while I was out shopping, then on to her parents' house.'

'Do you expect her back later?'

'She might not get back from her parents until after I've left tonight, so then I wouldn't see her until tomorrow.'

'Do you have her parents' telephone number?'

'Yes, I do.'

Schneider noted the number and dialled it straight after finishing with Lara, but it rang without answer.

His next call was to Stefan Hansel's office where an assisting Junker told him that Hauptsturmführer Hansel had left about eleven, 'And we don't expect to see him now until tomorrow. Some important papers he's delivering in Nuremberg for the Führer.'

It was then that Schneider jumped into his car and headed to Lichten Buchbinder.

His nerves already on edge, half-expecting the worst, he got there just ten minutes before they closed, when a young receptionist informed him that Herr Creutzen had left late morning, 'And we haven't seen him since. Said that he'll see us all tomorrow.'

Schneider decided to do one last check on Lukas and Elsa Creutzen's home four kilometres away, in case they were there and there was some reason they weren't answering their phone.

But the house looked dead, no lights on and no signs of life when he peered through the downstairs windows.

Just as he was getting back into his car, he noticed an elderly woman next door putting fresh seed on a bird table.

Catching his eye, as if in explanation, she commented,

'Have to put out seed for them in the winter, otherwise they get none.'

'Of course.' He smiled understandingly. 'I was actually looking for the Creutzen family. I wonder whether you've seen them today?'

'Yes, but not since earlier. And I doubt you'll see them now for a few days. They had suitcases with them when they went off with their son and young granddaughter.'

Schneider felt his chest tighten. 'And what time would that have been?'

'Eleven thirty or so.'

'Thank you.' Schneider got back in his car and started driving, his hands gripping hard on the wheel with the sudden cascade of events. At least now he had a rough time and a description of who was travelling together. If Edith Creutzen wasn't with her parents and daughter, then was it possible she was travelling separately with Hansel?

He had to get back to his office to urgently start making calls. He wondered whether he should even bother with a return courtesy call to Diestler.

With at least nine border posts to contact, that would simply eat into the time he needed to alert them.

59

As I watched the border guard leaf through our papers, I felt an itch high on my forehead. At first, I thought it was a fly before quickly discounting the idea. With the lying snow quickly turning to ice as the night-time temperature dropped, only insects buried deep underground would survive. I realized then it was a bead of sweat from my nerves and the heat of the car, but resisted the urge to wipe it away. That might just attract his attention more to it.

The guard, early twenties and heavy set with light-brown hair, had looked more or less satisfied with Teresa's and Xavier's papers and their cover story for travel to Switzerland: 'We're visiting a book exhibition in Zurich,' Teresa-Odette had explained. 'We plan to be there no more than four days.'

Now the guard looked at me more directly. 'I see that you, Fräulein Halpern, are attached to the Red Cross in Geneva?'

'Yes, I have some business first in Zurich before returning to Geneva.' I felt the sweat bead trickle further down my forehead.

Stefan had prepared a whole backstory for me about having visited Sachsenhausen camp, but had also advised me not to offer that information unless asked directly, '*Resist the temptation to overtalk.*'

She had switched cars earlier to ride with Stefan and then back again to Teresa and Xavier's car. Stefan had obviously spoken for himself at the Schweinfurt checkpoint. At that stage, he'd still been in his uniform with his Hauptsturmführer Stefan Hansel papers – but after a moment's checking, we'd been waved on, so at least there was no alert out yet in Berlin, or it hadn't reached that particular checkpoint if there was.

Now, Stefan was in plain clothes, two hundred metres back from us, observing. His identity, as were mine and my family's, also changed. I had no idea whether my family's new papers had passed muster, or if mine would. The only people going through on unchanged papers were Xavier and Teresa, still down as Luc and Odette Chastain from when they'd arrived in Berlin. The decision on them leaving had been last minute, so little time for new identity documents, and Stefan thought it unlikely they'd be instantly linked to me and an alert put out for them.

I watched the guard give their papers one last scan before handing them back, then he brought his attention again to mine. I looked straight ahead for a moment, didn't want to overtly stare at him.

Five hundred metres of floodlit, snow-dusted road between us and the Swiss border post, but it suddenly felt elusive, out of reach. My own recent forebodings gripped me again that doom was close at hand, we weren't going to make it – dark, shifting shadows of speculum images creeping into my vision, masking the stretch of road ahead.

Then suddenly the guard with a curt nod was handing my papers back, and I had to swallow the rising gasp in my throat, realizing I'd unconsciously held my breath. He nodded to another guard who lifted the barrier.

'Be careful as you drive through,' he said to Xavier-Luc behind the wheel. 'The road is quite icy.'

Kurt Schneider was frantic. He'd worked out the travel times from Berlin to the various Swiss border posts he'd notified; he'd even alerted the main border crossings into France and Austria, in case they'd decided to go through those less stringent checkpoints first, then go into Switzerland.

He should have heard something back from one of them by now.

He'd given all of them his home number to call back, having left his office four hours ago, stressing the urgency and that it was a matter of utmost importance to the Führer. They should have reached one of those border posts by now, surely?

Once he'd made all of his calls to the border posts, he'd decided to call Hans Diestler after all and bring him up to date on his findings.

'With all of them leaving at more or less the same time, yes, it does look suspicious,' Diestler agreed. 'But if it is just a coincidence, you'll face the Führer's wrath if you're wrong.'

'But probably preferable to the wrath I'd face if, knowing all of this, I simply let them get away. Which you'll have to worry about probably more than I, since Hauptsturmführer Hansel contacted you first.' Schneider couldn't resist a smug tone as he signed off from Diestler. 'So look upon it as something of a favour.'

But now with no call from any of the border posts,

perhaps Diestler had been right. It was just a coincidence. The Creutzen family away on a short break together somewhere, and Hansel, as his assisting Junker had advised, away on business in Nuremberg on the Führer's behalf.

The thought emerged as he pondered: They'd have known this situation would come up at some stage, so would likely have made their escape plans in advance, possibly involving changed names and identities. Which would then explain why there'd been no return calls as yet.

Another thought came on the tail end of that. The most recent link found at Colmar Bücher, the owners of which had arrived in Berlin from Paris at the same time as Edith Creutzen. Might they also have left at the same time, since there would be little point in them remaining once she'd gone?

What were their names again?

He leafed quickly back through the notes he'd made with Nikolaus Strohm, prodding one finger at the page when he found the entry: Luc and Odette Chastain.

They might have had new identity papers as well, but with the link to Edith Creutzen made by the SS only recently, of which they were likely unaware, no necessity would have been seen for that precaution. Certainly, now at almost 10.20 p.m. and still no return calls, it was worth trying.

Schneider picked up the phone and started dialling the first on his list of border posts.

From two hundred metres back, Stefan watched intently as Edith's car with Teresa and Xavier stood at the checkpoint. He'd pulled in as if to check the tightness of the tyre chains he'd put on when it started snowing eighty kilometres back, but then after briefly checking them, he'd stayed behind the steering wheel watching keenly. He hadn't wanted to be in the same car as Edith, in case a descriptive alert might trigger the guards' suspicions, but he also wanted to make sure the three of them were through safely before he approached the same barrier.

All seemed to be going smoothly, documents being examined then finally returned. He eased the breath he'd been unconsciously holding as the last papers were passed back and the guard nodded. The barrier lifted and they edged through.

But hardly had they gone forty metres when Stefan noticed another guard at the back of the small checkpoint hut on the phone, some agitated words between the two of them, then the guard who'd just handed their papers back was storming out of the hut with one hand raised.

His colleague by the barrier, who'd just started to lower it, wasn't sure if the stop gesture was aimed at him or the car that had just gone through. He stopped it a quarter-way down, in case his colleague wanted to run through after them. Swiss territory didn't start until two hundred and fifty metres past the barrier.

'Halt! *Stop!*' the approaching guard shouted, one arm still raised.

Stefan heard the shout from where he was, but Edith's car kept moving steadily away, now over a hundred metres past the checkpoint.

The guard ran ten metres past the barrier and shouted again.

'Halt . . . *Stop!*'

Stefan observed Edith's car still moving steadily forward, now over a hundred and sixty metres away and seeming to speed up. So, either they hadn't heard the guard's shout, or *had*, and were keen to escape as quickly as possible.

What the guard did next made Stefan's heart lurch. After one more quick shout of 'Halt . . . *Stop!*' he swung around the machine gun strapped over his right shoulder and aimed it their way.

Stefan started up and put his foot hard down, racing towards the half-raised barrier.

The first burst of fire was aimed high just above them, as if a final warning, and as the machine gun aim lowered, a silent scream rang out in Stefan's head, '*No . . . noooo!*' as he watched the volley of bullets rake Edith's car ahead.

The car swerved slightly, then straightened again as it sped off, now over two hundred metres away, fast approaching the Swiss section of the border. Two guards could also now be seen running from the Swiss border post, holding their arms up in alarm and waving frantically.

But the German guard seemed determined to get off one last volley before Edith's car crossed into Swiss territory.

Their car slalomed even more under another short burst, but the German guard broke off halfway through – perhaps from the shouts of his fellow guards, perhaps from the approaching high rev engine noise – realizing that a car was bearing down fast upon him.

The guard tried to step aside at the last second, Stefan purposely swinging in slightly to compensate, sideswiping the guard and sending him flying.

More shouts from behind as Stefan sped through, the other two guards snapping quickly into action.

A suspended moment, then the frantic volley of fire came from two machine guns behind, most of the bullets thudding into his own car, shattering the back and a side window with a blizzard of flying glass, swirling wildly with the snow now drifting in – but some still directed towards Edith's car ahead, which appeared to be a good three hundred metres away and well into Swiss territory.

Stefan was only eighty metres away from that same Swiss territory himself, but the gunfire from behind was relentless, bullets thudding into his own car and some still striking Edith's car ahead, which was now just at a crawl. Xavier Luc, who had been driving, must have been hit.

And as Stefan felt a searing pain and liquid warmth spreading, he realized that he too had been shot, gritting his teeth against it as that mid-point demarcation line fast approached – aware at the last moment of the Swiss guards running further out and now firing back towards the German guards, the hail of bullets from behind finally stopping just seconds before darkness claimed him.

60

Deià, Mallorca, October 1973

Heavy silence for a moment as Teresa finished, only the faint thrum of cicadas in the background. Robert Graves was the first to speak.

'And what happened to Edith and Stefan . . . And Xavier?' Obviously, asking Teresa's fate he saw as redundant, because she was right there before them telling the story.

Teresa took a sip of water, grimaced painfully. 'Sadly, both Edith and Stefan perished at that Swiss border point. Xavier was badly injured but recovered, though had to use a walking stick for a while.' She traced one finger on the terrace table next to her glass. *Tracing memories.* 'I still see him whenever I go back to Paris, and he's been out to see me here a couple of times.'

'And little Louise and the rest of Edith's family?' Jacob Bronowski inquired.

'They had got through their Swiss checkpoint without any problem an hour earlier. They stayed in Switzerland after the war, with Elsa only returning to Berlin at brief intervals to see her relatives there. Lukas and Elsa raised Louise alongside Tobias. And when she was eighteen she came to stay with me in Paris for three years while she attended the *conservatoire* there. Now she's in America, a concert pianist with one of their most famous orchestras. Her mother would have been proud. I still see her regularly, she's even visited me here a few times.'

Graves smiled briefly, nodded. 'Let us not forget the villain of this tale.' He twirled one hand in the air theatrically. 'Something I'm a fair expert on, having put villains and scoundrels at the heart of many of my books. So, what happened in the end to the obnoxious master-torturer, Kurt Schneider?'

'Sadly for his many victims, he went on to bigger and badder things in the remaining years of the war. Hitler gave him a promotion for uncovering Edith and Stefan's duplicity and bringing about their downfall, but also swore him to secrecy. The whole matter was then buried – the Führer not wishing it to be widely known that he'd been duped by a fortune teller and his close adjutant. Schneider was head of an SS death squad that went into ghettoes to kill Jews en masse or round them up to be sent to the camps.' Teresa looked down briefly, one hand clenching on the terrace table. 'His most notorious act was towards the end of the war. His squad came upon thirty or so Jewish children on the road not far from Treblinka. It wasn't clear whether they'd been set free or merely escaped as the camp closed. Russian troops were fast advancing, so Schneider didn't wish his squad to waste bullets they might need to defend against the Russians; instead he ordered that the children all be stripped bare and forced to bathe in a nearby freezing lake. Then they were left there. All but four had frozen to death or died of exposure or pneumonia by the time Russian troops got to them, finding some of the bodies as far as thirty kilometres away in their struggle to find shelter. The four that survived had been lucky enough to make it to nearby farms for help.'

'My God.' Bronowski closed his eyes for a second, shook his head. He'd probably heard a hundred stories like this, some even involving his own family, but still they chilled him to the core.

'He also continued to torture many remaining collaborators against Hitler.' Teresa forced a grim smile. 'Though at least this was impeded somewhat by how Stefan's death was announced.'

Bronowski raised a brow. 'In what way?'

'The RAF dropped a dead body disguised as a secret agent by parachute into enemy territory just over the old Polish border carrying a secret message for the Polish Resistance that Grey Wolf, aka Stefan Hansel, was dead. The man dropped was in fact a recently deceased vagrant, and the RAF purposely dropped him into tree-tops with a failed parachute to make it look as if the fall had killed him. That ruse allowed Canaris, Oster, Beck and other high-ranking officers to operate for a few years more without detection, the SS and military intelligence thinking the main source of leaks had gone.'

Graves took a sip of wine. 'And at the end of the war, did Schneider meet a suitably sticky end, like many of his fellow Nazis?'

'No. Unfortunately, he didn't. Although the full details aren't clear, it appears he got away, possibly through Genoa or Lisbon, and ended up in Brazil.'

Graves huffed. 'The devil takes care of his own, it appears.'

They were silent for a moment, perhaps dwelling on

the uneven fate of it all, Teresa considered: it was bad enough that both Edith and Stefan had not survived, but Schneider had also eluded justice.

'One major silver lining that mustn't be forgotten,' Teresa said with a fresh breath, as if to clear the poignant air: 'Edith succeeded in her main aim of misleading Hitler, getting him committed heavily on the Russian front to ensure the Allies won the war. Her and Stefan's sacrifice certainly wasn't for nothing.'

The two men stayed together for a while on the terrace after Teresa left, Graves looking contemplatively towards the surrounding mountains, as if seeking both inspiration and solace for the story they'd just heard.

'Quite some tale,' he commented to Bronowski, bringing his gaze back.

'Yes. Easy to see why it has been kept secret through the years.'

'Especially with ODESSA still quite active. Keeping the likes of Mengele and Schneider hidden away and protected from facing justice. I don't think they'd relish it becoming known that their beloved Führer had been duped like that.' Graves took a sip of wine, grimaced. 'So, it appears Hitler's insistence on secrecy persisted even after the war.'

'It appears so,' Bronowski agreed forlornly. 'But I was thinking as much of the Russians. Knowing that British Intelligence had a hand in a war that caused so many losses for them could be disastrous for diplomatic relations.'

'Damned on all sides, it seems. Not many secrets that *all* parties have an interest in keeping buried.'

Bronowski sighed. 'Not least Teresa, relating her and Edith's story now. She's done a pretty good job of keeping the truth buried all these years, so why now in particular?'

Graves lapsed into thought. 'Perhaps she felt it was safe at last, in the same way that some past war criminals are only now coming out of the woodwork. Don't forget, it was your own family's past association with the holocaust that made me feel you'd find her story particularly intriguing.'

'I suppose,' Bronowski conceded after a moment. 'I'm just overthinking it.'

Graves smiled tightly. 'My dear fellow, you've made an entire career out of overthinking things.'

61

Morro de São Paulo, Brazil, October 1973

Kurt Schneider leaned closer to the bathroom mirror as he trimmed the last of his beard. Through the window to one side, he could hear the gentle lapping of surf fifty metres away at the end of his manicured lawn; the same gentle shushing that had lulled him into his afternoon siesta three hours ago, as it had done for the past two decades. He looked over as a girl's voice came from the adjoining bedroom.

'Are you ready for your massage now, Senhor M?'

'Just two minutes more, Luana.'

She smiled briefly at him through the half-open door before moving away. At seventeen, she still looked disturbingly young, though she'd been only fourteen when she'd first arrived at his villa.

In another year, he'd probably trade her in for a newer model as he recommended customers to do at the Salvador Mercedes dealership he'd managed for the past twenty-five years. He might even pick the next one up at the same massage parlour where he'd found Luana. Their massage skills were amateurish at best, but the main fare had been table-top sex within twenty minutes.

Halfway through his second session with Luana, he'd asked if she'd like a more permanent arrangement so that she didn't have to sleep with so many men each day to help feed her family. Within a week, she was installed as his maid and cook, at which she was equally amateurish. But at least his main needs were satisfied, and a mixture of training and practice had gradually improved her other skills. Most important for him was to have only *one* person living in the house to cater for all his requirements.

More people and the chances of his true identity being uncovered increased. He'd kept the same first name, Kurt, but had opted for Müller as a surname. Probably the two most common German names. He'd also kept himself quite trim over the years, so that now in his early sixties he considered he cut a reasonable figure, not too grotesque a massage duty for his regular maids.

He'd never married. Too complicated, too many questions. Besides, he'd then also lose the option of trading them in every few years when their five-a-day, four-sugars-per-cup *cimbalinos* habit started to broaden their hips.

Halfway back across his bedroom, the phone started ringing. He paced to his bedside table and picked up, his brow furrowing after listening for a moment.

'You're not my normal contact,' Schneider said.

'No, I'm not. But your last contact was almost two years ago, and things change. The fact that I'm giving you the correct code number now, ODF 4638, should tell you enough.'

'You're one digit short.'

'Yes, that was my predecessor, 4637. I'm 4638, having taken over from him.' A clipped tone to the man's German the other end of the line. Impatient. 'Shall we get down to business?'

Schneider exhaled heavily. 'OK. Tell me. Why the need for contact now?'

'She's started talking. Or, at least, her friend and co-conspirator, Teresa Delmar, has started spreading the story.'

'I see.' Schneider felt himself go cold. Having been pledged to secrecy by the Führer at their last meeting towards the end of the war, he'd in turn promised to keep the story buried, if it should ever threaten to surface again.

'You of course appreciate the implications and the tarnish to the Führer if this tale should gain wings and become widespread?'

'Yes, I do. Very much.' It was one thing with ODESSA for the Führer to be painted as an arch villain and monster. They in turn, along with a fair body of the German public, painted Churchill as a gangster and mass murderer, not least because of excessive firestorm bombings like Dresden. But being made a mockery of and portrayed as a fool who was duped by a fortune teller was another matter. 'Are you planning to do anything about it your end?'

'No. I think this one is for you. At least, that is what I have been advised – because the matter is so personal to you.'

'Of course.' Schneider sighed, a mixture of resignation and satisfaction. 'Give me the details.'

62

Tel Aviv, October 1973

Alois Mayell tapped a pen on the table as he listened to the tape running.

'. . . And where will I find her?'

'A small village on the west coast of Mallorca, Deià,' replied Schneider.

'Do you have an actual address for her, or do I have to sniff around in the village to find her?'

'As usual, my contacts are efficient. They've in fact been aware of Delmar's location for some while, but only now has she started talking, precipitating this action. Here's the address . . .'

Alois made a note of it on a pad as Kurt Schneider read it out on tape.

'And you're in Paris now?' the SS man asked.

'Yes. I've been here for much of the past year.' The tone of the voice the other end of the line lifted slightly. 'When do you want this done by?'

'It has become urgent now, so with all due expediency. And I have to stress, this is a vitally important hit – so no mistakes.'

'No need to labour the point. I'm well aware of the history with Delmar and Edith Creutzen – what a major thorn this was in the Führer's side.'

'Glad that's clear.' A huffed sigh. 'There are direct flights from Paris to Palma de Mallorca, and Deià is no more than a forty-minute drive from there.'

'I'll get straight on it. Terms as before – half now, half on completion?'

'Yes. I'll arrange the transfer. How's your Spanish?'

'Quite good. I spent two years in Argentina, another year in Venezuela.'

Schneider exhaled tiredly. 'How easily I forget that so many of us have spent the years mostly in exile.'

The call ended shortly after. As his young assistant, Daniel, stopped the tape, Alois looked at him keenly.

'Do we know much about the hit-man hired, know his form?'

'His code name's Falke . . . the Falcon. Middle-aged now, but a strong track record. One of the best.'

Alois closed his eyes for a second, twirled one hand as he asked Daniel to rewind the tape to the first call.

'. . . The point where they're arguing the toss about the code number.'

Daniel wound back, hit play. As the tail of that first call came to an end, Alois nodded thoughtfully.

'Certainly seems like ODESSA, from the code and everything else. But do we know who his first contact was, have any record of that?'

'No. They've only been monitoring his calls for the last four months.'

Alois nodded again. Under normal circumstances, that would have been enough. They'd monitored Eichmann for only three weeks before grabbing him. But this time Alois had wanted a longer monitoring so that they might net a wider circle of Schneider's past SS comrades who had also hidden in Brazil courtesy of ODESSA. But only one other significant name had arisen, and now this – a threat to someone he himself, in league with the Swiss authorities, had gone to great lengths to keep hidden for the past thirty years.

Head of Field Operations for Mossad for much of that time, his original name had been Israel, but he'd changed it to help shield his Jewish identity in 1942, after most of his family had been sent to death camps. He'd then taken part in an identity-change network in his native Austria before moving finally to Switzerland, where many of the Jewish and Gypsy families he'd helped escape the Nazis had ended up.

After the war, he'd spent a year in Lisbon sharing an office with a fellow Austrian, Josef Weber, where much of their time was spent tracking escaping Nazis from a list provided by leading Nazi-hunter Simon Wiesenthal. Kurt Schneider had been the eighth name on Wiesenthal's list.

When Israel's bid for independence and the resultant war took place in 1948, he felt he had to take part. As a skilled intelligence operative with numerous international connections, his transition to Mossad seemed almost preordained. He'd considered at the time reverting to his original name, Israel, but felt that would be too obvious, would mark him as a Zionist wherever he went. He preferred operating in the shadows, so kept Alois.

For the same reason, he'd twice turned down promotions to become Head of Mossad. He didn't want to appear centre-stage or be deskbound. So he'd remained Head of Field Operations throughout.

Now just over seventy, he'd remained slim and wiry, and had shaved his head once his hair started thinning. Even just a few years ago, when he'd observed a group of new IDF recruits struggling over the standard assault course, he'd stepped forward and stormed through it to show them how it was done. But he was wise enough now to know that on an operation like this, he needed the hardest and sharpest back-up possible; a version of himself from thirty-five years ago.

'Is Izzy available right now?' he asked Daniel.

'Yes, I think so. He's not on leave.'

Alois grimaced tautly. Izzy had been alongside him in Beirut when they'd taken out Muhammed Al-Najjar and two other Black September terrorists. A busy year in the wake of Munich: he'd been only two away from Prime Minister Golda Meir as she'd slapped one hand on the conference table, 'Get them . . . get all of them!' He'd then over the coming weeks planned out how that retribution should take place.

'Tell Izzy to prepare a Customs shaving kit and meet me here. We should leave within the hour.'

A 'Customs shaving kit' was a polymer Glock gun, a stiletto and an explosive canister assembled into a mock shaving kit, which would pass undetected through Customs and scanners.

As Daniel went to the phone at the far end of the Ops Room, Alois briefly leafed through a notebook two drawers down in his desk and then dialled the number he had for Teresa Delmar.

As it started ringing, he looked anxiously at the clock on the wall. They'd already lost almost two hours getting the message relayed from the Mossad team in Brazil. It kept ringing. If Falke had left promptly from Paris, he'd already be halfway there by now. Whereas with no direct flight from Tel Aviv to Palma de Mallorca, the fastest was a connecting flight through Frankfurt, at least three hours behind Falke. Alois gave up after the eighth ring. There was nobody there.

He'd try again at Ben Gurion airport – but unless he got hold of Teresa Delmar before they boarded, he'd have to face that hard, unacceptable fact. They weren't going to make it.

63

Palma de Mallorca, October 1973

Falke, alias – he'd had so many aliases over the years he'd lost count, but for this quick visit he was Helmut Kühn, German tourist – sat eating a mixed-fish grill in Rififi, one of Palma's most popular seafood restaurants. He'd purposely picked a restaurant on its west side, so that he had a clear run to Deià without having to factor in the delay of city traffic. He also thought it a fitting name, Rififi, since that's how he envisaged this hit. In silently like a thief, three quick shots with a silencer attached, and out again.

Given the nature of his target, a woman in her early sixties living alone, it should be one of his easier assignments. A cakewalk.

He planned to visit in the dead of night when she was already asleep in bed, so decided to kill some time by stopping for a meal. Dining in Deià itself was out of the question, too close to the scene, and strangers in small villages were more readily noticed. The same applied to the communities and towns en route.

He'd taken a table at a sharp side angle to the entrance, as he did at practically every restaurant or bar he visited, so that he could see everyone coming in and out without being particularly noticeable himself. He wasn't a large man, just over medium height, had plain light-brown hair and no distinguishing features.

Following the same aim of blending in, he avoided bright or garish colours, opting for neutral beiges or light browns. The colour of his shirt and slacks today, respectively.

He glanced at his watch as he finished: 10.08 p.m. Still a couple of hours or so to go. Dining in Spain was a late affair; he noticed couples still coming in with young children as the waiter cleared his plate and he ordered crema Catalana to finish. An espresso with it, if nothing else to keep him alert during the possible wait ahead. He left the restaurant at close to eleven and went to his car parked fifty metres away.

A white Seat 127 he'd hired at Palma airport, it seemed that it was the most common car he saw on the roads, and practically all of them were also white.

A nondescript man in a nondescript car.

Nobody would remember him.

Falke kept one eye on the light in the upper-floor window in the house sixty metres ahead. A large village house on the end of a short row of similar stone houses, it had a flat-roofed extension that served as a terrace to the bedrooms above – probably over a lounge or kitchen, he surmised, having worked out the likely layout of the house within the first ten minutes of arriving.

No matter, he'd already seen a figure briefly at the lit window, without doubt the woman described as his target. Getting up onto the flat roof would probably be his best entry into the house.

All he had to do now was wait for the right time.

On the way to Deià, he realized he'd still be too early for the optimum time for the hit, so stopped off at a beach resort on the way. A large expanse of sand with only a single hotel at its centre, The Atlantic – hadn't anyone told them they were on the Mediterranean, he thought laconically – but it was an impressive stretch of sand with palm trees surrounding the colonial style hotel. It felt strange, night-time sightseeing, but there were a few young couples on the beach and some fishermen at the far end on some rocks. He doubted anyone would find his presence strange or, with the darkness, be able to see him clearly.

He'd stopped off again at a village called Esporles on the way, but there were fewer people on its streets as he took a quick stroll. Some drinkers in a couple of bars he passed – looked like locals and mostly men, a football match playing on a TV in one of them. He didn't go into either bar, didn't want to be remembered, simply continued with his stroll before returning to his car.

He tapped one finger on the steering wheel impatiently. If the light wasn't turned off soon, he'd drive around the block, then park in a different position in the street. It wasn't good to be seen parked in the same position for more than twenty minutes.

Just as he was about to start the engine, the light went out. He took a deep breath, composing himself. Ten more minutes to let her get to sleep, then he'd move in.

64

Alois and Izzy had watched the upstairs light in the house go off eight minutes earlier.

'Still no movement,' Izzy commented. 'Should we go in?'

Alois scanned the house quickly again, took a breath of the sea air. 'Let's give it a few minutes more.'

Thirty years this particular pot had been simmering. A few minutes more to make sure nothing was overlooked and it was done right seemed fitting.

Due grace.

Falke was only slightly out of breath from the strain of the short climb as he eased himself onto the flat terrace roof. A combination of the drainpipe and rough stone walling had made climbing quite easy. At just over forty and with his exercise regime, he considered himself in prime shape.

As he'd predicted earlier, a *cakewalk*.

He moved silently and stealthily across the terrace. He could see now from the two sets of French windows ahead that the terrace actually served two rooms. He decided to let himself in through the window that had remained in darkness – less chance of the minimal sound from the glass-cutting and the latch being turned disturbing her.

He moved to the window, attached the suction cup and had the glass cutter poised when he suddenly froze, his nerves immediately wire-taut.

Sudden sound of rustling movement from ten metres away. His breath trapped in his throat, he moved across cautiously to investigate. As he got to the far terrace edge, he could see another small flat roof five metres to the side at the back of the house. A cat's eyes glared back at him for a second before it slinked away.

He eased out his breath again, moved back to the French window. A fifteen-centimetre circle cut, he reached in, turned the latch and opened the window, closing it silently behind him. A small room with a desk and chair, an armchair to one side. Looked like a makeshift office.

He made his way swiftly to its door and opened it a fraction, a quick check of the short corridor outside through the gap. Then he moved along the corridor to what he knew was the bedroom with his target.

A suspended moment outside the door as he drew the Ruger with silencer attached from his waistband, a last listen out – a dog barking somewhere in the distance, no sounds from inside the house – then he stepped into the bedroom.

A moment for his eyes to become accustomed to the dark, then he could make out the shape of the figure beneath the covers, brown hair with grey streaks spilling out on the pillow. Without doubt his target, Teresa Delmar.

He raised the gun and aimed, pumped two quick bullets into the back, one of which he was sure would pierce the heart, then a final shot to the head.

He was just slipping his gun back into his waistband when something struck him as odd about the prone body. He moved in for a closer look.

Sudden sound of a door handle turning behind him, or perhaps a gun being cocked.

65

Alois and Izzy picked a lock on a downstairs door, then let themselves in silently and up the stairway to one side. They already knew which was their target's bedroom from the light going off twelve minutes beforehand.

They approached along the corridor stealthily, no noise from their footfall, then turned the handle on the door at the end.

No movement from the body on the bed beneath a cream counterpane.

Alois raised his Glock and fired two shots into the counterpane a few centimetres from the body.

The figure rose up sharply from the bed, stared at them with alarm.

'That got your attention,' Alois said.

Kurt Schneider continued to stare back at them, now rubbing his eyes, as if he didn't believe what he saw or was still not fully awake.

'What do you want?' Schneider inquired curtly.

Alois smiled dryly. 'Now is that any way to greet guests who've been waiting many years to meet you?'

'Who are you with? Who sent you?'

'Your colleague Eichmann was far sharper than you. He cottoned on straightaway.'

'*Israelis!*' An almost breathless exclamation, as if that

was Schneider's greatest dread. He held out one hand. 'And what did you do with my dogs?'

Alois nodded towards Izzy. 'They were taken care of.'

'*What?* You shot them?'

A small tic teased at the corner of Alois's mouth. Incredible that, just like Hitler, Schneider showed a compassion for animals that he was completely bereft of with humans. He made a mental note to be more wary of animal lovers in the future.

'Don't worry. We show a lack of mercy for only *one* type of animal.' Alois waggled his gun at Schneider. 'Your two dogs will wake up again in an hour.'

Izzy had thrown chunks of meat laced with ketamine over the back fence. Then the wait for all movement from the dogs to cease before they moved in.

'How did you find me?'

'Ways and means. And we found you months ago, have been monitoring your movements and calls ever since.' Alois smiled wryly. 'Gave us quite a bit of useful information and names.'

They'd gained only one worthwhile name and less information than they'd hoped, but it was satisfying to see Schneider's eyes dart, his mind panning back worriedly over who he might have spoken to and visited in that time. Alois watched his thoughts arrive at more recent phone calls.

'So, you heard my call about the Delmar woman?'

'That's what brought us here now.'

Now it was Schneider's turn to smile. 'If you listened to that call, then you should know it's already too late. She'll have been taken care of by now.'

'I think you'll find your man has a little surprise waiting for him. Which is why we're here rather than there.'

'You pathetic little Jew,' Schneider sneered. 'You think I haven't spent many years knowing this day might come? So what earthly extra surprises could you have for me?'

Alois contemplated Schneider coolly. He had tried Teresa's number again from Ben Gurion. *Still no answer.* Then he recalled the number of her neighbour to be contacted in an emergency, Jannik Lehmann. It was answered, and Alois explained the dire, urgent situation.

But rather than follow Alois's instruction to ensure Teresa stayed well clear of her house for the night, Jannik commented, 'Oh, we can go one better than that. I think we can plan a little surprise for him.'

'Don't risk it,' Alois urged. 'The man on his way to Teresa's home is a highly trained assassin. One of the best. Just make sure she stays well clear.'

'I'll make sure she's kept in the background.' Jannik sighed. 'But I think it's time to stop running. Put an end to this once and for all.'

'He's not been sent by who you might think,' Alois said flatly. Jannik on the other end stayed silent as Alois explained about the changed ODESSA code number and his main suspicions. 'So, is it worth confronting him?'

A moment's silence, then: 'The same would apply. Besides, having played a double game myself all these years, I'm hardly blind to the fact that others might play them.'

Alois was halfway through another plea when the line went dead. So, while he now emphasized to Schneider that 'surprise' mentioned by Jannik Lehmann, he prayed it went well. A lot of possible contingencies with a master assassin like Falke.

Minutes after the call, Alois had changed their flights to Brazil.

'So, what now?' Schneider held an arm out. 'You bundle me up and spirit me back to Israel to face a show trial, like you did with Eichmann?'

'You flatter yourself. You're not important enough for that, and we got enough grief from the international community for bringing back the death penalty just for Eichmann to want to repeat it.' Even if Schneider had been a bigger prize, they'd have needed a larger team to get him out of Brazil undetected.

A brief look down in resignation, as if realizing he wasn't going to make it out of this room, then a glance to one side. It was likely that someone like Schneider would keep a gun in his bedside drawer. Something to watch out for. Schneider raised his gaze to meet Alois's steadily.

'Eichmann was just a pen-pusher. He might have signed far more death warrants for Jews than me, but he wasn't hands-on like I was. Perhaps lacked the bravery to face them when he killed them like I did.'

That steady stare became piercing. But from the dry smile beneath, Alois suspected it was more gloating over those deaths than bravery. Alois felt his jaw clench. From the file he'd read on Schneider years ago, what had leapt out had been the cruelty of his interrogations with Betzner and the many later conspirators, then the various 'death squad' ghetto murders and finally the young children of Treblinka. Unlike Eichmann, he wouldn't even have been able to claim that he was 'just doing his duty'; Schneider had clearly revelled in those tortures and killings.

'You might think you're clever,' Schneider sneered. 'But you're just another worthless Jew.'

'Or perhaps just one of many you underestimated. Because not only did my team spend months monitoring you, undetected by either you or your pals in ODESSA – but I'm also the one here now holding the gun.'

Another brief eye-shift from Schneider, then he went for it, lunging for the gun in his bedside drawer. Alois had more to say to Schneider, but now there wouldn't be time.

He fired at the outstretched hand, saw the bullet sever the top part cleanly, taking the thumb and two fingers with it. Schneider watched in horror as his mangled hand bled out.

'No more plectrum playing for you,' Alois said. A moment's taste of what his victims suffered would have to suffice. He moved his aim to Schneider's chest. 'Paulos Betzner and the children of Treblinka send their regards.'

He fired twice, as did Izzy alongside him, then shifted up for a final head shot.

66

Deià, Mallorca, October 1973

Falke started to turn as the door opened behind him.

'Drop the gun on the bed,' the instruction came at the same time. 'I'll have shot you twice before you can even turn around.'

A firm voice, calm. Falke dropped the gun and turned fully to face the man behind as the light came on. Late fifties or early sixties, greying blonde hair, sharp grey-green eyes. In his hand was a Browning 9mm, pointed straight at him.

A woman appeared behind him at that point – brown hair with grey streaks – and Falke did a double-take as he glanced back at the figure on the bed. The factor that had made him move in closer at the last moment: even in the dim light, he could see no blood.

'Quite amazing what can be achieved with clothes bundled up right and a wig,' Jannik Lehmann commented.

'So, you obviously knew I was coming and got the drop on me,' Falke said. 'What now?'

'The main thing is for you to return a message to whoever sent you.'

'Why would that interest you?'

'Perhaps because we're both tired of hiding away and

feel it's time the game ended.' Jannik eased a weary breath, glanced to the woman behind him. 'And if I let you go now, the last thing I want is you or someone else coming back later to finish the job.'

'I don't see how a simple message passed through me might stop that.' Falke smiled cynically. 'You really think these people will just give up on their target?'

'It's more like an insurance policy.' Jannik pulled a piece of paper from his pocket. 'Whoever sent you did so to silence Teresa . . . or should I say, *Edith*.' If some didn't already suspect it, they'd know for sure once they read the letter. 'So that needs to be protected against.'

'Edith *Creutzen*? But she died years ago.'

'That's what everyone was led to believe.'

Jannik watched Falke's eyes dart from him to Edith, the recognition finally dawning.

'*Grey Wolf*,' Falke said breathlessly.

'That might be the natural assumption,' Jannik said curtly. 'But my main concern now is for Edith.' An ambiguous admission, but Jannik-Stefan could see the remainder gelling in Falke's mind: the link between him and Edith, and now confronting him. *Who else would attempt to brave that?*

Stefan stepped forward and handed Falke the letter, keeping his gun trained on him throughout as he moved back again and observed Falke keenly reading. A quizzical expression at first from the assassin, then a dry smile surfaced.

'As you can see,' Stefan prompted, 'it gives some vital background, then lays out firmly and clearly what will happen if there are any attempts on Edith's life or mine: a full exposé of exactly what transpired between British Intelligence, Edith Creutzen and Hitler between mid-1940 and late 1941 sent to Reuters and every major newspaper in Europe and the USA.' Stefan smiled primly. 'The aim of killing her to keep the matter secret will end up having entirely the opposite effect.'

Falke nodded, his countenance suddenly showing a twinge of concern. 'What makes you think they won't simply kill me – not only for delivering such a message, but for failing with this hit now.'

Stefan shrugged. 'That's a risk you'll have to take. Look at it this way: if you didn't have this message to deliver, you wouldn't be leaving this room now.' Stefan watched a reluctant acceptance dawn on Falke with another slow nod. 'Oh, and the people who ordered this hit now aren't who you think.'

Falke's brow knitted. 'But my instruction came from Kurt Schneider, and he's die-hard, old-school SS.' Under Stefan's unflinching stare, Falke became uncertain. 'I . . . I'll check back with him.'

'Don't bother. He won't be eating any more bratwurst. An Israeli team monitoring his calls paid him a visit, knowing I was holding the situation here. So, he drew the short straw.'

Fleeting glance down in respect of Schneider's demise. 'If not Schneider and ODESSA, then *who*?'

Heavy silence for a second, then Edith stepped forward, handed Falke a slip of paper.

'If you call the telephone number at the end, all will become clear.'

‘The clue is in the changed code number from Schneider’s usual ODESSA contact,’ Stefan prompted. ‘That’s the telephone number the call was traced back to.’ He watched Falke’s expression lift as he read the slip of paper. ‘As I say, not who you think.’

67

London, October 1973

Jeffrey Lutrell was still slightly out of breath as he walked into St Stephen's Tavern. Over half a mile from MI6's headquarters on Westminster Bridge Road, he'd have preferred to simply walk down the corridor at Century House for this meeting.

But he was a senior field officer, and the decision on the venue had been made by the Deputy Head of MI6, Charles Markham, a couple of pay grades above him.

He found Markham in his usual spot, tucked in a booth towards the back of the pub. 'At least provides some semblance of privacy,' Markham had informed him on a previous meeting.

Markham was convinced that the offices at Century House were not secure, too many potential Kim Philbys around. Aside from that, he hated the building, felt it looked 'hardly better than most council flat blocks'. Though the final factor in the decision on the venue now had come from his doctor, who after Markham's heart scare four years ago had advised him to walk at least a mile a day. So, he'd make the pleasant stroll every day over Westminster Bridge for some meetings.

Especially this one. As with their last meeting on the

same topic, it wasn't meant to take place, and hadn't been listed in any diary.

Markham half-guessed the news Lutrell was bringing from his downbeat expression.

'What happened?' Markham inquired as he took a seat.

A half-pint of lager had already been ordered and was on the table before him, indicating a short meeting. Markham was drinking port and lemon.

'It didn't end up fulfilled.' References to assignments, contracts or 'hits' were avoided. Too clumsy. 'The initial call was monitored and traced back.'

'Who by?'

'The Israelis.'

'Bloody Israelis.' Markham took a sip of his drink, grimaced. 'Sometimes they get above themselves.'

'You can hardly blame them. We've done little ourselves to chase past Nazi war criminals.'

'The CIA have far better operatives and contacts than us in South America. So, if you're looking to lay the blame anywhere, it should be there.'

'I suppose,' Lutrell agreed tamely, already starting to worry about Markham's reaction when he showed him the letter.

Markham snorted. 'Though I daresay they're still too preoccupied with communist domino theories in South-East Asia to trouble themselves with historic Nazis.'

Lutrell simply nodded, took a swig of lager.

'So, what happened exactly?' Markham pressed. 'Spell it out.'

Lutrell ran quickly through the sequence of events. 'In

the end, Schneider's man faced a small welcoming committee – in the shape of no less than our reincarnated "Grey Wolf" and Edith Creutzen herself.'

'My goodness. Quite brazen then – even though we've often had our suspicions.' Markham looked aslant for a moment. 'Though I suppose having relied so heavily on their ingenuity in the war, we can hardly be too surprised when they show it again now. And Schneider?'

'The Israelis took care of him.'

Markham nodded. 'And I daresay Grey Wolf did the same with the man Schneider sent.'

'No, he didn't.'

A moment's silence, Markham's brow creasing. 'Why not?'

'Because Grey Wolf had a message for him to pass back to us.' Lutrell took the letter from his inside pocket and handed it across. A stern, sour expression at first from Markham as he started reading, but as a faint smile emerged, perhaps in reluctant admiration at the audacity, Lutrell added, 'I think this one could possibly be filed under the ingenuity you mentioned earlier.'

Epilogue

Deià, Mallorca, October 1973

I was back at the terrace table with Robert Graves and Jacob Bronowski, but this time as Edith Creutzen rather than as my old friend Teresa Delmar. A bottle of wine sat on the table between us, which Graves had insisted upon as part celebration, although generally it didn't take much of an excuse for him to open a bottle.

Both Graves and Bronowski were aghast at points as I talked about the dramatic events of the night before.

Graves gestured at Stefan. 'Lucky you didn't actually kill your visitor last night. We haven't seen a murder here since the local baker killed the man he found *in flagrante delicto* with his wife fourteen years ago. Murder is a rare event here in Deià – so it would have caused quite a storm.'

'Don't worry,' Stefan assuaged, 'I wouldn't have shot him. I'd have taken him out at gunpoint to one of the clifftops, then bashed him on the head and tumbled him over. Made it look like an accident while he was out hiking.'

Graves smiled wanly. 'Ah, maybe there have been many more murders in the village over the years of which I have been completely unaware.'

Bronowski was looking at me keenly. 'Take us back to

the beginning, to when you both decided to change your names.'

I took a fresh breath as I explained that it had been Teresa who had sadly been killed that tragic night by the Swiss border. 'Xavier was severely injured, but after a long convalescence fully recovered. I was mostly untouched apart from some cuts from flying glass, and Stefan had only a leg injury.'

'In my case, I had a reversal of the usual dalliance with walking sticks,' Stefan offered with a soft smile. 'I used one for a while when I was younger, then when I was older no longer needed one.'

I picked up again, explaining that we both decided at that Swiss checkpoint that we would continue our lives under different names. 'We were convinced that if Hitler thought that we were still alive, he would seek retribution against us – possibly even sending agents and assassins after us in Switzerland while the war was still on.'

Stefan held out a hand. 'Or even after through the likes of ODESSA, as we've seen now. The only safe way forward, we felt, was to have changed names and identities.'

'I adopted Teresa's name. With us having been so close, it was a tribute of sorts, felt as if I was still keeping her spirit alive.' I looked towards Stefan.

'And Jannik Lehmann was my uncle's name, the one Hitler had put to death. And of course, Lehmann was also my mother's maiden name. Those were my tributes.'

Bronowski looked at Graves. 'I always had some suspicions it might have been Edith all along.'

Graves smiled tightly back. 'What? Too personal an account and all that.'

'It wasn't only that. It was also the fact that I felt the accent had more background German inflections than French.'

'Ah, now if you'd mentioned that, I'd have had my suspicions too. Knowing what a linguistic expert you are – having gone from your original Polish and Yiddish to speaking English fluently in only a year.'

Bronowski shrugged at the backhanded compliment. 'Well, I didn't say anything, because already you were commenting that I was overthinking everything.'

I smiled at the tame bickering between friends. 'Suffice to say that those identity changes worked and served us well through the years. Until just the other night.'

'That's the point I don't quite get,' Graves said. 'You felt sure that the assassin who visited you last night was sent by British Intelligence. Having recruited you initially and with you having benefited them so much all those years back – why on earth would they do that?'

I looked at Stefan, not sure for a moment which one of us should answer. Stefan went first.

'This was always a delicate, secret operation for British Wartime Intelligence, and even more so as we got into the depths of the Cold War.'

I nodded. 'If Khrushchev had got wind of the fact that British Intelligence had been responsible for influencing the tide of a war that had cost twenty million Russian lives, it could turn an already tense Cold War situation into something cataclysmic. Another Cuban missile crisis, but this time tipping over the edge.'

'They perhaps felt that drastic measures were needed to avoid that,' Stefan concluded.

Bronowski was pensive. 'And hoping to shift the blame onto old SS contacts and ODESSA – how was that done?'

I let Stefan explain about the ruse with an MI6 agent posing as ODESSA phoning Schneider in Brazil. 'The only problem was that an Israeli team had been monitoring Schneider's phone and movements for a few months and they picked up that it was a false contact and where it had originated from.'

'They knew that I was such a personal thorn to Schneider that he'd take action on it,' I came in on the tail end. 'And in the process the blame would have shifted to ODESSA.'

'And the Israeli team with Schneider?' Bronowski inquired.

'He went the same way as Eichmann,' Stefan said. 'But without the televised trial.'

Graves smiled smugly. 'Good to see he finally got his comeuppance.'

'Yes, we have enough Mengeles out there still evading justice,' Bronowski said, his countenance one of pained satisfaction.

'The head of that Israeli team, Alois Mayell, was a great asset to us,' I said. 'Even going back years when we first crossed into Switzerland.' I elaborated about Alois being part of an identity-change network in Switzerland for escaping Jews and Gypsies, 'In league with a Romany partner, his cousin, Deià, and her husband, Josef. They were in Lisbon after the war, and we spent almost five years there after Switzerland, then a similar period in Paris before finally moving here.' I'd noticed Graves's brow tweak at the mention of Deià. 'It was in fact Deià who first inspired me to visit here. Her original Romany name was changed later to Deià Reynes for her new Spanish identity, picking her Christian name up from a map of Mallorca. "A remote, idyllic artists' community on its west coast" was how she described it to me. Intrigued, we visited here shortly after Paris and fell in love with it. An ideal, peaceful hideaway.'

'I've always thought so,' Graves agreed. 'So, the account you related before as Teresa with Louise at the *conservatoire* in Paris, she was with you and Stefan all that time?'

'Yes. And now she visits here regularly from America.'

'So, that's the young woman I often see in the village with you,' Graves confirmed. A mute nod from me, and he sank into thought again. 'And the young man I sometimes see with her – he seems a bit young to be her boyfriend.'

I looked at Stefan. The other secret we'd long withheld.

'No, that's our son.'

'My goodness,' Bronowski exclaimed, beaming. 'Mazel Tov!'

'No doubt conceived while Stefan, posing as your German neighbour, was borrowing a cup of sugar,' Graves teased. 'Or while you were watching *Estudio 1* together?'

I chuckled. 'No, that happened many years back, while we were in Lisbon. Joachim is now on a postgraduate engineering course at MIT. He flies over with Louise when she visits, so that we can all be together.'

'My uncle Jannik was studying to be an engineer before the war intervened,' Stefan added, as if to partly explain.

I touched Stefan's hand on the table, smiled at him. 'My parents are a bit frail now, so have only visited us here with Tobias a couple of times. But we visit them each year in Switzerland, as do Louise and Joachim.'

'Tobias is still alive?' Graves inquired.

'Yes, he's another to have defied the odds.'

Robert Graves surveyed the surrounding mountains for a moment, clearly buoyed by our account, before bringing his gaze back.

'I think that calls for a toast,' he said. He topped up our glasses, raising his own with a glint in his eye. 'To two worthy survivors. The perfect end to an all but perfect day. May there be many more ahead.'

All but perfect day.

Although I knew that it wouldn't be completely perfect without my usual daily visit to the promontory on the edge of the village with its sweeping valley and sea view.

I breathed in as my eyes drifted across the glorious, uplifting vista – the memories of the dramatic view from Hitler's Kehlsteinhaus now thankfully distant. Though today the view started to blur as my eyes filled.

Stefan gently clasped my hand as my gaze fell to the graveyard just ahead. Only thirty gravestones in the small patch with a similar view, with my own gravestone, marked Edith Creutzen, directly ahead. Except that it was Teresa's ashes buried there. I'd had the urn with me all those years in both Lisbon and Paris before I finally found a resting place that I felt was ideal.

Although perhaps part of that was because I couldn't bear being apart from her, even just in ether spirit – not only because I planned to spend the rest of my days here, but also because this would be my final resting place too. Louise when she visited had been able to pay her respects to the woman who had helped raise her as a baby. Xavier too had been out a few times to lay flowers, one of those visits also with his wife and two children, both girls – one of whom he'd named Teresa.

'I'd like to keep her name, Teresa Delmar,' I muttered.

'Are you sure?' Stefan gently hugged me. 'We can be free now, don't need to live double lives any more. We can live under our old names again.'

'I know. But I want to continue doing this as a mark of respect. Otherwise, it might seem she's just been forgotten.'

I'd spent enough years voicing my guilt over Teresa's death to go over the same ground now. That if I hadn't gone back to Berlin, Teresa wouldn't have joined me there – a trip she ended up paying for with her life.

'I understand.' Stefan grimaced, hugging me tighter for a second. 'And I suppose it would at least save all the raised eyebrows in the village with having to explain how and why we'd reverted to our old names.'

'Yes. Probably a bit too much shock and drama for a place this size.' I smiled through my tears.

We were silent, lost in thought for a moment, the only sound the gentle surge and lapping of waves far below.

'I think I'd be happy too, sticking with the name Jannik Lehmann,' Stefan said at length. 'My own small tribute to my uncle.'

Tribute. I'd never felt entirely comfortable with my 'epitaph': *The woman who brought down Hitler* – the millions who had lost their lives in the Russian winter of 1941–42 now long forgotten, only the political significance remaining – so perhaps now it was as much to assuage our guilt. That equally we wouldn't feel comfortable living our lives without paying part tribute to those who had lost theirs on the way.

Those who had also played their part in Hitler's downfall.